THE MUTANT FILES
REDZONE

WILLIAM C.
DIETZ

THE MUTANT FILES
REDZONE

TITAN BOOKS

THE MUTANT FILES: REDZONE

Print edition ISBN: 9781783298761
E-book edition ISBN: 9781783298778

Published by Titan Books
A division of Titan Publishing Group Ltd
144 Southwark Street, London SE1 0UP

First edition: July 2015
2 4 6 8 10 9 7 5 3 1

Printed and bound by CPI Group (UK) Ltd, Croydon, CR0 4YY.

This one is for Lawrence Kane . . .
my first self-proclaimed fan!
Thanks for sticking with me. I really appreciate it.

ONE

Deputy Chief Ross McGinty had been dismembered by a serial killer called the Bonebreaker—and his body parts dumped next to a freeway. Unfortunately, that was the same fate that had befallen Cassandra Lee's father two years earlier. And now, as the long procession of police cars and limos followed the black hearse toward LA's Evergreen Cemetery, there should have been a sign. Rain perhaps . . . to match the mood. But no, the sky was blue, and it was going to be a nice day. For most people, anyway.

Lee was seated in an unmarked car along with Assistant Chief Sean Jenkins and two other members of the LAPD's Special Investigative Section (S.I.S.). It was the unit McGinty had led prior to his death—and was supposed to hunt down the Bonebreaker.

Lee was the only member of the force who had encountered the serial killer and lived to tell about it. "I am the Avenger," the Bonebreaker had told her. "I'm the one God sent to kill the monsters and their progeny. That's why you're going to die the way your father died."

That threat had been hanging over her ever since. But if the Bonebreaker was hunting her, she was hunting *him*, and had been for years. "I'm going to miss the chief," Jenkins commented. He had dark skin, green eyes, and was seated next to her.

"Yeah," Lee agreed. "Me too." And that came as a surprise. McGinty and her father had been partners once. But they had fallen for the same girl, got into a fight, and wound up as enemies. Some of that hostility had been apparent in the way McGinty treated her. Although, truth be told, Lee knew that some of the friction stemmed from her rebellious personality. Then the Screed kidnapping brought them together. And that was when Lee learned that there was a lot to like about McGinty, who, as it turned out, had a legitimate reason to dislike her father.

A brace of motorcycle cops led the funeral procession into the cemetery and its carefully kept grounds. The graveyard had been there since 1877 and was very crowded. Thickets of markers lined both sides of the gently curving road. *I won't let them bury me here,* Lee decided. *When I go down, there won't be any police cars, bagpipes, or mourners. I'll leave instructions for a couple of motorcycle riders to scatter my ashes along a good stretch of road. Highway 26 out of Stockton would do . . . The last thing I want is a box and a hole in the ground.*

Then Lee remembered McGinty's coffin and why it was so light. The Bonebreaker liked to keep his victims' limbs. So all McGinty's family had to bury was a head and a torso.

Later, once the flesh had been removed from McGinty's arms and legs, the killer might send some of the bones to the police, members of the press, or relatives. But he kept most of them for himself. Maybe they were buried somewhere. But Lee figured that the Bonebreaker kept the missing bones close to him, so he could look at and touch them. Including those that belonged to her father. She shivered.

The vehicles ahead of them were pulling over by that time, so Detective Yanty did likewise. Lee opened the door, got out, and was forced to squint in the sunlight. She put on a pair of sunglasses and was following a column of mourners into the maze of markers, when a reporter stepped out from behind a large monument. She looked like a fashion model and was holding a microphone. Her cameraman hurried to frame a two-shot. "Detective Lee! I'm Carla Zumin with Channel 7 News . . . The Bonebreaker killed your father. Now Deputy Chief McGinty is dead as well. How do you feel about that?"

Suddenly, everything that Lee felt, all of the emotions that were bottled up inside of her, came boiling to the surface. The result was a roundhouse right that struck Zumin in the temple. Lee felt the impact all the way up her arm, saw the lights go out in the reporter's eyes, and watched the blonde slump to the ground. "That's how I feel," Lee said, as Jenkins knelt next to the reporter. "I hope that helps." Then she walked away.

There was a great deal of fuss as medics were summoned to revive the reporter, her peers converged on the scene, and Channel 7's footage of the knockout was sent back to the station.

Meanwhile, most of the mourners remained unaware of the dustup as bagpipes played and a large crowd gathered around the open grave. Then, after a lengthy eulogy and a prayer, McGinty's coffin was lowered into the ground.

Lee turned to watch the woman everybody referred to as "McGinty's companion." Her name was Cheyenne Darling, and Lee had seen her at parties but had never exchanged more than a couple of words with her. Darling's blond bangs fell to a point just above her eyebrows. She had high cheekbones, a well-proportioned nose, and a generous mouth.

Like the rest of the mourners, Darling was dressed in black but with a difference. She was wearing silver jewelry, her dress was a little too short for the occasion, and her heels were red. It wasn't typical widow wear by any means, but Darling was crying, and that was when Lee realized that she wasn't.

Should she cry? Should she have to *think* about crying? What the hell was wrong with her anyway? Such were Lee's thoughts as her eyes scanned the crowd. Was the Bonebreaker present? Feeding off the misery? And feeling superior?

If so, he was pretty damned stupid because police officers dressed as reporters were salted throughout the crowd. Their job was to photograph the mourners so that detectives from the S.I.S. could check them over later.

The coffin was in the ground and a final prayer was being said as Lee sensed movement beside her. She turned to find that Jenkins was there. Their eyes met, and he shook his head sadly. "I'm sorry, Cassandra," he said. "But I've got to place you under arrest. Let's go to the car. Do not, I repeat *do not*, interact with the press. And that includes punching reporters. Do I make myself clear?"

Lee nodded contritely. "Sorry, boss. Is she okay?"

"Yes," Jenkins said, "or so it seems. When Zumin came to she looked up at her camera operator, and said, 'Did you get that? Did you *fucking* get that?' So I think she's going to survive."

Lee laughed as they returned to the car, but she knew the incident wasn't any laughing matter. It could, and probably would, cost her her badge.

Things went from bad to worse once Lee entered the car and was ordered to surrender both her weapons and her ID. Then, with the other officers listening in, Jenkins read her her rights. "Okay," he said, once the formalities were complete, "take us to the MDC."

The Metro Detention Center was located downtown, a short walk from LAPD headquarters. The process of being booked was something that Lee, like every police officer, was very familiar with. She'd never been through it herself however— and was struck by how powerless she felt. Plus, there was the shame that went with the abrupt transition from police officer to accused criminal.

After being searched and forced to surrender the rest of her belongings, Lee had to sign for them. Then she was given an opportunity to lawyer up. Something she definitely needed to do. But it was evening by then, and she feared that it might be difficult to reach people.

Lee knew dozens of lawyers, but there was only one she wanted, and that was a wily old legal lizard named Marvin Codicil, or "Coddy" as he was known at the courthouse. How many times had she arrested a scumbag only to see Coddy get him off? A dozen? At least that. Lee hoped he was still in the office.

After arriving home from work, Marvin Codicil took his clothes off and forced himself to stand in front of a full-length mirror. Not because he was vain but because he was a mutant and had to be vigilant. That included looking at all the things he would have preferred to ignore, including the pasty white skin, the paunch, and the bushy pubic hair. None of it was pretty—but all of it was normal. And that was the key. To *look* normal even though a third kidney was growing inside his body.

Yes, a small number of norms were born with a third kidney, but his situation was different. Codicil had been born with *two* kidneys, but had contracted *Bacillus nosilla*, and begun to grow a third shortly thereafter. That was in the year 2038, when a terrorist who called himself Al Mumit (the taker of life) turned the plague loose on the world.

The bioengineered bacteria was delivered to *Kaffar* (unbelievers) all around the world by 786 *Shaheed*, or martyrs, each of whom had been selected because they had light-colored skin, were elderly, or only a few months old. Babies turned into weapons. The thought of it made Codicil sick to his stomach.

The results were everything that Al Mumit hoped for. *Bacillus nosilla* spread quickly. Billions fell ill, and of those who did, only 9 percent survived. Most of the survivors went on to develop mutations. Some were good, but most were bad, and frequently disfiguring.

Hundreds of thousands of such people were declared communicable, some mistakenly, and herded into hastily organized "recovery" camps. And by all rights, Codicil should have been one of them. But his mutation was internal and would have remained a secret even to him had it not been for some emergency surgery in 2040.

"You aren't a carrier, Mr. Codicil," his doctor told him during a private conversation. "But you *are* a mutant. A third kidney is growing between the others. That shouldn't cause you any distress, and odds are that you'll die of something else. But the mutation could be a harbinger of things to come. So examine yourself frequently and seek help if you see unusual changes. In the meantime, I recommend that you keep this condition to yourself. You know what will happen if you don't."

And Codicil *did* know. It hadn't been long before the "recovery" camps evolved into "relocation" camps—and untold thousands of people were loaded onto trucks and sent east into the states of Idaho, Nevada, and Arizona. The sudden influx of mutants caused the "norms" in those states to flee in the *other* direction. And, so long as they were *B. nosilla* negative, they were allowed to immigrate. A policy that wasn't as generous as it seemed since the people along the West Coast were going to need workers with a wide variety of skills.

Meanwhile, other parts of what had been the United States of America were going through a similar sorting process. The result was a patchwork quilt of so-called red zones, where mutants lived, and green zones, which were occupied by norms. Soon the zones and collections of zones gave birth to nations like Pacifica. It consisted of what had originally been the states of Washington, Oregon, and California.

During that same period, the Republic of Texas annexed Idaho, Utah, and Arizona, which, based on what Codicil had heard, liked to keep government small and taxes low so that citizens could enjoy their full measure of freedom.

The phone rang. It was sitting on his dresser, and since his office number was set up to forward to Codicil's cell phone, chances were that a client was calling. A DUI probably . . . Or a pimp. Either of which would be boring. He picked up the phone. "This is Marvin Codicil."

The voice on the other end of the line was female. "Mr. Codicil? I don't know if you remember me . . . This is Detective Lee. I could use some help."

Codicil walked over to look at the flat-screen TV mounted on the wall of his bedroom. Channel 7 was playing the head-punch video for what? The billionth time? "Yes," Codicil said, as Zumin hit the ground again. "You could definitely use some help."

"So you've seen the footage?"

"I think it's safe to say that everyone in LA has," Codicil replied dryly.

"Yes, I suppose so," Lee said. Her voice was subdued. "I'm being held at the MDC. Can you get me out of here?"

"Of course I can," Codicil answered confidently. "First, I'll try to get you released on your own recognizance. Failing that, I'll get you out on bail. In the meantime, keep your mouth shut."

"Maybe I should plead guilty."

"Don't be silly," Codicil said condescendingly. "I plan to get you off."

"But *how*?" Lee wanted to know. "You've seen the tape."

"Have faith," Codicil replied. "Punching a reporter in the

face was stupid—but the decision to hire me was brilliant. Sit back and relax. I'll keep you informed."

Lee started to say something, but Codicil thumbed the phone off. A boring day wasn't boring anymore. And for that, the attorney was grateful.

In order to protect her from the people she had arrested in the past, Lee was placed in a jail cell by herself. That was SOP for such situations, and Lee was glad. Otherwise, she might have been locked up with somebody who was drunk, coming down from a meth-induced high, or just plain stupid.

But with no TV, and nothing to read, time passed slowly. So much so that Lee had begun to lose faith in Codicil when a jailer arrived. "Good news," the woman said as she unlocked the cell. "You're out of here. Come with me."

Lee's spirits rose as the jailer led her through a maze of halls to a heavily secured door. There, she had to show her wrist tag and sign a log before being allowed to enter the room where she'd been processed six hours earlier. Marvin Codicil was waiting for her.

Codicil was bald on top with white hair that was combed back along both sides of his head. His cheeks were hollow, and that made his face appear gaunt. A pair of glasses, a thin mustache, and a neat goatee completed the look. Codicil was dressed in a blue windbreaker and a polo shirt with khaki pants. "There you are!" he said warmly. "I was able to get you out on your own recognizance. No need to thank me now—the bill will arrive later. Come on . . . Let's get your belongings, and I'll take you home."

It took ten minutes for Lee to retrieve her belt, a lipstick, and a wallet from the man behind the bulletproof glass. Then she had to sign yet another piece of paper before following Codicil out into the cool night air. His *especiale* was sitting in a clearly marked handicapped parking zone. And as Lee got in, she saw the permit that was dangling from the rearview mirror. "You aren't handicapped," she pointed out. "I should give you a ticket."

"Yes, you should," Codicil agreed, as the car pulled away from the curb. "But you can't. Not until you get your badge back."

Lee couldn't help but laugh. "You're incorrigible."

"Look who's talking," Codicil replied. "Now here's the plan. You aren't just *any* cop . . . You're the detective who killed nine bank robbers in a single gunfight—and had the ovaries to go after human traffickers in the red zone. And that makes you something of a folk hero. So the mayor and the chief of police will have to hold at least five meetings and consult a PR agency before they can decide what to do. I'll use that time to work my magic. *You* will use that time to watch TV and paint your toenails. At no point will you communicate with anyone other than me. Is that clear?"

"Yes. Can I ask what you plan to do?"

"No."

Lee looked at him. "Is that because you don't know what you're going to do?"

"Yes."

Lee smiled. "Well, at least you're honest about it."

"Never fear," Codicil said, as the car pulled into her driveway. "I promised to get you off, and I will. All you need to do is sit tight."

Lee thanked him, got out, and made her way up the drive to the kind of four plex that critics referred to as a "dingbat." Meaning one of the formulaic 1950s-era apartment buildings that were still common throughout California. Frank Lee had lived there until his death. Lee had moved in a month later, hoping to find a clue among her father's effects. An overlooked something that would lead her to the Bonebreaker. She was still working on it.

But, as Lee climbed the stairs to the second floor, she came to a horrible realization. Were she to lose her badge, it would be difficult if not impossible to find her father's killer. And that prospect frightened her. Lee felt that she owed it to the man who had raised her all by himself even if she didn't like him as much as she wanted to.

But there was another reason as well. Something she was conscious of but didn't want to fully confront. Somewhere along the line, finding the Bonebreaker had become central to her life. The hunt was her mission, her purpose, and her reason for existing. Healthy? Hell, no. But there it was.

The door opened, and the lights came on as Lee's fingers flipped the familiar switch. "Man-cave modern." That's how one friend described the apartment. And for good reason. The kitchen, which was off to her right, was a tiny space hemmed in by dark wood cabinets. And the appliances were black. Bought on sale probably—by the dingbat's penny-pinching owner.

The kitchen opened into a small eating area, and the living room beyond, where closely drawn floor-to-ceiling curtains made everything seem smaller than was necessary. Brown paint added to the gloomy feel. She could change those things, of course . . . But that would require her to make a commitment to the place.

The bath was to the left, with the bedrooms beyond. It felt good to shed the black pantsuit and get into some sweats. Since it was too late for a predinner jog, Lee went straight to the kitchen and opened the freezer. It was half-full of three-hundred-calorie prepackaged chicken and veggie dinners. Lee popped one of them into the microwave and took a moment to check her mail. There were forty-six voice mails waiting, along with a couple hundred e-mails, all from various media outlets.

The microwave beeped. So Lee pulled the entree out, plopped the steaming tray onto a dinner plate, and took it into the living room. That was where she usually ate, which explained why the salt and pepper shakers were on the coffee table. A quick check served to confirm her worst fears. "The punch" was still getting a lot of play on the local twenty-four-hour news channel. Lee sighed, switched to a documentary about how *B. nosilla* was causing animals to mutate, and ate her dinner. She'd seen how the virus could change dogs, and it was scary.

Then, after throwing the empty tray into the garbage and brushing her teeth, Lee went looking for a gun. She never slept without one, not since the Bonebreaker had threatened her in Tucson, and wasn't about to start.

The solution was the venerable Colt .45 double-action semiauto that her father had liked to carry off duty. It was a reliable weapon although Lee would have preferred a larger magazine. Still, beggars can't be choosers, so she placed the pistol next to her bed. It had been a long and stressful day. But sleep came easily, as did the dreams, and all the things Lee wanted to hide from.

Lee was negotiating a maze, looking for a way out, when her alarm went off. She opened her eyes, saw the horizontal bars of sunlight on the far wall, and knew she'd overslept. On second thought, she *couldn't* oversleep. Not while she was on administrative leave. That meant the sound was emanating from her phone rather than her clock. A member of the media then? Some dickhead who had been able to get a hold of her unlisted number? Probably. Lee let the call go to voice mail. Then it started again.

Lee swore, rolled out of bed, and made her way over to the dresser. The phone continued to ring as she picked it up. She was about to turn the instrument off when she saw that the incoming call was from Marvin Codicil. She thumbed the green bar. "This is Cassandra."

"Finally," Codicil said. "It's nine thirty for God's sake . . . I have good news for you."

Lee felt a sudden surge of hope. "Really?"

"Yes. You can go back to work as of 1:00 p.m. this afternoon if you do exactly what I say."

Lee felt the hope start to fade a bit. "Which is?"

"Which is to participate in a twelve-minute sit-down interview with Carla Zumin at noon today. If you agree, she'll refuse to press charges. That will force the DA to drop the case, and you'll be in the clear."

Lee could imagine it, sitting there under the lights, being grilled for twelve long minutes. It was her idea of hell and would constitute the first such interview she had ever granted. Codicil cleared his throat. "Are you still there?"

"Yes," Lee said, as she sat on the bed. "There's no other way?"

"We can go to trial, the DA will play the tape, and we'll lose. Then I'll ask for a suspended sentence. If we're lucky, he or she will agree but order you to get counseling."

"So, I would lose my job."

"Yes, you would."

Lee considered that. To lose her badge was to lose the Bonebreaker, and she wasn't ready to live without him. "Okay," she said finally, "I'll do it. But I'll have to get a clearance first."

"No need," Codicil said cheerfully. "I proposed the arrangement to Deputy Chief Jenkins an hour ago—and Chief Corso agreed. And why not? If Zumin drops the charges, that's good for the department."

Lee frowned. "Did you say *Deputy Chief* Jenkins?"

"Yes I did. Jenkins has been promoted into McGinty's slot."

"He deserves it," Lee said.

"If you say so," Codicil said. "Now get dressed and be ready in half an hour. I'll pick you up. And, Cassandra . . ."

"Yes?"

"Work on an apology. Something sincere." And with that, the phone went dead.

Lee rushed to shower, put on some makeup, and get dressed. She chose to wear a dress rather than a suit. Hopefully, that, plus some low-key jewelry, would help soften the rogue-cop persona that the media had assigned to her.

Three news teams were parked out front, all hoping for the sort of scoop that Zumin was about to get, so Lee waited for Codicil to pull up before running the gauntlet. Reporters yelled questions at her. "Detective Lee! What was it like in jail?" "Channel 5 here . . . Has a trial date been set?" "Detective Lee . . . Is it true that Carla Zumin stole your boyfriend in high school?"

Lee managed to get through without shoving anyone, jumped into the car, and pulled the door closed. Codicil nodded. "Don't worry, we'll drop the press release immediately after the interview. By this time tomorrow, they'll be focused on something else."

Both remained silent until the car pulled into the lot next to Channel 7. "Are you ready?" Codicil inquired.

"No."

"Well, do your best. Remember, your badge is at stake."

"I'll remember."

"And don't hit anyone."

"I won't."

"Good. Break a leg."

* * *

It was Jenkins's first day as deputy chief and he was already knee deep in crap. Prior to the boss's death, he'd been good cop to McGinty's bad cop—and served as a buffer between the no-nonsense head of the S.I.S. and the team's most controversial member.

But now, as he entered Chief Corso's office, Jenkins had a far better appreciation of why McGinty had been pissed off at Lee so much of the time. And the fact that her latest screwup had taken place at McGinty's funeral was ironic to say the least.

As befitted his station in life, Corso had an enormous office, a large desk, and a wall covered with photos of himself. They included Corso with the president, Corso with the governor, and Corso with the mayor. And in keeping with his political ambitions, the chief had movie-star good looks. His carefully combed hair was just so, his features were boyishly young, and his teeth were unnaturally white. He looked up from his computer terminal as Jenkins entered the office. "So what do you think, Sean? Will she implode?"

"I hope not," Jenkins said grimly. "Codicil promised me that everything would go smoothly."

"Let's hope so," Corso said as he aimed a remote at the wall-mounted flat-screen TV. "The mayor wants this story to go away, and so do I."

It was almost noon, and they had to watch a commercial before the Channel 7 news logo came spinning onto the screen. Jenkins took a seat as the technical director faded up onto a wide shot. And there, seated behind a curving Plexiglas desk, were the noon hour's anchors. The eternally perky Dolly Day was screen left, while square-jawed Tom Cole sat in the middle, with weather nerd Art McGee standing on the right.

Cole wasted no time teasing Carla Zumin's big get. "Good afternoon. By now I think most of our viewers have seen the footage in which Los Angeles Police Detective Cassandra Lee punched one of our reporters in the face. But just in case you missed it—here's what took place when Carla Zumin approached Lee to ask a question."

As the anchorman spoke, the three-shot was replaced by the now-notorious clip. So Jenkins, Corso, and thousands of viewers could enjoy the footage in delicious slow motion as Lee's fist came around to impact the side of Zumin's head. Spittle flew out of Zumin's mouth, and the reporter's eyes rolled back in her head as she collapsed.

"Ouch!" Day said, as the director came back to her. "That had to hurt! But now, in a Channel 7 exclusive, the two women are face-to-face in Studio B. Carla?"

The picture dissolved to a different set, where two women were seated across from each other at an oval table. "Oh my God," Corso exclaimed. "Look at that! Lee is wearing a dress."

Jenkins saw that it was true and felt a new sense of respect for Codicil's powers of persuasion. The director was on a tight shot of Zumin by then. Amazingly enough, the reporter still looked pretty in spite of the black eye. As far as Jenkins could tell, no attempt had been made to conceal the damage with makeup, and, for all he knew, the people at Channel 7 *wanted* to emphasize it. "Good afternoon," Zumin said. "My name is Carla Zumin—and I'm here with LAPD Detective Cassandra Lee. As Dolly indicated I was covering Deputy Chief McGinty's funeral, when I saw an opportunity to approach Detective Lee and ask her how she felt. That was when Detective Lee hit me."

"That's bullshit," Jenkins growled. "I was there. The bitch ambushed us."

Corso nodded as the director went to an over-the-shoulder shot of Lee. A halo of black hair framed her face. Her skin was brown, she had big eyes and full lips. Jenkins would never admit it to anyone else, *couldn't* admit such a thing, but he thought she was beautiful. Lee spoke as the camera zoomed in. "I would like to take this opportunity to apologize for that," she said. "Counting my father, and Deputy Chief McGinty, the Bonebreaker is believed to be responsible for murdering *nine* members of the LAPD over a period of sixteen years. That makes me angry every time I think about it. Still, there's no excuse for what I did, and I hope you'll accept my apology."

"Well done!" Corso said admiringly. "I didn't know she had it in her."

"Apology accepted," Zumin said, as the director cut to her. Then the reporter took the opportunity to ask Lee about the status of the Bonebreaker investigation, the now-famous bank shootout, and the well-publicized Screed case. All of which were subjects Lee hadn't discussed publicly before. A scoop to be sure.

"So," Corso said, when the interview came to an end. "She performed well. Once the DA drops the charge, you can take her off administrative leave. I would suggest a desk job somewhere. Not in media relations, though."

Going one-on-one with the chief was a new experience for Jenkins. And Corso made him nervous. But he was determined to overcome that and took the opportunity to assert himself. "I understand where you're coming from, sir . . . But I would like to suggest an alternative."

Corso listened, skeptically at first, but it wasn't long before a smile appeared. "I can see that I promoted the right man! You are one tricky son of a bitch, Sean . . . Make it happen."

Although the overall plan worked as advertised—Codicil was wrong in one respect. Rather than being allowed to return to work the day of the television interview—three days passed before the DA's Office got around to dropping the assault charge. But that was okay, all things considered, so Lee was in a good mood as she locked the front door and made her way down to the first-floor garage.

When Lee wasn't driving an unmarked car, her sole means of transportation was a postplague replica of a Harley Road King Police Edition motorcycle. Lee kept the bike under a tarp and always looked forward to seeing it again. It was a brutish motorcycle, with a huge headlamp, a teardrop-shaped tank, and saddle-style seat. A pair of white panniers completed the look.

Lee pulled the black-helmet-and-visor combination down over her head, turned the key, and listened as the bike came to life. Even though it hadn't been manufactured in a Harley factory, the big hog produced a satisfying rumble nevertheless. Lee kicked the stand up out of the way, toed the bike into gear, and let it roll down the driveway and onto the street.

From there it was a short trip to a tiny restaurant called Maria's. That was where Lee purchased a breakfast burrito every morning, and because she was usually late, took it with her. That morning was no exception, which meant Lee would have to warm the burrito up once she arrived at work.

From there it was a ten-minute journey through Monday-morning traffic to LAPD headquarters and the ramp that took her down to the point where a steel pipe barred the way. She put the motorcycle in neutral and used her feet to prevent it from rolling downhill as she removed the helmet and shook her hair out. That allowed the officers who were on duty to see her face. "Sorry," Lee said. "I don't have my ID on me. You can call Deputy Chief Jenkins if you need to."

"There's no need for that," one of the patrolmen said. "I *love* the video . . . That shit never gets old. Welcome back."

And that, as it turned out, was a good indicator of the way most of her fellow cops felt. It was a rare police officer who hadn't had some sort of run-in with the media during the course of their careers—and watching Lee punch a reporter had a cathartic effect. So the trip from the parking garage up to the sixth floor was a celebration of sorts complete with fist bumps, high fives, and raucous greetings.

Lee was already running late, and all of the social interaction made her later, as did the need to microwave her breakfast in the break room. So by the time she arrived at roll call, Jenkins was halfway through the morning agenda and, like McGinty before him, was anything but pleased. "I'm glad you could fit us in, Detective Lee . . . How many times have you been told to eat your breakfast *before* you come to work?"

"I don't remember," Lee replied blandly as she took her place at the conference table. The other detectives grinned. It was a classic Cassandra Lee moment, and they'd seen all of it before. Jenkins had something new up his sleeve, however.

"Okay," Jenkins said. "Maybe this will help you remember . . . From now on every time you're late you'll have to deposit ten bucks in the S.I.S. party fund. Cough it up."

That produced a round of cheers, and Lee made a face as she

pulled a wad of nubucks out of a jacket pocket and threw a badly crumpled ten on the table. Jenkins put the bill in a screw-top jar and picked up where he'd left off. Lee took the opportunity to chow down.

The meeting came to an end fifteen minutes later. And as the other detectives began to leave, Jenkins crooked a finger at Lee. "Come with me."

Lee followed the deputy chief into what had been McGinty's office, where she sat on a guest chair as Jenkins circled the desk. He opened a drawer and began to remove items one at a time. "Here you go," he said. "Your Glock, Smith & Wesson, and your badge. Welcome back."

Lee stood to retrieve her belongings. The pistols went into their respective holsters, and the ID slid into a pocket. She felt whole again. "Thanks, boss . . . I appreciate it."

"Okay," Jenkins said, as he sat down. "I have some good news for you."

"What? They're going to close the cafeteria?"

Jenkins smiled. "No, but almost as good. We're putting you in charge of the Bonebreaker investigation."

Lee felt a sudden surge of excitement. "Really? But what about the conflict of interest? The Bonebreaker killed my father."

"We'll be up front about it," Jenkins replied. "We'll admit that it could be a problem but promise to monitor the situation. Imagine the headline: 'Detective Lee leads the search for her father's killer.' The press will love it."

All sorts of thoughts flitted through Lee's mind. The promotion was like a dream come true. She wouldn't need to look for the Bonebreaker in secret anymore—and she would have a team of detectives to help her. What could be better?

But there was something about the assignment that didn't feel right. She'd never been popular with the brass, and she was coming off a suspension, so why give her the equivalent of a reward unless . . . Lee eyed Jenkins. His face was professionally blank. That served to confirm her suspicions. "You rotten bastard! You're going to use me as bait! Putting me in charge of the investigation is like giving the Bonebreaker the finger . . . He'll come for me, and you'll use a shadow team to nail him.

Unless he gets past them . . . And then you'll find my head and torso next to the Santa Monica Freeway."

Jenkins formed a steeple with his fingers. A boyish smile appeared on his face. "So," he said. "Are you in?"

Lee stared at him for a moment. Then she nodded. "I'm in."

TWO

Even as a little girl, Lee had found it difficult to get up in the morning, and nothing had changed. So Lee set *two* alarms and placed both of them well away from her bed. When the first one went off, she managed to muffle the sound by pulling a blanket up over her head. Even so, the second and more shrill alarm was still audible.

Finally, swearing like a sailor, Lee threw off the bedcovers and hurried to silence both machines. That was when the true extent of her accomplishment struck her. She was running on time! And a good thing, too, since she was supposed to attend a very important meeting at 8:00 a.m. Lee hurried to shower, dress, and leave the apartment.

Calling her police car "unmarked" was something of a misnomer because it had exempt plates and was therefore a target for graffiti. Lots of it. So, with a small GPS and cell-phone detector in hand, she circled the car looking for trackers and concluded that it was clean.

After stopping at Maria's for breakfast, Lee set off for work. Fifteen minutes later, she entered Conference Room B on the seventh floor of the LAPD headquarters building. There were some familiar faces and a few she didn't know. And that made sense since Chief Corso had stolen resources from a variety of organizations in order to staff Operation Thunderstorm.

Lee chose to sit next to Detective Dick Yanty. He was balding, wore a pair of wire-rimmed glasses perched on the end of his nose, and was dressed in the usual sports coat. Or maybe he had two jackets that were identical. He raised a doughnut by way of a salute. "Good morning, Cassandra . . . Where's the burrito? Are you on a diet?"

Lee made a face. "No wonder your parents named you Dick . . . They knew how things would turn out."

Yanty laughed. "What do you think? Are we about to take part in a huge circle jerk? Or is this for real?"

Lee shrugged. "I don't know . . . But I hope it's for real. I want to take this asshole down."

All of the participants were seated by then, and as Lee looked around, she counted twenty-five people. Jenkins was the only person still on his feet. He cleared his throat. "Welcome to Operation Thunderstorm. Our mission is to find the serial killer known as the Bonebreaker and bring him to justice.

"The fact that you are here, sitting in this room, means you are one of the best and brightest that the department has to offer. Congratulations on making the cut. Your reward will be the same pay you're already receiving, longer hours, and the satisfaction that flows from working on a high-priority case."

Jenkins's eyes roamed the room. "Okay, enough rah-rah. Let's get down to brass tacks. Operation Thunderstorm is going to be structured in an unusual way. The people in this room will be divided into *two* teams. Detective Cassandra Lee will lead the first team—which will be referred to as the 'public team.' Their job will be to pursue the existing investigation and do so in a manner calculated to attract the Bonebreaker's attention. According to the psychological profile our shrinks put together, he may perceive the public team's activity as a personal affront and try to kill Lee or one of her detectives.

"That's where the shadow team comes in. They, which is to say most of you, will report to Lieutenant Brianna Wolfe here . . . You may be familiar with her role in breaking the Troba drug operation. Brianna, please stand up so everyone can see you."

Lee didn't know Wolfe and hadn't paid any attention to the woman until then but saw that she was quite striking. The first and most jarring aspect of her appearance was the blond crew cut she wore. But rather than make her look masculine, the severe hairstyle served to emphasize her femininity. Wolfe was dressed management-style, in a nicely tailored suit and some tasteful jewelry.

Wolfe looked around the room, nodded to some of the people she knew, and paused as her eyes came to rest on Lee. A spark seemed to jump the gap. Not a sexual spark . . . but something akin to recognition in spite of the fact they didn't know each other. And that was the moment when Lee knew that Wolfe was a potential enemy.

But *why*? The obvious answer was competition. In spite of her aversion to publicity, Lee had a high public profile, and Wolfe didn't. And the other woman was on her way somewhere. To deputy chief? Yes, Lee would have been willing to put money on it. Then the moment was over as Wolfe took her seat, and the briefing continued. "The shadow team will watch over the public team twenty-four hours a day," Jenkins said. "And that will require a lot of resources—so the public team is going to be small.

"The next few days will be spent putting electronic surveillance gear into place—and working out the details required to keep the operation running. Once we accomplish that, we'll hold a press conference, with Detective Lee standing front and center. Will the Bonebreaker take the bait? Let's hope so. But if he does, and the shadow team fails, then someone on the public team will die."

There was total silence as Jenkins looked down at a piece of paper. "Okay, last, but not least . . . This is a *secret* operation. Do not, I repeat do not, disclose any aspect of what we are doing to other members of the LAPD, to your family, or to the press." Jenkins finished with a nod. "That's it . . . Let's do this thing."

A day had passed since the briefing, and Lee was about to meet with her two-person team. They were gathered in a small conference room on the sixth floor. Detective Dick Yanty was taking the opportunity to eat his lunch. It consisted of the P&J sandwich that his wife prepared for him every morning plus a carton of milk. Milo Prospo was digging into a meal purchased in the cafeteria. Lee wrinkled her nose. "What *is* that?"

Prospo looked up. He had black hair, bushy brows, and a perpetual five o'clock shadow. "It's meat loaf with mashed potatoes. You should try it."

"Right . . . When I want to go on medical leave, I'll jump on that. Okay, first things first. What's wrong with you two? Jenkins told me that you volunteered! That's crazy."

Yanty smiled vaguely. "Not my brightest moment, that's for sure. But I've been working on the Bonebreaker case for years . . . And you're going to need someone who is familiar with the evidence. A historian, so to speak. Assuming you plan to work the case, that is."

Yanty pushed his glasses up onto the bridge of his nose and looked Lee in the eye. The challenge was obvious. Was the public team going to investigate? Or sit around and wait for the serial killer to attack one of them? Lee nodded. "I'm glad you raised that issue. Damned right we're going to work the case. And hard, too . . . So your familiarity with the evidence will be a huge help. What about you, Milo? Why did you volunteer?"

Prospo barely contained a belch, and said, "Sorry." When he frowned, two bushy brows became one. "McGinty was a friend of mine. So this is personal. I hope the Bonebreaker comes for me because if he does, I'll kill the bastard."

It was said matter-of-factly—and without a trace of humor. Prospo was serious. Never mind the score, which was the Bonebreaker nine, police zero. Or the fact that the detective was well past fifty and at least twenty pounds overweight. Prospo saw himself as a stone-cold killer. Lee considered some sort of lecture and decided against it. "So," Yanty said. "When's the press conference?"

"At three," Lee answered. "The media-relations people figured that would provide the TV stations with plenty of time to get the story on the evening news."

Prospo used a piece of bread to soak up the last of the gravy. "And then?" he inquired.

"And then I'm going to reinterview Cheyenne Darling. I read the original transcript, and there's no color. It's a straight-on ticktock of what time McGinty went out, when Darling became worried, and so on. I'm hoping for something more.

"Meanwhile, I'd like to see you guys go through the list of people the team talked to in the past and follow up. How many of them were in the slammer when the chief disappeared? How many have some other alibi? And how many are dead? Let's narrow the list."

"Sounds good," Yanty said, as he threw his brown lunch bag into a trash can. "Have fun at three."

"Watch your six," Lee replied. "The Bonebreaker could come after any one of us."

"Roger that," Prospo said, as he carried his plate out of the room. "I'll be waiting for him."

The LAPD headquarters building had opened for business in 2009, was known for its angular appearance, and cost $437 million old bucks to construct. The façade had been damaged by a rocket attack five years earlier and was awaiting repair. But so long as the weather was good, the outside plaza was the perfect spot to hold press conferences. And that was where Lee had been told to report.

About fifteen members of the LAPD were present, including Corso, Jenkins, and Wolfe. Lee nearly missed the latter because she was dressed in a full-on blue uniform complete with hat. But, that said, why was Wolfe there since she was in charge of the shadow team? The answer was glaringly obvious, as Wolfe leaned in to say something in Corso's ear, and he laughed. Lee was looking at a grade-A suck-up.

Her thoughts were interrupted as one of the department's media-relations specialists appeared in front of her. The PR rep had a mop of dark hair, wide-set eyes, and a pointy chin. "Detective Lee? My name is Molly. The chief will speak first, followed by Deputy Chief Jenkins, and you. There will be some Q & A, so be careful . . . If a reporter asks a question about traffic lights, find a way to steer the conversation back to the Bonebreaker. Okay?"

"No problem," Lee said, but that was far from the truth.

Speaking to the press wasn't one of her strong points. Maybe that explained why her palms were sweaty.

Corso stepped up to a portable podium a few seconds later and flashed one of his thousand-megawatt smiles. Then, as the TV cameras zoomed in, the police chief delivered a carefully crafted thirty-second sound pop intended to remind the public of who the Bonebreaker was and why they should care.

Next it was Jenkins's turn to address the crowd. His job was to say all the things Lee couldn't say about herself. After a mention of the now-famous bank shoot-out, and the recent trip into the red zone, he went for the punch line. "And that," Jenkins said, "is why Detective Lee has been named to lead a new investigation into the Bonebreaker murders. And not only is Detective Lee supremely qualified to do the job, she's the daughter of LAPD Sergeant Frank Lee, who is one of the Bonebreaker's nine victims. So who better to track this despicable killer down and put him behind bars? Detective Lee?"

Lee knew that was her cue and felt slightly light-headed as she stepped up to the podium. Then, as the well-rehearsed words began to come out of her mouth, she felt slightly disassociated. As if out of her body and watching herself speak.

Fortunately, that sensation began to fade once the thirty-second statement was over, and the Q & A began. Carla Zumin was there, her eye only slightly discolored, and she cut right to the chase. "The Los Angeles Police Department has been investigating the Bonebreaker murders since 2053 without any significant success. Why should we believe that *this* effort will be any more successful?"

Lee was ready. "That's a good question, Carla . . . For one thing, we plan to devote an unprecedented amount of resources to the case. I can't get more specific without compromising security, but I can assure you that what I say is true.

"Additionally, we're going to put some custom-designed software to work analyzing all of the existing data and looking for significant patterns, and we're going to take advantage of some breakthrough profiling techniques to help us focus on the killer."

Both of those initiatives were entirely fictitious . . . But the

Bonebreaker didn't know that—and maybe the prospect would spook him. "Okay," a second reporter put in. "But what about the issue of objectivity? How can *you*, the daughter of a murder victim, bring the necessary objectivity to the situation?"

"That's where Deputy Chief Jenkins comes in," Lee said with a smile. "He'll be looking over my shoulder. And remember . . . While I may not be entirely objective, I care about this investigation in a way that only a murder victim's daughter can."

That was the perfect exit line, and Molly knew it. So she stepped in to bring the press conference to a close. The trap was set, the bait was in place, and the waiting had begun.

The light was dim inside the underground ossuary. That was a matter of preference as well as necessity since power was precious. The Bonebreaker's electricity was drawn from an illegal tap and piped into the crypt through a carefully camouflaged cable. Not an easy thing for most people to do, but the Bonebreaker wasn't most people and had plenty of time to work with.

So, except for the pool of light provided by a single overhead fixture and the glow that emanated from a flat-screen TV set, the main room was unlit. That was why the Bonebreaker always wore a headlamp as he moved through the tunnels that radiated out from the ossuary like the spokes of a wheel. It was perpetually chilly belowground—but three layers of clothing were sufficient to combat the cold.

Plus, the Bonebreaker was busy. *Very* busy since each time God called on him, there was a lot of work to do. First he had to plan the abduction. A task that could require weeks if not months of observation. Then he had to create a disguise, wait for the right moment, and strike.

Of course, that was only the beginning. Then came the moment of dismemberment, a rather messy process, and the flensing. Or what the Bonebreaker thought of as the holy trinity.

At the moment, he was still in the process of preparing one of Deputy Chief McGinty's bones prior to inscribing it with the police officer's name, date of birth, and a short message. The blade made a scritching sound as he scraped the last bits of tissue off a femur.

Then he took a moment to examine the shaft, using a jeweler's lit headband magnifier. Hopefully, McGinty appreciated the care and respect shown his earthly remains even as his soul burned in hell. Now it was time to put his tools aside, clean the surface of the table, and watch the news. Something he did every day at 5:30 p.m. Channel 7 was already on, so all he had to do was aim the remote and touch MUTE. The lead story had to do with the increasingly serious conflict between the Republic of Texas to the east and the Aztec Empire to the south. The tecs believed that all of the lands that had once been part of Mexico should be returned to them, regardless of the treaties and purchases signed in the past. The Bonebreaker didn't give a shit.

The next story had to do with a terrible house fire in which two adults and three children had perished. He didn't care about that either.

Then, in the number three slot, was a story he *did* care about because it was all about him. The Bonebreaker turned up the volume in order to hear Chief of Police Corso clearly. He was followed by a man named Jenkins and the person God wanted him to kill next: Detective Cassandra Lee. They'd met once, and he could have killed her then, except for one thing. It would have been too quick and painless. That's why a stay of execution had been granted. Now, according to Lee, she was going to hunt him down. Never mind the fact that God was on *his* side. Still, the bitch could get lucky.

The Bonebreaker felt a mishmash of conflicting emotions, including a flush of pleasure at being so important, a sense of superiority that went with having been able to operate with impunity, and just a tinge of fear. And that made him uncomfortable.

It was the first day after the press conference, and as Lee got out of bed, she was very conscious of the fact that eyes were watching her every move. The hidden camera was there to protect her—but it also meant a tremendous loss of privacy.

Rather than the tee shirt and panties that Lee normally wore to bed, she was dressed in plain pajamas. Her plan was to give the males on the shadow team very little to talk about. It was a short trip to the bathroom, which was the only place in the apartment that wasn't bugged. It felt good to close the door and be by herself.

After completing her morning routine, Lee emerged from the bathroom fully dressed. Then, with a wave to the nearest camera, she left the apartment. Lee felt the first drops of rain on her skin as she made her way down to the street. LA had been suffering through a minidrought, and the moisture was welcome.

So Lee was in a relatively good mood as she performed a 360 on the sedan and slipped behind the wheel. That car was equipped with *two* trackers. A primary and a backup that was extremely difficult to access. The hope being that even if the Bonebreaker located the first one, he'd miss the second. Lee pulled away from the curb and was on her way to Maria's, when her phone rang. Lee eyed the number, saw that the call was from Jenkins, and thumbed it on. "Hey, boss . . . What's up?"

"Nice jammies," Jenkins replied. "I have some that are nearly identical to yours."

Lee groaned. "Pervert."

Jenkins chuckled. "Where are you headed?"

"To reinterview Cheyenne Darling."

"Okay . . . But take it easy on her. Cheyenne is a nice lady, and she's been through hell."

"Roger that."

"Can you make it into the office by one?"

"Sure."

"Good. They filled my previous slot, so the new guy will be running the operation, and the sooner you meet him, the better. Lieutenant Wolfe will attend the meeting as well."

Lee wanted to say, "Oh, goody," but managed to restrain herself. "So, who is he?"

"His name is Purdy Ayeman."

"Never heard of him."

"That isn't surprising. We hired him away from San Diego. He was head of HR there."

"He was head of *what*?"

"Don't go there," Jenkins said sternly. "Ayeman was a detective prior to that. Corso wants to bring well-rounded people onto the force."

"I'll bet he's well rounded. People who ride a chair all day usually are."

"Just do your job," Jenkins growled. "And keep your lips zipped. I'll see you at one." The call ended.

It was raining harder by then, and the wipers slapped back and forth as Lee took the exit to Laurel Canyon Boulevard and turned north. Upscale homes lined both sides of the road. The car's nav system told her when to turn off.

Once Lee spotted the correct address, she turned onto the two-car-wide concrete platform that jutted out from the side of a steep hill and parked next to an expensive-looking sports car. That was when she remembered the lunch with McGinty months earlier and the vehicle he'd been driving then. The *same* vehicle, judging from appearances.

Lee locked the sedan and followed a flight of concrete stairs down to a modernistic house that was partially cantilevered out over the hillside and surrounded by well-kept vegetation. Water gurgled as it passed through the downspout located a couple of feet away from a red door. Raindrops pattered all around as she pushed the button and heard a distant chime. That was followed by the sound of footsteps and a metallic click.

As the door opened, Lee saw that Darling's bangs were just so, there was a slightly sleepy look in her eyes, and she was holding a blue mug. The smile came quickly. "Detective Lee! I know we haven't met, but it *feels* as though we have. Ross spoke about you frequently—plus I've seen you on TV. Please . . . come in."

Lee wondered what McGinty had said. Odds were that it was negative since the two of them hadn't been on friendly terms until two months before his death. "Thank you . . . My! What a beautiful home!"

"It's an endless project," Darling said, as she led the way into the living room. "I'm an inveterate tweaker. The unending changes drove Ross crazy. Can I get you something to drink? Coffee perhaps?"

"No, thank you . . . I drank some on the way over." Lee could see that every picture, every lamp, and every piece of furniture was part of a carefully orchestrated whole. A marked contrast to the way she lived and a sure sign that Darling wasn't the sort of person to speak off the cuff.

Wall-to-wall sliding glass doors fronted the living room and could be opened during good weather. Not at the moment, though, since the only thing Lee could see was mist and rain. "Please have a seat," Darling said. "That was Ross's favorite chair over there . . . the one with the unobstructed view of the TV set!"

Darling smiled, which caused Lee to wonder if the chair and its location had been part of a private joke. She chose to perch on the couch instead. "Thank you for agreeing to see me. I'm going to record our conversation if that's okay." Lee leaned forward to place a small recorder on the coffee table. She pushed RECORD and a red light came on.

"That's fine," Darling said, as she kicked her shoes off in order to curl up in a well-upholstered chair. "I'll do anything I can to help." She was wearing a white blouse over blue jeans. A simple outfit but one that looked like a classic on her.

"Some of my questions are personal, perhaps painfully so," Lee began.

Darling shrugged. "A little more pain won't make much difference."

"How long had the two of you been together?"

"Almost twenty years."

"And you were married?"

"Not in the legal sense, no."

"May I ask why?"

Darling turned to look outside for a moment before turning back. "Ross said that getting married would be a mistake. He said he might not come home one day." A tear trickled down Darling's cheek, and she wiped it away.

"So he thought he might be killed in the line of duty."

"I guess so," Darling said uncertainly. "But he had nightmares. Terrible dreams that caused him to cry out in his sleep. He wouldn't tell me what they were about."

This was new information. The sort of stuff not included in the previous interview. By choice? Or because the investigator failed to ask? Of course, just because it was new didn't mean that it was important. "So you think that the dreams were connected with his decision not to marry?"

Darling plucked a tissue out of the box on the table next to her and dabbed at her eyes. "I don't know," she said. "But he refused to live here. He would visit nearly every day, and sleep for a few hours on occasion, but always went home afterwards."

Lee tried to remember if she'd read anything about McGinty's home but couldn't come up with anything and made a note to follow up. "So, was that a quirk in your estimation? Or something else?"

"Ross said I'd be safer that way . . . That if someone came after him, they wouldn't hurt me."

"I see," Lee said. "Was that a general concern that he had? Or was he trying to protect you from the Bonebreaker?"

"I thought it was general before his death," Darling replied. "But now I realize that I was wrong. His attitude changed immediately after the Bonebreaker killed the second policeman years ago."

"Larry Evans."

"Yes, Ross made his decision shortly after that. I'm sorry about your father by the way. This must be very difficult for you as well."

"It's tough," Lee admitted. "But maybe we can prevent the Bonebreaker from killing another cop. I have one more question. Was there anything different about the night the chief disappeared?"

Darling shook her head. "No. We ate dinner here. Then he watched the second half of a baseball game and went home. Assistant Chief Jenkins called the next day and asked to speak with him. That was when the two of us realized that something was wrong."

Lee knew the rest of it. How two days passed before a patrol unit found the red sports car parked in a supermarket parking lot—and how another three days elapsed before McGinty's head and torso were found next to the freeway.

The interview came to an end shortly thereafter. Darling saw Lee to the door and gave her a hug. "Be careful, Cassandra," she said. "And keep me informed to the extent that you can."

Lee promised to do so. And as she climbed the stairs to the parking pad, she noticed that the rain had stopped. If that was an omen, she had no idea what it meant.

After performing a 360, Lee got into the car and began the trip downtown. There were plenty of things to think about but the most central issue had to do with McGinty's motivation. Were his actions those of a cop who, knowing that other police officers had been murdered, had taken reasonable steps to protect the woman he loved?

Or, did the chief have a particular reason to be afraid? Something he'd done that could make him a target? Of course, that would imply that all nine victims had something in common other than their status as police officers. That was a possibility that had been considered more than once over the years, and maybe it was time to do so again.

Lee was still thinking about the case as she pulled into the LAPD garage, showed her ID to a patrol officer at the checkpoint, and went looking for a parking slot. She arrived on the sixth floor ten minutes later. It was only a few minutes past noon, which meant she could spend some time in her cubicle. There were lots of e-mails to answer plus the usual pile of paper in her in-box. Lee was only halfway through it when she ran out of time.

In an effort to put her best foot forward, Lee stopped by the ladies' room to check herself in the mirror before making her way to Jenkins's office. Wolfe was already there. For how long? Lee wondered. And talking about *what*?

Wolfe nodded as Lee entered, but her face was empty of expression, and Lee had no way to know what the bitch was thinking. *Why think of her that way?* Lee asked herself. *She hasn't done anything to you. No,* the other Lee replied, *not yet anyway.*

Jenkins smiled. "How did it go?"

Lee discovered that she didn't want to share the information, not with Wolfe, but knew that was stupid. She gave the other officers a brief rundown and finished by saying, "So, it looks like

McGinty believed he was a target."

"That's interesting," Jenkins said. "I had no idea that the chief was so concerned. I wish he'd said something."

Jenkins might have said more, but Ayeman chose that moment to enter the office. He was well over six feet tall, and in spite of his time in HR, there was nothing round about him. Lee figured he was a runner—although he could have been anything. A tennis player, perhaps? In any case, the man had perfect hair, piercing blue eyes, and a gleaming smile. Ayeman spotted Wolfe right away and went over to shake hands with her. "Lieutenant Wolfe? This is a pleasure . . . I read about the way you solved that drug case. Nice work!"

The two of them were still holding hands when Jenkins cleared his throat. "Lieutenant Wolfe is in charge of the shadow team, as you know. But it's Detective Lee and her people who are working the Bonebreaker case."

"*And* serving as bait," Ayeman said admiringly as he turned to greet Lee. "I'm familiar with your work as well . . . Although I hope you won't have to shoot nine people while we're working together! Yes, I know, the public ate that up. But there's no 'I' in 'team,' is there? And that's what Operation Thunderstorm calls for . . . teamwork."

Lee felt the anger boil up inside of her and saw the frown appear on Jenkins's face but couldn't stop herself. "I didn't get up that day looking for an opportunity to get on TV. The perps were robbing a bank."

Ayeman smiled apologetically. "Sorry . . . It looks like I hit a nerve. No, of course you didn't. But the point remains. Teamwork. That's the ticket to success."

Lee saw the corners of Wolfe's mouth turn up and wondered what she was thinking. Was Wolfe drinking the Kool-Aid? Or did she think Ayeman was a loon as well? It was impossible to tell.

"By the way," Ayeman said, as he dropped into the remaining chair. "This is an excellent time to talk about the importance of good documentation when managing a team. I'm going to ask each supervisor to complete a personnel assessment form for each person who reports to them. That's what we'll use to set goals, measure performance, and make decisions about whom to promote."

Lee looked at Jenkins. How did he feel about the suggestion that his work had been less than adequate? But if the deputy chief was offended, there was no sign of it on his face. So either he agreed with the initiative—or had decided to give his new guy some rope. To what extent had Jenkins been involved in hiring Ayeman anyway? Was the desk jockey *his* choice for the job? Or had Chief Corso done all of the choosing for him? "I'm kind of busy right now," Lee said. "What's the deadline on those forms?"

Ayeman smiled lazily. "The day after tomorrow at roll call. I hear you have a tendency to show up late, Detective Lee. Here's a piece of advice: Don't."

It wasn't easy, but Lee managed to extricate herself from the meeting without running her mouth. She should have gone to work filling out personnel assessment forms for Yanty and Prospo, but there was no fucking way. Not until she managed to cool off.

So Lee went down to the garage, got in the sedan, and left the building. It was a relatively short drive to the LAPD Academy and the shooting range there. Her days at the academy seemed like ancient history now. She parked in the lot, and as Lee made her way through the facility, various people said hello to her. It felt good to mingle with *real* cops after spending twenty minutes with Ayeman.

Having neglected to check the schedule before coming over, Lee was relieved to discover that the range was currently open for monthly qualifications. A requirement that every officer had to comply with.

After checking in and picking up some standard safety gear, Lee followed a uniformed patrol officer out into the open area, where a dozen lanes led to the same number of head and torso targets. Lee and two other police officers took their positions as the range master put them on standby. That was followed by the command to advance and fire.

In order to qualify, each person had to score a minimum number of hits at twenty-five yards, fifteen yards, and seven yards. At each distance, it was necessary to draw, fire, and reload. Firing weapons was something that Lee not only was good at but enjoyed. And by pretending to shoot at her new boss, Lee managed to release most of the tension that had built up during the meeting.

The .9mm Glock was her primary weapon, but Lee took the opportunity to fire her backup as well and was pleased to see the tight grouping the Smith & Wesson produced from seven yards. Then it was time to pick up her brass and find out how she'd done. A passing grade was 147 out of a possible 210. Her score was 192. Not bad . . . Not bad at all.

Lee was feeling pleased with herself as she walked out into the sunshine. She looked up, saw that rays of sunlight were slanting through broken clouds, and noticed something else as well. What looked like a toy airplane was circling above her. A small drone? Yes. The shadow team was watching over her.

Lee took comfort from that as she crossed the parking lot to the spot where the sedan was parked. It beeped, and the parking lights flashed when Lee thumbed her key. The scanner was in her pocket. She removed the device and turned it on. And it was then, just as Lee prepared to circle the car, that she heard the mosquito-like whine. So she looked up and was startled to see that the drone was diving straight at her! She ducked as the miniature airplane struck the vehicle. There was a flash of light, a clap of thunder, and the world went dark.

THREE

As Lee came to, she could hear the muffled sound of the siren and feel the ambulance sway as it rounded a corner. When she tried to sit up, her head hurt. The EMT put a hand on her shoulder and shook her head. She had a softly rounded face and was wearing a stethoscope. "Don't move, hon . . . The doctors need to look you over."

Lee remembered the drone and the split-second decision to duck. Had that been the difference? She was alive, so maybe it had. "I need to make a phone call," she croaked.

"No you don't," the EMT countered. "We know who you are, the police department was notified."

So all Lee could do was lie there while the ambulance pulled into the hospital's parking lot and came to a stop in front of the entrance to the emergency room. She wanted to get off the stretcher and walk in, but the EMT wasn't having any of that.

So Lee was forced to remain where she was as the attendants pulled the stretcher out of the van, allowed the undercarriage to deploy, and wheeled her inside. There was a brief pause near the front desk, followed by a short trip to the treatment area. Then came a flurry of activity as a nurse took her vital signs, and Lee stared up at the stylized sky on the ceiling. She could see the sun, plus some fluffy clouds, but no drones.

Then the privacy curtain parted to admit a small woman. She was wearing a white coat over OR scrubs. "Hello," she said.

"I'm Doctor Wu . . . How do you feel?"

"As if I was hit in the head."

Wu laughed. "Your sense of humor is intact . . . That's a good sign. Do you feel dizzy? Or nauseous?"

"No, but my head hurts."

"I'm sure it does," Wu said sympathetically. "Please turn your head to the left. Let's see what we have."

Lee turned her head, winced, and tried to look stoic as the bandage was removed. "You have a scalp laceration," Wu announced as she examined the wound. "But I'd say you got off easy given what happened. Five stitches, maybe six, and you'll be good as new! We'll have to shave a small area around the wound. Sorry about that."

"Can I go home?"

"Probably," Wu replied. "We'll see how you're doing once the stitches are in place."

Wu injected a local anesthetic into the area around the cut and went to work. It took less than fifteen minutes for Wu to close the gash, apply a small bandage, and declare Lee fit for release. A nurse gave her some pain pills, and she took two.

That was when Jenkins appeared. There was a frown on his face and a look of concern in his eyes. "Cassandra? Damn, girl . . . You scared the hell out of me."

"Sorry," Lee said. "The sky fell in."

Jenkins turned to Wu. "Can she leave?"

The doctor nodded. "Yes. She should be fine. But if she feels dizzy or nauseous, bring her in."

Lee thanked Wu, allowed herself to be wheeled outside, and felt a little light-headed when she stood. But that passed as Jenkins helped her into the passenger seat of his car. "So," Lee said, as Jenkins got behind the wheel. "What the hell happened?"

Jenkins pulled out of the loading zone and steered the car toward the street. "That's a damned good question. Wolfe's looking into it. But, pending further investigation, it looks like the Bonebreaker took the bait."

"Really? With a *drone*? That's way outside his MO."

"True," Jenkins conceded. "But who else would do such a thing? Maybe the press conference spooked him . . . Maybe he's scared. I'll check with the shrinks to see what they think."

"Good idea," Lee said. "What's Ayeman up to? Is he busy updating my personnel file or something?"

Ayeman was her supervisor. Normally, *he* would be the one to rush to the hospital, and Jenkins was well aware of that. He kept his eyes on the road. "Ayeman has a lot of meetings scheduled for today. I left a message for him."

Lee smiled thinly. "Tell him not to worry . . . I'll turn the personnel assessments in on time."

Lee made a point out of arriving on time the following morning and took a lot of good-natured ribbing as she crossed the bull pen. "Hey, Lee," one detective said, "don't sit near a window!" She flipped him the bird and kept walking.

The drone attack was all over the news by then, and Lee had been forced to say, "No comment," over and over again as she hurried from her apartment to the car that had been sent to pick her up. Now, as she entered the conference room, there were more jokes mixed with a bit of sympathy. "The motor pool wants their car back," one officer said. "What happened to your hair?" another wanted to know. "It took a hit."

"Ignore the cretins," Yanty said as he pulled a chair out for her. "We're glad you're okay."

Ayeman entered as Lee sat down. Wolfe was two steps behind him. And when he took a seat, Wolfe sat next to him. "Good morning," Ayeman said. "As all of you are aware, someone tried to kill Detective Lee yesterday. Thankfully, they failed.

"We have no way to know who initiated the attack, but unless we receive information to the contrary, we're going to assume that the Bonebreaker was controlling the drone. The shrinks think he's scared. If so, that could explain his departure from his past MO."

Yanty raised a hand and got a nod. "Regardless of *who* did it, where was the shadow team at the time?"

Lee smiled. Yanty might *look* like a CPA—but he had some balls. Based on their facial expressions, it was easy to see that neither Ayeman nor Wolfe were pleased. They couldn't dodge the issue, though. "Would you like to take that one?" Ayeman inquired, as he turned to look at Wolfe.

Lee watched as Wolfe's eyes shifted from Yanty to make contact with hers. "Of course . . . The simple answer is that the possibility of a drone attack never occurred to us. We fucked up. It won't happen again."

Lee was pleasantly surprised. Wolfe was willing to take responsibility. That made quite a contrast to pass-the-buck Ayeman. *Maybe I was wrong about her,* Lee thought to herself. *And maybe you weren't,* the other Lee countered. *It ain't over until it's over.*

Having successfully avoided any blame, Ayeman nodded. "I, for one, appreciate Lieutenant Wolfe's honest appraisal. Now that we know about the danger, we will take steps to prevent such attacks.

"Detective Lee, if you feel up to it, please make yourself available for a press conference at one o'clock. We're going to pull the Bonebreaker's chain. Who knows? Maybe he'll show up in person next time. If he does, we'll nail him."

Roll call went downhill from there as Ayeman covered a variety of topics including a ten-minute dissertation on how important the personnel assessment process was. Prospo fell asleep halfway through the lecture—but came to when Lee nudged him.

Once the team was dismissed, Lee returned to her cube, where she forced herself to fill out assessment forms on both of her subordinates, studied the statement Molly had e-mailed to her, and took a pain pill before reporting to the sun-splashed plaza.

The second press conference was similar to the first except that it had a more militant tone. "There's a coward out there," Ayeman said as he read from a prepared statement. "A lunatic who tried to assassinate Detective Lee with a homemade drone. But I'm happy to say that the attack failed—and she's standing here beside me. Detective Lee?"

That was Lee's cue to step in front of the mike, look perky, and deliver a largely fictitious report about how much progress had been made. The press had lots of questions about the drone attack, but experts were present to deal with the technical stuff, and that meant Lee could fade.

She was supposed to meet Yanty down in the garage at two and got there with time to spare. By visiting the personnel department, and raising a fuss, Yanty had been able to obtain McGinty's *real* address. A place the first set of investigators missed because they, like everyone else, assumed that the chief lived with Cheyenne Darling.

Yanty was at the wheel and clearly knew where he was going as they drove to the south side of the downtown area. It appeared that McGinty, like Lee, preferred to live close to work. The address they were looking for was emblazoned on the front of a nondescript apartment building. It was a boxy affair that had an ugly parking lot out front with two graffiti-covered Dumpsters sitting off to one side.

After parking in a slot marked VISITORS, Yanty told her to wait while he went looking for the manager. He had spoken to the woman earlier and was armed with a search warrant. Under normal circumstances, Lee would have gone with him but was grateful for the chance to take it easy. The detective was back ten minutes later. Lee got out of the car. "The manager says McGinty wouldn't let anyone enter the apartment unless he was notified ahead of time," Yanty said. "So we're the first ones to go in since his death."

Yanty led her inside. An elevator with a cracked mirror and threadbare carpet carried them up to the fourth floor, where the smell of what Lee recognized as Indian cooking permeated the air. Yanty led her to apartment 407, inserted the key into the lock, and motioned for her to move aside. Then he unlocked the door, took a step to the right, and gave it a push.

The double-barreled shotgun went off with a roar—and sprayed the opposite wall with double-ought buck. Both detectives drew their weapons as Lee called out, "Los Angeles Police! Drop your weapon and come out with your hands up!" A man down the hall stepped out into the hall to look around and went back inside when Yanty flashed a badge at him.

Not having received a reply, Lee took a peek around the corner. Gun smoke eddied in the air. The shotgun was clamped to a sawhorse. Wire cables led from it to pulleys and from there to the door. "It was a booby trap," Lee said. "How the hell did you know?"

"I didn't," Yanty confessed. "It pays to be careful, that's all."

"You are a fucking genius," Lee said admiringly. "I'll call the bomb squad. Who knows what else might be waiting in there."

It took twenty minutes to get the bomb squad on-site, and Lee had a headache by then. Yanty took her back to headquarters, where she requested another car and drove it home. Lee knew that the walls had eyes, but she was too tired to care. The moment her jammies were on, she went to bed. Sleep pulled her down.

Lee overslept the next morning, missed roll call altogether, and went to visit Jenkins. If he was upset about her tardiness, there was no sign of it on his face. "There are two possibilities," he said, as Lee took a seat. "The first and most obvious is that McGinty hoped to bag the Bonebreaker. But it could have been the other way around as well. What if the Bonebreaker killed McGinty, went to the apartment, and rigged the shotgun?"

"And?" Lee prompted.

"And we don't know yet. Not for sure. But it's my guess that McGinty's fingerprints are all over that shotgun. That's why he told the manager not to enter the apartment without talking to him first."

"That makes sense," Lee agreed. "Plus, prior to the drone attack, the Bonebreaker always did things the same way. And it's a stretch to think that he abducted the chief, locked him up somewhere, and went to the apartment to set a trap."

"Exactly," Jenkins said. "We'll see what, if anything, the forensics people come up with. They're processing the apartment now."

"Good," Lee said. "In the meantime Yanty, Prospo, and I are going to look at all of the past suspects. Who knows? Maybe we'll get lucky."

"Be careful out there," Jenkins cautioned. Lee promised that she would and left.

Thus began the long, tedious process of checking to see

which suspects were still alive, which ones were on the loose, and where they'd been on the day of the abduction. And in the wake of the drone attack the police had another filter to apply. Given the complexities involved in building a drone, even one that came in a kit, the profilers had reason to believe that the Bonebreaker was an educated man.

So days went by, the headaches disappeared, and Lee's hair grew back. During that time, the team took a second look at a retired science teacher with a penchant for sadomasochism, a computer programmer who enjoyed killing cats, and a priest who had switched his allegiance to Satan.

But the science teacher was confined to a wheelchair, the programmer was in prison the day McGinty disappeared, and the priest had been killed in an auto accident. And Chief Corso was getting antsy. Operation Thunderstorm was sucking up a lot of valuable resources, and the department had nothing to show for the effort thus far. And that was bad for Jenkins since the whole thing was his idea. But things changed when Prospo phoned Lee and asked her to join him and Yanty in a conference room on the seventh floor.

Lee got off the elevator and made her way down a long hallway to Conference Room 7-J, which was located next to an emergency stairwell. When Lee opened the door, it was obvious that Yanty and Prospo had converted the tiny space into their own mini–operations center—complete with pieces of paper taped to the walls and a big stack of cardboard boxes, all of which were marked as EVIDENCE.

A table occupied the center of the room, and both men were seated at it. Prospo was halfway through a candy bar, and Yanty was typing on his laptop. "What the heck is *this*?" Lee inquired as she took a look around.

"It's where we drink coffee and take naps," Yanty replied. "And every once in a while, we do some work. That's how we came up with a grade-A, number one suspect for you."

Lee felt a rising sense of hope. Prospo and Yanty were good detectives, so if they had a suspect, there was bound to be some there-there. "I like it," Lee said as she sat down. "Tell me more."

"His name is Arnold Kaplan," Prospo said, as he pushed an

eight-by-ten mug shot across the table. The man in the picture had a receding hairline, dead eyes, and a soul patch on his chin. "This piece of shit was halfway through medical school when he stabbed his wife to death, dismembered her in the bathtub, and used a secondhand vacuum sealer to package the body parts. Then he took the packaged parts out of the apartment house one or two at a time and drove to who knows where. He never told anyone."

Lee's eyebrows rose. "How do we know all of this?"

"We know because Kaplan's wife thought he was banging her sister—and placed tiny surveillance cameras all over their apartment three days before he killed her," Yanty replied. "And when Kaplan reported his wife missing, and a couple of patrolmen asked to take a look around, he couldn't say no. Not without looking like he had something to hide. One of the boys in blue was a sharp cookie. He came across the wireless recorder, checked to see what was on it, and blamo! Case solved."

"Okay," Lee said. "But the guy's in the slammer, right?"

"Wrong," Prospo said. "All this took place back in 2051. About a year later, the bastard escaped custody while being transported from the North Kern Prison to Tehachapi. And he hasn't been seen since."

"The first murder took place in 2053," Lee said. "So he was out and about at the right time. But *why*?"

"Revenge, pure and simple," Yanty suggested.

"It fits," Lee said cautiously. "Kaplan is educated, has a demonstrated willingness to kill, and knows how to butcher a body."

"So?" Prospo said hopefully.

"So let's find the bastard."

Even though Arnold Kaplan would have preferred to delegate such chores, it was his experience that "pickups" couldn't be left to others, not if he wanted to keep the donors in tiptop condition. He was riding shotgun in the long, gleaming hearse as it oozed through traffic. *Check all of the lights before you depart and drive at five miles per hour under the limit.* Those were just two of the rules that Kaplan's employees had to obey.

And, if the police stopped the hearse, what would they discover? What they *expected* to discover ... A body in a coffin. Never mind the fact that the wino wasn't dead but heavily sedated. That would escape all but the most rigorous examinations, and very few people wanted to get up close and personal with a dead body. Cops included.

Of course, transporting the donor was the easy part. Identifying a good "pick" was more difficult. Age was the chief criterion, because the older a homeless person was, the more damage one could expect to the donor's liver and kidneys. And Kaplan prided himself on supplying top quality "meat" to his clients in the red zone.

Although nearly all mutants were disfigured in some way, most could live fairly normal lives. But there were those, perhaps as many as 5 percent of the mutant population, who would die without an organ transplant. Most had to settle for hearts, lungs, or livers harvested from other mutants. But that was far from ideal.

No, those who could afford to pay wanted to receive *normal* organs. And to get them, they had to depend on suppliers like Kaplan, who maintained a citywide network of "spotters." It was their job to locate healthy candidates and summon the hearse. Then, once the order was filled, Kaplan would ship it east.

The driver turned into the drive and followed it up and around to the rear of the two-story funeral home, where Kaplan's staff hurried out to meet it. The wino would be dead in fifteen minutes, fully processed by 10:00 a.m., and on the way to the red zone by noon. Then it would be time to make the drive to Malibu and Kaplan's oceanfront home. Life was good. And so, come to think of it, was death.

After sharing the information about Kaplan with her superiors, Lee received the go-ahead to follow up early the next morning. Eleven years had passed since Kaplan's escape, and the case was ice-cold. That made it difficult to know where to start.

The team was gathered in Conference Room 7-J for a

brainstorming session. "Kaplan will have a new identity by now," Lee predicted. "And chances are that he'll look different as well."

"True," Yanty agreed. "But his skills are the same. He can't practice medicine, but he could get work as an orderly, a lab tech, or something like that."

"Good thinking," Lee said. "Although it will be damned hard to sort through such a large population."

There was a moment of silence followed by a comment from Prospo. "There's another thing he can't change . . . And that's his relatives. Maybe he cut them off, and maybe he didn't."

"That seems like the best place to start," Lee said. "Eleven years is a long time. Even if he was careful not to contact them in the beginning, he could figure that it's safe to do so now. Let's go out and talk to every damned one of them."

That, as it turned out, was easier said than done. Kaplan had a brother and a sister. His mother was still alive, as was *her* mother, and any number of uncles, aunts, and cousins. Lee elected to start with Kaplan's mother, while Yanty and Prospo went off to interview the murderer's siblings.

Mrs. Kaplan lived in the working-class neighborhood of Glendale. And as Lee pulled into a parking place across the street, she saw that the house she was looking for was a two-story Craftsman. According to the information she'd been able to dig up, Kaplan's mother was a retired nurse and therefore likely to be home. Lee hoped so as she got out and locked the car.

But what about Kaplan? Did *he* live there, too? After such a long time, anything was possible. And if she surprised him, all hell could break loose. But that was what the panic button in her pocket was for. All she had to do was press it, and the shadow team would swoop in to save her ass. Lee took a quick look around and was pleased to see that none of Wolfe's people were visible.

She crossed the street, climbed a flight of stairs, and approached the door. The green paint had started to peel. Lee pushed the doorbell, waited for a while, and pushed again. The door opened to reveal a pleasant-looking woman clad in a light sweater and slacks. She had the wary expression of someone who is ready to tell a stranger no. She smiled. "Yes?"

Lee presented her badge case. "I'm Detective Lee . . . Are you Mrs. Kaplan? If so, I'd like to ask you some questions."

The response was sad to see. The woman's face fell, and there was sorrow in her eyes. "Yes, I'm Beth Kaplan. Is this about Arnie?"

"Yes, I'm afraid so."

"Is he dead?"

"No, not so far as I know. We're looking for him. Is he here?"

Lee's thumb was resting on the panic button as she watched Mrs. Kaplan's expression. But it remained unchanged. "No, he isn't. I haven't seen him since the day they sentenced him to life in prison. They should have executed him. Would you like to come in?"

Lee thought the juxtaposition of the two comments was somewhat jarring. She nodded. "Yes, ma'am. I would."

Mrs. Kaplan led Lee into a well-kept but slightly dated living room. A picture was hanging over the fireplace. The color photo was of a man wearing a white hat and a dark uniform. "That's my husband, Bill," Mrs. Kaplan said, as Lee paused to look at the picture. "He was a fireman. *B. nosilla* killed him. Arnie got sick, too—but he recovered."

Lee took note of that. There were cases where people infected with *B. nosilla* had mental problems as a result. Was Arnold Kaplan one of them?

"Please," Mrs. Kaplan said. "Have a seat. May I ask why you're here? It's been a long time since anyone spoke to me about the case."

Lee sat on the couch. A cat jumped down and scurried away. There was no reason to lie. The strategy was to flush the Bonebreaker out. So if his mom warned him, that was fine. Her phone line and her e-mail were being monitored and would continue to be until Lee said otherwise. Besides, Lee had been on TV talking about the Bonebreaker case, so it was only a matter of time until Mrs. Kaplan remembered her. "I'm in charge of the Bonebreaker investigation," Lee said.

Mrs. Kaplan frowned. "That's right . . . You were on the news. Does this mean that you think Arnie is the Bonebreaker?"

"We think it's a possibility," Lee replied.

"What he did to Carol was horrible," Mrs. Kaplan said, as she looked away. "I don't know what went wrong."

"Such things are always hard to understand," Lee said sympathetically. "Your son never tried to contact you?"

Mrs. Kaplan's eyes swung back to make contact with Lee's. "No. Arnie knows I would turn him in."

"What about other members of the family? How do they feel?"

"His brother and sister feel as I do," Mrs. Kaplan answered. "As for my mother, well, she lives in a state of denial. She believes that Arnie is a doctor."

"I see," Lee said. "Can I speak with her?"

"Of course, but it won't do you much good. She's senile. But I'll write the address down and let the assisted-living center know that you're coming."

"Thank you," Lee said. "I would appreciate that. Would it be okay if I took a look around?"

Mrs. Kaplan made a face. "I can't say that I like the idea, but I guess there's no point in saying no. I'm sure you can get a search warrant if you want to."

"I will be as nonintrusive as possible," Lee promised. It took about fifteen minutes to check all of the rooms. Not for little things but to see if another person was living in the house. And as far as Lee could tell, Beth Kaplan was telling the truth.

As Lee left, Mrs. Kaplan gave her a piece of paper with an address on it. "Please take it easy on my mother. She's eighty-six and in poor health."

"Of course."

"And one more thing," Mrs. Kaplan said, as they stepped out onto the porch. "If you run into my son, don't turn your back on him." And with that, she went back inside.

It was still morning, so Lee decided to visit Kaplan's grandmother. And since the assisted-living facility was only two miles away, the trip didn't take long. As Lee pulled into a large parking lot, she saw that the building was three stories tall, nicely painted, and surrounded by a well-kept lawn. Before leaving the car, Lee got on the radio to let the shadow team know what she was up to. And as she got out of the vehicle, Lee couldn't help but look up to see if a drone was circling above. The sky was clear.

Lee entered the lobby via a wheelchair-friendly automatic door and crossed over to the point where a reception desk fronted one wall. The woman seated behind the mahogany bulwark had a pleasant appearance and a somewhat exaggerated manner. It was as if she believed that every word she said had to be amplified. Her name tag read, WILMA. "Good morning!" she said, in a voice loud enough to be heard on the other side of the room. "How are you?"

"I'm fine, thank you," Lee answered. "My name is Cassandra Lee. Mrs. Kaplan said she would call ahead."

"Yes," Wilma said brightly. "You're here to see Mrs. Kelly . . . Please sign the guest book. Then I'll call Margaret and let her know that you're here."

Lee took a ballpoint pen out of a cup with a smiley face on it, and was about to sign the register, when something occurred to her. "Tell me," she said, "does Margaret get a lot of visitors?"

"Her daughter comes at least once a week," Wilma answered cheerfully, "and her grandchildren visit regularly as well. Then there's Dr. Duncan . . . He drops by one or two times a month."

Lee frowned. "Really? Her doctor comes *here*?"

"Wonderful, isn't it?" Wilma gushed. "I wish more doctors would do that. It's difficult for residents like Margaret to get out and about."

"Yes," Lee said, as she flipped through the pages in front of her. "It is."

Wilma knew something was up by then and frowned. "I'm sorry, Miss Lee, but I can't allow you to . . ."

Lee produced her ID case and flipped it open so Wilma could see the card and badge. "I'm here on official business," Lee said as she put the leather folder away. "Please keep my visit to yourself. And that includes Margaret. Okay?"

Wilma swallowed. "Of course."

"Good. If it isn't too much trouble, please make a copy of *this* page . . . the one with the doctor's signature on it."

The receptionist stood and stepped away to make the copy. Lee took the opportunity to look around the room. Three women and a man were playing cards at a table. A fire was burning in the gas fireplace despite the fact that it was seventy-five degrees outside. And there, up in a corner, was a surveillance camera. "Here you go," Wilma said, and Lee turned to receive the copy. "So you won't be going up to see Margaret?"

"No," Lee said. "Not today. I notice you have a surveillance system. I would like to look at the tape that corresponds to the last time that Dr. Duncan came by."

"You'll need to talk to Eva about that," Wilma said. "I'll get her."

The manager turned out to be a young woman named Eva Mendez. She had a pageboy haircut, bright red lipstick, and matching nails. Once Lee identified herself, Mendez took her into an office and closed the door. They watched the video together, found the snippet that featured the man who called himself Dr. Duncan, and froze it.

That was when Lee had a moment of self-doubt. Duncan looked very different from Arnold Kaplan's mug shot. *But that makes sense,* Lee told herself. *He worked hard to change his appearance—and he's eleven years older.* "Can I take this with me?" she inquired.

"I don't see why not," Mendez replied. "Especially if you could make a copy for me. We're supposed to keep the tapes for ninety days."

"Done," Lee said. "Thank you very much . . . Please don't mention my visit to Mrs. Kelly or anyone on your staff."

Mendez frowned. "Is Margaret in danger?"

"No," Lee answered. "She isn't. But if Dr. Duncan is who we think he is—we may need your help in order to catch him. I'll let you know."

Lee's heart was beating just a little bit faster as she left. Was the doctor Margaret Kelly's grandson Arnold? Who, in spite of his history as a murderer, had a soft spot for his maternal grandmother . . . Or was Lee grasping at straws? She could contact every Dr. Duncan in LA and ask whether Mrs. Kelly was a patient. But most of them would insist on a CYA court order before they would divulge such information. Fortunately, there was another way to get the confirmation she needed.

From the assisted-living facility, Lee went straight to LAPD headquarters and Conference Room 7-J. The evidence boxes were still there, and Lee could hardly wait to dive into them. After fifteen minutes of searching, Lee had six samples of Arnold Kaplan's crabbed handwriting.

With those sheets of paper in hand, she went over to the table where she compared those to Dr. Duncan's signature. It looked as though there were a lot of similarities so she put in a call to the Criminalistics Laboratory. The person who answered referred her to a forensic document examiner named Alvin Soltis. He listened to her description of the situation, and said, "Come on up . . . I'll take a look."

So Lee went up to the eighth floor, entered the lab, and went looking for Soltis. He had carefully mussed hair, was wearing a pristine lab coat, and was clearly heterosexual. "My, my," he said, as they shook hands. "My television set doesn't do you justice."

"Thanks," Lee said, as she pulled her hand free. "But I'm here to get your opinion on a handwriting sample, not my appearance."

Most men would have been put off, but not Soltis. He produced a boyish grin. "Did I come on too soon? No problem . . . I'll try again later. Let's see what you have."

The next twenty minutes were spent comparing the signature from the guest registry to the other writing samples. And once the process was over, Soltis delivered his judgment. "I wish we had more than the one signature to work with . . . But based on the sample we have, I'd say there's a high degree of probability that the Duncan signature was made by Arnold Kaplan."

"That's it? Just 'a high degree of probability'?"

"Yup."

"Okay, put that in writing and e-mail it to me."

"I could deliver it at dinner."

Lee smiled sweetly. "Thanks for the offer . . . But I have fourteen cats—and they have to be fed at six."

With the match to rely on, Lee returned to the assisted-living facility, and after a second conversation with the manager, was allowed to take the guest register. Subsequent analysis proved that Dr. Duncan's visits occurred twice a month, generally around the first and the fifteenth.

It was the twelfth, so Lee put in a request for surveillance during the day, when visitors were allowed to enter the facility. It was approved.

The long, seemingly interminable days crawled by. Hundreds of people came and went. A fire alarm went off on day one. It rained for a couple hours on day two. And an old lady backed into the van on the morning of day three. Then, having no idea that people knew what she'd done, the woman took off.

Finally, at about 10:00 a.m. on day four, came the moment they'd been waiting for. Lee was sitting in back near the com tech, listening to some R&B, when her phone rang. She had to remove the earbuds to take the call. "Cassandra Lee."

"This is Wilma," the receptionist said conspiratorially. "Dr. Duncan is here . . . He went up to visit Mrs. Kelly."

Lee felt her heart try to beat its way out of her chest. "Excellent . . . Well done. What's he wearing?"

"A sports coat, open-collared shirt, and khaki pants."

"Okay, we'll take it from here," Lee said. Then she brought a handheld radio up to her lips. "This is 1-William-3. The suspect is inside the building. He's wearing a sports coat, open-collared shirt, and khaki pants.

"We'll pick him up as he comes out and tail him. The shadow team will follow and take over after a mile or two. Do you read me? Over."

"This is 1-Union-6," a male voice responded. "I read you."

1-Union-6 was Wolfe's second-in-command. Where was Wolfe anyway? Not that it mattered.

Prospo drove the van through the parking lot to a position adjacent to the single exit. That would allow Lee to track Dr. Duncan to his car and put out a description. Then Prospo was supposed to tail the vehicle prior to the switch. Maybe Duncan would go home, and maybe he wouldn't. But the plan was to follow him until he did. Because if he was Kaplan, and Kaplan was the Bonebreaker, that was where Lee was likely to find evidence linked to eight murders.

She turned to the tech. He was wearing headphones and

seated in front of a control panel. "What are they talking about?"

It had been easy to plant listening devices in Mrs. Kelly's apartment though largely a waste of time. "She's complaining about her back pain," the tech replied. "The suspect wants her to get more exercise."

The next twenty minutes were agonizingly slow. But finally, after what seemed like an eternity, the tech said the words that Lee had been waiting to hear. "They said good-bye to each other. She called him 'Arnold.'"

Lee felt her heart leap. The entire team had been 99 percent sure that Duncan and Kaplan were the same man, but now it was a certainty! "Okay," Lee said over the radio. "Stand by. The visit is over. He'll be out in a minute or two."

Lee trained a pair of binoculars on the entrance to the building. A man pushed an empty wheelchair out. A woman carrying a cardboard box went inside. Then the suspect appeared. Sports coat, check. Shirt, check. Pants, check.

Lee watched Kaplan pause to look around. The murderer had more hair now. A wig? Implants? Anything was possible. And he was wary, the way a wild animal is wary, always on the lookout for danger. But the white van didn't *look* dangerous. So Kaplan's eyes slid across the vehicle without so much as a pause.

Then, satisfied that it was safe to do so, Kaplan cut across the parking lot to an end slot, where a gray *especiale* was parked. "He's getting into his car," Lee reported. "It's a metallic gray two-seater with California plate Six-Mary-Boy-Victor-Three-Three. Now he's pulling out. We're on him. Stay back until I call you forward."

Kaplan pulled out of the lot, and Prospo followed. The key was to stay one or two cars back but to keep the *especiale* in sight. At one point, Prospo had to run a red light in order to keep up but managed to get away with it.

Lee scrambled to get into the front passenger seat as Prospo swore. "Shit! There's some sort of roadblock up ahead!"

Lee looked, saw that two squad cars were parked nose to nose, with a small gap between them. Their light bars were lit, and cops with shotguns were standing to the left and right. Lee was about to get on the radio when Ayeman's voice was heard.

"This is the SLO (Senior Lead Officer). We have the suspect in the box. Close it."

But it quickly became clear that Kaplan wasn't about to cooperate with Ayeman's plan. He hit the gas, aimed the sports car at the gap, and slammed into the sedans. Both vehicles gave, which allowed the *especiale* to pass between them. Some of the police officers opened fire. "Stay on the bastard," Lee ordered, as the van's grill lights and siren came on. "Don't let him get away!"

Her mind was spinning. Why had Ayeman taken control? Where was Kaplan going?

"Break it off!" Ayeman shouted over the radio. "Break it off *now!*"

He's scared, Lee thought to herself. *Scared that civilians will get hurt. Never mind the fact that a cop killer is getting away.* "We didn't hear that," Lee said flatly. "Get him."

"Hear *what*?" Prospo said, as he put his foot to the floor. The van barely fit through the gap between the two police cars and a police officer fired at it reflexively. Shotgun pellets pinged the van. Ayeman was yelling contradictory orders over the radio as Kaplan made a series of random turns. Or were they random? His general direction was north.

Suddenly, a helicopter appeared up ahead. A police chopper . . . or a helicopter owned by one of the TV stations. That's what Lee assumed until the aircraft turned to expose an open door. The machine gun was clear to see. "Holy shit!" Prospo exclaimed, as the gunner opened fire, and bullets threw up columns of asphalt from the street.

Rather than tilt up, the guy on the gun let the van run into the stream of fire. Lee heard a series of overlapping impacts as bullets hit the hood, smashed the windshield, and passed between them. Both Lee and Prospo were unhurt, but as Lee looked back she saw the tech was slumped sideways in his seat. Her first thought was to go back and help but there was no reason to do so. Half his head was missing.

Then the van was in the clear, but steam was pouring out of the engine compartment as Prospo took evasive action. "This is 1-William-3," Lee shouted into the radio. "We are taking fire from a hostile aircraft . . . Officer down . . . Need assistance."

"No, no, no!" Ayeman shouted. "Stop it!"

But it was too late for that. "He's going somewhere," Prospo said, as he swerved to miss an oncoming car. "A place where the chopper can pick him up."

Lee swore. She should have thought of that . . . Even worse was the fact that she had assumed Kaplan was the Bonebreaker and a loner. The possibility that he could summon a helicopter had never occurred to her. Stupid, stupid, stupid.

Focus, Lee told herself. *Where is the bastard going?* She fumbled with the laptop. There . . . The GPS-enabled map was on the screen. She could see the arrow that was the van, and looking ahead, a sports park! The perfect spot to land a chopper. "He's headed for Chavez Park!" she exclaimed.

The words were nearly drowned out as the helicopter passed low over their heads. Then it swept over Kaplan and continued north. Proof that the theory was correct. "Don't let him reach that helo," Lee said grimly. Prospo didn't answer. His eyes were glued on the street ahead. The steam pouring out of the engine compartment had turned to smoke. That made it difficult to see. A car backed out of a driveway. That forced Prospo to turn, bump up and over the curb, and circle through a yard. Lee heard a screech as the tires hit the road again.

Then she saw the cyclone fence, light standards in the distance, and wooden stands off to the right. An entrance was located directly ahead of the van, but a row of four-foot-high metal pipes blocked the way forward. Kaplan brought his car to a halt, jumped out, and began to run.

Prospo braked, lost control, and slid sideways. There was a loud crash as the left side of the van hit the rear end of the *especiale*. Flames erupted from the engine compartment.

Lee opened the passenger-side door and hit the ground. She was a better-than-average runner—and so high on adrenaline that it felt as if she could fly. Her legs pumped, the Glock was in her hand, and she saw the distance begin to close. Meanwhile, the chopper was settling into to a miniature dust storm of its own making on the baseball diamond.

Kaplan skidded to a stop, turned, and fired a pistol. The shots went wide. He whirled and took off again. Valuable ground had been lost. Lee was closer by then, but not close enough, as the machine gunner opened fire. The bullets drew a line in front of her as Kaplan dashed in under the rotors. Lee couldn't catch up. That was obvious now. So she knelt, took aim, and fired. Not once, but seventeen times, until the weapon clicked empty.

Kaplan was up on a step by that time, reaching for the gunner's outstretched hand, when at least one of the .9mm slugs struck him in the back. The body pitched forward, slid sideways, and fell. Kaplan's corpse was consumed by a manmade dust storm as the helicopter took off, skimmed the neighborhood to the east, and continued to gain altitude.

There were sirens after that, and a dozen blue uniforms swept onto the field. Lee just stood there, body shaking, her pistol pointed at the ground.

It had taken Detective Prospo a long time to cover the necessary distance, and he was out of breath when he arrived. A moment passed while he stood with hands on knees. Then he straightened up. The body lay near the pitcher's mound. "Nice job," Prospo said as he put an arm around Lee's shoulders. "Let's go home."

FOUR

Lee had been in the conference room before. It was a soulless environment that was home to a dying plant, some institutional art, and a much-abused conference table. What was the record for shooting reviews anyway? Three? Four? Five? It didn't matter. Lee felt certain that she would win. Or lose. Depending on how one chose to look at it.

Two weeks had passed since Kaplan's death. And as the shooting review board convened for a third day, Lee's badge was on the line yet again. Because, unlike her previous reviews, the outcome of this one was anything but certain.

The morning had been spent on a list of alleged failures which, according to Assistant Chief Purdy Ayeman, Lee was guilty of. That included disobeying an order from him, public endangerment, and telling a superior officer to "fuck off." The officer in question was Ayeman himself.

Now it was Lee's turn. Which was to say, Marvin Codicil's turn, and the attorney was ready. "So," Codicil said, as he took to the floor. "Let's review the facts. Detective Lee was in control of the stakeout. A plan had been agreed upon. And, in accordance with that plan, Lee and Detective Prospo were to follow the suspect as he left the assisted-living facility.

"Then as soon as it seemed prudent to do so they were to switch off with another car to escape notice. The goal being to follow the suspect to his home where there was reason to believe that the team could obtain evidence related to *eight* unsolved murders. We know this plan was shared with, and approved by, Lieutenant Wolfe because we have a signed document to that effect."

Codicil's back was to Lee and the rest of the observers as he eyed the members on the review board, all of whom were seated behind the long, narrow table. "So far so good," Codicil concluded.

"But then, unbeknownst to Detectives Lee and Prospo, Assistant Chief Ayeman assumed command of the operation. This, as we learned during his testimony, was due to the fact that Lieutenant Wolfe was ill. And had Chief Ayeman been content to allow Wolfe's second-in-command to take over for her, the odds are good that we wouldn't be here today."

That produced a loud objection from Ayeman's attorney—as well as a rebuke from the deputy chief who was in charge of the panel. "This is not a courtroom, Miss Tangent. Objections have no place here." Then, with a nod to Codicil, "You may continue."

Codicil nodded. "Thank you. The reason I said what I did is that Chief Ayeman made what he admits was a unilateral decision to depart from the agreed-upon plan and to do so without providing Lee's team with any warning. Rather than try to follow Mr. Kaplan to his residence, Ayeman decided to establish an ad hoc roadblock in an attempt to capture the suspect after he left the assisted-living facility. His justification was that, as he put it, 'I was afraid that the public team would lose the suspect in traffic.'

"That," Codicil said, "sounds like a reasonable concern. But one that would normally be addressed during the planning stage of such an operation. A process that Ayeman was invited to take part in but chose not to. And we know what happened next. The suspect blew through the impromptu roadblock, thereby triggering the very chase that Detectives Lee and Prospo have been criticized for taking part in."

Codicil paused at that point to let his words sink in. "Then," Codicil said ominously, "the suspect headed north. Chief Ayeman claims to have given orders at that point . . . And there are tapes to substantiate his testimony. On those tapes he can be heard ordering Detectives Lee and Prospo to break off the chase. But here's the problem . . . For some reason the two detectives didn't *hear* that order. Perhaps a technical glitch was to blame. Or maybe it had something to do with the fact that they were taking fire from a helicopter.

"Of course there was a *third* person in the van. A com tech named Dewey Lambert. Ideally, *he* would be able to shed some light on this matter. But, unfortunately, Lambert was killed as a direct result of Chief Ayeman's incompetence and dreams of personal glory."

That triggered an objection from Ayeman himself. "That's a lie!" he shouted.

"Is it?" Codicil asked rhetorically. "Then explain why you called an editor at the *Los Angeles Times* immediately after the suspect left the assisted-living facility and invited her to dispatch a reporter to that location?"

That was a new revelation, and it produced a storm of consternation, commentary, and expressions of outrage. Codicil smiled beatifically, said "Thank you," and returned to his seat. Lee and Prospo were cleared forty-six minutes later.

The shooting review had taken place on Friday. And Lee had the weekend off. After changing the linen on her bed and cleaning the apartment, she went out for a three-mile run. When Lee returned she made her way back to the stairs. And there, chained to the wrought-iron railing, was a three-wheeled bicycle. It was a strange-looking affair that boasted an old-fashioned squeeze horn, a flashlight in place of a headlight, and a small radio mounted on the handlebars. The rear cargo area was full to overflowing with bottles of water, camping gear, and a folding lawn chair. Lee had never seen the rig before but assumed that it belonged to a visitor.

She climbed the stairs and, as she made her way along the walkway, saw that a man was seated with his back against her front door. His head was down, and it looked as if he was reading. Then, as he heard her footsteps, the man scrambled to his feet. The electronic reader disappeared into a side pocket, and his hands dangled loosely at his sides.

The man was well over six feet tall and skinny as a rail. His hair was long and stringy, his eyes looked huge because of the goggle-style glasses he wore, and his clothes were filthy. Worse yet was the fact that she could smell him from six feet away. The Bonebreaker? No, she didn't think so. But her right hand was on her hip just inches away from the Smith & Wesson holstered at her back. "Yes?"

"W-Wally," the man said. "M-my name's W-Wally. Are y-you C-Cassandra Lee?"

Lee frowned. "Yes."

"G-good. I h-have something f-for you. A l-letter."

"You don't look like a mailman."

"I'm a c-courier," Wally replied. "I w-work for R-red Zone L-logistics."

Lee had heard of the company. Most people had. Since it was impossible to send a letter or package into the red zone, or to receive something *from* the red zone, a variety of companies had stepped in to fill the need. The most prominent of which was RZL. Their couriers were freelancers. Men and women who were paid to pick up letters and small packages from one of the company's distribution stations and deliver them to their final destinations.

But only within their respective countries because mutants weren't allowed to enter the green zone, and the norms didn't want to visit the red zone. "I see," Lee said. "So you have a letter for me."

"Y-yes," Wally replied.

"How much?"

"F-fifty nu."

"That's a lot of money for a letter."

Wally wiped his nose with a crusty sleeve. He, like all of his kind, was familiar with cheapskates. People who didn't care about the hundreds of miles he pedaled under a hot sun, the bribes that had to be paid in order to obtain addresses, and the nights spent hunkered down next to contaminated creeks. His response took all of that into account. "O-okay . . . N-no problem. I-I'll w-wipe my ass with it."

Lee couldn't help but laugh. "Okay, Wally . . . You win. Fifty nu it is. What were you reading?"

"T-the P-postman, by D-David Brin."

"Never heard of it," Lee replied. "But that's what you are. A postman. Wait by your bike. I'll get the money and be right down."

Lee watched Wally disappear down the stairs before unlocking her door and going inside. She had only one friend who lived inside the red zone, and that was Ras Omo, a deputy with the Maricopa County Sheriff's Department. They had worked together on the Screed case. So, assuming the letter was from him, she was eager to read it.

Lee opened her purse, found her wallet, and removed sixty nu. Then she left the apartment and made her way down to the bottom of the stairs where Wally was waiting. "Here you go," Lee said, as she gave him the money.

Wally counted the bills and looked up at her. "Th-thanks for the tip."

"You're welcome."

Wally withdrew the letter from the inside pocket of his ragged jacket and gave the packet over. Lee saw that her name had been written on the outside of the RZL all-weather envelope. But there was no return address.

Wally was busy freeing his bike from the railing by then. "Hold on," Lee told him. "Before you leave, I'd like to make sure that there's a letter inside and that it's intended for me."

Wally waited while Lee tore the package open. A *second* envelope was waiting within. The return address read: "Alala Lee, C/O Myra Meo, 1432 Mountain View Lane, Heartbreak, Nevada."

The name came as a tremendous shock. *Alala Lee . . .* Her *mother's* name! And written with the same loopy handwriting she'd seen on the various documents Alala had left behind. The most notable being a notebook filled with poetry. It had been what? Thirty-four years earlier? When she was *two?* Yes, that was when Mrs. Frank Lee had packed a bag and left for parts unknown.

Lee could feel the tears starting to build up as she turned to Wally. Then she said, "Thank you," and ran up the stairs. Once inside the apartment, she locked the door—and stood with her back pressed against it. Her mother was alive! Lee wasn't sure if that was good or bad. She'd been angry at her for a long time. Then the dam broke, and deep sobs racked her body . . . Lee stumbled into the living room, where she collapsed on the couch, the letter still clutched in her hands.

It wasn't until five minutes later that she stood on wobbly legs and went into the kitchen to get a knife. It cut through the envelope to reveal a single piece of paper and a photo. Even though she hadn't seen her for decades, and even though the woman in the picture was a good deal older now, Lee recognized her mother right away. And more than that, herself . . . Because in spite of the age difference there was a remarkable resemblance between them. Then realization hit . . . Every day Frank Lee looked at his daughter he'd been reminded of the woman who'd left him! Had that colored their relationship? Of course it had.

According to the date, the letter had been written four weeks earlier. "Dear Cassie," it began. *Cassie?* Nobody called her Cassie. Nor did she want them to.

Dear Cassie,

I read about you honey . . . It was in the paper. According to the article, you're a detective now. And you're in the red zone looking for a girl who was kidnapped. I'm proud of you Cassie, real proud, but not so proud of myself.

I shouldn't have left you honey, that was the wrong thing to do, and not a day goes by that I don't regret it. But I was young . . . Too young. And your father? I told him how I felt, but he didn't understand. So I felt trapped—and when the two of you were away, I ran. That was wrong, Cassie . . . But what is, is. There's no way I can go back and fix it now.

I called myself Freedom for a while—and drifted from place to place. Eventually, I wound up here, in Heartbreak, Nevada. It's a mining town and not an easy place to live if you're a norm. But you've been in the red zone, and you know what I'm talking about.

Anyway, here's the thing . . . I've been sick for some time now, and the doctors tell me that I'm going to die. That's okay 'cause all of us are going to die—but I'd like to see you one last time before I go. I'd like to look into your big brown eyes and tell you that I love you.

Of course you might not receive this, or if you do, you might be too busy to come. Or, and I wouldn't blame you, there's the distinct possibility that you won't want to come. Should that be the case don't worry about it. Believe me, I understand.

With all my love,
Your mother

Lee spent the rest of the day, and much of the evening, reading and rereading her mother's letter. There was so much to consider. Alala had apologized, and that was good. But how much was such an apology worth? More than three decades had passed since Alala had walked out on her husband and daughter. And now, as her mother's life was about to end, she wanted *what*? Comfort? A reconciliation? Forgiveness?

There was a part of Lee that was willing to grant some or all of those things assuming that it lay within her power to do so. But another part, the *cop* part, was hard and unyielding. *Alala made her choice,* the cop identity said. *Now she has to live the consequences of her decision. That's how it should be.* But another, softer her disagreed. What was the famous quote? "To err is human; to forgive, divine." And it wasn't as if Lee hadn't made mistakes herself. There was a lot to think about.

The Bonebreaker awoke with a start. Another bad dream. He was lying on his bed in what had once been a storage room, surrounded by concrete walls, and protected by a steel door. But even the vault couldn't protect him from Cassandra Lee. Because she was him, and he was her. She hated the way *he* hated, she schemed the way *he* schemed, and she lived to kill just as he did. Both of them were good at that, each in their own way, and meant to battle each other. He for God and she for Satan.

And Lee was winning. She was using the police department to put pressure on him, to strike fear into his heart, and to force him out into the open. His response was to build and launch the drone. He's seen her through the camera, approaching the sedan, and sent the explosive-laden plane straight at her. Anyone else would be dead. But in the fraction of a second that preceded impact, the Bonebreaker had seen her look up! As if she knew . . . As if Satan had told her.

But that wasn't all. Rather than hide, and skulk about the way Roscoe McGinty had, Lee redoubled her efforts to find him. And in doing so stumbled across some fool who had been murdering transients and selling their organs. A miss . . . Definitely a miss. But indicative of what the she-devil could accomplish. So what to do? Hide in the ossuary? Or strike back? Put like that, the question was no question at all.

The shooting review board's finding, and Assistant Chief Ayeman's decision to accept an HR job in Big Bend, Oregon, went largely unnoticed by the press. And the reason for that was clear. The investigation turned up *another* serial killer, and Kaplan was generally considered to be an even greater threat than the Bonebreaker.

How many people had the Kaplan gang killed anyway? It was impossible to know for sure since the organ jackers didn't keep records, but based on preliminary estimates, the number was likely to be well over a hundred.

So with no one to hand the follow-up investigation to, the detectives assigned to Operation Thunderstorm had no choice but to work on the newly revived case. A total of forty-six arrests had been made subsequent to Kaplan's death. Among those awaiting trial were the organ jacker's so-called spotters, pickers, and harvesters. All of whom were questioned to whatever extent their attorneys would allow. Then deals were struck as suspects agreed to rat each other out. That drove *more* interviews, all of which had to be cross-checked. It was a time-consuming business.

Meanwhile, the LAPD Adult Missing Persons Unit was working overtime in an attempt to match their list to the partial descriptions and muddled recollections obtained from various gang members. The situation was made all the more difficult by the fact that once a donor's organs were harvested, the rest of the body had been cremated within hours. As a result there was nothing for the forensics people to run DNA tests on.

One week after the hearing, Lee and the rest of the team were putting in long days in an attempt to clear all of the Kaplan-related issues. And because of that, Lee had been forced to put her mother's letter, and the question of what to do about it, on a back burner.

In an effort to catch up with all of the administrative crap she had to do, Lee had decided to work into the night. An hour had passed, and Lee was nearing the bottom of her in-box when she came to a cardboard mailer. She glanced at the return address, saw that the package was from Cheyenne Darling, and tore it open. There was a thumb drive within but nothing else. Information that pertained to McGinty perhaps?

Lee pushed the USB drive into one of the ports on her computer. A single file appeared. It was labeled FRANK LEE. Lee felt a fluttery sensation in the pit of her stomach as she clicked PLAY. At first it was very difficult to know what she was looking at. The lighting was murky and the camera work was erratic. Then she saw the specially designed metal framework and the man strapped inside of it. It was her father! He was naked, filthy, and held in place by a complicated system of metal bars, pulleys, and cables. All working together to render him helpless. She'd seen such a machine once before and recognized it right away.

Lee felt the bottom drop out of her stomach as the camera moved in over a tripod, where it wobbled for a moment before being secured in place. Then her father's eyes tracked movements she couldn't see. "*Please,*" he begged. "Don't do it!"

There was no reply as a man in a white scream mask entered the shot and began to wrap rubber tubing around her father's extremities. In each case the tourniquet was applied as close to Frank Lee's torso as possible. The police officer was shaking the cage by then in a desperate attempt to escape. But the effort was to no avail.

Once the tourniquets were tightened the Bonebreaker stepped out of the picture. Lee knew what would happen next—

and ordered herself to stop the tape. But for some reason she couldn't. Then came the unmistakable sound of a chain saw starting up. Her father began to scream at that point. And he continued to scream as the Bonebreaker reentered the picture carrying the saw. Gray exhaust shot out into the air as the Bonebreaker pulled the trigger all the way back. Then the chain began to chew its way through her father's leg.

Lee was sobbing by then, and screaming, *"No! No! No!"* as the blood flew. Then the world began to spin, the floor seemed to disappear, and the endless fall began.

Lee was deep below the surface of the ocean. She could see light, and was kicking her legs in an effort to reach it, but couldn't breathe. "You can't sleep forever," a male voice said.

Her father? Calling to her from the hallway outside her room? No, he was . . . Then Lee "saw" blood spraying away from the chain saw and screamed. Or tried to . . . But nothing came out. A hand touched her shoulder and suddenly she was there, at the surface, sucking air. "It's all right, Cassandra . . . Everything is all right."

As Lee looked toward the sound a face came into focus. The man's hair was cut short. That served to emphasize a high forehead. He had a straight nose, even features, and was wearing a suit. "There you are," the man said. "That's better . . . I'm Dr. Kane. How are you feeling?"

Lee was scared. But she couldn't say that. Not and maintain her rep. Images stuttered through her mind. Pictures of her father being murdered. She clutched the sheets. "Fine, I feel fine."

Kane smiled. "Denial isn't going to work, Cassandra . . . What you saw was real, and so were all of the emotions you felt. The first step is to acknowledge that."

Lee frowned. "What are you? A shrink?"

Kane smiled. "Yes."

"And I'm in an insane asylum?"

"No. You're in the Buena Vista Treatment Center. It's located on the ocean. Once you feel better you can go out and walk on the beach."

"Screw that . . . I have work to do."

"Eventually, yes. Once your recovery is complete you can return to duty. But not until I say so."

"Who says?"

"Chief Jenkins put you on medical leave with full pay."

"How long have I been here?"

"Two days."

"And I was unconscious?"

"Part of the time, yes. But you were sedated as well."

Lee's eyes narrowed. "On whose authority?"

"It seems that you don't have a next of kin on file. So Chief Jenkins agreed to make decisions on your behalf until such time as you can make them for yourself."

Lee felt sorry for herself. Everyone was against her . . . Even Jenkins. "Go away."

Kane nodded. "Get some rest. Press the red button if you need anything. I'll drop by this evening."

Lee continued to lie there for a while, too exhausted to get up. Now some memories were coming back. Snapshots really . . . An ambulance. Concerned faces. A dimly lit room. And a haggard face in a mirror. *Her* face? Yes.

Lee thought about that. A mirror. A bathroom. She needed to pee. Slowly, like a woman twice her age, Lee sat up and put her feet on the floor. Her feet were bare and the tiles felt cold. The room was large, well decorated, and the sunlight was attempting to find a way past the heavy drapes.

Lee stood, felt dizzy, and paused. Then, by placing one foot squarely in front of the other, she tottered into the bathroom. She winced when she saw the woman who looked back at her from the mirror. The creature's hair was matted down, there were dark circles under her eyes, and a small bandage was visible on her forehead. Had she fallen when things went black? Probably.

Lee did what she needed to do and left the bathroom with plans to open the curtains. According to Kane she was near the ocean. Could she see it? But before Lee could complete the journey to the window, a wave of anxiety swept over her. The bed beckoned and the sheets took her in. Lee awoke to the sound of a knock and a female voice. "Miss Lee?"

She opened her eyes to see a young woman standing just inside the door. She was dressed in khaki slacks and a dark blue polo shirt. "Yes?"

"Deputy Chief Jenkins is on the phone. He would like to visit you at four o'clock. Is that okay?"

Lee wondered why the people who ran the place would send someone to tell her that. Then she glanced at the bedside table and realized that there was no telephone. And her cell phone was nowhere to be seen. She sat up. "What time is it now?"

The girl glanced at her watch. "Five after three."

"Tell him yes, thank you."

The woman nodded, indicated that she would return at 3:55, and withdrew. Lee got out of bed and made her way into the bathroom. She had to look good for Jenkins. Good enough so he would allow her to leave and go home. With that goal in mind she entered the shower, washed her hair, and emerged feeling better.

The next twenty minutes were spent drying her hair, and combing it, but without any of the stuff she normally used. The results were far from perfect but would have to do. Fortunately, there was a tube of lipstick in her purse, and it was sitting on the dresser. There was no sign of her phone or weapons however.

By then it was time to get dressed, and Lee was pleased to discover that the outfit she'd been wearing two days earlier had been washed, pressed, and was hanging in the closet. So she got dressed and was ready to go by the time the woman returned. "Hi! My name is Cindy," she said. "Chief Jenkins is downstairs. Would you like me to show you the way to the lobby?"

Lee knew that the high level of personal service was a good way to keep track of her. But it wouldn't do to pitch a fit about it. Not if she wanted to get out of there. She smiled sweetly. "That would be nice, thank you."

Lee followed Cindy down a hall to an elevator that took them down to the main floor. From there it was a short walk to a substantial reception desk and the spacious lobby beyond. There were carefully placed plants, clusters of comfortable-looking chairs, and the Pacific Ocean's sparkling presence beyond the enormous windows.

Jenkins got up from a chair and came forward to meet her. "Cassandra! How are you feeling, girl? You look good."

Lee accepted the hug and took the chair next to his. "Thanks, boss . . . And I *feel* good. So how 'bout bailing me out of here?"

Jenkins laughed before turning serious. "I know you want out . . . And you have the legal right to leave whenever you want. But here's the deal . . . I can't clear you for a return to work until Dr. Kane tells me that you're ready."

Lee started to reply but Jenkins raised a hand. "Hear me out . . . The Bonebreaker is feeling the pressure. The shrinks think he's just normal enough to be frightened. And he's scared of *you*. Put that together with the run-in you had with the bastard in the red zone, and it's likely that you're on his mind twenty-four / seven.

"But he couldn't attack you directly," Jenkins continued. "Not without exposing himself. So he launched a psychological attack instead. Think of it as a bullet. The slug hit you, and it caused damage, but you survived. Now you're in rehab, and it will take time to heal."

"Okay," Lee said. "So how 'bout this? I agree to see Dr. Kane as an outpatient and you let me go home."

Jenkins nodded. "I'll talk to him. If he's okay with the idea, then so am I."

After that the conversation turned to Operation Thunderstorm, the effort to resolve all of the issues related to the Kaplan murders, and the manner in which Wolfe had stepped up to the plate. Jenkins was clearly pleased with her performance—and Lee wondered if the lieutenant was a candidate to replace Ayeman.

Jenkins left after that, and Lee discovered that she was hungry. After checking with the front desk she learned that the facility had a dining room, which was open for dinner.

Lee went in, took a table by the window, and was looking at the ocean when Kane arrived. "I heard you were up and around . . . May I join you?"

Lee smiled. "Of course."

Kane sat down, and a waitress arrived seconds later. Lee ordered the pan-fried sole, and Kane chose a shrimp salad. "So," he said, as the waitress left. "You spoke with Chief Jenkins."

Lee's eyebrows rose. "You're very good at tracking my movements."

Kane laughed. "I can see how it might seem that way—but I ran into the chief as he was leaving. So we talked."

"And?"

"And I think it's fine for you to go home. But I'd like to see you every other day for a while."

"Okay. I won't pretend that I like it, but I can hack it, if that's what I have to do. Since you're my doctor, I have a request."

"Which is?"

Lee told Kane about the security measures that had been installed in her apartment, and concluded by saying, "I want them taken out. Yes, I need some protection, but having people stare at me all day is too much."

The food arrived at that point, and Kane waited until it had been served before making his reply. "I agree . . . I'll talk to the chief."

The conversation that followed was a good deal more relaxed than what Lee had expected. Rather than interrogate her the way a cop would, the psychologist took the long way around to some very perceptive questions. That led to answers Lee hadn't been planning to give.

A good example of that was when he asked if she thought of her father as a friend. And the answer was no. Lee went on to say that while she felt a sense of gratitude toward her father, she didn't like him all that much, which made her feel guilty.

"And," Kane said, "watching him die made you feel even *more* guilty. Even though he was a man you weren't all that fond of."

Lee felt a piece of the emotional puzzle fall into place. "I guess that's true."

Lee took that concept with her as she checked out of the treatment center and went home the following morning. The technicians came that afternoon. And once the cameras and microphones had been removed, she felt better. So much so that she decided to clean house. Except for the second bedroom, that is. It had been converted into her own mini–operations center back before she'd been allowed to work on the Bonebreaker case openly. And now, after viewing the footage of her father's death, Lee didn't want to go in there. So she didn't.

But she had time to read and reread the letter from her mother. And now, after watching her father die, Lee felt an increased level of interest in her mother. One parent was dead—the other was dying. Should she ignore that? *Could* she ignore that?

Lee met with Kane the following afternoon for a walk on the beach. She half expected him to show up in the same dark suit he'd been wearing the first time she had seen him. But he was wearing a tee, board shorts, and flip-flops. And the vibe was different too . . . More of a guy-girl thing. Was Kane interested in her? And trying to suppress that because of the doctor-patient relationship? Or was that wishful thinking on her part? Because there was some pull. Quite a bit of pull, actually . . . From her perspective anyway.

The conversation was trivial at first. Then Kane asked what she'd been up to, and she told him. "I cleaned my apartment. Except for the room where I keep the stuff related to the Bonebreaker investigation."

Kane looked at her. "So you have a room filled with material related to your father's death—and you don't want to enter it. Not even to clean."

Lee produced an awkward laugh. "It sounds so symbolic when you put it that way!"

Kane smiled. "You don't need the things in that room. Why not pack them up and send them to your office? Or put them in storage?"

There was more give-and-take, but Kane's suggestion stuck with her. She couldn't get rid of all the memories related to her father nor did she want to. But what about placing at least some of them in storage? The images of his death included?

With that in mind Lee went home and had storage boxes delivered to her apartment the next day. Once she was ready Lee steeled herself for the task, unlocked the door, and entered the bedroom. Then, with the same single-minded determination that had gotten her through college and the police academy, Lee went to work. Printouts, notes, and maps went into boxes equipped to handle hanging files. Memorabilia and all sorts of other objects were placed in carefully labeled containers. After making a call to the storage facility she was done. They would come and take her father's life away. Was that wrong? Maybe, but it *felt* good, and that would have to do.

It was a beautiful day. The sun was shining down, the surf was up for those who cared, and lots of people were visiting the beach. Two of them were barefoot and walking along the uncertain line of demarcation that separated land from ocean. The part of the experience Lee liked best was the moment when a wave came in, slid up over the sand, then swirled around her ankles. She turned to look at Kane. He felt like something more than a doctor now. A friend? Or something else?

Whatever the case it seemed as if Kane was increasingly important to her. And that made it difficult to lie to him—which was what she intended to do. Because after much soul-searching, she had decided to visit her mother. And that was something that Kane, never mind the police department, wouldn't approve of. "So," she began. "I'm feeling better."

"No," Kane said. "You can't go back to work. Not yet."

Lee laughed. "You're predictable if nothing else. But that isn't where this conversation is headed. I'd like to take a couple of weeks and head north. To the San Juan islands. I hear it's beautiful up there at this time of year. I'll kick back, rest up, and call you when I return. And at that point I hope you'll let me return to duty."

Kane was silent for a moment as if thinking the proposal over. "That could work," he said finally. "You wouldn't be able to take part in therapy sessions—but the opportunity to get away from LA and your work environment would be a good thing. And you can call me anytime you want to."

Lee got the feeling that he *wanted* her to call . . . and knew that she would be tempted. Kane understood her in ways that other people didn't. Was that why she liked him? Because he let her ramble on about herself? While other men wanted to talk about themselves? Or sports? If so, that was the professional him. A paid listener. But she didn't think so. The walk continued. And, as the ocean pushed its way higher up the beach, her footprints disappeared.

Jenkins heard the knock and turned to see Cassandra Lee standing in the doorway to his office. She looked good, better anyway, and he motioned her in. "Have a seat . . . Dr. Kane tells me that you're feeling better."

"Yeah," Lee replied as she sat down. "I am. And that's why I'm here. I spoke with him about the possibility of a trip north . . . Up to the San Juans in Washington state. If it's okay with you, I'd like to spend a couple of weeks there. Then, assuming the doc clears me to do so, I'll return to work."

Lee was lying and Jenkins knew it. First because there were still a couple of cameras hidden in her apartment. And carefully chosen members of the shadow team had been watching her. Not to snoop but to protect her since there was no reason to believe that the Bonebreaker was done with Cassandra Lee.

But it was a very touchy situation since Lee had requested that all of the cameras be removed and didn't know she was being spied on. The only people allowed to see the video feeds were female—but that wouldn't appease Lee if she found out. And understandably so.

That wasn't all however . . . Jenkins was under a great deal of pressure to find the Bonebreaker, and crazy or not, Lee was the best bait he had. So, once the RZL courier left, he had given Wolfe permission to search Lee's apartment while she was visiting with Kane. What if the RZL letter was from the Bonebreaker? But the letter *wasn't* from the Bonebreaker, and since Wolfe didn't have a search warrant, Jenkins couldn't admit that he knew about it. Nor could he call Lee out even though she was clearly getting ready to enter the red zone and visit her mother. A very dangerous proposition indeed.

Still, according to Dr. Kane, while the act of watching her father's death had been very traumatic for Lee . . . a lot of her pent-up anger stemmed from having been deserted by her mother. That meant there was a possibility that the trip could be therapeutic. "If Dr. Kane is okay with the trip, then so am I," Jenkins said finally.

"I could take vacation instead of sick leave."

"There's no need for that," Jenkins assured her. "You're covered for up to six months of leave for a job-related injury. But remember this . . . I can't send any LAPD officers along to watch over you up in Washington state. And even if I could, the cost would be astronomical."

The complete lack of protection scared Lee—but not enough to abandon her plan. "No problem," she said. "I understand. Chances are that the Bonebreaker will keep his head down for a while . . . If I'm careful he won't notice that I'm gone. Or, if he does notice, he won't know where I went."

"Sounds good," Jenkins said. "But keep your phone on in case I need to reach you."

"Sure," Lee said. "Thanks for the slack . . . I appreciate it."

Jenkins rose and circled the desk to give Lee a hug. "You take care, girl . . . And watch your six."

It wasn't until later, as Lee took the elevator down to the parking garage, that the words echoed in her mind. "Watch your six." That was a strange thing to say to a person who was headed out on vacation. The doors slid open. The trip into the red zone had begun.

FIVE

ee felt the bus jerk to a stop and opened her eyes as the
driver spoke over the PA system. "All out for Halloran," he
said. "The restrooms are in the motel. The bus will depart in
fifteen minutes."

Lee sat up and stretched. Most of her fellow passengers were
blue-collar types who lived in the town of Primm, which was an
hour and fifteen minutes east of Halloran. Primm had once been
a place where gamblers could test their luck on the way to Las
Vegas or lose their winnings on the way back to LA.

But that was then. Primm was a military town now, a staging
point for the army should the relationship with the Republic
of Texas deteriorate, and one of the entry/exit points through
which people could legally enter or depart the country of
Pacifica. The second being easier than the first.

Lee was seated toward the back of the bus. So she had to wait
for the passengers in front to disembark and that included the
man seated next to the aisle. Once he was out of the way Lee
stood, pulled her backpack down from the overhead bin, and
made her way forward. The plan was to travel light and blend
in. The only items in the much-abused pack were a change of
clothes and some toiletries.

Unlike the rest of the passengers Lee was planning to stay the
night in the town's single motel. It was called the Arrowhead,
and as Lee stepped off the bus, it was directly in front of her. It

looked as though the three-story-tall structure had been built before the plague and hadn't fared well since. A line of sixteen-wheelers were parked off to one side—and Lee figured the truckers were the ones who kept the place in business.

That impression was reinforced as she entered a shabby lobby and approached the reception desk. The woman behind the counter had garish red hair, faded blue eyes, and a face with plenty of mileage on it. "Good evening," she said. "What can I do for you?"

"I have a reservation," Lee answered. "The name is Travers. Tina Travers."

After consulting her computer, the clerk nodded. "I have you down for one night, a nonsmoking room, and a queen-sized bed."

"Perfect."

"That will be ninety nu . . . In advance, please."

Credit cards were okay in LA . . . but not that close to the border. There weren't very many norms who wanted to enter the red zone, but there were a few. And once over the border it would be very difficult for the motel to get its money.

Lee slid two fifties across the counter. As the woman made change Lee scanned her surroundings. The whole purpose of staying the night in Halloran was to check for a tail. The Bonebreaker had followed her before . . . Would he do so again? If so he'd be a lot easier to spot in a town that consisted of a motel, a gas station, and a sun-baked trailer park.

But as Lee eyed the people from the bus, many of whom were starting to stream outside with cold drinks in hand, no one looked back. No one other than the soldier who had tried to hit on her back in LA. He waved, and she waved back.

"Here you go," the woman said, and Lee turned to discover that ten one-nu coins were waiting on the counter, the hope being that Lee would drop them into one of the motel's sleek slot machines. She said, "Thanks," and swept the money into her left hand.

"Here's your keycard," the woman said. "Room 203 is on the second floor. The elevator is out of order, so you'll have to take the stairs."

Lee accepted the card, took her pack off the floor, and made her way back to the stairwell. Judging from the planter in front of the elevator doors the lift had been out of service for a long time. Lee made use of the card to access what turned out to be a very bare-bones room. Everything about it looked worn, and Lee wasn't about to slip between the sheets.

Unpacking consisted of dumping the pack on the floor. Then Lee went over to peer through a dirty window. The sun had started to set by then and there was nothing to see other than a parking lot, Highway 15, and the desert beyond.

Lee was hungry. So she left the room, paused to tear a piece of clear tape off a dispenser, and placed it across the crack that separated the door from the jamb. After that she followed a worn set of stairs down to the first floor. The bus had left, and Lee kept her eyes peeled for any passengers who had stayed behind. But she didn't recognize anybody as she left the lobby and entered the restaurant. Lee spotted a table where she could sit with her back to a wall and made her way over to claim it. Once seated she scanned the room to see if she was attracting any attention. A couple of truck drivers were eyeballing her, and Lee knew that what they were talking about had nothing to do with the Bonebreaker.

A tired-looking waitress waddled over, blew a wisp of gray hair out of her eyes, and popped the question. "So, hon . . . What'll it be?"

"I'll have the grilled cheese sandwich and a tossed green salad."

"Dressing?"

"Ranch."

"And to drink?"

"A Diet Coke, please."

"Got it," the woman said, and turned away.

The food arrived about fifteen minutes later. And as Lee began to eat, she had time to reflect on the fact that while she was perfectly happy to eat alone while sitting in her apartment, it felt awkward to do so in public. Why was that? The best solution was to bring something to read. But having failed to anticipate the moment Lee was forced to stare into space and wound up eating her food too quickly. So it was a relief to finish the meal, pay her bill, and depart.

Lee knew that another bus would pass through Halloran the next afternoon—but she didn't want to sit around waiting for it. She went outside and made her way over to the area where a dozen big rigs were parked. Maybe she could hitch a ride.

There was plenty of illumination thanks to the sodium-vapor lamps mounted on tall poles. And as Lee walked along a line of trucks, she noticed that some of the drivers were preparing to leave, while other rigs were parked for the night. Were the drivers sacked out in their sleepers? Or were they drinking beer in the motel's bar? The problem was that the first group wouldn't appreciate a knock on the door—and those in the second would assume she was a hooker.

So Lee was about to give up, and return early the next morning, when she saw light and movement up ahead. As Lee got closer she could see that a woman was working on one of the trucks. A work light was positioned above the point where the trailer was hooked to the tractor. "Hi there," Lee said. "It looks like you have a problem."

The woman straightened up, turned, and frowned. "Yes, I do . . . And I'm looking at it."

Lee felt foolish. The woman was skinny as a rail, had leathery skin, and was wearing a black eye patch. "Sorry to bother you . . . I'll . . ."

"You'll *what*?" the woman demanded. "Are you going to unbother me? It's too late for that. So spit it out."

It was difficult to intimidate Lee, but the truck driver had succeeded in doing so. "Well, I . . . That is . . . I was hoping to catch a ride. I can pay."

"That ain't no bus," the woman replied, as she hooked a thumb at the truck. "That's Big Bertha . . . And I'm her bitch. Here, hold this."

Lee took the wrench and held it ready as the woman bent to her task. "This is called a gladhand," the woman explained, as she held a doughnut-shaped part up for Lee to examine. "And don't ask me why. Men name these things, and most of 'em ain't very smart.

"See the flaplike things inside it? They seal the gladhand and keep it shut whenever the hose is disconnected. That keeps dirt and moisture out of the air line—and that's important for those of us who like to have brakes that work. But the ass wipes in the bar? Half of them should be out here doin' what I'm doin', but they aren't, so they're gonna pay. Who are you running from?"

The question came out of nowhere. So did Lee's answer. "My boyfriend."

The driver nodded. "Been there, done that. Where you headed?"

"East."

"The name's Annie. You got a place to stay?"

"Yes. In the motel."

"Okay. You be here at 5:00 a.m., and I'll give you a ride to Primm. Don't be late, because if you are, I'll leave you like a bad habit."

Lee nodded. "Yes, ma'am."

When Annie smiled, her face broke into leathery lines. "Don't worry, hon . . . Put the shithead in your rearview mirror and move on. Everything will be fine in the end."

On that unexpectedly cheerful note, the two women parted company. Lee returned to the motel and went up to her room, where she paused to check on the piece of tape. It was intact. So it was unlikely that either the maid or the Bonebreaker had opened the door.

Assumptions could be fatal however, so Lee had one hand on the Glock as she opened the door and slipped inside. Both the room and the adjoining bath were empty.

As Lee got ready for bed, she kept her clothes on—but removed the Smith & Wesson from the small of her back and placed it on the bedside stand. Then she set the alarm, checked the lock, and slipped a wedge-shaped stop under the door. It was a cheap but effective way of making sure that people with keycards, be they good or bad, couldn't get in.

Still fully dressed, Lee stretched out on the bed, managed to pound a lumpy pillow into submission, and put her head down. So far so good. Dreams were waiting . . . They were filled with ghosts.

* * *

In spite of her tendency to ignore alarms, the clock radio woke Lee up with an overly cheerful, "*Buenos dias, mutantes!* And good morning to our brothers and sisters in the green zone . . . We're all people, *sí*? And that includes one-eyed freaks like myself!"

That was followed by a wild cackle of laughter, and a song that Lee recognized as "Flor D'Luna" ("Moonflower"), by a preplague genius named Santana. It was a tuneful reminder that the red zone was only sixty or seventy miles away.

Thirty minutes later Lee approached Big Bertha with the pack on her back and a cardboard tray in her hands. It was loaded with two supersized coffees and two maple bars. Annie's eyes lit up when she saw it. "Now that's what I call a copilot! Right on time with fuel for the driver. I'll take that . . . You'll need both hands to climb up into the cab. Go ahead and throw the pack into the sleeper."

Lee did as she was told, and they were ready to pull out five minutes later. The coffee was hot, Lee's maple bar was sinfully good, and the view of the desert was spectacular. "Hang on, honey," Annie said, as Bertha lurched into a higher gear. "We're outta here."

It was just past 5:00 a.m., and the sky turned bloodred as the sun cleared the mountain range to the east. That was followed by an explosion of pink light as two Heevy brothers waited for the third.

"It's a nice day for it," Hoss Heevy said, as he puffed on his pipe. He was the oldest, the biggest, and the one who looked the most like the family patriarch, "Boss" Heevy. He had long hair, a full beard, and wore an enormous Stetson on his lumpy head. The black duster was large enough to serve most people as a tent—and hung down over the Clydesdale's flanks.

Bruce Heevy was the walleyed progeny of Boss Heevy's second wife, Monica. He was wearing a cowboy hat as well but preferred a fleece-lined leather jacket to a duster, along with a pair of faded jeans. He made a face. "Where's James? He said 5:00 a.m., and it's ten past."

Hoss produced a puff of smoke and lung-warmed air. "The

supreme one will arrive when he's good and ready."

Bruce knew that was true. James Heevy, the son produced by his father's third wife, Alala, was the old man's favorite. There were lots of reasons for that. James was significantly more intelligent than his siblings were—something their father made frequent reference to. And James was better-looking as well. Because even though James was a mutant, he *looked* normal . . . And that meant a lot to the Boss. Having a near-normal son was like having a big house, the best horse, and the finest cigars. It made a statement. "Here he comes," Hoss said. "Sound the trumpets."

Bruce looked back toward the house. And sure enough . . . Jimbo was strolling down the path from the house with a footman trailing along behind. The "house" looked a lot like a castle and was located on high ground at the head of a long, narrow valley.

Unlike his siblings James favored formal attire for such outings and was dressed in a shooting jacket, riding breeches, and tall boots. Both he and the servant stopped just short of the horses so that James could take a final sip from the stirrup cup before turning to place the object on a silver tray. "Well," he said cheerfully. "Here we are . . . Three amigos all ready to do our father's bidding."

Bruce didn't approve of the mocking tone—but knew better than to object. James didn't like people to push back and always found a way to punish them when they did.

James mounted his horse with ease, settled into the saddle like the natural he was, and drew the Browning A-Bolt III out if its leather scabbard. It was chambered for .300 magnum bullets and equipped with a preplague Bushnell Elite 4-12X40 scope on Leupold STD bases. The old man had given the rifle to James on his sixteenth birthday and it was his pride and joy. A quick check confirmed that the box-style magazine was full up and ready for action. God help his groom if it wasn't.

James returned the weapon to its scabbard and kicked the big Morgan into motion. And, in keeping with the well-established pecking order, James took the lead. They followed the road at first as it switchbacked down past a checkpoint manned by a dozen members of the family's security team. The mercenaries knew the brothers and waved at them as they rode by. Half a mile down the road James pulled his horse's head to the left and sent the animal down the narrow trail that led out to the top of a ridge. It ran west to east along the south side of the valley.

The path rose and fell every now and then, meandered through stands of whitebark pine, and clung to sheer cliffs. That was when Bruce had the opportunity to look down into Heartbreak Valley. It had been given the name back during the California gold rush, when men came for precious metals, but failed to find any. What they didn't realize was that the *real* bonanza was an enormous deposit of rare earth metals—including lanthanides and quantities of scandium.

It wasn't their fault of course since products like super magnets, fluorescent lightbulbs, and the components required for missile-guidance systems had yet to be invented. And now, as Bruce looked out over the vast open-pit mine that his father operated, he knew that most of what the family took out of the ground would be sold to companies in Pacifica.

That was unfortunate since the Republic of Texas and Pacifica had been at each other's throats in the past and might be again someday. But most of the people who ran the Republic were suspicious of technology and believed that the plague had been sent by God to punish an increasingly secular society. So to their way of thinking rare earth metals were part of the problem rather than part of the solution.

Would that change as the Aztecs continued to push up from the south? And missiles continued to fall in Texas and Arizona? Boss Heevy thought so . . . But in the meantime, he was happy to sell his product to the people who had the money, regardless of which country they were in.

Both the valley and the mine disappeared from sight as the trail angled to the right and slipped behind an outcropping of lichen-covered rock. A short time later, James led his brothers out onto a spur, where they stopped next to a wind-twisted pine. "This is the spot," he said. "I spent three hours here two days ago. Bruce, I'd like you to serve as my spotter. Hoss, you will be in charge of security. And that's an important job! How would I explain it to the old man if some yahoo was to sneak up and shoot Bruce in the ass?"

Hoss wasn't amused, and Bruce knew why. The truth was that Hoss wasn't willing to act as the shooter *or* the spotter, because in his words, "It ain't right." Was that his mother talking? Quite possibly—since she was a Bible thumper. Of course that didn't keep her from living in luxury even as she offered up all sorts of holier-than-thou bullshit.

James dismounted as Hoss pulled the Clydesdale around and turned back. "Okay," James said, as his boots hit the ground. "We'll leave the horses here and proceed on foot."

After tying the animals to low-hanging branches, the brothers took their long guns and made their way onto the rocky spur. It narrowed quickly, and since there was no cover to speak of, it was necessary to crawl. "Take your hat off," James ordered, as they arrived at the edge of the precipice. Bruce did as he was told and cursed himself for failing to think of it.

As the brothers looked down into the valley they could see the hundreds of shacks that lined both slopes. Many had tiny, carefully terraced gardens, chicken coops, and goat pens. A few were flanked by old jalopies. These were the homes that the workers lived in. Most of whom were barely literate and, lacking the skills required to do something else, had no choice but to perform manual labor.

Still, ignorant or not, there were natural leaders among the people of Shack Town. Men and women who, because of their personal charisma, could urge others to unionize. The solution was a process that the Boss referred to as "culling the herd." Because by removing the so-called "bad breeders" from the workforce, the family could prevent potential leaders from causing harm. And stop the spread of their DNA.

That was where Bruce differed from Hoss. He didn't enjoy culling the herd, but he understood the necessity and considered it a duty that had to be fulfilled. It was something that James and he could agree on. Bruce had a spotting scope in addition to his rifle. He brought the telescope-like device to bear on the shacks that were almost directly below them. "What am I looking for?"

James was looking through the Bushnell by then. "The

target's name is Luigi Bravo. He's been agitating for better medical care. See the shack off to the left? The one with the red blanket hanging out to dry? That's where he lives."

Bruce panned over to the dwelling with the red blanket and made a small adjustment to the focus. There was a small yard behind the hovel. Half of it was taken up with piles of firewood, some rabbit pens, and a pile of rusty auto parts. But there was an open area in the middle—and that's where the little boy was playing. He had a brightly colored toy and was pushing it around. "I see a kid," Bruce said. "Right in the middle of the backyard."

"That's Luigi's son," James replied. "It's Sunday, so Luigi will be home. I will shoot the boy in the leg. He'll scream. That will bring dad out into the open. I'll put him down. If the wife comes running out of the house so much the better. Do you have any questions?"

Bruce's mouth was dry. James made it sound so easy, so routine, but the thought of shooting the little boy made Bruce feel queasy. *But you don't have to shoot him,* Bruce reminded himself. *James will take care of that.* "No," Bruce said. "I don't have any questions."

"Good. Check the range . . . What have you got?"

Bruce eyed the mil-dot reticule, did the math, and gave his answer. "About three hundred yards, give or take." That was well within the Browning's reach. What would make the shot difficult was the extreme downward angle, the persistent down-valley breeze, and the fact that the little boy was moving around.

Of course James knew all of that . . . and was making calculations of his own. Bruce shouldn't have been surprised when the rifle fired, the bullet blew a divot out of the boy's thigh, and the child began to scream.

Just as James had predicted Luigi came charging out through the back door and rushed to assist his badly wounded son. One of his legs was shorter than the other, and that forced him to limp. Then the rifle cracked again, the sound echoed off the other side of the valley, and a piece of Luigi's skull flew off.

As the miner fell Mrs. Bravo came out shooting. She didn't know where the sniper was, and the shotgun was the wrong weapon for the job, but that didn't stop her. She stood over her husband's body and fired at the ridge above. "You have to give her credit," James said, as he worked the bolt on his rifle. "The woman has balls."

Bruce had to agree. And he knew something else as well. Mrs. Bravo *wanted* to die. James took care of that for her. The bullet hit her chest at a downward angle and exited through the small of her back. She fell across her husband.

"Okay," James said matter-of-factly, "mission accomplished."

"What about the boy?"

The child was still making a lot of noise, and the neighbors could be seen peeking out of their windows trying to see what was going on. "Right," James said. "My bad." And with that, his eye went back to the scope. The Browning thumped his shoulder and the crying stopped.

The city of Primm was anything but. The town was mainly devoted to the bars, honky-tonks, and strip joints that gave soldiers something to do. Though originally located in Nevada, and officially part of the Republic, the community had gradually evolved into *two* towns. West Primm was located in California, while East Primm remained in Nevada, and the border fell in between.

But before Lee could cross over into the red zone, she needed to purchase some transportation. Because it was one thing to ride buses and hitchhike in Pacifica, and another to do so in the Republic of Texas, where a norm female was worth tens of thousands of dollars on the black market. So Lee asked Annie to stop shortly after they entered West Primm. "I'll hoof it from here," she said. "Can I pay for your fuel?"

Annie laughed. "Hell, no . . . You don't have that kind of money—and I topped the tanks back in Halloran."

"Thank you."

"You're welcome. Now go out there and get happy. That's an order."

Lee grinned. "Yes, ma'am."

Lee took her pack, opened the door, and jumped to the

ground. She waved as Big Bertha pulled away. And that was when she noticed the plate on the trailer. "1EYEONU." That caused Lee to laugh out loud.

The next few hours were spent walking up and down both sides of the highway. There were a lot of nightspots, and a lot of soldiers wandering in and out of them, but plenty of car lots as well. And that's what Lee was interested in. So she talked to sleazy salesmen, took test drives, and tried to figure out which wreck to buy.

Eventually, with her decision made, it was time to have a couple of tacos in a mom-and-pop restaurant, before circling back to Larry's Used Car Emporium. Larry was right where she'd left him, boots on his desk, watching TV. He looked up as she entered the office. He smiled wolfishly. "You're back . . . Which one will it be?"

"That depends," Lee countered. "It's down to a van at Jumpin' Jack's, or the old 4x4 I drove earlier. Pay me two hundred nu, and I'll take that piece of shit off your hands."

Larry threw his head back and laughed. "You got some nerve, girl . . . But I like that in a woman. Let's go out and kick the tires. They're in good shape by the way . . . There's at least twenty thou on those puppies."

Larry was dressed in a white shirt, bolo tie, and boot-cut jeans. A sizeable paunch hung down in front of a silver rodeo belt, and a cloud of cologne followed the salesman wherever he went. But there was a crafty mind behind the turquoise blue eyes, and Lee had her hands full as negotiations got under way. Finally, in a show of exasperation, Larry threw up his hands. "Okay, okay . . . Twelve-hundred nu. And not a penny less."

The starting price had been eighteen hundred, so Lee was satisfied. "It's a deal," she said, as Larry's hand swallowed hers. "*If* you fill the tank, give me a spare, and throw in the high lift jack that's leaning on the wall over there."

That produced a string of choice swearwords, but Lee got what she wanted, and took possession of the rig an hour later. The SUV was equipped with knobby tires, widely flared fenders, and lots of dents. The truck had been red once. But, after years in the desert sun, what remained of the paint was pink. And that was fine with Lee. She wanted a vehicle that would look like it belonged, wasn't worth stealing, and could handle some rough terrain should that become necessary. The Republic of Texas plates were a big plus as well. How had the truck come to be in Pacifica? If Larry knew, he wasn't telling.

The engine started with a roar, the truck rattled loudly, and a whiff of exhaust wafted up through a hole in the floor as Lee pulled out onto the street. Compared to her motorcycle, it was like steering a ship, and Lee was careful to keep both hands on the gigantic steering wheel as she drove east.

It was late afternoon by that time, but the stores were still open, and Lee had a list of things she needed to purchase. It didn't take long to find a surplus store where she could pick up some basic camping gear and a map of Nevada. "We don't sell very many of these," the man behind the counter confided in her, as he blew some dust off the map. "Are you sure you know what you're doing?" He had thinning hair, a permanent suntan, and a fatherly manner.

Lee nodded. "Yes, sir."

"If you say so," the man said doubtfully. "That'll be 212 nu."

Lee peeled the correct number of bills off her steadily shrinking roll and stuffed the rest of the cash back into her pocket. After loading the purchases into the truck, Lee had dinner at a fast-food joint before setting off to find the campground that the man in the surplus store had told her about. A lot of the streetlights were burned out, making it difficult to see street signs. Lee took a wrong turn and drove north for a while before realizing her mistake.

The second attempt was successful. The facility was about half-full. And, judging from the elaborate manner in which some of the campers, trailers, and motor homes were set up— quite a few of the residents were full-time residents.

Lee had been watching for a tail all day and hadn't detected one. So odds were that the Bonebreaker was still back in L.A. But just to make sure, she planned to sleep in the rig. A strategy that would lessen the chance that the killer would place a tracker on the vehicle.

The backseat had been removed at some point—which made

the cargo area that much larger. Big enough for the newly purchased air mattress and sleeping bag with room left over. After a quick trip to the women's restrooms and showers, it was time to place the Smith & Wesson within easy reach, and lock herself in.

Someone's car alarm went off just after 2:00 a.m. But, other than that, the night passed peacefully. Bright sunlight woke Lee up. Then came the uncomfortable process of getting out of the bag, making what felt like a twenty-mile hike to the shared bathrooms, and performing her morning ablutions side by side with a prostitute who had just returned home from work. She was tall and dressed in a tank top/miniskirt combo that left very little to the imagination. "Hey," the woman said. "Did you have a good night?"

That was when Lee realized that the woman had mistaken her for a hooker. "I spent it sleeping," Lee replied, as she dried her face.

"Good for you," the woman replied, as she removed her wig. "It's hard to sleep during the day."

Lee agreed and returned to the truck where she eyed herself in the rearview mirror. Did she look like a streetwalker? No, not in her opinion anyway. Her normal hairstyle had been left back in LA and replaced with a do that was so short she might have been in boot camp. That made her look different, boyish even, which was the plan. Her cheeks were hollow though . . . And there were circles under her eyes. All since watching the video. Was she doing the right thing? Should she go into the red zone? But, if she wanted to meet her mother, what choice was there? *None*, Lee told herself. *None at all.*

After a quick breakfast Lee made her way to the main drag and a lane marked BORDER CROSSING. There was quite a backup— and that was to be expected. Because while mutants weren't allowed to *live* in Pacifica, they could apply for visas, and cross the border to conduct business. Once they were in-country the mutants had to comply with a long list of strict health regulations. Meanwhile, very few norms wanted to risk their lives by entering the red zone. That meant 99 percent of the vehicles in front of Lee belonged to mutants.

The line jerked ahead in fits and starts. In between Lee had plenty of time to inspect the businesses that lined both sides of the main drag. Most were straight-up stores unlike the seedy bars, strip clubs, and dance halls Lee had seen west of town. There were still lots of soldiers walking the streets, but they were mixed in with dependents and the townsfolk who made their livings off the military.

Eventually, after a half-hour wait, Lee arrived at a concrete hut and the striped drop arm that blocked all further progress. She'd been through the process before and knew what to expect. It began with the look of amazement on the soldier's face as he peered in through the driver's side window and saw her ID. He had to be at least eighteen to join the army but looked two years younger. "A cop? You must be shitting me."

"Yup," Lee confirmed. "A cop. Let's get on with it, shall we? You're going to call for an NCO. He or she will take a look, say something stupid, and summon an officer. So let's start with the officer. What do you say?"

The soldier said, "No." It seemed that privates weren't allowed to send for officers. Only a sergeant could do that. So the situation played out exactly the way Lee predicted it would. And after fifteen minutes of waiting, an officer appeared. Lee had been ordered out of her vehicle by that time and searched. The fact that she was carrying two pistols seemed to confirm the private's belief that she was up to no good—even though the police ID should have been sufficient to put his concerns to rest.

The officer was a dull-eyed specimen not much brighter than the private. But he knew that it was perfectly legal for norms of every description to enter the red zone. And since there was no "stop and hold" order out on Detective Cassandra Lee, he had no legitimate reason to bar her way.

So he asked Lee to sign a release that would prevent her from suing the government of Pacifica should she be infected with *B. nosilla*, raped, or murdered while out of country. The implication being that all three possibilities were likely. Once that was out of the way, he ordered the private to return her weapons and tossed a casual salute. "Have a nice trip," he said. "And good luck." The *you're going to need it* was left unsaid.

Lee got into the truck, started the engine, and eased her way forward. That was when she saw an equivalent security post waiting up ahead. It was unmanned. The overhead sign said, WELCOME TO THE REPUBLIC OF TEXAS. The red zone took her in.

SIX

Lee passed under a steel bridge as she left East Primm and saw the remains of an old roller coaster next to the road. It was a symbol of sorts—a monument to better times.

A jagged mountain range could be seen on the horizon. It, like the rest of the landscape, was an unrelieved beige color. It looked as though every drop of water that had ever fallen on the state of Nevada had been absorbed by the thirsty sun. And the air grew steadily warmer as the fiery orb continued to rise in the east. Lee turned the AC on, or tried to, but the only thing the unit produced was an impotent whirring sound.

Lee rolled the window down but couldn't reach the one on the other side of the truck. So she pulled over to the side of the road, got out, and circled around. The passenger-side door made a creaking sound when she pulled it open. A package of flesh-colored antibacterial masks was sitting on the seat, so she took the opportunity to put one on. Not for the purpose of protecting herself from *B. nosilla*, not yet, but as a disguise. Because even though the muties weren't required to wear one in the Republic of Texas, some chose to do so. Not to protect themselves from a disease they already had—but as a way to hide a badly disfigured face. And that was the impression Lee hoped to convey.

Lee checked the mask in an outside mirror, liked what she saw, and pulled a baseball cap onto her head. It had the initials

LA on it and looked like she'd been wearing it for years. The hope was that most people would mistake her for a man or a boy. With her disguise in place Lee circled the truck, slipped behind the wheel, and pulled away. The slipstream was warm and buffeted her face.

The occasional truck passed her going in the opposite direction. And a car went by ten minutes east of Primm. But most of the vehicles she saw were riddled with bullet holes and had been sitting next to the road for months if not years.

Had they been shot up with people inside? Or used for target practice after being abandoned? Both scenarios were possible because the roads belonged to bandits during the hours of darkness—and anyone foolish enough to travel them was taking a chance.

That's why long-haul truckers formed convoys just before sunset and paid mercenaries to escort them from one city to the next. Could the bandits operate as mercenaries? And vice versa? Of course they could. And did.

It didn't have to be that way. The Republic's citizens could hire more cops. But then they would have to pay more taxes and increase the size of government, which most of them were loath to do. So the people who lived in the red zone got what they deserved. Or so it seemed to Lee.

Lee had been waiting for the turnoff that would take her to the town of Goodsprings. When the road split, she stayed to the left and drove generally north. She saw occasional signs of life, including a white contrail, a patch of green tucked in between two hills, and a wild horse standing on a rise. But such sights were few and far between.

Lee had just passed a burned-out truck stop when she heard the familiar rumble of motorcycle engines. She glanced at her rearview mirror, saw a column of bikers coming up from behind, and felt a sudden stab of fear.

As she watched, the column split in two so that a line of bikes could slip up along both sides of the truck. Some of the riders wore helmets, including football helmets, but most didn't. The gang members were dressed in a wild assortment of clothing that included a lot of denim, leather, and bits of metal. Most rode alone, but there were deuces too . . . And, as the lead biker pulled level with the truck's cab, his passenger was close enough to thump the door with a club.

Lee considered swerving to the left and right. Both columns of bikers were so close that at least some of them would be killed. But what about the rest? Could she outrun them? No. Could she kill them with her pistols? Hell no. So she held the wheel steady as the chopper on the left fell back and the driver stared at her. A spiral horn was protruding from his forehead, and his lips were pulled back to reveal rows of rotting teeth. Was that a smile or a grimace? It was impossible to tell.

At that point, Lee heard a shout and turned her head to the right. A woman with slits rather than a nose was peering in through the passenger-side window. Lee waved as if to say, "Hi," and saw the biker flip her off. That seemed ominous, and Lee figured things were about to get ugly, when horn head opened his throttle and surged ahead. The rest of the column followed.

That was the signal for the riders on the shoulder to pass the truck as well—and Lee felt a profound sense of relief as the gang merged and pulled away. *Luck,* she thought to herself. *I got lucky.* Although it was likely that the unassuming truck, the ball cap, and the mask had been helpful as well.

It wasn't long before the Pahrump sign appeared. As the highway split, Lee veered left onto Highway 160. Mountains rose to the right and there were places where hills hugged the road. There wasn't much traffic at first, but when Lee hit a long, sloping hill, it was necessary to pass three semis before arriving on the flats beyond.

From that point forward the trip to Pahrump was uneventful. As she approached the town, a series of signs appeared. All of them said the same thing: PREPARE TO STOP. ENTRY FEE 20 NU. Nu being the currency of choice in the red zone even though it was issued by Pacifica.

This was something Lee hadn't seen before. Apparently, the folks in Pahrump had chosen to raise funds by taxing travelers rather than themselves. Could she go around the town? Drive cross-country if necessary? Maybe. But the effort wasn't worth it. And the citizens of Pahrump were counting on that.

Half a mile later Lee was forced to slow down and stop at the end of a relatively short line. It jerked forward until Lee was level with a wooden shack where a man with a saggy face and a couple of two-fingered hands took her money.

From there Lee drove into town. She was hungry and was on the lookout for a Mexican restaurant. Not having seen one she pulled into the lot that fronted Bob's Barbecue.

She got out of the truck, locked it, and went inside. The walls were lined with boards that might have been salvaged from an old barn—and the picnic tables were covered with checkered tablecloths. The place was about half-full, and as far as Lee could tell, none of the customers was paying special attention to her. So far so good.

Lee went to the counter and ordered a brisket sandwich, fries, and a Diet Coke to go. There was no other choice since she couldn't eat inside the restaurant without removing the mask and exposing herself to *B. nosilla*.

As Lee waited for her order, she noticed that most of her fellow customers were wearing pistols. That was the way of things in the Republic, so no one would question the fact that she was armed as well.

After they called her name Lee paid the cashier, took her food out to the truck, and went in search of some shade. She found it under a tree two blocks away. The brisket was tender, the fries were greasy, and the Coke hit the spot. Thus refreshed it was time to find the town of Heartbreak.

It wasn't necessary to pay on the way *out* of Pahrump, but Lee decided to stop at the station on the edge of town, and top off the truck's oversized tank. Fuel was a nice thing to have out in the desert.

Once on the highway, with the hot air pummeling her face, Lee felt a rare moment of happiness. Freedom really . . . And a sense of anticipation. Things had gone smoothly so far, and even though her emotions had a tendency to vacillate, Lee was looking forward to meeting her mother.

Nearly featureless desert stretched off in every direction as Lee followed the badly faded white line north. Highway 160 to

Highway 95, where, according to the map, she should take a right. Eventually, if she continued east, Lee knew she'd wind up in Las Vegas.

A railroad track paralleled the highway on the left. And, judging from how shiny the tracks were, it was used frequently. After fifteen minutes or so, she spotted an intersection in the distance and slowed to read a large sign. HEAVY MINING. AUTHORIZED PERSONNEL ONLY. TEN MILES. An arrow pointed to the left. That was when Lee saw a smaller sign that read, HEARTBREAK HWY, and knew she was in the right place.

It was necessary to wait for an oncoming car to pass before Lee could turn left. There was a slight rise where the track crossed the side road, and she felt a couple of bumps as the truck rolled over the rails and entered the narrow passageway that separated the hills on the left from the hills on the right. The Heartbreak Highway took her north.

Lee drove for ten minutes or so. Then, as she rounded a curve, the checkpoint appeared. It was located at a natural chokepoint between two sleep slopes. The guardhouse was painted an eye-searing white, was topped with a HEEVY MINING sign, and straddled both lanes of traffic. All for what purpose? To keep bandits out? Or to keep people *in*?

Lee had no choice but to slow down and come to a stop in front of a striped drop bar. A uniformed security guard was sitting on a stool in the strip on the east side of the guard station. There was no sense of urgency in the way he got up and ambled over to the truck. He looked normal except for the goiter that was growing at the base of his throat. According to the name badge clipped to his shirt pocket the guard's last name was Tuel. "Good afternoon. Do you have a pass? If so, please place it on the inside surface of your windshield."

"I don't have one," Lee replied. "I'm here to visit someone."

Tuel shook his head. "Sorry . . . The company doesn't allow visitors except on Sunday—and you would need a guest pass to enter then."

Lee felt a growing sense of frustration. *Sunday?* That was three days away! "How would I go about obtaining a pass?"

"You'll need to apply for it," Tuel answered. "The company

has an office in Indian Springs. You can submit a request there."

"How long will the process take?"

"About a week," the guard replied. "A car is waiting behind you. I'll raise the arm so you can circle around and go back the way you came. Have a nice day."

Lee had no choice but to follow Tuel's instructions. She drove the truck around the guard station, waited for the southbound arm to lift, and let the clutch out. The truck jerked ahead. Lee felt a mix of disappointment, frustration, and anger as she drove back to Highway 95.

Why hadn't her mother warned her? Where was she anyway? The address on the letter was care of someone else. And then there was the Heevy mining company. A business that operated much like a government. And a dictatorial one at that. The whole thing was strange to say the least.

Lee took a left on Highway 95. Was there a back way into the town of Heartbreak? No, that was ridiculous. The people who had gone to such lengths to close the highway off weren't likely to leave a secondary route unguarded.

But Lee had to go somewhere while she thought things over. The obvious choice was to turn around and go home. But her mother was dying . . . And Lee wanted to see her for a variety of reasons. It would be a chance to reach some sort of closure where the mother-daughter relationship was concerned, and if she was lucky, get a chance to get a fresh perspective on her father too.

Such were Lee's thoughts when she spotted a driveway up ahead and an unexpected splash of green back behind it. It was a place to turn off so she did. Then she saw the ruins of a house and the outbuildings beyond. Was the place deserted? If so, she could pause there and decide what to do.

Cautiously, in case the house was occupied, Lee drove up the drive and turned into an unpaved parking spot located behind the sagging house. The farmhouse had been occupied by squatters judging from the graffiti and piles of trash. But they were gone, and the house made the truck impossible to see from the highway.

As a precaution Lee pulled wide and backed into the parking

place so that she could depart quickly if necessary. It was an old trick practiced by patrolmen everywhere.

Lee took a bottle of water off the passenger seat and carried it with her as she got out. The grove of palm trees she'd seen from the road hinted at the presence of a spring and explained why the house had been built there. Lee made her way into the shade, blew a layer of dust off of an old bench, and sat down. The water was warm but wet.

Bees were buzzing around the wildflowers that had taken root in and around the old garden, and the occasional cricket could be heard, but that was all. With nothing else to do Lee took her phone out and turned it on. Maybe an important message would be there waiting for her. Something that would help guide her actions. But there was no service in that part of Nevada. She put the device away.

An old path led past the garden and wandered uphill. Lee followed the trail past an old chicken coop to a fence. The gate was long gone, but the path continued up along the side of the hill.

Lee knew that Heartbreak Valley lay what? About five miles beyond the top of the hill? Yes, that was a reasonable guess. So what about hiking up and over? She had her pack, plus the camping gear purchased back in Primm, and some exercise would feel good. Not in the sun, however . . . No way. Such a journey would best be carried out at night.

But what if she ran into more security? *I'll turn around and return here,* Lee thought to herself. *And that will put an end to it.*

Lee made her way down the side of the hill. The more she thought about the hike the more she liked it. And by the time she returned to the truck, the idea had morphed into a plan. She would sleep if she could, eat dinner, and leave just before sunset. As for the truck, well, it would be there when she got back. Especially since she was going to disconnect the ignition coil. Could someone make the proper diagnosis and hot-wire the vehicle? Sure, but it was unlikely.

After pulling the wire loose, Lee went to work on her pack. She hoped to reach the town of Heartbreak by sunup, blend in, and find the woman named Myra Meo. But what if she failed?

What if she had to spend the next day under the hot sun?

With that possibility in mind Lee filled her pack with bottles of water from the case in the truck. Four in all. Those plus the sleeping bag, a change of underwear, some toiletries, her gun kit, and a box of energy bars would be enough. The rest went back into the truck.

Lee spread a tarp out under the trees, made a pillow out of her jacket, and tried to sleep. That didn't seem likely because of the heat. But then she awoke to discover that it was 5:30 p.m. She felt groggy and it took a major effort to stand up, find a place to pee, and return to the truck.

Lee couldn't risk a fire and the smoke it would produce but didn't have to. After boiling water over a tiny backpacking stove, she made a cup of instant coffee and poured the rest of the hot liquid into a foil bag labeled CHICKEN AND RICE. She'd eaten the freeze-dried meal before—and actually liked the glutinous mixture. So after consuming about half of the bag's contents, and washing it down with instant coffee, Lee felt better.

It was six thirty by then. The light had begun to fade, and half an hour had passed since a vehicle had rolled by, so Lee figured it was safe to go.

So after a final look around she shouldered the pack and set off. The trail was steep, but the air was a good deal cooler by then, and she felt a sense of anticipation. What would it take? Four hours? Six? Then she'd be there. After that, well, time would tell.

A rocky overhang jutted out from the side of a hill to provide a patch of shade during the hottest time of day. As the sun went down, and the temperature fell, the pack began to stir. The animals weren't dogs or wolves. They were an unholy mixture of both. And thanks to mutations caused by *B. nosilla*, they were even more dangerous than their ancestors had been.

One Ear was an excellent example of that. He looked like an oversized Rottweiler rather than a wolf. But to a large extent One Ear *thought* like a wolf. A smart wolf who weighed 150 pounds, had senses keener than those of his predecessors, and possessed some primitive social skills. All of which helped to explain why the mutimal and his mate Silver were alpha dogs. Meaning the pair from which most of the pack was descended—and to whom the rest of the animals looked for leadership.

So when One Ear began to stir, the rest of the pack watched to see what he would do. Like the rest of them One Ear had fleas. So the first order of business was to scratch himself. Then it was time to pad over to the shallow basin where cool, clean water was waiting. One Ear didn't wonder why the liquid was there—or give thanks for the fact that it was. What was, was. He drank his fill as Silver looked on.

She was lying on her side so that six hungry pups could suckle at her teats. She knew she would be left behind when the pack went out to hunt. Then, once One Ear ate his fill, he would return to regurgitate some food for her.

Gimpy couldn't run very well, not since the epic battle with the canyon dogs, but he was a good fighter. So he would stay with Silver and protect both her and One Ear's pups from harm. Then, once the kill was made, he would be summoned to feed on the carcass. That level of specialization was a relatively recent development but one that was consistent with the wolf-dog instincts of the past and the natural extension of greater intelligence.

Silver produced a whining noise and One Ear went over to nuzzle and lick her. Neither one of them could speak nor did they need to. Both understood their roles and the nature of the relationship that bound them together.

But the moment was brief. One Ear was hungry and knew that the others were as well. So as he made his way out into the bone-strewn common area, his supersensitive nose was sampling the evening breeze. He, like the rest of the pack, could discriminate between thousands of different odors. Hundreds of them were associated with food. But none of those were in the offing, so the pack would have to go out and search for prey.

All of the hill dogs were ready, their bodies quivering, waiting for their leader to make the first move. But some of the pack's best trackers were missing. That included Loner and Spot. One Ear threw his head back and produced a long-drawn-out howl that could be heard from miles away.

Loner heard the call and answered with a series of distinctive yips followed by a howl of his own. Spot, who was off to the south, joined in. He was following some meat—and not that far away. The hunt began.

Lee heard the first howl and the blood-chilling chorus that followed. The sound of it caused her heart to race. Dogs. *Mutant* dogs. Everyone knew how dangerous they could be . . . especially at night.

How far had she gone? A mile and a half maybe? It felt like more since she'd been trudging uphill. What should she do? Continue on? Or retreat? But because there was no way to know where the dogs were, either move could prove fatal.

Lee swore, shrugged the pack off, and opened a side pocket. She had a laser sight. It was designed to slip onto the rail under the Glock's barrel just forward of the trigger assembly. That could be useful at night.

But, to ensure accuracy, she should mount the sight, aim through the pistol's iron sights, and fire at a target. Then she would use a small wrench to align the laser with the open sights. That would produce a lot of noise however. And noise could attract the very dogs she was afraid of. So Lee decided to forgo the procedure and take her chances.

Suddenly, what had been a simple night hike had been transformed into a terrifying trek through a scary landscape. Each dimly seen bush, each rock, could be a mutimal. What would Lee notice first? The rattle of stones as toenails sought purchase in the gravelly soil? A chorus of howls coming from all around? Soon to be followed by an onslaught of wiry bodies?

Lee knew she would fall at that point, firing wildly, as the dogs swarmed her. Chances were that she'd be conscious when they ripped her belly open. It was a terrifying thought and Lee discovered that it was difficult to hike and look over her shoulder at the same time. She hurried up the trail.

* * *

Spot was black except for the patch of white that rode his back like a saddle. One Ear was his father, Silver was his mother, and he would try to take over if One Ear was killed. Meanwhile he was hunting with the big dog, even leading the way at times, completely unaware of the fact that One Ear *wanted* him to do so. Especially when they were hunting a two-leg. That was because the alpha knew that most of the two-legs carried bang sticks. And the first dog to attack such a creature was likely to die. So it was better to be the second, or even the third dog, if he hoped to survive.

Spot paused next to a rock and sniffed all around it. A two-leg had been there. He knew that because of the complex combination of odors that hung in the air. He produced a throaty growl and surged up the trail. One Ear, Jitters, and Short Tail followed.

Lee had two choices. She could try to outrun her pursuers, a hopeless task if there ever was one, or fort up and face them. By using the flashlight she'd been able to examine various possibilities as she climbed. The key was to find a place where she could put her back against something solid and thereby force the dogs to attack one at a time. Unfortunately most of the hill was open, bare of significant vegetation, and therefore indefensible.

So it was only when Lee arrived on the summit that she saw what might be a possibility. There were lots of shadows. But, thanks to the starlight, Lee could see that part of the hilltop had sloughed away at some point. The result was a flat area and a big pile of rocks. And it was within that tumble of boulders that Lee sought safety.

It was also a natural lair for mutant rattlesnakes that, according to pictures she'd seen, could be eight feet long. But Lee couldn't concern herself with that. All she could do was follow a natural passageway back to a dead end, place her back against a rock wall, and get ready for what promised to be a desperate battle. Doing so made her feel better. So much so that she stripped the foil off two energy bars and threw them into the passageway.

"Here, doggy," she called. "Come and get your treat."

There was no reaction. Each minute felt like an hour. There were no more howls, and Lee was left to ponder the meaning of that. Had the pack lost her trail? Were they off chasing a rabbit? Or were they only twenty yards away—preparing to charge up the narrow corridor?

The answer came in the form of a huge beast that attacked from *above*. Having found its way up onto the rocks, and done so silently, it dropped into the passageway not six feet away. Lee tried to pin the green dot on the target and fired. Both bullets went wide.

Lee didn't know if that was as a result of her failure to zero the laser sight earlier or a bad case of nerves. Whatever the reason she resolved to rely on her natural talent and triggered the flashlight. The dog was airborne by then. Lee fired and saw a splash of blood where the bullet struck but knew that the mutimal would hit her. It did. And the force of the blow drove all of the air out of her lungs. Had a second dog attacked the fight would have been over. Fortunately, none did. And as Lee tilted the flashlight down she saw that the dead dog had a white spot on its back. It twitched, and she shot it again.

Silence settled over the scene. Lee checked her watch. It was 10:22. Dawn was still a long ways off. Should she venture out? Or wait for sunrise? Daylight would even the odds quite a bit. With that in mind Lee resigned herself to spending the rest of the night where she was. The first order of business was to reload the Glock—plus the magazine that had been in the Glock.

Once that was accomplished Lee took an energy bar and a bottle of water out of the pack, put them off to one side, and turned the flashlight off. The batteries were relatively new, but she didn't have any backups. Then, with the Glock and flashlight within easy reach, Lee ate the energy bar and drank half a bottle of water. The air was cold . . . And she was wearing everything she had.

There was the sleeping bag, though, which she could unzip and drape around her shoulders. That helped, but as the adrenaline began to fade, she felt sleepy. A sudden chorus of bloodcurdling howls took care of that. Lee suspected that the pack knew that one of their members was dead—and this was their way of mourning him. She braced herself for another attack, but none came.

The minutes and hours seemed to crawl by. Lee heard movement from time to time and was on guard against another drop-in. But it appeared that the dogs were smart enough to avoid making the same mistake twice.

Then the sun rose. And as the lavender light found its way down into the passageway, Lee got a better look at the animal sprawled in front of her. And that was when she noticed the collar around the dog's thick neck. What did *that* mean? That the big brute was a stray? Probably. Such things were common. There were tens of thousands of such dogs in Pacifica . . . And police officers had to shoot hundreds of them each year.

As the light level continued to increase Lee knew that the time had come. She held a pistol in each hand as she stood. Everything else would be left behind. Assuming she won the battle, the supplies would be there waiting for her. If she didn't, it wouldn't matter. Maybe someone would find her badge and mail it to LA.

There was a queasy feeling in the pit of Lee's stomach as she stepped over the body and made her way forward. She paused just short of the open area and took a careful look around. There was no sign of the dogs other than piles of fresh feces. Had they left? Or were they hiding? There was one sure way to find out.

Lee sprinted out into the very center of the open area, brought both weapons up, and started to turn. The targets seemed to materialize out of nowhere. They were crouched low, teeth bared, ready to attack. If Lee had a gift, it was the ability to shoot. One-handed, two-handed, it didn't matter. But with *four* dogs coming at her from different directions that talent might not be enough. Add to that the necessity to put at least two slugs into each mutimal, and the task was even more daunting.

But Lee knew that the trick was to let go, and she did. The Smith & Wesson seemed to go off of its own accord. The first bullet entered the dog's open mouth and blew a large chunk of meat out through the back of its head. The second clipped an outstretched paw but did no additional damage.

Lee wanted to fire at the first animal again but knew that would be a mistake. So she sidestepped the incoming body even as she fired three rounds from the Glock. The first bullet missed the dog charging in from the left. That meant it was only four feet away when she fired three slugs into its hindquarters. One of them severed the mutimal's spine, causing it to fall. It snapped futilely as it tried to sink its teeth into her.

All of which was good—but not good enough. What felt like a sledgehammer hit Lee in the back. The force of the blow threw her forward. She hit the ground hard, the Glock popped loose, and skittered away.

There was barely enough time to turn over before the remaining dogs were on her. One of the slavering beasts straddled her body and was about to go for her throat when the .357 magnum went off. The stubby barrel was only an inch away from the animal's rib cage so the hollow point made a small hole going in and a *big* hole coming out. The dog died instantly and collapsed on top of her.

Lee struggled to push the body off, and the corpse served as a temporary barrier between her and the last dog. It was a big beast with one ear and a black muzzle. It growled at her. And Lee, whose weight was resting on her left elbow, growled back. "Eat lead, asshole."

The bullets hit One Ear in the nose, an eye, and his throat. He went down in a welter of blood. Lee swore, rolled free of the body, and stood. Her legs were wobbly, and she felt dizzy. That went away after a moment, and she was about to return for her belongings, when she heard a whining noise. It came from the dog with the severed spine.

As Lee went over to look at him she was surprised by the way she felt. The formerly frightening dog looked pitiful now, its brown eyes pleading with her as it tried to pull itself forward. "I'm sorry," Lee said. And was surprised to discover that she meant it. She pulled the trigger, and the report echoed off the face of the nearby cliff.

For the first time Lee had an opportunity to look north. A huge open pit mine was located directly in front of and below her. As she looked on, toy-sized earthmovers were being used to load the trucks that would haul the raw ore to the railroad for shipment west. Lee could hear the distant growl of their engines and imagine how hot the pit would be by midafternoon.

The town of what she assumed to be Heartbreak was laid out grid-style, and consisted of low one- and two-story buildings, very few of which appeared to be homes. No, based on what Lee could see, most of the local residents were living in the shacks that clung to the slopes of the valley west of the mine. Was that where she would find her mother? Lee was determined to find out.

Lee made her way back into the passageway where she had to step over the dead dog in order to retrieve her belongings. She hauled everything out into the open where it would be easier to repack, and was busy stuffing the sleeping bag into its sack, when she heard a distant buzzing sound. As Lee turned toward the sound, she saw that a small helicopter was flying straight at her from the west end of the valley. Her first impulse was to run. But she wasn't ready to depart—and there was no place to run to.

So Lee turned back to the task at hand and was finished by the time the chopper circled the top of the hill. Sunlight glinted off the aircraft's bubble-shaped canopy—and she could see two people inside.

By that time it was clear that the helicopter was going to land on the flat area adjacent to the sprawl of bodies. All Lee could do was stand and wait as the chopper settled onto its skids. The rotors made a whup, whup, whup sound as a man got out and paused to survey the carnage. Both barrels of his shotgun were resting on his right shoulder as he came forward to speak with her. But Lee knew that he could level the weapon in a heartbeat and fire just as quickly. He was wearing a cowboy hat, a fleece-lined leather jacket, and jeans. And once the man was closer Lee could see that he was walleyed. The face mask was ready, and she pulled it on.

The man stopped. "You're a norm," he stated flatly.

"Yes."

"We don't get a whole lot of norms out this way," the man said conversationally. "What did you use on the dogs? A machine pistol?"

"Nope. A Glock and a .357 revolver."

The man uttered a low whistle. "That took some fancy shootin'. The old man's gonna be pissed though . . . Them were *his* dogs."

"I thought they were wild."

"They *are* wild," the man replied. "Or they were. But that don't matter. The old man owns *everything* around here. And that includes the wild dogs. When they went off-line, he sent me out to take a look."

Lee frowned. "Off-line?"

"You didn't notice the collars? And the trackers? She-it, girl . . . Those animals were part of the company's security system. So I've got to ask you to surrender those pistols. Then we're gonna have a little meet and greet with the old man. Maybe you can work the cost off at the mine."

"And if I don't?"

The shotgun dropped so that both barrels were pointed at Lee's chest. "Then I'm going to blow you in half."

Lee remained as she was. "And you are?"

"Bruce Heevy. Boss Heevy's son."

"I see. Okay, I'm going to open my jacket real slow and remove the Glock . . . Then I'm going to reach for the Smith & Wesson. It's holstered at the small of my back. I will place both weapons on the ground and take three paces back."

Bruce nodded. "Sounds like you've done this before."

"I'm a cop."

"Get serious."

"I *am* serious. I have a badge and everything."

"Show it to me."

"Okay . . . I'm going to remove it from the inside pocket of my jacket."

Once the case was out in the open Bruce crooked a finger. "Toss it here."

Lee watched him make the one-handed catch and flip the case open. Bruce glanced at the ID card inside. "Cassandra Lee . . ." His eyes met hers. "What brings you to the town of Heartbreak, Detective Lee?"

"I'm looking for my mother."

"And her name is?"

"Alala Lee. Or Freedom Lee."

A look of surprise appeared on Bruce's face. "Does she have dark skin?"

"Yes. Darker than mine."

Bruce was silent for a moment. Then he laughed. "She-it! The old man's gonna have a cow . . . Put those weapons on the ground, girl . . . And welcome to the town of Heartbreak."

SEVEN

After surrendering her weapons and submitting to a pat down, Lee was ordered onto the helicopter. She had ridden on choppers before—but never one so small. The backseat was barely wide enough to accommodate both her and the pack.

Once Lee was belted in, Bruce secured her hands with a plastic zip tie he connected to the U-bolt mounted on the back of the front seat. A sure sign that the aircraft had been used to transport prisoners before.

Then Lee and the pilot had to wait while Bruce retrieved all the dog collars. Would they be used to track another pack? Probably.

Finally, after Bruce strapped himself into the front passenger seat, the chopper took off. The aircraft angled forward as it sped out over the mine and turned west. Its shadow blipped over excavators, support buildings, and the town of Heartbreak.

It wasn't until the noise thing was gone that Silver emerged from hiding. She couldn't comprehend what had taken place—but she was very familiar with the smell of death. And as Silver went over to nuzzle One Ear's body, she made a whining noise deep in her throat.

Then, overcome with emotion, she threw her head back and uttered a long, mournful howl. The sound was audible on the other side of the valley. A miner heard it and made the sign of the cross.

Lee's thoughts were churning. Bruce Heevy was acquainted with her mother! And, more than that, seemed to feel that Boss Heevy would be interested in the fact that Alala had a daughter. *Why?* Lee caught a glimpse of a castlelike house as the helicopter circled it. Then the structure was behind her as the pilot brought the machine in for a soft landing on a pad just south of the mansion.

Once on the ground Lee had to wait while the engine shut down and Bruce got out. He gave the dog collars to a man in blue overalls before turning back to Lee. His pocketknife was sharp enough to free her with a single cut. "Come on," he said. "Word travels quickly in our house . . . And I want to be there when the old man gets the news! You can leave the pack . . . A servant will bring it in."

The great room was truly great. The fireplace at the north end of the room was at least six feet tall and twelve feet wide. That made it large enough to roast a cow should Boss Heevy choose to do so. Plus, there was enough seating to handle thirty people, all of which was arranged to create interlocking conversation areas. Those walls not devoted to large windows were hung with dozens of hunting trophies. Some of them were nightmarish creatures that owed their existence to *B. nosilla* rather than the hand of God. Unless one believed, as some did, that *B. nosilla* had been sent by God to punish the human race.

But Boss Heevy's province was at the south end of the vast room, a good seventy-five feet from the fireplace, on a platform originally intended for use as a stage. It had been constructed so that Heevy's sister could dance while their parents looked on. But Belinda had been gone for a long time—as were the man and woman who adored her.

That left Heevy to use the platform as he saw fit—and it was a good place for his desk, some guest chairs, and the bookcases located to the right and left. And he loved books. Not for the sort of romantic nonsense that Belinda had favored. No, he liked books about geology, mining, and economics. All subjects that he'd been required to master in order to maintain the company and expand it.

But who would follow him? Who would take the operation to the next level? That was the question that haunted Heevy. Hoss was too soft for the job, Bruce lacked the necessary intelligence, and James lacked ambition. Yes, the boy could be prodded into action. But when left to his own devices he preferred to play rather than work. Of course he was young, and with the passage of time . . .

Such were Boss Heevy's thoughts as he heard a commotion and looked up to see Bruce enter the room. Bruce and a boy, no, a girl, who was wearing a spit mask. An ugly then . . . Someone so hard to look at that she chose to hide her face. Was she the one responsible for killing 90 percent of pack two? No. It would take a group of people to accomplish that. Troublemakers most likely . . . Miners trying to leave the valley without paying what they owed to the company store.

Bruce stopped just short of the stage so the girl did as well. "I'm back," Bruce said.

Heevy stood to circle the desk. His body was normal from the waist up. But his legs were so twisted that two canes were required in order to walk. "Yes," Heevy said sarcastically. "I can see that. Who is this creature?"

Bruce was enjoying himself. "This," he said importantly, "is Detective Cassandra Lee. She's looking for her mother . . . A woman named Alala."

Heevy frowned. "That's what she told you? And you were stupid enough to believe it?"

Lee took a deep breath and removed the mask. A look of wide-eyed shock appeared on Heevy's face. "No! It can't be!"

Lee pulled the mask back into place so that she could breathe. Now it was clear that both Heevys were acquainted with her mother. "Yes," Lee said. "It can be—and it *is*. It seems that you know my mother. Where is she?"

Heevy had regained his composure by then. His lower lip stuck out farther than the one above. And that gave him the look of an eternally petulant child. He forced a smile. "I'm sorry to say that she's ill and has been for some time. She's upstairs in her bedroom."

"She lives *here*?"

"Of course. All three of my wives do."

Now it was Lee's turn to feel a sense of shock. Married! And one of *three* wives? That was a surprise to say the least— although Lee knew that polygamy was legal in the Republic of Texas. Her head was spinning. "Can I see her?"

Heevy made his way down a flight of three stairs. "She sent for you?"

"Yes. I had no idea where she was until I received the letter."

"May I ask what she told you? What brought you into the red zone?"

"She said that she's dying."

Heevy nodded. "Yes. I'm sorry to say that's true. I will miss her greatly."

As Lee looked into Heevy's brown eyes, she could see that it was true. Regardless of whether Heevy was good or bad, he was in love with her mother. And that possibility had never occurred to her. That someone could love the person who abandoned her. "I see," Lee said awkwardly.

"I will let Alala know that you're here," Heevy said gently. "And, assuming she feels up to it, I'm sure she'll want to see you. In the meantime I have a question . . . Bruce mentioned that you're a detective."

"Yes. With the Los Angeles Police Department. That's how my mother knew where to find me. She'd seen me on television."

Heevy looked skeptical. "Here in the red zone?"

"Yes. I followed a kidnapping victim across the border. That got some press down in Arizona."

Heevy nodded. "I'll bet it did." The *real* question, which was why Alala had chosen to keep Lee's existence to herself, remained unsaid.

"She's a very good shot," Bruce volunteered. "She took pack

two down with a couple of pistols."

"How interesting," Heevy said mildly. "That's quite an accomplishment—and more than a little annoying. Normally, there would be severe consequences for such a thing. But, since you're a member of the family, we'll put it down to a misunderstanding."

Lee didn't know how to feel about her sudden induction into the Heevy family—but assumed it was to her advantage. "Thank you. Can I have my guns back? I feel naked without them."

Heevy laughed. "Of course. Bruce . . . give the girl her weapons."

Bruce was carrying the pistols in his belt. He offered them butts first. Lee took them, and was in the process of putting the Smith & Wesson away, when Heevy spoke. "See the buck hanging over the fireplace? The twelve pointer? My father shot it through the heart. I want you to put a bullet between its eyes." It was a strange challenge—but Lee was in a strange place.

So she checked to make sure that the Glock was loaded, brought it up with both hands, and took the proper stance. The gun fired. The deer was at least twenty-five yards away, and Lee knew that most shooters would be happy with a three-to-five-inch pattern at that range. How close was she? Bruce went down to the other end of the room for a closer look. "She was a few inches to the right," he announced. "The bullet went through its left eye."

Heevy had bushy eyebrows, and they rose. "There's only one other person who could get that close from this distance—and that's your half brother, James. He's down at the mine right now . . . But you'll meet him at dinner. Bruce, tell Mrs. Dustin that Cassandra will be staying in the blue room and to look after her needs."

Lee was stunned. And even though the lower part of her face was covered Heevy could see the reaction in her eyes. He smiled bitterly. "It appears that your mother kept secrets from you as well . . . She's consistent if nothing else."

Mrs. Dustin had appeared by then. She was a kindly-looking woman with a short trunk in place of a nose. "Come with me, dear . . . I'll show you to your room."

* * *

It was Heevy's custom to visit Alala every morning at 10 a.m. That gave Myra Meo the time necessary to bathe her mistress, help her dress, and change the sheets on the bed. Once Alala was back in bed a kitchen servant would arrive with a breakfast of tea and dry toast. Both of which were likely to stay down. So when the knock came, Alala looked at herself in a hand mirror. There was no need for a mask now that *B. nosilla* was ravaging her body. And, all things considered, Alala thought she looked reasonably good. She put the mirror down. "Come in!"

The door opened, and Heevy entered. His canes produced a thumping sound as he passed through the shaft of sunlight that was streaming in through a high arched window. *His* chair, the one kept in the room especially for him, was positioned next to Alala's bed. It had been what? A year since they had slept together? Something like that. Fortunately Heevy had Monica and Bethany to take care of his needs. "Good morning, darling," Alala said. "How are you?"

"I'm fine," Heevy replied. "More to the point—how are *you*?"

"The pills keep the pain down," Alala replied. "But they make it hard to stay awake."

"Don't worry about that," Heevy replied. "Sleep as much as you want."

Alala smiled weakly and reached out take his hand. "You're so good to me." That was a lie, of course . . . Since she caught *B. nosilla* from *him* while they were having sex.

"I want to see your face," he had insisted. That was when he tore the mask off. And infected a person he loved. Did her husband feel guilty about that? Yes, Alala believed that he did.

Heevy smiled. "I have a surprise for you."

Alala's eyes widened. "A surprise? Whatever could it be?"

"Your daughter, Cassandra, is here. She's staying in the blue room."

Alala felt a brief moment of joy quickly followed by a stab of fear. "I'm sorry, Hiram . . . I should have told you."

"Yes," he said tightly. "You should have. Why didn't you?"

Though calm, Heevy was angry. Alala could see that, and it came as no surprise. Because while Heevy loved her in his own way, he had very high standards for his wives, and would perceive her omission as a lie. That was why Alala had hoped to see Cassie in private. At Myra's house.

But now, looking back, Alala knew how unrealistic that plan had been. Her health had deteriorated a great deal over the last few months and it was no longer possible to leave the house. But somehow, some way, Cassie had been able to find her. "I was scared," Alala told him. "I wasn't sure you would want me if you knew." That was only half-true but enough to assuage Heevy's ego.

"I would want you no matter what," Heevy said gallantly. "And I must say that your daughter is a very impressive young woman. She hiked through the hills to reach the valley, was attacked by pack two, and put most of them down. It's the sort of thing James might do."

That was a compliment of sorts. An indirect way of saying that Alala's son was superior to the rest. But Alala was careful to ignore that. Or seem to. "Yes, all of your boys are competent, and I know that's a comfort to you."

"Yes," Heevy agreed, "it is. Well, time for me to go. Cassandra would like to see you . . . Would 1:00 p.m. be convenient?"

Alala would have preferred to see Cassie right *then*—but rather than betray the strength of her emotions she nodded. "Yes, darling . . . That would be fine. Thank you for your understanding where this matter is concerned. I'm the luckiest woman in the world."

Heevy stood, bent to kiss her cheek, and left. Alala's thoughts were racing. Cassie! There in the house . . . The first part of the plan was in place. Now for the second. Alala felt better than she had for a long time.

The blue room was not only large and nicely furnished, it had a bathroom of its own. And that included a big tub. So Lee filled it with hot water and took the opportunity to wash all the dirt and grime away. Then she got out, toweled off, and discovered that new clothes had been laid out on the bed. Not a shirt and jeans but a summery dress! The sort of thing she rarely wore.

Still, clean was better than dirty, so she put it on. And there were shoes, too . . . strappy things with high heels. Who was dressing her anyway? Then it struck her. Frank Lee had seen his wife in his daughter, and Boss Heevy did, too. Was her mother required to wear dresses? Lee had a feeling that she was. There was a knock at the door.

Lee pulled a mask down over her face before going to open it. A girl with a linen-covered tray was waiting in the hall. She looked nervous. "A bite to eat, Miss . . . And a note from Mr. Heevy."

Lee said, "Thank you," and took the tray. As the door closed she carried it over to the ornate makeup table and put it down. When Lee removed the cover she saw the envelope. She tore it open. The card read: "Your mother knows you're here—and would like to see you at 1:00 p.m. Her maid will take you there. Affectionately, Hiram."

Lee felt her spirits soar. She looked at her watch and saw that it was 11:50. The salad looked good, so she tried to eat it, but she had no appetite. Her mother . . . After all of those years. She cried.

Like his brothers, James was required to spend every third day at the mine. "You need to learn the business," their father told his sons. "I won't live forever."

And that was true. But both Hoss and Bruce knew James was the favorite, so why bother? And James knew he could rely on the mine's manager, a crusty old coot named Barrow, to run the operation far more effectively than he could. So it was his habit to make an appearance at the mine, follow Barrow around for a while, and fade. Of course he needed a place to go—so he was renting a small apartment above Heartbreak's single feed store. As for Barrow, he knew that James would be in charge one day and wasn't about to complain.

Meanwhile Bruce's mother, a beauty named Monica, went into town on a frequent basis. The ostensible purpose of the visits was to volunteer at the company-run school. But her *real* objective was to escape her husband and the stifling environment at the house for a few hours. And that was how the affair had begun. James and Monica kept running into each other in town and became confidants. So it wasn't long before James invited his father's second wife to his secret hideaway for an informal lunch. Time passed, the visits grew routine, and the inevitable occurred.

Now, many weeks later, Monica was naked and lying on the rumpled bed with her legs parted and James kneeling between them. He never tired of looking at her. Though more than twice his age Monica was very pretty. Part of that was related to a girlish figure. But a lot of it, more than James cared to admit, was related to the iridescent scales that covered large portions of Monica's anatomy. They made her look exotic in a way that none of the local girls could.

But that wasn't all. James knew that part of the attraction was the opportunity to punish his father for infecting his third wife with *B. nosilla*. "Don't make me suffer, James," Monica said huskily. "Give me what I want . . . what I *need*."

As James lowered himself into place she took him in. Her arms wrapped around him, a moan escaped her lips, and the bed began to squeak. Revenge was sweet.

Eventually, after what seemed like an eternity, Lee heard a knock on the door. She hurried to open it. The woman who stood there was dressed in a gray-and-white maid's uniform. She would have been pretty had it not been for a bulging forehead. "Good afternoon, Miss . . . My name is Myra. Your mother is waiting. If you're ready, I will take you to her room."

"Thank you."

Lee followed Myra down the hall to a central staircase, then up to the third floor, which was entirely dedicated to members of the Heevy family. From there it was a short walk down the hall to a door that stood slightly ajar. "This is it," Myra announced, and stood aside to let Lee pass.

Lee heard the door close as she entered the room and saw the woman who was sitting up in bed. "Cassie!" Alala said, as she held out her arms. "My precious Cassie!"

If you're so precious, why did she abandon you? the voice in Lee's head inquired.

But Lee *wanted* to believe and made her way over to the bed. An awkward embrace followed. Then, as Lee straightened, Alala spoke. "Hold your breath, Cassie dear . . . Let me see your face. Just this once."

So Lee took a deep breath, removed the mask, and let her mother look. Then she put the mask back on, "You're beautiful," Alala said. "So very, very beautiful. Even with short hair! You had an Afro in the pictures I saw."

"It will grow back," Lee assured her. "But short hair made sense for the trip."

"Thank you for coming," Alala said. "It must have been very difficult. Hiram told me about the way the dogs attacked. That must have been very frightening."

So Lee told her about the trip and was truthful for the most part, except for the claim of having hitchhiked into the area. She hadn't told Bruce or his father about the truck and saw no reason to mention it then.

Once the story was over the two women stared at each other for a moment. Alala broke the silence. "What I did was wrong . . . very wrong. And I apologize."

Lee looked into her mother's eyes, saw the emotion there, and nodded. "Thank you. So tell me . . . How did you wind up here?"

Alala shrugged. "It's like I told you in the letter. Things weren't going well with your father . . . And I felt overwhelmed. I wandered up the coast, lived in Oregon for a while, and eventually met a man named Ted. He had plans. Lots and lots of crazy plans. Schemes that would make the world better. One of which was to make a documentary about life in the red zone. A film that would show how similar norms and mutants are. And that seemed like a wonderful idea to me. So we saved our money, bought the necessary equipment, and entered the red zone."

Lee frowned. "You're joking."

Alala shook her head. "No, I'm serious. Things went well at first—and we were capturing some really wonderful footage. But our luck ran out in Nixon, Nevada. Bandits hit the town while we were there. Ted was killed, I was taken prisoner, and they sent me south. Norm females are worth a lot of money, as you know. So they put me up for sale at an auction in Indian

Springs. Hiram made the winning bid."

"So, he bought you."

"Yes," Alala agreed. "But he also married me . . . And I had nowhere else to go. But enough about me. I want to know about *you*! About all of the things I missed."

Lee did her best. She told her mother about school, about college, and her decision to follow in her father's footsteps.

And when Alala asked about men, and whether there was a man in her daughter's life, Lee told her about Kane. More than that, she told her mother about how nice he was—and was surprised to hear herself speak at length. Had there been someone else she felt that way about? Not that Lee could remember.

That was when Lee realized that she and her mother were having the sort of talk that both of them had missed. The realization made Lee feel sad, but she did the best she could to keep the emotion hidden.

Finally, having laid the necessary groundwork, Lee told Alala about the video, and the gruesome nature of Frank Lee's death. "So, I feel guilty," Lee concluded. "About the nature of our relationship. He was a hard man to like."

Tears were streaming down Alala's cheeks. "Oh, Cassie, I'm so sorry. And believe me, I understand. Frank was a fine man in many ways. But there was a darkness in him. Something he wouldn't talk about. And there were dreams. *Terrible* dreams that caused him to thrash around at night. That's part of why I left. Looking back, I realize that I should have stayed for your sake . . . or taken you with me. My failure to do so still haunts me."

Lee gave Alala a hug at that point—but the cop in her was thinking. According to Cheyenne Darling, McGinty had bad dreams too . . . And the men had been partners. Was there some sort of connection?

Lee was about to pull back when Alala took hold of her wrists. "I have a favor to ask," she whispered. "It's something that would mean a great deal to me. But I'm the one who owes you— not the other way around. So if you say no, I'll understand."

Lee said the only thing she could. "What is it?"

"Hiram told you about James."

"Yes."

"You'll meet him tonight . . . He's a god boy. Like you in many ways. And Hiram's favorite. But there's a darkness in Hiram just as there was in your father. My luck isn't very good where men are concerned. Not very good at all. So I want you to take James with you. To Los Angeles, where Hiram can't reach him. James is a mutant—but he isn't communicable. The right tests will prove that, and with you to sponsor him, the authorities will allow him to live in Pacifica. I know that . . . I did my homework."

Lee wanted to cry. There it was . . . the thing the other part of herself had feared. She'd been lured into the red zone for a purpose. Two purposes really . . . To assuage her mother's guilty conscience—and to take her half brother into the green zone. But in spite of the way she felt Lee managed to maintain her composure. "I see . . . And how does James feel about your idea?"

"He doesn't know," Alala confessed. "There was no reason to raise the possibility if you said no."

"And your husband?"

Alala's eyes grew wide with fear—and her grip was like steel. "He'd be furious! He's depending on James to take over. He would kill you if he knew . . . So this has to be our secret."

Lee felt a lump of cold lead form in the pit of her stomach. Her mother was trying to use her—and Heevy would make a dangerous enemy. So why place herself in danger? Then something occurred to her. Something she should have asked earlier. "Tell me, Mother . . . You lived here for many years without contracting the plague. What happened?"

Alala looked away and back again. Her eyes brimmed with tears. "Hiram can be very rough at times. Especially in bed. He tore my mask off. S-s-so he could look at m-m-me."

Lee swore. "Okay . . . You tell James this . . . If he wants to go, I'll take him."

There were rules in Boss Heevy's house, one of which was that every member of the family would show up for dinner, and do so on time. That had been made clear to Lee by her mother. So, at 5:50, Lee descended the stairs to the main floor, where one of the house servants directed her to the dining room. It was a long, relatively narrow space with six tall windows on one side and cabinets on the other. The shelves were filled with mineral specimens that had been chosen for their beauty rather than their intrinsic value. Large geodes had been sliced in half to reveal the glorious layerings within, there were all sorts of crystals to admire, and one section of the display was dedicated to chunks of quartz. All were lit by strategically placed lights.

But Lee had scant time to examine the specimens because the butler was there to receive her. He stood at least six and a half feet tall—and was so thin that he resembled a living skeleton. And if he thought that the sudden appearance of a norm was strange, there was no sign of it on his long, lugubrious face. "Good evening, Miss Lee," he said in a deep baritone. "My name is Manley. Please allow me to show you to your seat."

Lee's seat was on the other side of the dining room table with her back to the windows. Though set for nine the linen-covered table was long enough to accommodate twice that number. It was replete with candelabras, gleaming silverware, and all manner of glasses. Others were filing in by that time, and Lee found herself sandwiched between Bruce Heevy, and a large man who introduced himself as Hoss. Both brothers were nicely dressed.

"So," Bruce said, "it's nice to see you again. How's your room?"

"Very pleasant, thank you."

Bruce had just started to say something more when James entered with a woman on each arm. Lee knew it was James because she'd seen a photo of him in her mother's bedroom. A picture that hardly did him justice. He had black hair, skin about the same color as hers, and shockingly blue eyes. Not shocking because of their color so much as the intensity of his gaze. "There she is!" he proclaimed, as he looked at Lee. "My long-lost sister! Welcome to Heevy house, Cassandra . . . I'm James. The lovely lady on my left is Monica—and the lovely lady on my right is Bethany."

Chairs scraped as the other brothers came to their feet, and both women said their hellos. James made a show out of seating them—and that gave Lee a moment to form an impression of each. Lee was immediately struck by how different the two women were. While Monica had high cheekbones and a shapely body, Bethany was a stocky woman with a doughy face and glaring eyes. "I hear you killed some of our dogs," she said accusingly.

"I ordered them to surrender," Lee replied. "But they refused. That left me with no choice." Bethany scowled, James laughed, and Bruce joined him. Hoss looked down at his plate.

Meanwhile a girl who looked as if she was in her late teens entered the room. She was wearing too much makeup, an excessive amount of jewelry, and a party dress. James stood to seat her. "This is Dawn. She's Bethany's daughter and Hoss's sister. Dawn, it's my pleasure to introduce my sister, Cassandra. She's from Los Angeles."

"Do you know any singers?" Dawn wanted to know. "Or movie stars?"

As Dawn took her napkin off the table Lee saw that the girl had a single finger and thumb on each hand. "No," Lee answered. "I'm a police detective. So I spend most of my time with cops and criminals."

"Of which there are many from what I've heard," Bethany said acerbically.

"We have our share," Lee allowed. "But we can drive from city to city without being attacked by bandits."

Bethany's expression soured even more, and she was about to reply, when Heevy wheeled Alala into the room. She was seated in a wheelchair, but nicely dressed, with a blanket across her lap. Her eyes sought Lee and went to James before surveying the rest of the room. "Good evening, everyone. Sorry I'm late."

All of the brothers stood as their father pushed Alala into the slot next to Monica. From there he went up to take his place at the head of the table. "I would like to extend a special welcome to a new member of our family tonight," Heevy said solemnly. "As I'm sure you know by now, Cassandra is Alala's daughter by a previous marriage. I, for one, am glad to have her here.

"Bethany? Would you be so kind as to say grace? You do it so well."

But what ensued was more than a simple prayer. It was a three-minute-long rant in which Bethany called upon God to cleanse the world of sinners, "Especially those who look normal—but are filled with hate." An apparent reference to Lee, and one that caused James to wink at her from across the table, since he *looked* normal as well.

Finally, when the tirade was over, Heevy nodded. "Thank you. Cassandra's meal will be served in her room in order to guard her health. Manley, you may serve the rest of us."

Having been raised by a single father who wasn't around much Lee was amazed by the procession of dishes that came in one after another. And by the family's proficiency with an array of highly specialized eating utensils. A challenge she was happy to forgo.

Lee noticed that while all of the Heevy men had hearty appetites there was a good deal of variation among the women. Monica left most of her food on a succession of plates. Alala appeared to be on a special diet and consumed only half of what she was given. And Bethany, by contrast, gobbled her food and called for another dessert.

In the meantime, Heevy was leading the conversation in much the same way that a moderator would question a panel. Each person was presented with a provocative question, given a chance to answer, and rewarded with some sort of comment. In Lee's case, the question was political. "So, Cassandra . . . it sounds like the Aztec Empire's army may overrun all of Arizona . . . What, if anything, can we expect Pacifica to do in response?"

Lee toyed with one of three forks. "I have no way to know, of course. But, if I had to guess, I'd say that Pacifica will side with the Republic of Texas."

Heevy seemed to be genuinely interested. "And why," he wanted to know, "is that?"

"Both the Republic and the Empire are controlled by mutants," Lee answered honestly. "So both pose a potential threat. But we have ties with the Republic some of which are quite strong. Take your mine for example. As I entered the area I noticed that you have railroad tracks that lead east and west. But the shiny ones run west . . . And that tells me that you are selling ore to Pacifica. Would the tecs honor the agreements that are in place?

Who knows? So why take the chance?"

Heevy put his dessert fork down and turned to Alala. "You have a very intelligent, not to mention observant, daughter." Then he turned back to Lee. "It happens I'm in talks with certain individuals inside the green zone. And, based on their comments, I think Pacifica *will* side with the Republic." Heevy's eyes roamed the table. "Are they telling the truth? Time will tell."

"But enough of that," Heevy said lightly. "It's time for some entertainment. And, if I'm not mistaken, Dawn has prepared something special for us."

Lee looked at Dawn and saw her face light up. This, it appeared, was something she'd been looking forward to.

As Dawn stood her eyes took on a dreamy look. Then she began to sing "Ave Maria." She had no accompaniment; nor did she need any. Her voice was pitch perfect and all the more impressive for being a capella. Lee sat transfixed as the girl sang. Was the angelic voice the result of a positive mutation? Or was it a gift that would have been hers regardless? It didn't matter. What was, was. And Dawn was extremely talented.

There was silence for a moment as the song came to an end. Then Lee stood and began to clap. The rest of the family did likewise. All except for Bethany. She remained seated. That was when Dawn burst into tears and rushed out of the room. Dinner was over.

Dawn had grown up in the mansion and knew every square inch of the house and the surrounding grounds. And that included every squeaky floorboard, the way the furniture was placed, and how each shadow fell. So, with a small suitcase in hand, she was able to leave her room shortly after three in the morning—and glide down the central staircase without making a sound. Once on the main floor, it was a simple matter to enter the deserted kitchen and head for the back door.

The security system was on. But, like every member of the family, Dawn knew the code. So it was easy to disarm and reset the alarm. Dawn knew that doing so would trigger a tone in any room that was equipped with a keypad. And that included her father's. But she also knew that he was a sound sleeper. And even if Daddy heard the beep, he'd assume that a family's retainer was arriving for work.

So Dawn left the mansion undetected. Her heart was racing, and she felt a heady combination of excitement and fear. This was the moment she had long fanaticized about. The moment when she would leave home and start the next phase of her life.

But she wasn't free yet. Far from it. There was a security checkpoint to pass through at the foot of the driveway—and another one along the Heartbreak Highway. Dawn had an ally however . . . even if he didn't know it yet.

She smiled, paused to put her shoes on, and slipped shadow to shadow across the well-kept yard to the garage. Then she paused to listen. Nothing. So far so good.

The door wasn't locked. She turned the knob, stepped inside, and was careful to pull the door closed behind her. A great deal of planning had gone into the escape plan, so the flashlight was out and ready for use.

Dawn followed the blob of light past the delivery truck to the stairs that led up to the second-floor loft. Dawn knew that the second tread from the bottom would creak if she stepped on it, so she didn't.

Moments later, Dawn was at the top of the stairs in the space where the family's twenty-five-year-old driver was allowed to live. The furnishings consisted of a narrow bed, a dresser with three legs, and a cast-off armchair. A couple of mismatched lamps completed the décor.

And it was there, some six months earlier, that Dawn had chosen to surrender her virginity to Mickey. It was partly a matter of curiosity. But Dawn had something more in mind as well. Because from that point forward, she owned Mickey. And the investment was about to pay off. She put the suitcase on the floor and went over to kneel beside his bed. "Mickey," she whispered. "It's me, Dawn."

Mickey rolled over and reached for the bedside lamp. Light flooded his face. "Dawn? What are you doing here?"

"We're going to Las Vegas, Mickey. You're going to drive, and I'll ride in the back of the truck."

Mickey sat up. He wasn't especially bright, but even he could understand the implications of what Dawn proposed to do. "You've got to be kidding! Your father would kill us."

"Las Vegas is a big city," Dawn countered. "And I've got enough money to keep us going for a couple of months. We'll hide. Then, when they stop looking for us, I'll find a job as a singer."

Mickey frowned. "What about me?"

"You're good with cars," Dawn replied. "So you'll change your name—and work in a garage."

"But we'll be together?"

"Of course we'll be together," Dawn lied. "Forever and ever."

"Okay," Mickey said. "Take your clothes off. Let's do it."

"No," Dawn said firmly. "Not until we get to Las Vegas. Then we'll do whatever you want."

"Okay," Mickey said. "But we can't leave until sunup. The security people would know something was up if we did. So let's get some sleep. You can lie next to me."

So she did. But there was no need to sleep in order to dream.

EIGHT

fter returning to her room, Lee enjoyed an excellent dinner before taking a bath and going to bed. It had been a long day—and she fell asleep within a matter of minutes. By the time she awoke, light was trying to slide in between the curtains, and someone was knocking on her door. "Just a minute," Lee called out. "I'm coming."

After placing a self-adhesive mask over her face, Lee padded to the door and pulled it open. "Yes?"

A maid was standing in the hall. "Sorry, Miss," she said. "But Mr. Heevy would like to see you as soon as possible."

"Did he say why?"

The maid shook her head—but Lee could tell that she was lying. "Okay, I'll get dressed and come down right away."

The maid curtsied and hurried off.

Lee brushed her teeth, washed her face, and got dressed. Her own clothes had been washed and she wasn't going to wear the summer frock all day. She planned to visit her mother, find out what James wanted to do, and get the hell out of town. But first, she had to humor Heevy.

Once she was ready, Lee made her way down the stairs to the main floor, where she entered the great room. Heevy was meeting with a small group of mercenaries in front of the platform. "So," he said, "be ready at eleven."

One of the mercs nodded. "Yes, sir."

"Okay, that's all for the moment."

Lee waited for the mercenaries to leave the room before approaching the platform. Heevy saw her coming and clomped forward to greet her. "I'm sorry to bother you with our domestic difficulties," he said. "But I wonder if you would be willing to do me a favor."

"What's wrong?" Lee inquired.

"You met Dawn last night," Heevy replied. "And you heard her sing."

"Yes, she has a beautiful voice."

"I agree," Heevy said. "She hopes to be a professional singer one day . . . I'm willing to give her that chance. But Bethany says no. She says that entertainers are sinners."

"I see," Lee replied noncommittally.

"So Dawn took off early this morning," Heevy said ruefully, "*with* my driver. An idiot named Mickey. And it doesn't take a genius to figure out that the two of them are headed for Las Vegas."

Lee raised an eyebrow. "And?"

"And I made a few calls. The police were there to intercept our truck as it rolled into town. Dawn is still seventeen, so they're holding her for us. As for Mickey, he will be charged with grand theft auto, and will most likely spend some time in prison."

"Okay . . . Where do I come in?"

"You're a cop," Heevy said. "And even though you're a norm—the police in Vegas will respect that."

"They might," Lee agreed. "Or they might not. I ran into both kinds in Arizona. What do you have in mind?"

"I would like you to accompany Hoss to Las Vegas. He isn't much of a conversationalist, and there will be questions to answer. You could provide him with help if necessary."

Lee's bullshit detector was going off by then. It sounded as if the pickup was cut-and-dried. There was no need for her to accompany Hoss. So Heevy wanted to get her out of town for some reason. *Why?* "Perhaps James or Bruce should go," Lee suggested.

"*No,*" Heevy said emphatically. "They're busy. So, if you're willing, I would appreciate it."

Lee couldn't see a way out. Not and keep things friendly. "Okay," she said. "Does Hoss know that I'm coming along?"

"Yes, he does. Meet him at the helicopter in half an hour."

"Got it," Lee replied. "Maybe I can grab something to eat in the meantime."

"Of course," Heevy said. "Just stop by the kitchen. And thanks for the help."

After scoring a bacon-and-egg sandwich in the kitchen, and washing it down with two cups of hot coffee, Lee made her way out to the helo pad where Hoss was waiting. There was a pained expression on his misshapen face. "Good morning, Cassandra. I'm sorry my father dragged you into this."

"Don't be," Lee told him. "I doubt you'll need any help, but if you do, I'll do what I can. Tell me something, Hoss . . . just between you and me. How do *you* feel about Dawn's running off to Las Vegas?"

There was a whining sound, followed by a roar, as the helicopter's rotors started to turn. Hoss had to yell in order to be heard. "I think Dawn should be allowed to sing." Then he turned away. Had there been tears in the big man's eyes? No, that seemed unlikely.

Lee made her way over to the chopper and climbed up into the back. Hoss more than filled the seat in front of her. Once the preflight checks had been completed the aircraft took off. The ground dropped away, and they passed over the town of Heartbreak a minute later. Lee was looking forward to putting the place behind her.

Monica had her own car and drove it herself. A privilege she insisted on even though her husband would have preferred to have Mickey drive her around. The same Mickey who had run off with Dawn! The theory was that Mickey could protect her should some ruffian accost her. But was that the *real* reason? Or was it Hiram's way of keeping an eye on her?

Not that it mattered. Hiram knew when to give up and had. So as Monica left the school, and made her way out into the parking lot, she felt a momentary sense of freedom. And more than that, a rising sense of excitement. What was the relationship with James anyway? A pleasant distraction? Proof that she was still attractive? Or a bad habit? Maybe it was all three. A change would have to be made eventually. But not yet.

There were errands to run. Some were necessary, and some weren't, but both helped to justify her presence in town. It was a matter of routine by then. Park well away from the apartment, make her way to the drugstore, and leave through the rear exit. It opened onto a small parking lot and the alley beyond.

After a quick look around Monica crossed the lot, entered the alley, and walked west. Then it was a simple matter to enter the feed store through the back door and follow a flight of wooden stairs up to the second-floor apartment. And that's where James was waiting for her. He got up from a chair and opened his arms wide. "Mom! It's good to see you."

Monica frowned as she put her packages down. "Don't talk like that, James . . . It isn't nice."

"Sorry," James said contritely. "Would you like a drink?"

"Yes, please." Alcohol was forbidden at the mansion thanks to Bethany's influence—and the drinks were something that both of them looked forward to. James poured Monica a glass of white wine and made a Bloody Mary for himself. "So how 'bout Dawn?" he said, as he delivered the glass. "You have to give her credit. The girl has guts."

"Yes," Monica agreed. "I hope she gets away with it."

"She won't," James predicted. "In fact, based on what I've heard, the police already have her. Father sent Hoss and my sister to pick her up."

"Your sister? *Why?*"

James shrugged. "Beats the heck out of me . . . I would expect the old man to go . . . or to send me. But I like it. Spending some quality time with you beats the heck out of flying to Vegas."

"I'm glad to hear that," Monica purred as she came over to sit on his lap. She could taste the Bloody Mary when they kissed. Then the drinks were put aside as his right hand cupped a breast. That was when the mercenary kicked the door in.

* * *

James didn't know who he was up against; nor did he care. His first priority was to survive. So he dumped Monica off his lap and drew the .9mm Browning. Monica screamed, and was back scooting across the floor, when the merc fired. James heard the bullet whip by his head and squeezed the trigger. His slug blew a bloody chunk out of the man's skull and dumped him onto the floor.

The side splatter hit the second merc and blinded one eye. So when he triggered his submachine gun, the three-round burst went wide. That gave James the opportunity he needed. The first bullet went through the shooter's neck and still packed enough punch to kill the man behind him.

James waited for a fourth target to appear but none did. So he jammed the Browning back into the shoulder rig and went over to one of the room's two windows. It opened onto Front Street, and Monica was screaming his name as he threw it open. Then he was out on the hot metal roof and sliding toward the edge. A woman produced a yelp of surprise as he landed next to her. James apologized. Then he ran.

Monica's heart was beating like a trip-hammer as she struggled to her feet. The mercs weren't in uniform, but she recognized them, and knew they were acting on her husband's behalf. He knew. Somehow, some way, the bastard knew. A nosy townsperson probably . . . or a treacherous servant.

James was aware of that, of course . . . which had everything to do with why he had left her behind. Now she knew the truth. It was all about sex and nothing else. She was still in the process of buttoning her blouse when Bruce appeared. His anger was clear to see. "Where is he?"

"He went out the window," Monica replied. "Listen, Bruce . . . It isn't what you think. I . . ."

"*You* are a cheap whore," Heevy said, as he arrived in the apartment. "No, a slut . . . Whores get paid. And you give it away."

"You have it all wrong," Monica objected. "I didn't want to do it! James threatened me. He said . . ."

"Shut up," Heevy said coldly. "Don't shame yourself any

more than you already have. Bruce? This is *your* moment, son. You know what to do."

Bruce felt a host of conflicting emotions. Anger at his mother for the way in which she had betrayed his father, and more than that, betrayed *him*. But there was love, too . . . Because in spite of her faults Monica was his mother. The one person in the house he could trust. Or thought he could trust. Now it was clear that she preferred James to him.

Bruce brought the Colt .45 up and aimed it at her. Monica's eyes were wide with fright, tears were streaming down her cheeks, and her hands were extended palms out. "No, please . . ."

The rest of Monica's words were lost as a .45 caliber slug hit her chest and slammed her into the wall. She looked surprised, and her body seemed to hang there for a second, before slumping to the floor. That exposed a patch of blood on the wall and the hole that marked the middle of it. "Well done, son," Heevy said grimly. "*You* are the one that I was looking for."

Everything had gone smoothly. Or as smoothly as could be expected given the circumstances. The police were waiting for Hoss in Las Vegas. Once he signed some forms Dawn was given into his custody. And she was an emotional mess. As they made their way out to the police helo port, Hoss was subjected to fits of crying, angry tirades, and impassioned speeches. Dawn insisted that the authorities should let Mickey go. No one listened.

Therefore, all Lee could do was try to comfort a distraught Dawn during the ride home. Fortunately it was a relatively short trip. And as Lee left the helicopter she could tell that something was wrong. Dozens of mercenaries were stationed around the house—many of whom were using binoculars to scan the surrounding hillsides.

Bethany came out to escort Dawn inside. That freed Lee to return to her room. She was halfway to the house when she glanced to her right and saw something that shouldn't have been there. Her truck! In all its faded glory. It was parked on the south side of the house in an area reserved for guests. That brought Lee to a halt. How long had Heevy known about the truck? From day one probably—and she'd been naive enough to think that the vehicle had gone undiscovered. So why reveal it now? Because Heevy wanted her to leave. And did that have something to do with whatever had taken place in her absence? Probably.

Lee entered the house and followed the stairs to the third floor. She half expected someone to try to stop her, but no one did. So she made her way back to her mother's room and knocked on the door. The response was a faint, "Come in!"

Lee opened the door and stepped inside. Shafts of sunlight threw puddles of gold onto the wood floor. Alala was in bed and struggled to sit up. "Cassie! I'm so glad you came."

Lee went over to stand next to the bed. "How are you?"

Alala forced a smile. Her eyes were red as if she'd been crying. "I've been better . . . But that doesn't matter. Did you hear what happened?"

"No," Lee said. "Tell me."

"I'm not supposed to know," Alala said. "But Myra told me."

"Told you what?"

"It seems that James and Monica were having an affair! Hiram heard about it from someone in town, and he was furious. So he sent mercenaries to kill James. But James killed them and ran. Then Bruce and Hiram went in and one of them shot Monica."

Alala began to sob at that point—and Lee tried to comfort her. Now everything made sense. She'd been sent to Las Vegas to get her out of the way while they killed her brother. And now Heevy was eager to get rid of her. And that explained the truck. "But what about the police?" Lee inquired. "What are they going to do about Monica's death?"

Alala used a handkerchief to dab at her eyes. "The town marshal works for Hiram . . . as do his deputies. It's time for you to leave, Cassie . . . And I mean right now."

Lee had to agree. A murder had been committed, but she was powerless to do anything about it. "What about James? Did you talk to him?"

"Yesterday evening. He said no. Why leave when you're going to inherit a town? That's what he said. But that was before they shot Monica. Now he's on the run. Go home, Cassie . . . And thank you! It was brave of you to come here."

It was stupid, given the way Alala planned to use her, but the knowledge that she would never see her mother again brought tears to Lee's eyes. Alala reached up to thumb them away. "Get out, Cassie. There's nothing you can accomplish here. Bethany says that all of us are sinners—and I have to admit that she's right. We made this mess, and we have to live with it."

Lee bent over to plant a kiss on her mother's forehead. Then, with tears trickling down her cheeks, Lee left the room.

From there it was a short trip down to the second floor and her room. What few belongings she had were in the pack—and she took a moment to check her weapons before returning them to their respective holsters. Lee didn't think it would be necessary to shoot her way out of the house but figured it was better to be safe rather than sorry.

With the pack hanging off one shoulder, Lee made her way down to the main floor, where she entered the great room. Heevy was visible at the far end of it where he was talking to Bruce and a man Lee hadn't met.

Heevy spotted her, said something to the other, and started her way. They met in the middle of the room. Lee was surprised to see how haggard Heevy appeared. Pale even, as if feeling something, but *what*? Guilt? Remorse? Fatigue? Or, and the final theory seemed more likely, was Heevy afraid? Not of the law but of retribution? James was on the loose after all . . . And, according to all accounts, he was very good with a long gun. That would explain the mercenaries stationed around the house. "So," Heevy said, as they faced each other. "You're leaving."

"Yes," Lee replied. "Thanks for having someone bring my truck around."

Heevy's eyes glittered. Some of the usual braggadocio could be heard in his answer. "You're welcome."

"About my mother," Lee said. "Take care of her all the way to the end. Do you understand me? Because if you don't, and I learn of it, you'll have more to worry about than James. Do we understand each other?"

Heevy's pale skin took on a grayish hue. He nodded.

"Good. I'll see myself to the door."

In spite of the fact that Lee was leaving her mother behind she felt a sense of peace as she left the house. Because even though she didn't like everything her mother had done, or would do if given the chance, she knew her now. And in some oblique way that made Lee feel better about both of her parents. Each had good qualities and each had flaws. And none of it was *her* fault.

Once Lee arrived at the truck it didn't take long to discover that it had been hot-wired. A toggle switch dangled from two wires, and when she flipped it, the engine roared to life. And the gas tank was half-full. So she threw the pack in the back and got behind the wheel.

Lee didn't slow down at the checkpoint; nor did the mercenaries try to stop her. From there it was a straight shot to the Heartbreak Highway and the beginning of the trip home. So she turned the radio on, found some country western music to listen to, and let the warm slipstream buffet her face.

About three songs later, Lee saw the second security checkpoint up ahead, and knew she'd have to stop. So she braked, came to a stop just short of the drop bar, and waited for the guard to emerge from the little building. But when the door opened, it was her brother James who stepped out of the hut! There was a big smile on his face as he came over to the truck. "Hi, sis! I've been waiting for you."

Lee's first reaction was one of shock. The second was anger. Not only was Alala still intent on sending her son to live in Pacifica—she was using Monica's death to her own advantage! "Don't tell me, let me guess," Lee said. "Mother called you the moment I left."

"It was Myra," James answered lightly. "But what's the difference?"

"Did you kill the guard?"

James looked offended. "No, of course not . . . I tied him to a chair."

Lee looked up at the camera mounted on a metal pole. If Heevy wasn't watching live, he would see the footage soon. And he had a helicopter. "All right, get in . . . They'll be on us soon."

James turned to the guard shack and went back in. As he

came out he was carrying a pack and a rifle. When he touched a button Lee heard a whining sound and the bar rose up and out of the way. After placing his gear in the back, James slid in next to her. "This isn't much of a ride, sis . . . How much money do detectives make?"

"More than *fugitives* do," Lee said pointedly, and let the clutch out. The truck jerked each time she shifted gears. Lee took the rig up to seventy and wondered how much time they had.

James put an arm on the windowsill. "So what's the plan?"

"I want to reach Highway 95 before they catch up with us."

"And then?"

"And then we'll bail out. Where did you get the rifle anyway?"

"I charged it to my father while he was yelling at Monica," James replied. "And the pack too."

Lee glanced at him. "You father didn't just yell at Monica . . . He shot her! Or Bruce did. That isn't clear."

James looked shocked. "*No!* They wouldn't."

"They did. Your mother . . . *our* mother told me. She got it from Myra."

"B-but why didn't Myra tell me?"

"Here's a guess," Lee said tightly. "Mother wanted you to hook up with me—and was afraid that you would kill your father. She's needs him."

James was silent for a moment. Then he nodded. "Yeah . . . That fits. She never liked the red zone—and always thought I'd be better off in Pacifica."

Lee waited for some mention of Monica, some expression of sorrow regarding his role in her death, but none was forthcoming. That was a disappointment—but Lee didn't have time to dwell on it. Highway 95 was up ahead, and she knew they were operating on borrowed time. "Okay," Lee said, as she began to brake. "I'm going to pull over. Take both packs plus your rifle into the rocks next to the railroad track. Find a place to hide and prepare to shoot at the helicopter. But don't fire unless they do. Understood?"

James frowned. "You're kidding."

"No, I'm a police officer . . . And so long as they don't shoot at us, we'll leave them alone."

"Whatever," James said, as the truck came to a halt. "I'll do my part."

As James got out of the truck and pulled the gear out, Lee made her way up to the front of the vehicle where she raised the hood. A metal rod was available to prop it up. Once that was accomplished, she poured half a bottle of water onto the hot manifold. Steam billowed up and out from under the hood. Hopefully, their pursuers would see it, assume that the truck had broken down, and focus on that while James took aim at them. Because in spite of what Lee had said earlier—she was confident that Heevy's thugs would open fire.

A minute passed and nothing happened. So Lee poured *more* water onto the engine and wondered if she was wrong. Maybe they wouldn't come . . . *Be patient,* Lee told herself. *Give the plan some time.*

The steam dissipated and Lee dumped the last of the water on the manifold. That was when she heard the sound of an aircraft engine and looked to the right. Sunlight glinted off the helicopter's bubble-shaped canopy as it came straight at her and flared into a hover. The aircraft's starboard side door had been removed and a man with a machine gun was sitting sideways in the passenger seat. As he opened fire she began to run. "Shoot the bastard!" she shouted, as bullets threw up gouts of dirt all around her.

But the order wasn't necessary. As Lee arrived at the pile of rocks she heard the crack of a rifle shot and turned to look back. The merc wasn't strapped in. So when the bullet hit him in the stomach he folded over, and with nothing to keep him aboard, toppled forward. The body and the weapon fell separately—but hit the highway at the same time.

As luck would have it, that was the moment when a man in a beetle-shaped blue sedan turned off 95 and onto the Heartbreak Highway. The motorist tried to brake but wasn't fast enough. The front wheels of his car hit the body and rolled over it. He was getting out to see what had occurred when James shot the helicopter's pilot.

It was a truly amazing feat of marksmanship. Lee heard the report, saw a jagged hole appear in the canopy, and knew that whatever remained of the slug was unlikely to hit its target. But James knew that too . . . And the second bullet passed through the hole created by the first!

The response was immediate. With no living hand at the controls, the helicopter rolled over onto its side and fell onto the truck! There was a crash, followed by a loud boom, and pieces of debris fell all around as Lee ducked.

Then, as she stood, Lee saw a mushroom cloud of orange fire and black smoke rising into the sky. The blue sedan's driver was staring up at it when Lee approached him. "I'm sorry," she said, "but I need to borrow your car. Please go over to the side of the road. You'll be safe there—and help will arrive soon."

The man had a parrotlike beak and holes where his ears should have been. He looked as if he was about to object to the order when he saw the Glock. It was pointed at the ground but that was sufficient. He raised his hands and backed away.

As Lee entered the car James came on the run. He was carrying both packs and the rifle. The key was already in the ignition and the motor was running. Doors slammed as James threw things into the backseat and slid in next to her. "Sorry about the truck, sis."

"Don't call me 'sis,'" Lee replied as she threw the car into reverse. The engine roared, and the car bucked as one of the front tires passed over the merc again. Then it was time to turn the wheel and shift into drive. Lee could see the smoke in the sedan's rearview mirror as she turned left onto Highway 95.

"We're headed east," James observed calmly. "Last I heard Pacifica was west of here."

"Yeah," Lee said. "And your father knows that. So he'll send people to cut us off. We'll find a different ride, spend the night in Las Vegas, and depart for LA from there."

"Sounds good," James said mildly. "Except that the guy who owns this car saw us turn *left*. So, assuming he shares that with my father's mercs, they'll follow us to Las Vegas. Maybe you should have shot him."

"And maybe you should shut up," Lee replied, although the thought had occurred to her. The difference was that she wouldn't do it and James would.

But like him or not, Lee knew that James was correct. So it was important to reach Indian Springs quickly and get rid of the sedan before Heevy could mobilize the local cops. Fortunately, the town was no more than twenty minutes away.

Lee took the car up to seventy and kept it there as they drove through open desert. It was late afternoon by that time and hot. But unlike Lee's truck the sedan had air-conditioning that actually worked. So Lee felt delightfully cool as James twiddled with the radio until he came across some news. There was no mention of them—but it sounded like the war was heating up. And the Republicans were hoping that Pacifica would side with them.

That reminded Lee of LA, her job, and the Bonebreaker. She wanted to return to work. Could she convince Kane? And Jenkins? She would do her best. But at the moment there were more pressing problems to deal with. As the car passed a sign that read, INDIAN SPRINGS, 5 MILES, she had to focus on the present. "We're almost there," she said. "I'm going to pull over when we cross the next bridge. That will be your opportunity to get rid of the rifle."

"Get rid of the rifle?" James inquired. *"Why?"*

"Because even though it's legal to do so, very few people carry rifles," Lee replied patiently. "And we need to blend in. Besides, the pistol you're carrying is enough."

"You noticed?"

"Of course I noticed. Now get ready . . . I'm about to pull over."

The concrete bridge was no more than a hundred feet long— and one of many that crossed a myriad of dry riverbeds. "Watch for cars," Lee instructed, as she brought the sedan to a stop.

James said, "Yes, Mother," as he opened the door and left it that way. The sudden influx of hot air quickly overwhelmed the air conditioner, as James opened the back, and removed the rifle. Then, after a quick glance in each direction, he went over to stand in front of the rail. There was a distant clatter as the weapon landed on the rocks below. The door slammed as James got in. "I hope you're happy," he said sourly. "That was a very nice rifle."

Lee chose to ignore his comment as she put her foot on

the gas and steered the car onto the highway. The preplague air force base had a new name now—but it was still located just north of Indian Springs. And as they neared town Lee could see the steady stream of planes taking off and landing. Were they flying missions into Arizona? To fight the tecs? Lee would have been willing to put money on it. "Okay," she said, as they took the first off-ramp. "We're about to lose the car. So be ready."

As was often the case in small communities there were lots of car lots on both sides of the main drag, along with a few stand-alone businesses and some fast-food restaurants. And when Lee spotted a large used-car dealership she pulled in. It was called Fast Eddie's Automobile Emporium, and there were at least a hundred vehicles lined up next to the mobile home that was Eddie's office.

Lee followed a lane to the back row and hooked a right. Then, when she saw an empty slot, she pulled in. "Grab your stuff," she said, "and follow me."

After retrieving her pack from the back Lee left the car unlocked with the key in the ignition. She was concerned lest a salesperson intercept them but none did.

"That was slick," James said admiringly, as they walked towards town. "The cops will have to pay close attention to find it."

"It should take a while," Lee agreed. "But this town is too small for us to hide in. So we need to find another ride. How well do you know Indian Springs?"

"Pretty well," James replied. "I've been coming here all my life."

"Do you know where the post office is?"

"Sure, it's about four blocks south of here, and off to the west."

Lee glanced at her watch. It was 4:33. "Okay, we'll need to hurry. Chances are that they close at five."

Lee increased her pace and James hurried to catch up. "So what? Why do we care?"

"Back when I was a patrol officer, my partner and I had to deal with lots of car thefts . . . And a surprising number of them occurred at the local post office. That's because some people like to run in and leave their engines running. And the local car thieves knew that. Who knows? Perhaps some of the locals do that too.

"We can't stand around though," she added. "That would attract the wrong sort of attention. We need to spot a car, jump in, and take off quickly. Then we'll head back to the highway and put this town behind us. Las Vegas is less than an hour away."

"Got it," James said. "You are one very bent cop. And I mean that as a compliment."

"Thanks," Lee said, as the post office came into sight. "And one more thing . . . Don't shoot anyone."

The sun was just about to set, and dark shadows lay everywhere, as the chopper roared up the valley. It looked like what it was—a machine made for killing people. And it was no more related to Heevy's helicopter than a dog is to a wolf. The barrel of a minigun protruded from the ship's nose, a pair of stubby wings were hung with rocket launchers, and machine guns were mounted just inside both doors.

The helicopter circled the Heevy mansion twice before flaring in for a landing on the well-lit helipad. That was when Crystal Bye felt a gentle thump and stood. She was wearing a headset and knew that the team could hear her. "Okay . . . You know the drill. Let's put some security around the ship and keep your eyes peeled. Remember, *Qui confit amittit*. He who trusts loses." And Bye took her motto seriously. She heard half a dozen mike clicks as she jumped to the ground.

A man in Western garb came out to meet her. "Howdy," he said. "My name is Bruce Heevy . . . I'm one of Hiram Heevy's sons." He extended a hand, which Bye chose to ignore.

"My name is Crystal Bye—and I own the Dragon Security company."

Bruce let the hand fall. "Glad to meet you," he said lamely. "My father is waiting."

As Bye followed Bruce toward the house, two of her operatives fell in behind her. Enough to put up a very good fight if she was attacked. They were clad in military-grade body armor—

and equipped with stubby submachine guns. The threesome followed Bruce to a side door—and from there into the house.

Hiram Heevy struggled to push his way up out of a leather chair as Bruce entered the great room. Then, with his canes to stabilize him, he waited for the party to march the length of the room. "Father," Bruce said, "this is Crystal Bye. She owns Dragon Security."

Heevy was surprised to say the least. Bye was at least six feet tall, appeared to be about thirty years old, and had shoulder-length white hair. Her eyes were pink and her skin was the color of milk. An albino then . . . Just one of the many thousands of mutations produced by *B. nosilla*. Bye was dressed in body armor over a skintight bodysuit, and was armed with two mini Uzis, one holstered on each of her slim thighs. For looks? No, Heevy didn't think so. He cleared his throat. "Welcome to our home, Miss Bye. Please . . . Have a seat."

"I prefer to stand," Bye responded. "You have an assignment for us? What is it?"

"You get right to the point," Heevy said approvingly. "I like that. Yes, I have an assignment for you. Unfortunately, one of my sons murdered one of my wives, and . . ."

"Please spare me the details," Bye said dismissively. "How many targets are there?"

"Two. One male and one female."

"How much of a head start do they have?"

"About six hours."

"Do you know where they were headed?"

"Yes."

"Good. That will be two hundred thousand nu—half of which is payable now. So would you like to hire us? Or should we leave?"

Two hundred thou? That was more than twice what Heevy expected to pay. Maybe he'd been wrong to contact Dragon Security. Maybe he should . . . Bruce interrupted his thoughts. "We don't have much choice, Father . . . Not if we want to leave the house, stroll the grounds, or visit the mine."

Heevy thought about that. Bruce was right . . . James was likely to be angry. *Very* angry. And James could shoot people from a long way off. So like it or not, he would have to pay. "Yes," Heevy said reluctantly, "I want to hire you."

NINE

Lee's right foot was all the way to the floor, and the pickup was barely doing 35 mph, much to the frustration of the drivers who came up behind her. Many of them flashed their lights or offered her an obscene gesture while passing.

Part of the problem was the full load of hay bales in the bed of the truck. But the main issue was an ancient engine that was in need of a complete overhaul. All of which meant that the fugitives wouldn't be able to run should the police come after them.

Beggars couldn't be choosers however, and the ancient *especiale* was the only vehicle that had been left running outside the post office, probably because the owner feared that once they shut it down, they wouldn't be able to start it again. Lee had the same concern and wasn't about to turn the engine off until they were in Las Vegas. And now, with only ten minutes left to go, the odds of making it into the city looked good.

Lee figured that the authorities in Indian Springs had notified the Las Vegas police about the car theft by then, but every police force of any size received hundreds of such reports each day, and typically gave them a low priority. Still, the sooner they got rid of the vehicle the better. Lee took the first exit she came to—which led her to the oddly named Horse Drive.

From there they followed an arterial into a poorly lit maze of mostly uninhabited two and three-bedroom homes. Lee figured the area had been a prosperous suburb at one time but that was prior to the plague. Now it was an ocean of abandoned houses, graffiti-covered walls, and looted strip malls.

There were islands of civilization, though . . . Places where one, two, or three families had banded together to create an urban fortress. Outposts that often had watchtowers, defensive walls, and free-fire zones. It looked like a tough way to live.

As the truck lurched through potholes, and was forced to navigate around burned-out wrecks, it didn't take a genius to figure out that the neighborhood was a dangerous place to be. Especially at night. So rather than dump the pickup there— Lee drove it south through mostly deserted streets into the community of North Las Vegas.

The farther south they went the more streetlights there were. Well-kept houses lined the streets, the amount of vehicular traffic increased, and pedestrians could be seen. They even passed a patrol car headed in the opposite direction. Lee watched the taillights in the rearview mirror as she waited to see if the cruiser would execute a U-turn and come after her. It didn't. But how long would their luck hold?

Lee began to look for a place to park—and wound up choosing a slot next to a feed store. Perhaps people would assume the load of hay was related to the store in some way. If so, they wouldn't report the pickup for a day or so. "The cops don't know we were the ones who stole the truck," she said. "Not for sure anyway . . . So let's wipe it down. There's no point in leaving prints behind. By the way . . . are you carrying a cell phone?"

James nodded. "Yes."

"Is it on?"

"No."

"Good. Leave it off. They can use it to track you otherwise. Okay, let's get to work."

The wipe down was complete ten minutes later and they could walk away. Once again the key was left in the ignition. Hopefully, if things went well, the vehicle's owner would be able to retrieve the load of hay.

The next step was to find a place to stay—and James wanted to go downtown. Because, according to him, "there will be lots of people there—and we'll be less noticeable."

Lee couldn't argue with his logic so she went along with the suggestion. After getting directions from the clerk in a convenience store, they walked two blocks to a bus stop. Twenty minutes passed before a bus arrived—and once they got aboard there was standing room only. That was when Lee realized that most of the passengers were headed for work. A lot of servers, clerks, and maids were required to run a casino-hotel complex. And the bus offered them a cheap way to commute.

It wasn't long before the bus turned onto South Las Vegas Boulevard, and ten minutes later they were rolling down the so-called Strip, with hotels and casinos on the left and right. Except that many of them were little more than empty shells now. After millions died, and the worldwide economy tanked, there were a lot less people who were willing to risk what they had on a roll of the dice.

So brightly lit towers had been transformed into dark, brooding places, many of which were infested with what James referred to as "human rats." That was why the bus didn't stop at the Trump International Hotel, the decrepit Palazzo, or the fire-ravaged Imperial Palace. All of which lurked in the shadows as if ashamed to be seen.

But at least half the city's famous casinos were lit up, still open for business, and providing jobs for the people on the bus. And when the bus paused in front of the Monte Carlo, James urged Lee to get out. "I stayed here before," he said. "And the rooms are nice."

Lee had no reason to object so she didn't. James led the way into the hotel. There was a constant stream of people headed in both directions. Most were in a good mood—and appeared to be having fun. Once in the hotel's cavernous lobby they paused. "I'll register for both of us," Lee said. "And I'll try to get adjoining rooms."

James shrugged. "Works for me."

Lee was forced to wait in line before she could approach the registration desk and make her request. She knew cameras were tracking her every move. But the security system was there to serve the casino complex rather than Hiram Heevy. So it was unlikely that the mining magnate or his employees would see the video.

After providing false names and enough cash to cover two rooms, Lee made her way over to where James was seated. "Okay, here's your keycard. And here's a slip of paper with the room number on it. Are you hungry? If so, there's a restaurant on the other side of the lobby."

As it turned out James *was* hungry, and although Lee couldn't eat with him, she could get something to drink. So they went over, were shown to a booth, and took their seats. James ordered a large meal—while Lee had a Diet Coke with a straw.

Once the waitress left Lee thought the conversation might turn to Monica and the love affair that precipitated her death. It didn't. As far as Lee could tell, James felt little or no remorse and spent most of his time living in the moment. Talk centered around the hotel, the people seated near them, and what he could expect in Pacifica. "Mother told me that you are noncommunicable," Lee said. "Once the authorities confirm that they'll turn you loose."

James took a sip of beer. "Then what?"

"That's up to you," Lee replied. "Perhaps you should go to school and get a degree."

James frowned. "I didn't like school . . . It was boring."

Lee shrugged. "Maybe you should consider a vocational school . . . Lord knows we need carpenters, plumbers, and electricians."

James didn't object, but Lee got the impression that her brother wasn't excited about the prospect of going to any kind of school, *or* having a job. Both of which would be necessary once he was admitted to Pacifica.

After James finished his dinner, they left the restaurant and made their way over to a bank of elevators. "I'll do some research tonight," Lee promised. "Maybe we can take a bus to Primm . . . Or rent a car. In any case let's get an early start. How does that sound?"

"It sounds painful," James said. "But I'll be ready."

"Good. And, James . . ."

"Yeah?"

"Don't party. Stay in your room. If you go downstairs the mercs might spot you."

"Yes, downstairs, Mother." He said it with a grin, so Lee let it go.

Their rooms were next to each other, and James waved as he slid the keycard into the lock, opened the door, and disappeared.

Lee's room was what she expected it to be, which was to say nice, but somewhat worn. It was as if a thousand people had slept in it since the last reno. Lee dropped the pack onto a chair and went over to the phone. She was ravenous by then—and the room service lady promised to send her meal up within twenty minutes.

Lee made use of the intervening time to unpack, surf the local Internet via the terminal on the desk, and make some phone calls. A bus was scheduled to leave for Primm at 8:15 a.m., and she planned to be on it. Would James show up? Lee wasn't sure. But if he didn't, that would be the end of the relationship. Lee intended to honor her mother's wishes as long as James continued to cooperate. But if that stopped then she would leave him to deal with his father on his own.

When the knock came Lee was careful to eyeball the busboy through the peephole before letting him in. And even as he placed the tray on the desk, Lee was holding the Glock behind her back. The food wasn't as hot as Lee would have preferred, but the lukewarm steak was still reasonably good even if the fries were limp.

After finishing her meal Lee decided to take a bath before going to bed. She locked the door, turned the water on, and got undressed. The hot water felt good. *Very* good. And the combination of a full stomach and heat made her feel sleepy. So when the man kicked in the door, the action caught her by surprise. He was wearing a black hood over his head and pointing a pistol at her. A noise suppressor was screwed to the end of the barrel. *"Hola, chica,"* he said cheerfully. "I like your tits. Where do you want it? Left tit or right tit?"

All sorts of things flickered through Lee's mind. The ease with which Heevy's hired killers had closed in on them, her failure to shove the rubber stop under the door to the hallway after receiving the meal, and the fact that she didn't want to die.

So Lee brought the Smith & Wesson up out of the bathwater and pulled the trigger. Because of the angle the hollow point passed through the top of his mouth, pulped part of his brain, and blew a hole through the top of his skull. He toppled back through the doorway and hit the floor with a thud. "What an asshole," Lee said, as she got up out of the tub.

She was reaching for a towel when James appeared just beyond the dead assassin. The Browning was ready. His eyes grew bigger as he stared at her naked body. "What happened?"

"What do you *think* happened?" Lee demanded crossly. "Now stuff your eyes back into your head—and call the front desk from your room. Tell them you heard a shot, opened the door, and saw a man run down the hall. Hurry!"

As James left Lee hurried to pull her mask on and dry herself. It was necessary to step over the dead body to reach the room beyond. Then she made a call to the front desk. "Reception . . . How can I help you?"

"I heard a loud noise," Lee complained. "Like a firecracker going off. It woke me up."

"I'm sorry to hear that," the man on the other end of the line said. "Other guests have complained as well—and security has been notified. Are you okay?"

"Yes, I'm fine," Lee replied. "Or will be if I can get back to sleep." And with that she hung up.

"I made the call," James said, as he entered the room via the connecting door. Lee had wrapped herself in a towel by then. "Good. Pack your stuff. If the security people come by, tell them you heard a bang, and nothing more. Got it?"

James nodded. "Got it." He disappeared.

Lee had to step over the body again to enter the bathroom. That was when she flipped the revolver open and emptied the cylinder. The bullets rattled as they spilled onto the counter. The weapon was made of stainless steel and not likely to rust. But it was better to be safe rather than sorry. So Lee placed the handgun on the counter, aimed the hotel's hair dryer at it, and turned the device on. A strategy she had used before.

Then it was necessary to search the body. Unfortunately, the assassin's bowels had emptied shortly after his death, and the stink was horrible. But Lee forced herself to go through the assassin's pockets. That effort turned up a backup magazine for the .22 plus the keycard that had been used to enter the room. How was such a thing possible? Hundreds of maids worked for the hotel. Lee figured that one of them was a little bit richer than she had been that morning.

In addition to the keycard Lee found a small two-way radio, a comb, and a hundred nu in a variety of denominations. No ID though . . . And that made sense. Professional hit men don't carry items that could lead the police to their employers.

Lee put the pistol, the extra mag, the money, and the radio on the dresser while she hurried to get dressed. Then she went over to empty her pack onto the bed. That's what she was doing when James reentered the room. "Lord . . . It stinks in here."

"Really?" Lee inquired. "I hadn't noticed. Shit! Here it is."

James came over to look. "Here *what* is?"

"A tracker," Lee said, as she held the tiny transmitter up for him to look at. "Your father had someone place it in my pack. That's how they found us. I'll get rid of it on the way out."

So Lee slipped the tracker into a pocket rather than throw it away. Then it was time to scoop up the assassin's money and the two-way radio, which she turned on. If the mercenaries were sloppy there was the possibility that she could monitor their conversations.

But it soon became apparent that someone could tell that the unit was on. "Pedro? Where the hell are you?" a female voice demanded. And, "What happened?"

Lee turned the radio off rather than run the risk that the mercenaries could track it somehow. Then she dropped the device next to body as she entered the bathroom. After checking to make sure the .38 was dry Lee took the moment required to reload and holster it.

James was ready and waiting as Lee reentered the room. She took her pack off the bed and turned to the door. "Come on . . . Let's get out of here."

A preliminary peek confirmed that the hallway was clear. The security people had come and gone by then. Lee led James down the hall to the elevators and, after a short wait, onto a car that took them to the first floor.

Even though it was nearly midnight there were a lot of people in the lobby—and the pair fell into step with a group of businesspeople headed for the Strip. "There are plenty of hotels," James said. "Let's turn right. I know that end of town quite well."

Lee paused long enough to toss the tracker into the bed of a parked pickup truck and nodded. The plan was to find another place to stay, hole up until morning, and get out of town. So they fell in behind a group of teens and were making good time when something slammed into her pack, and shoved her forward. A hand slap? No . . . A bullet! Fired from a silenced weapon up high and to the rear somewhere. "Sniper!" Lee yelled. "Run!"

"We'll head for the Trump International!" James replied. "It's up ahead."

The hotel was hard to miss. Lee figured it was at least sixty stories tall and large enough to have a thousand rooms. But it was the building's gold glass skin that made it memorable and reflected light from all around. Random sections of the exterior were missing, making the outside look like a black-and-gold checkerboard. And deep within some of the black rectangles, flickering lights could be seen. "What about the people who live in there?" she wanted to know. "How will *they* react?"

But James couldn't hear her. He was leading the way and zigzagging back and forth to foil the sniper. There was a cyclone fence around the tower—but it was riddled with holes created by the people who lived there. Lee had to remove her pack in order to follow James through one of them—and then hurried to put it back on.

They followed a well-worn trail through mounds of trash to a huge entrance. Other than the glow produced by a single burn barrel the interior was dark. "Hey!" a male voice shouted. "Hold it right there! Nobody enters *my* hotel without paying admission."

"Nobody except *me*," James replied, as he fired his pistol. Lee heard somebody cry out and realized that James could see in the dark! There was no other explanation for that kind of shooting.

And it made sense. He was a mutant after all . . . One with a talent instead of a disfigurement.

But Lee *couldn't* see and was forced to use the flashlight. As the beam of light swept the area ahead Lee saw mutant faces, people dressed in dirty clothes, and piles of garbage. No wonder the Las Vegas Police Department didn't want to go in and clean the place out.

Lee had no idea of where to go but figured the main hallway was a good bet. So she led James past the empty reception desk and into the gloom. That was when someone said, "Get 'im!" and she heard a growl. The dog came barreling out of the darkness and was almost upon her when Lee shot it. There was a thump as the body hit the floor and a howl of anguish from the shadows.

As Lee continued on she saw that luminescent arrows had been painted onto the floor. Did they lead to a stairway? There was only one way to find out. A can skittered away from Lee's boot, she heard the muted sound of music, and was forced to use the light again. Bingo! An exit sign.

Lee followed it to a steel fire door, pulled it open, and began the laborious climb. Trash covered the stairs and the walls were coated with layers of squirming graffiti. She'd been operating on adrenaline. And now she was running on empty. A face with one eye peered out from the third-floor doorway as they passed. The mutant pulled back—and the door closed behind him.

Then it was up through an area bordered by bullet-pocked walls, over the remains of a barricade, and onto the fourth-floor landing. *Keep going,* Lee thought to herself, as they continued to climb. *The higher the better.* Her lungs were on fire by then, her legs felt as if they were made out of lead, and each step required a conscious effort.

The fifth floor was marked by a sloppy, handwritten "Do Not Enter" sign, and what might have been a gang mark. Then they were on what Lee hoped would be the final stretch. And as she arrived on the sixth floor, the beam from Lee's flashlight wobbled onto an additional sign: POOL DECK. She paused to catch her breath. James, by contrast, seemed to have enjoyed the climb. "This is high enough," James said. "I'll go in first."

That made sense given his night vision so Lee nodded. So, Glock in hand, she opened the door for him. James went in with the Browning raised—and Lee was ready for a flurry of shots. None came. She followed.

They were in a lobby of sorts, which led through double doors, and out onto the pool deck. There wasn't much to see other than some forlorn pieces of furniture and the empty pool. Well, a *nearly* empty pool, since a good deal of garbage had been dumped into it over the years. Still, it did appear that the six-story climb had been sufficient to keep most of the hotel's rats on the lower levels.

A section of windows had been broken out, but that did nothing to diminish the full impact of the awesome view. The surrounding hotels were lit—and like beacons in a different world. And some of that light glazed the surface of things inside the pool area.

The roar didn't mean anything to Lee at first until a helicopter appeared outside! They were only six stories up, which meant the aircraft was relatively low, so Lee assumed that the LVMPD was getting into the act. But then the gunship's nose began to swivel her way. That was when she saw the minigun and knew what would happen next. "In the pool!" she shouted, and made the jump. Layers of trash acted to cushion Lee's landing as the pilot opened fire and 7.62X5mm rounds blew the remaining windows out and swept the pool deck. Although it seemed to last forever, the assault was actually quite brief. "Shit!" James said, as he made his way to Lee's side. "Where did *that* come from?"

"From your loving father," Lee replied. "The bastards followed us, and they know where we are. These people are the real deal compared to the wannabes that hang around the mansion. And you know what that means."

James sounded uncertain for the first time. "No, what?"

"They aren't going to fight their way up from the street," Lee told him. "They're going to land on the roof and come *down* the stairs. And the helicopter will leave before the boys and girls in blue can do anything about it."

James hadn't thought of that. "So what can we do?"

"Ambush the bastards," Lee said. "There can't be more than six of them given the size of the chopper . . . That's three apiece."

"Yeah," he said happily. "That's right."

Lee sighed. "Okay, the pool deck is as good a place as any to take them on. The chopper's on the roof by now, and since it's all downhill, we'll have company soon. Let's find the doors and block all but one of them."

"I like it," James responded brightly. "I'll nail the bastards as they enter! I can see in the dark, you know."

"I noticed that," Lee said dryly. "Come on . . . Let's climb up out of the pool."

Once on the pool deck Lee used the flashlight to locate what turned out to be four entrances. One for each side of the building—and one for each locker room. They worked feverishly to drag furniture in front of the doors knowing that the assassins could arrive at any moment.

Finally, having completed their preparations, the couple took cover. Lee was crouched behind a long, narrow planter, while James knelt next to a thick support column. As soon as three or four assassins were in the area, they'd open fire. Lee would have preferred to let all of the bastards get inside, but knew the group would disperse, and attempt to flank their targets. Something she couldn't allow.

That was the plan . . . And Lee thought it was a good plan until she heard glass shatter and turned to see dark forms silhouetted against the lights outside! The assassins were smarter than she'd given them credit for. Rather than walk into a possible ambush, they had chosen to rappel down from a higher floor!

Lee was about to shout a warning when James turned toward the windows. There was a loud report, and a muzzle flash marked his location, but his aim was true. One of the black silhouettes jerked and fell out of sight.

In the meantime two killers had entered the pool deck via the open windows and stood with their boots planted on the floor. They were armed with machine pistols, which chattered madly. Bullets pinged all around Lee as she scuttled away. They could *see* her! And, since the mercs were wearing night-vision gear, she was the only combatant who *couldn't* see.

Lee tripped, fell, and rolled. That put her behind the waist-high wall that ran along the northern perimeter of the pool. She went to one knee with the Glock in hand. The laser sight was in place, and Lee fired as the red dot swept onto a body and wobbled there. The assassin flinched and fired in return. He was wearing body armor! Lee made an adjustment and the Glock jumped. His head snapped back. Asshole down.

James was firing again by then, and Lee heard someone scream. Three. Three of them had been eliminated. That meant . . . Lee heard the crunch of broken glass and turned to find an assassin standing *behind* her! The unlocked door . . . They were coming down the stairs too.

Lee fell sideways as the killer fired. She was momentarily blinded by the flash but triggered three shots anyway. At least one of them must have struck the target because she heard a loud grunt. A leg shot perhaps . . . The Glock went off again at that point and the assassin crumpled.

Bullets. How many bullets remained in the Glock? Six? Or seven? It was important to keep track. Lee heard firing in the background as she crawled to the body, ripped the helmet free, and put it on. Her surroundings had a greenish hue, but now she could see!

Lee turned, careful to stay low, and saw a white flash as James fired. But the killers had surrounded him. And as one assassin hit the floor, the rest pulled their triggers.

Lee heard herself utter a roar of rage as the Glock bucked in her hands, the dot flowed from target to target, and the targets fell in order. Then the weapon clicked empty and the Smith & Wesson came out.

There was silence as Lee got up and made her way over to where James lay. She could tell that he'd been hit at least a dozen times. None of the wounds were lethal by themselves. But James had lost a lot of blood and wasn't going to make it no matter how many bandages Lee put on him. She knelt at his side. Their eyes met. James tried to smile but produced a grimace instead. "So much for Plan A," he said. "Time for Plan B. Get the hell out of here, sis . . . Tell Mom . . . Tell her . . ." Then he was gone.

Lee swore. But there was no time to grieve. And, come to

think of it, very little reason to do so. Maybe it was his fault and maybe it wasn't. But her brother had been a shallow, self-centered jerk. Would she let Alala know? Lee would make that decision later on. Her first priority was to escape the hotel.

Lee put the revolver away and took a moment to reload the Glock as she considered her options. She could leave the way she had come in. Or she could slide down one of the ropes still dangling outside the windows. Yes, someone could sever the line from above, but would they? Lee didn't think so. It would be difficult for an assassin, if any were left, to see who he or she was cutting loose.

The decision seemed to make itself. Lee went over to retrieve her pack from its hiding place, slipped her arms through the straps, and went looking for gloves. That part was easy since all of the assassins were wearing them.

Thus equipped Lee made her way over to the windows. The LAPD had taught her how to fast rope out of a helicopter many years before. Fast roping was different from rappelling in that the rope wasn't attached to the person via a descender. It was a dangerous maneuver however . . . especially without gloves.

But with gloves on, Lee was able to jump out and grab the thick rope. Her hands and feet served as brakes. It took less than a minute to land next to the building, release the line, and depart. Then all she had to do was slip through a hole in the cyclone fence and step onto the Strip. Sleep. She needed sleep . . . So Lee set off to find it.

The pack was a burden. But by wearing it Lee identified herself as a drifter, a tourist on a budget, or a homeless person. And that meant that the city's street people saw her as one of their own and were happy to provide advice. That was how Lee found her way to a low-rent motel called the Blue Lagoon. Never mind that the lagoon was a trash-filled hole out front.

All Lee cared about was the fact that a room could be had for fifty nu per night, the sheets were clean, and the steel fire door was strong enough to keep people out. Just to make sure Lee threw both bolts and pushed the rubber stop in under the barrier.

After a quick shower, she got ready for bed, a process that consisted of brushing her teeth and placing handguns on both of the bedside stands. Sleep fell on Lee like a ton of bricks. She slept hard and woke feeling stupid.

It took a moment to orient herself, check the time, and discover that it was nearly noon. Later than she had intended, but still early enough to catch the 3:15 bus to Primm. And like it or not, that was the way she would have to get there.

Lee had the money taken from the hotel assassin but was still running low. Perhaps she should have searched the dead bodies for cash, but the thought hadn't occurred to her, and it would have taken time. So Lee would have to escape the red zone using the money on hand. And that could be difficult if they were still looking for her. James was dead. Did that mean the contract had been fulfilled? Yes. Maybe. Hopefully. But assumptions could be fatal.

Lee completed her morning routine, got dressed, and shouldered the pack. After leaving her room, she made her way down the long hallway to a shabby office. The night clerk had been replaced by a woman with broad cheekbones, a flat nose, and a pair of dangerous-looking canines. "Good morning, hon . . . What can I do for you?"

"I'm looking for a breakfast burrito," Lee replied, as she placed the keycard on the counter. "And I'm checking out."

"I would suggest the Mariachi," the clerk replied. "It's two blocks south of here. You were in 108. Hold on, hon . . . I have an envelope for you. Someone dropped it by last night."

Lee figured it was a mistake. She didn't know anyone in Las Vegas. But when the clerk handed her the envelope Lee saw that her name was written on it! That was scary. "What did this person look like?" Lee wanted to know.

"I wasn't on duty," the clerk replied, "so I don't know."

Lee thanked the woman and took the envelope outside, where she tore it open. There was a piece of paper within. The words were written in block letters. "PAYBACK IS A BITCH, BITCH. YOURS IS COMING." The note was signed, Crystal Bye. *Crystal Bye?* Who the hell was *she?* A mercenary, that's who. Lee sighed. There was nothing she could do except be careful. Perhaps a disguise would help. But breakfast was the first priority. She was starving.

So Lee walked the two blocks, entered the restaurant, and chose a booth that would allow her to monitor the front door. Now, after reading the note, *everyone* looked suspicious. Fortunately, none of the employees or customers tried to shoot her, and the burrito was excellent.

After paying the bill Lee made her way out into bright sunlight and began the walk to the bus station. She stopped every once in a while to check her six but saw no signs of a tail. And that made her feel better. About halfway to her destination Lee passed a secondhand store, paused, and went back. The place was packed with all sorts of things, including a rack of multicolored burqas. The perfect garment to hide in.

So she bought one, traded the pack for a small roll-around suitcase, and emerged from the store with a very different profile. It was hot by then and even hotter in the burqa. Fortunately the station was only three blocks away, and, when Lee arrived, she was delighted to find that the interior was air-conditioned.

Lee bought a ticket to Primm and took a seat in a corner. There were all sorts of people around her, but they were generally working-class types, many of whom were surrounded by all manner of packages.

The wait was only forty-five minutes long, but it seemed to take forever. Eventually the bus arrived, passengers got in line, and were forced to stand there for ten minutes until they were invited to board. Lee wound up sitting next to a woman who had a wicker cage resting on her lap. There was a rooster inside and it crowed from time to time. Luckily, the trip to Primm would take less than an hour.

Lee put her earbuds in and listened to music until the bus pulled into the town of Jean, where half the passengers got off. She knew it would be more difficult to get at her on the bus, so she remained on board, and felt a sense of relief when it departed ten minutes later. At that point she was only twelve miles away from the border and Pacifica. She was going home.

TEN

Lee woke up in Los Angeles. She was on a bus, curled up on the backseat, where she had fallen asleep an hour earlier. As Lee sat up she realized that the bus was empty. Somehow, she'd managed to sleep through both the driver's announcements and the commotion the passengers made as they departed. None of them had bothered to wake her. Why?

Because you're in the city, that's why, Lee told herself. *And for all they know you're a meth addict, a wino, or a head case. Welcome home.*

It had been a long, difficult trip. After arriving at the border and showing her ID, Lee had been arrested for impersonating a police officer and thrown in jail. More than twelve hours passed before the military police got around to contacting the LAPD. And when they did, one of the clerks in HR told them that the *real* Cassandra Lee was vacationing in the San Juan islands. Insofar as the army was concerned that raised the possibility that the woman who claimed to be Cassandra Lee had murdered the police officer and taken the woman's ID. Never mind the fact that the person in custody looked exactly like the cop in question.

So *another* eight hours passed while Lee pleaded with them to call Deputy Chief Jenkins. Once they did so she was released. That was good except it meant Jenkins was going to be pissed. She had lied to him after all—and that was a definite no-no.

Such were Lee's thoughts as she grabbed the suitcase, stood

up, and exited the bus. It was 10:36 a.m., and the bright sunlight caused Lee to squint as she stepped down onto the ground.

From there it was a short walk through a mostly empty terminal and out onto the street, where two cabs were waiting. Both were decorated with murals, lots of chrome, and plenty of unnecessary accessories. Lee entered the first one and gave her address to the driver.

As the *especiale* pulled away from the curb Lee thought about how good it was to be back in the green zone—and wondered how her mother was doing. Did she know that James was dead? And that his killers worked for her husband? Maybe Heevy had told Alala so as to punish her for giving birth to James. Or maybe he was keeping the entire episode to himself. Not that it mattered. There weren't many secrets in the Heevy mansion, and if Myra knew, then Alala knew. But Lee was determined to let the whole thing go. The Heevy family had created the mess—and they would have to sort it out. Her mother included.

"That'll be ten nu," the driver said as he brought the car to a stop in front of the apartment house. Lee was forced to pay with some badly crumpled ones and a handful of coins. She didn't have enough money to give him a tip—and the driver muttered something as she got out.

After losing the truck, which Lee had come to appreciate, she'd been worried about the motorcycle. But the big Road King was right where it was supposed to be, hiding under its gray cover. Lee made a mental note to thank her downstairs neighbors for keeping an eye on the bike as she climbed the stairs to her apartment.

The door was intact, something most people would take for granted but something Lee had reason to worry about. The interior was a bit dusty, mostly dark because the curtains were pulled, and it felt like her father was still living there. *It's time to move*, Lee told herself. *It's time to get a place of my own.*

It was also time to dump the contents of the suitcase onto the bed and shed the dirty clothes. A few minutes later she was in the shower where she let the deliciously hot water pummel her skin before washing her hair. She was standing on the bath mat, using a towel, when the cell phone rang. It was outside the bathroom on the hallway table. "This is Cassandra Lee."

"And this is your boss," Jenkins replied. "We need to talk."

"Yeah," Lee said contritely. "We do. Thanks for bailing me out."

"Be in my office at two," Jenkins said. Lee winced as the line went dead.

After starting a load of laundry and getting dressed for work, Lee went down to the garage. The hog started right away, and Lee rode it downtown. The cops in the parking garage said, "Hi," and welcomed her back as she passed through security.

Then began what could be a fateful trip upstairs. She was officially on administrative leave rather than vacation—and that meant she was supposed to be available to her superiors. So Jenkins could fire her if he chose to. Then what would she do? The thought caused her stomach to churn.

As Lee crossed the bull pen on the third floor there were some greetings but none of the friendly insults that she could normally expect. And there was something else as well . . . It seemed as though a pervasive feeling of gloom was hanging over the area. But why? Lee couldn't stop to ask without being late. So she made a note to find out what the problem was as she continued on her way.

But when she arrived outside Jenkins's office it was to discover that the chief had a visitor. So Lee was forced to sit and worry until the woman left, and Jenkins waved her in. The guest chair was still warm when she sat on it. There was a serious expression on the chief's face. "How are you feeling?"

"Good," Lee replied truthfully. "Very good. Listen, I want to apologize for . . ."

"Never mind that," Jenkins said brusquely. "You didn't watch the news this morning, did you?"

"No," Lee confessed. "I didn't."

Jenkins nodded. "Yeah . . . Well, the Bonebreaker struck again. The victim was a patrolman named Rudy Vasquez. A kid really, only a year out of the academy. A road crew came across his body this morning."

Now Lee understood the black cloud that hung over the bull pen. *Another* cop had been murdered. "Was the body found on the Hollywood Freeway?"

"Yes. Which means that traffic has been backed up all day, and the mayor is pissed." Jenkins scowled. "I wonder which she cares about most . . . Vasquez or the traffic. No, strike that, she has a city to run."

Lee nodded. She understood how Jenkins felt. How *all* cops felt. "Had the body been dismembered?"

Jenkins made a face. "Yes."

Lee remembered the video of her father's death. "Shit."

"Yeah. So Lieutenant Wolfe is working the case along with your guys. And she wants you back on the team if you're up for it."

Lee frowned. "Why? Because she could use another detective? Or because my involvement will make the Bonebreaker even crazier?"

"For both reasons," Jenkins answered. "Do you have a problem with that?"

"No. I would do anything to bring that sick son of a bitch in. So I'm back on duty?"

"Yes."

"And Dr. Kane agrees?"

"He will."

Lee smiled. "Good." She was looking forward to seeing Kane again.

"So," Jenkins said. "How did it go with your mother?"

The question came as a shock. Jenkins knew! But *how*? Lee frowned. "You left cameras in my apartment?"

Jenkins nodded. "Yes. For your own good. And we may have to install more."

"And you read the letter my mother sent me?"

"A copy . . . Yes."

Lee stared at him. "So you knew where I was going and why."

"No," Jenkins said. "I *didn't* know. Not for sure. Had I known, I would have had to take disciplinary action against you."

Lee couldn't help but smile. "You are a grade-A son of a bitch."

"And you are an insubordinate pain in the ass." Both of them laughed.

Jenkins stood. "Come on . . . The right-hand lane of the

Hollywood Freeway is still closed—and I promised the mayor that our people would pull out before rush hour. I want to see the scene firsthand—and I imagine you would as well."

Lee felt mixed emotions as she followed Jenkins out of the office, through the bull pen, and toward the elevators. It was good to be back. But another policeman had been murdered. And by returning to active duty she was about to remind the killer that she was still alive. Would that stir him up? Definitely. The reality of that frightened her.

Most of the department's "unmarked" cars had been tagged by members of LA's graffiti underground who, having done so, liked to post photos of their "kills" on the Internet. And the sedan that had been assigned to Jenkins was no exception. In fact the letters TIACC, (This is a cop car,) had been scrawled across the trunk in bright pink paint.

It took less than five minutes to merge onto U.S. 101 northbound—a road also known as the Hollywood Freeway. The right lane and the shoulder next to it had been coned off and closed to regular motorists. That slowed traffic to a crawl but allowed the police car to make good time. It wasn't long before flashing lights appeared ahead, and Jenkins had to pull over.

As they made their way along the line of cruisers and "creepers," Lee knew that the passing motorists were staring at her and the cops processing the crime scene. It wasn't the first time since she'd been a street cop and worked lots of accidents. The army of looky loos, gawkers, and bloodthirsty ghouls were part of the job. And that was one aspect of what the Bonebreaker wanted . . . lots and lots of attention.

There were five lanes and a narrow shoulder on the right. It was hot, and Lee enjoyed a brief respite from the sun as they passed under a bridge. She turned to look back over her shoulder as they emerged and saw that at least four TV cameras had been set up on the overpass. All of which had a perfect view of the crime scene up ahead. Was Carla Zumin looking down at her? Probably. Although panels of blue fabric had been set up to protect the crime scene from prying eyes.

With the exception of some patrol officers and the CHP personnel, Lee and Jenkins knew all of the people who were working the scene. So there was no need for introductions. Lieutenant Wolfe was standing next to one of the department's Incident Command Post units. The vehicle was roughly the size of a bus—and equipped to provide a variety of support services. Wolfe wiped the sweat off her forehead. She had to raise her voice to make herself heard over the roar of traffic. "Chief, Detective Lee, welcome to the frying pan . . . We're almost finished. We'll pull out by five thirty."

"That won't be good enough for the mayor," Jenkins predicted gloomily. "But nothing is. Can you give us a walk-through? Lee's going to rejoin your unit and, given her media profile, will have to share the shitstorm with us. Which reminds me . . . Molly has a press conference scheduled for six thirty, and all three of us are supposed to be there."

Wolfe made a face. "Oh, goody. Yeah, let's take a stroll. There were three black garbage bags," she said, as they walked north. "They were removed a couple of hours ago but cones mark where they were found."

Lee could see that technicians were still on the scene, still taking measurements, and still snapping photos. She stopped next to the first marker and eyed the others. It looked as though the cones were roughly thirty feet apart. "The bags were spread out?" she inquired. "They weren't in a single pile?"

"Correct," Wolfe replied. "And I know what you're thinking. Prior to this murder, the Bonebreaker always left the bags in a pile. So this represents a deviation from his past MO."

Lee nodded. "There's something else as well . . . If I remember correctly, the Bonebreaker used to dump bodies next to the *southbound* lanes of the freeway."

"That's right," Wolfe said. "Plus, he dumped the bags under the bridge where the traffic cameras couldn't see him. So, thanks to the switch, we can look at the footage from the nearest cameras and who knows? Maybe we'll get lucky."

Jenkins frowned. "You're sure it's him?"

"Hell no," Wolfe answered. "We're not sure of anything at this point. But the odds are pretty good. After all, if it *is* him, this wouldn't be the first time he made changes to his MO. Sometimes he contacts us—and sometimes he doesn't. And he sent a drone after Lee . . . But the general location is consistent with his MO—as is the fact that the body was dismembered."

"It will be interesting to read the autopsy report," Lee said, as they arrived at the third cone. "He used a chain saw on my father. We know that for a fact. So we'll find out if he's still using that methodology."

Lee was surprised by the cool, emotion-free way in which she was able to talk about it. And, judging from their expressions, the others were as well. "Right," Wolfe said. "Assuming the chief agrees, I'd like you and your team to work on Vasquez. Who was he really? What, if anything, did he have in common with previous victims? And what was he doing the night he disappeared?"

Lee nodded. "Got it. We'll get to work."

"One more thing," Wolfe said. "The fact that you are working on the case could provoke another attack. So I'm going to reactivate the shadow team. Your bathroom will be safe—but don't parade around the apartment naked."

After looking at the crime scene, Lee and Jenkins returned to LAPD headquarters, where they met with the department's public-affairs rep and Wolfe prior to reporting to the plaza for the press conference. It was late afternoon by that time, and the light was starting to fade as Jenkins stepped up to a portable podium, and read a prepared statement.

"At approximately 5:30 a.m., a state highway crew found what appeared to be three bags of human remains next to northbound SR 101. Patrol cars were dispatched to secure the scene and worked with units from the California Highway Patrol and the highway department to shut down the right lane of the Hollywood Freeway.

"Shortly thereafter, members of the LAPD's Robbery-Homicide Division arrived on scene and began their investigation. Later it was determined that the remains were those of LAPD Patrol Officer Rudy Vasquez, who had been reported missing three days earlier. Officer Vasquez's family was notified early this afternoon and requests that the media respect their privacy during this difficult time. A memorial service will be held on a date to be announced later in the week."

Jenkins paused to survey the faces in front of him. "Many of you are aware that certain aspects of this murder are reminiscent of the murders committed by an individual who calls him or herself 'the Bonebreaker.' And while we acknowledge there are some similarities, we urge you not to make assumptions regarding this murder. It may or may not be connected to the previous killings. Once an autopsy has been performed, and various test results are back, we'll let you know if we think there's a connection.

"Now I would like to introduce Lieutenant Brianna Wolfe, who is leading this investigation with assistance from Detective Cassandra Lee. They will answer your questions to the extent that they can—remembering that there are topics we can't discuss at this time."

Lee had to give Wolfe credit. She handled the barrage of questions with considerable finesse. Yes, there were three black garbage bags. No, she wouldn't comment on the contents of the bags. Yes, there was a message from a person claiming to be the killer. No, she wouldn't say what was in the message, or whether it was from the Bonebreaker.

And so it went. In fact, the whole thing was so smooth that Lee thought she was going to skate until Carla Zumin called her name. "Detective Lee! You've been working on the Bonebreaker killings for a long time now—and he tried to kill you. Do you have a message for him?"

Lee felt a surge of anger, opened her mouth, and heard herself speak. "Yes, I have a message for the bastard . . . No matter where you are, no matter what hole you live in, we will find you." And *that*, needless to say, was the sound pop that all of the TV stations led with.

The Bonebreaker's work was done for the day. The current task was to inscribe the words from Matthew 25:46 onto Chief McGinty's femur. After many hours of painstaking work using an air-powered engraving tool, the phrase, "Then they will go away to eternal punishment," had been successfully inscribed onto the bone. He planned to finish the job soon. The *full* inscription, the one the Bonebreaker would send to McGinty's whore, was going to read: "Then they will go away to eternal punishment, but the righteous to eternal life." The "righteous" being those who had suffered at McGinty's hands.

It was 10:42 p.m. by then, although time had very little meaning in the ossuary, and the Bonebreaker was hungry. The camp stove was located on a counter next to an improvised sink. Fixing dinner was a simple matter of dumping a can of chicken noodle soup into a pan and lighting a burner. That, plus a piece of Melba toast, was the Bonebreaker's idea of a hearty meal.

Once the soup came to a boil, the Bonebreaker took it and the piece of toast over to the stainless-steel worktable, where he put both items down next to McGinty's femur. Having worked through the 5:00 p.m. newscast, the Bonebreaker wanted to watch Channel 7's 11:00 p.m. *News-Wrap* while he ate.

He was slurping soup out of a large spoon as the anchors appeared. The Bonebreaker knew both of them well, or felt that he did, and liked square-jawed Weston Smiley the best. It was blue-eyed Mary Rollit who read the first story, however. "I'm sorry to say that another Los Angeles police officer has been murdered. And, based on preliminary evidence, the killing may be the work of the notorious Bonebreaker."

The real Bonebreaker stopped eating as Rollit described the black trash bags, where they had been found, and the miles-long traffic jam that resulted from the discovery. The Bonebreaker felt a rising sense of rage. He was innocent! Of *that* murder anyway . . . And had never heard of Officer Vasquez before.

So he was already upset when the press-conference footage appeared. A police official was speaking, but the Bonebreaker had very little interest in what the man had to say. His eyes were on Cassandra Lee! The bitch had returned from wherever she'd been hiding. He called upon God to strike Lee dead. *No*, the voice in his head said. *You are my servant on Earth . . . It is your task to punish the evildoers.*

Lee took a question from one of the reporters as the press conference began to wind down. "Detective Lee! You've been working on the Bonebreaker killings for a long time now—and he tried to kill you. Do you have a message for him?"

"Yes," Lee said. "I have a message for the bastard. No matter where you are, no matter what hole you live in, we will find you."

The Bonebreaker uttered a scream of rage and threw his spoon at the TV set. It hit, bounced off, and clattered to the floor. "I didn't do it!" he shouted. But no one heard him other than a hungry rat—and it wasn't impressed.

Lee had no difficulty waking up on the morning after the press conference. That had a lot to do with the fact that there were cameras in her home including the bedroom.

The first thing Lee did as she rolled out of bed was to give the people who were watching her the finger as she left for the bathroom. The one place where she could be sure of some privacy. After completing her morning routines Lee left the apartment, went down to the street, and performed a 360 on the sedan. The lack of response from the handheld detector suggested that the vehicle was clean, except for the police department's tracker, that is.

Rather than head downtown for roll call, Lee chose to check in with Wolfe by phone. "I'm going to visit the Vasquez family," she said. "And Yanty is hard at work trying to get access to Vasquez's phone records, e-mails, and online activity."

"Sounds good," Wolfe said. "What about Prospo?"

"He's working on a search warrant for Vasquez's apartment," Lee replied.

"Roger that," Wolfe said. "Keep me informed."

Lee promised to do so, broke the connection, and pulled into a strip mall. Ten minutes later, she emerged from the local coffee shop with a grande mocha and a blueberry scone in hand. In a clear violation of departmental policy and a couple of laws, Lee ate breakfast while she drove.

The working-class community of Glendale was north of where she lived, had taken a heavy hit during the plague, and was still on the long road to recovery. But it looked like roughly two-thirds of the houses were occupied. And, judging from the numerous neighborhood-watch signs, the local homeowners were doing their part to keep crime under control.

After a wrong turn, Lee got back on track, and had to wind her way through an old subdivision before arriving in front of the Vasquez house. She couldn't park there however since the driveway was full of cars—and at least a dozen vehicles were parked on the street. Friends and relatives? Probably. And based on previous experience, Lee knew that the presence of so many mourners could make her job more difficult.

Lee parked the creeper half a block away and walked back. The Vasquez residence was a ranch-style home with a brick façade and a raised planter that ran along the front. Judging from the profusion of flowers someone had a green thumb.

Lee rang the bell and heard a distant chime, followed by the sound of footsteps. The door opened to reveal a pleasant-looking woman with carefully arranged black hair. Her eyes were red as if from crying. "Yes? Can I help you?"

"I'm Detective Lee," Lee said, as she opened her ID up for the woman to look at. "I called last night. Are you Mrs. Vasquez?"

"Yes," the woman replied. "Please come in. My husband and I have visitors, but we can talk in the kitchen."

In order to reach the kitchen it was necessary to pass through a living room packed with people, including a Catholic priest, who nodded to Lee as she passed by. Halfway to the kitchen a man whom Lee took to be Mr. Vasquez got up off a chair and fell in behind her.

The house had been built back before open interiors became popular and had never been remodeled. So, with the exception of a pass-through, the kitchen was partitioned off from the dining area. Three children were seated at a table playing a board game—but left when Mrs. Vasquez ordered them into the backyard. "Please," Mrs. Vasquez said. "Have a seat. This is my husband, Jorge. And this is Detective Lee . . . Would you like something to drink? Coffee perhaps?"

The words had a robotic quality—as if Mrs. Vasquez was going through the motions. "No, thank you," Lee replied. "I'm sorry to intrude. I know this is a very difficult time for you and your family. But the department wants to apprehend the person or persons who murdered your son and bring them to justice as quickly as possible. And that's why I'm here . . . to collect any information that might help us solve the case."

Mr. Vasquez was sitting across from her. He was small, wiry, and starting to go bald. "Thank you for coming," he said. "But I'm not sure that we'll be of much help."

"You never know," Lee said, as she placed a small recorder on the table between them. "Let's start with the last time you spoke with Rudy."

Mrs. Vasquez started to cry at that point and began to snatch tissues out of a box. So it was up to Jorge to field Lee's questions. It seemed that Mrs. Vasquez had spoken to their son on the phone about a week prior to his disappearance. It had been a routine call, the kind young men make to keep their mothers happy, and lasted about ten minutes.

As the interview continued Mr. Vasquez said that no, they didn't know of anyone who would want to harm their son, nor were they aware of any problems in his personal life. "He was a good boy," Mrs. Vasquez insisted, as she blotted her eyes. "He liked to listen to music, ride his bike, and play baseball. But most of all he loved his job. He was five when he told me that he was going to be a policeman."

There were more tears after that—and Lee figured that she had what there was to get. Many eyes followed her progress as Mr. Vasquez led her through the living room and out onto the front porch. Once there he looked around as if to ensure that no one else could hear. "I know you," he said solemnly. "You're the cop that killed those bank robbers. Promise me this . . . When you find the people who killed my son, shoot them. "Do you hear me?" he demanded, as the tenor of his voice rose. "Kill the bastards."

And with that, he turned around and went back into the house. The door clicked as it closed. The interview was over.

After leaving the Vasquez residence Lee pointed the car downtown. There was a ton of administrative crap waiting for her with more coming in all the time. Her phone rang. "This is Lee."

"It's Prospo," the voice on the other end of the call said. "I have the warrant."

"Outstanding . . . Give me the address. I'll meet you there."

Lee pulled over to jot the address down, and saw that it was in West Hollywood, an area sometimes referred to as WeHo. A place where a lot of gay people had chosen to live. Did that mean Vasquez was gay? No, but it raised the possibility. And his sex life might or might not be relevant to the case. "Thanks," Lee said, as she pulled away from the curb. "I'm on the way."

Lee took Hyperion Avenue to Santa Monica Boulevard, which led straight to West Hollywood. The four-story apartment house was on the east side of Martel Avenue and looked like thousands of other flat-topped white stucco buildings.

Prospo was there, along with a slightly overweight, middle-aged crime-scene investigator whom everyone called "Moms." Having already obtained a key from the on-site property manager, they were ready to enter the apartment that Vasquez had occupied for most of the last two years. It was on the second floor, facing out onto a shared walkway and the street beyond. What could have been his bike was chained to the metal railing.

Prospo opened the door and pushed it back out of the way so that he could eyeball the interior. Then, confident that they weren't about to step on any evidence, he let the others in.

Moms had something like a thousand investigations under her belt and didn't need any instructions. Her camera whirred, and light strobed the walls, as the detectives gave themselves a tour of the one-bedroom apartment. It was decorated man-style, with leather-covered furniture and a couple of dying plants. Sports stuff, including free weights, were scattered about. An old surfboard had been hung over the couch, which sat across from a huge flat-screen TV.

There was some cop memorabilia too . . . including a class photo from the academy on one wall and a framed lifesaving medal on another. All of which was consistent with Lee's expectations, and sadly enough, not that different from her apartment. *I need to move,* Lee thought to herself for the second time in twenty-four hours. *I need a fresh start. I need to call Lawrence.*

As for Vasquez's sex life, that wasn't clear. Snapshots of men *and* women were pinned to the refrigerator with magnets so it could go either way.

"I don't see any signs of violence," Prospo said. "Nothing that would suggest that Vasquez was abducted from the apartment. And that's consistent with the Bonebreaker's MO. None of his victims were taken from their homes. Not so far."

"I agree," Lee replied. "I think we should talk to his partner next."

"She's scheduled to meet with us at 2:00 p.m.," Prospo said. "Back at the cop shop."

"Nice work," Lee said. "Come on . . . I'll take you to lunch. Maybe we can find a Mexican restaurant that serves meat loaf and mashed potatoes."

Lee was sitting at her desk, working her way through 247 e-mails, when Officer Syndy Seko appeared. She was dressed in her blue uniform and looked like a recruiting poster. A black band was wrapped around her badge to symbolize the loss of a fellow officer. "Detective Lee? I'm Syndy Seko. I was told to report to you at two o'clock."

"Thanks for coming," Lee replied as she stood up. "Come on . . . We'll grab Detective Prospo and find a place to talk."

The place turned out to be a nearby conference room, which, judging from the mostly eaten cake, had been used for somebody's birthday celebration earlier in the day.

Seko had vaguely Asian features, almond-shaped eyes, and a freshly scrubbed appearance. If she was nervous Lee couldn't see any sign of it. "So," she began. "Let me start by saying how sorry we are about your partner's death."

Seko produced a short, jerky nod. And her lower lip quivered for a second. That was when Lee realized that Seko was battling to keep the lid on her emotions. "Thank you," Seko said simply. "I miss him."

"I know this is hard," Prospo said sympathetically. "But partners have a special relationship with each other. Chances are that you know things about Rudy that his family isn't aware of."

Seko shrugged. "Probably . . . What would you like to know?"

"Did Rudy have enemies?" Lee inquired. "People on or off the force who might want to harm him?"

Seko shook her head. "No, not that I know of. People liked Rudy."

"How 'bout his private life?" Prospo inquired. "Did Rudy have a girlfriend? A boyfriend?"

"He had a boyfriend," Seko replied. "But they broke up three months ago."

"Was the breakup amicable?" Lee wanted to know.

"Yes," Seko said. "I know Marty . . . And he would never do anything to harm Rudy. Not physically anyway."

"So, was Rudy out and about?" Prospo wanted to know.

"We worked a lot of overtime," Seko answered. "But when Rudy could, he liked to hang out at the Hi-Jinx Club. That's where Rudy met Marty—and he hoped that lightning would strike twice."

"But no current lovers?" Lee inquired.

"Not that I know of."

The interview continued for another ten minutes and ended with a request that Seko call them should something relevant come to mind. Once she was gone, Prospo looked at Lee. "Don't tell me . . . Let me guess. We're going to visit the Hi-Jinx Club."

"You *can* read minds!" Lee said. "I'm impressed. Here's hoping we find some sort of lead there . . . Because at this point, all we have so far is a whole lot of nothing."

Lee spent the rest of the afternoon working her way through administrative tasks and was about to catch up when Prospo appeared. "Are you ready?" he inquired. "The Hi-Jinx is open, and the manager is expecting us."

"Yeah," Lee said, as she logged out. "Do you want to meet me there? Or would you like a ride?"

"I'll meet you at the club," Prospo replied. "I'll go home from there."

Lee nodded, and they rode the elevator down to the garage together. Once in her car, and on the way, Lee checked her six. There was no sign of a tail, so she allowed her thoughts to wander. She had lied to Kane. So how would he react when Jenkins told him the truth? Lee figured that Dr. Kane would receive the news with equanimity. But what about the *man*? Would he be angry? Perhaps. Or maybe he wouldn't give a shit. Maybe he viewed her as another whack job. A wayward patient in need of a steadying hand. That would be horrible.

The Hi-Jinx Club fronted on the tree-lined Santa Monica Boulevard. The parking was out back, and it was early, so there were plenty of parking places to choose from. As Lee slid into one of them, Prospo pulled in next to her.

On the way into the club they passed the restrooms, *huge* fish tanks on both walls, and the door to the kitchen. The lighting was so subdued that it was hard to see across the room. Round tables and chromed chairs were arranged around a dance floor and the table where a DJ would sit later on. There were some customers but not many. The bar, which was supported by a beautifully lit fish tank, took up most of the right-hand wall. Prospo went over to speak with the bartender. "We're looking for Andre . . . He's expecting us."

The bartender responded with a nod. "Sure, I'll tell him." Then he turned toward a door labeled OFFICE.

Lee was still looking around when a man emerged from the office and came out to meet them. "Hi, I'm Andre . . . Welcome to Hi-Jinx."

"I'm Detective Lee—and this is Detective Prospo."

"Right," Andre said, as he shook hands with Prospo. "We spoke on the phone."

"So you know why we're here," Lee said as she shook hands with the bar owner. "We're trying to find the person or persons who murdered Officer Rudy Vasquez. His partner says he came here on a frequent basis."

Andre had very little hair and what remained had been cut short. He had well-groomed eyebrows, high cheekbones, and the body of a runner. He nodded. "Yes, Rudy was a regular. I liked him. Everybody did."

"So, how 'bout it?" Prospo inquired. "Was Rudy here on the night of the sixth?"

"I don't know," Andre replied. "Hundreds of people come and go every night. I can't keep track of them; nor do I try."

"How about those cameras?" Lee inquired as she pointed

them out. "Do they work? And do you keep the footage?"

"They work," Andre assured her. "And we keep everything for a rolling thirty days."

"Can we look at the images from the sixth?" Prospo wanted to know. "Or will we need to get a warrant?"

"There's no need for that," Andre replied. "You can watch it in my office. Follow me."

In order to enter the office it was necessary to walk behind the bar and pass through the door located at the far end of it. The room was about the size of a large walk-in closet and furnished with an ancient safe, a built-in computer station, and a couple of mismatched chairs. The walls were lined with DIY shelves that were laden with binders, piles of marketing materials, and a collection of bowling trophies. "Sorry about the mess," Andre said. "Have a seat at the desk. I'll show you how to access the video files."

Prospo plopped down in front of the screen, followed the directions that Andre gave, and caught on rather quickly. "Good," Andre said, as Prospo shuttled back and forth. "I need to excuse myself if it's okay with you. Happy hour is about to begin, and that's when things start to get crazy."

"No problem," Lee said. "Thanks for the help."

As Andre left Lee took up a position directly behind Prospo, where she could look over the other detective's shoulder. Video started and stopped as he worked his way through the fifth and moved into the sixth. Vasquez had been working shift two that day—and it ran from 7:00 a.m. to 3:30 p.m. So Prospo chose 4:00 p.m. as a starting point.

There were multiple cameras and all four shots appeared on the screen at once. So that, plus the poor lighting, made viewing difficult. One camera was pointed straight down at the cash register, however—so they could ignore that.

The next twenty minutes were spent starting, stopping, and rewinding. Every now and then, Prospo would tap one of the boxes, causing the image to pop full screen.

But it wasn't until the rolling time stamp read 05:36:27 p.m. that they hit pay dirt. That was the moment when Vasquez strolled into the club and paused to speak with the bartender.

The patrol officer was wearing an open-necked sports shirt that hung out over his jeans. To hide his off-duty weapon? Probably . . . And that was something Lee had long wondered about. How had it been possible for the Bonebreaker to subdue not one, but *nine* armed cops? It was a mystery within a mystery.

At that point they had Vasquez on the day he disappeared in what could have been the place where he was abducted. Lee felt a rising sense of excitement as the footage continued to roll. Prospo had three speeds to choose from: normal, kind of fast, and a blur. "Kind of fast" was the best for their needs.

They watched as Vasquez left one camera shot and entered a second one. He did some table-hopping before settling down at a spot near the front entrance. And that's where he was when a man joined him fifteen minutes later. They talked for a while, danced, and consumed two rounds of drinks. The time stamp read 07:22:19 p.m. when they got up and left. "Bingo!" Prospo said. "They went out through the back door."

"Yeah," Lee said grimly. "Vasquez's car was found in the lot, so I figure Mr. Goodbar drove. Back up . . . I want another look at him."

Prospo backed the video up, hit PLAY, and clicked the box labeled CAMERA 3. The image was large but the angle was far from ideal. Still, Lee could see the man sitting across from Vasquez. He was a good-looking guy, with a head of dark hair, a straight nose, and a nice mouth. Still another good-looking gay guy . . . What a waste.

Once they stood, Lee was able to see that the two men were roughly the same height, and since Vasquez was five feet eight inches tall, that meant Mr. Goodbar was too. "I'll get Andre," Lee said. "Maybe we'll get lucky . . . Maybe he knows who the pickup artist is."

Lee went out into the bar, waited for Andre to complete a conversation with a customer, and asked him to return to the office. Once there Andre watched the video three times. "I'm sorry," he said finally, "I don't know him."

"Damn," Lee said. "Please keep your eyes peeled, and if he shows up, let us know right away. Here's my card."

"Yeah," Prospo said, "and here's mine. One of our techs will come by to copy that video. In the meantime please don't erase any part of that video file—and don't let anyone else have access to it."

"No problem." Andre said. "I'll keep the office locked."

"Good," Lee said as she took one last look at the man who, based on what they knew so far, had to be the Bonebreaker. There was a problem though . . . A significant problem. The face on the screen was too damned young to be the Bonebreaker's. No one knew how old the Bonebreaker was exactly—but he'd been killing cops for a long time, and Lee figured that Mr. Goodbar was thirty or so. So what the hell did that mean? It could mean that a copycat killer was responsible for the Vasquez murder. But how to prove it?

ELEVEN

Despite the fact that Lee didn't like having cameras in her apartment, they did provide her with an additional sense of security, and she slept well as a result. So she woke up feeling rested and was only ten minutes late when she arrived at work. And that was the same thing as being on time in her book.

After sitting through roll call, Lee went to her cubicle, where she was scrolling through her e-mail, when Yanty plopped down on her guest chair. "Good morning," he said cheerfully. "I have bad news, good news, and bad news. In that order."

"That sounds like a shit sandwich," Lee replied sourly. "Okay, what's the first piece of bad news?"

"We were hoping to recover video of the Bonebreaker dumping the garbage bags next to the freeway," Yanty said. "Unfortunately, the nearest camera was dead. Somebody put a high-velocity rifle slug into it."

Lee frowned. "The Bonebreaker?"

Yanty shook his head. "We don't think so. I'm told that gang members and vandals use cameras for target practice on a regular basis. So odds are that the Bonebreaker had nothing to do with it."

The occasional report of gunfire was part of LA's eternal sound track along with the wail of sirens. And Lee could imagine gang members shooting at the cameras for fun and to reduce the extent to which authorities could keep an eye on them. "Okay, that sucks. So what's the good news?"

Yanty smiled. "We got lucky. A passing motorist *saw* the bags being dumped and is willing to tell us all about it."

"Uh-oh," Lee said. "Something about the way you said that tells me that I'm about to receive the second piece of bad news."

"Yup," Yanty confirmed. "Unfortunately, the aforementioned motorist is none other than a four-time loser named Mr. William Rawlings . . . A man better known to his friends, neighbors, and cellmates as Slick Willy. At the moment he's over at the Metro Detention Center waiting to be arraigned for grand theft auto."

Lee eyed the other detective. "Don't tell me, let me guess . . . On top of the fact that he's an ex-con, Slick Willy was driving a stolen car when he witnessed the bags being dumped. A fact that would make his testimony less credible."

Yanty's grin grew wider. "You're smarter than you look."

"And he wants to cut a deal."

"Exactamundo. That's why they call him Slick Willy. He refuses to say what he saw unless the DA cuts him some slack."

"And will he? Cut Willy some slack?"

Yanty nodded. "Given the nature of what we're working on, he's willing to drop the charge from grand theft auto to theft. Even though Rawlings was driving a car worth 40 thou."

Lee knew that the lesser charge was likely to result in a shorter sentence, and nodded. "Good work . . . So let's stroll over to the MDC and see what Mr. Rawlings has to say."

The jail was a short walk from the headquarters building. Once inside Lee and Yanty had to show ID to get past the reception desk. Then they had to show it again once they arrived at a checkpoint, where they were asked to surrender their weapons.

After logging in the officers were herded through a metal detector and a health screening before being escorted to one of the interview rooms. The walls were lime green, ceiling-mounted cameras were ready to capture the interview from two different angles, and the table was bolted to the floor. Brightly colored plastic chairs completed the décor.

The detectives sat down, and Lee continued to work on her e-mail via her phone until the door opened, and Slick Willy was shown in. He had longish brown hair that was parted on the right, a high forehead, and slightly protuberant eyes. A neatly trimmed mustache and Custer-style goatee completed the look. "Cuffs on? Or cuffs off?" the uniformed guard wanted to know.

"Cuffs off," Lee replied. "Thank you."

"Dial five when you're finished," the jailer said, as he pointed to a wall-mounted phone.

"Got it," Yanty replied. "Thanks."

"Have a seat," Lee said, as the guard left. "So you're the famous Slick Willy."

Rawlings liked that description of himself, and his expression brightened as he sat down. "Yeah . . . That's what they call me."

"I'm Detective Lee—and this is Detective Yanty. We hear that you have some information regarding the Vasquez murder. We're all ears."

Rawlings frowned. "Not so fast . . . What's in it for me?"

"That depends," Yanty responded. "What sort of information do you have? If you can ID the killer, we'll carry you out of here on our shoulders."

"I don't know who killed Officer Vasquez," Rawlings said cautiously. "But I saw the Bonebreaker guy dump the bags. You know . . . the ones filled with body parts. I saw a report on TV."

Lee pretended to yawn. "Whoopee. We have video of that taken from the other side of the freeway. This is a waste of time."

"Not so fast," Yanty said. "Rawlings had a different angle on what took place . . . Maybe he noticed something important."

"Whatever," Lee said dismissively. "I'll tell you what, Mr. Rawlings . . . You tell us your story, and we'll ask the DA to reduce the charge from grand theft to theft. You've been through the grinder before—so you know that's a righteous deal."

Rawlings appeared to think about it. Then he nodded. "Okay . . . I'm in."

"Excellent," Yanty said. "So, give . . . Tell us what you saw."

"It was about 4:30 a.m.," Rawlings began, "and I was headed north on the Hollywood Freeway."

"In someone else's car," Lee reminded him.

"Maybe," Rawlings said with a quick glance at one of the cameras. "There wasn't much traffic, but I had a big pickup in front of me. It had a canopy on the back. Suddenly, the flashers came on and the truck swerved over onto the shoulder of the road. I figured the guy had a flat tire, but that was when the tailgate fell, and the first garbage bag tumbled out."

Lee remembered the scene—and the way the bags were spaced out. "Okay . . . Then what?"

"Then a second bag fell out—quickly followed by a third," Rawlings said. "That was when the flashers went off and the truck veered onto the freeway. I figured the bags were filled with trash until I saw the news reports later that morning."

Lee's mind was racing. *Two* people. It would take two people to dump the bags. One to drive the truck and one to kick the containers out over the tailgate. And the Bonebreaker was a loner. Never, not once, had there been any evidence of an accomplice. Not until now. That suggested that a minimum of two people took part in the Vasquez murder. And that was a big deal.

Three hours had passed since the interview with Slick Willy. Lee, Jenkins, and Wolfe were seated in Chief of Police Corso's private conference room. They were about to take part in the kind of meeting that Lee hated the most, which was to say a meeting that Corso was involved in. The walls were decorated with artistic black-and-white photos of the "new" LA; there were a lot of green plants, and the redwood conference table was large enough to seat twenty people.

A good fifteen minutes passed before Corso entered the room. The thousand-megawatt smile was on, and he was dressed in a beautifully cut blue suit. Corso was careful to acknowledge each person in the room before getting down to business. "I understand you have a new theory regarding the Vasquez murder," Corso said. "Please proceed."

"There have been a couple of developments," Jenkins said carefully, "neither of which is definitive. But taken together they raise the possibility that the Bonebreaker *didn't* kill Vasquez."

Corso was visibly surprised. "Really? What makes you think so?"

Jenkins turned to Lee. "Cassandra? You did the legwork—tell the chief what you discovered."

It was an attempt to give Lee credit for what she'd

accomplished. She knew that. But the effect was to grant her full ownership of the theory. And she was fully aware that such ownership could cut both ways.

With all eyes upon her Lee told Corso about the video of the last person to be seen with Vasquez, the way the bags had been spaced out on the freeway, and what Slick Willy Rawlings had seen. "So," she concluded, "it's possible that we're dealing with a copycat killer. Or killers, since it would require two people to dump the bags out of a moving pickup."

Corso had been a street cop once, and as Lee watched his face, she could see him processing what she'd said. But Corso wasn't a street cop anymore. He was a cop/politician. And one who wanted to become mayor. So his analysis was bound to be more complicated than hers. And that was reflected in the noncommittal response. "That's interesting . . . Very interesting. I'm scheduled to meet with the mayor this afternoon. I'll share your theory with her. In the meantime let's keep the lid on this . . . An announcement, if any, will require some planning. Is there anything else? No? Okay . . . Thanks, and keep up the good work."

Corso left at that point, and Lee felt a sense of disappointment. Shouldn't they start looking for Mr. Goodbar and his accomplice? Why wait? But Jenkins was more philosophical. "Don't let it bother you," he said, as they got onto the elevator. "Ignore the bullshit. Things will come right in the end."

The decision had been made the previous evening. That was when one of Channel 7's reporters announced that an individual who identified himself as the Bonebreaker had called the LAPD to take credit for the Vasquez murder! And that constituted an outrage insofar as the *real* Bonebreaker was concerned. First because he was innocent, and second because the name Bonebreaker belonged to *him*, and him alone. It was *his* brand . . . And woe be to the asshole who was trying to hijack it. The solution was obvious. Find the impersonator and kill him.

So when the Bonebreaker rolled out of bed the next morning he had a long list of things to accomplish. The first of which was to find out where the Vasquez family lived. And that wasn't easy because phone books were a thing of the past, and the media were part of a police-led conspiracy to keep the information private.

But the date and time for the memorial service had been announced along with the name of the cemetery where Vasquez's body parts were to be buried. The *same* graveyard to which most of the Bonebreaker's victims had been sent.

It was a simple matter to call the cemetery's business office, schmooze the female secretary, and claim to be an undertaker who wanted to confirm the exact location of the Vasquez gravesite. "Hundreds of people will be there," he said. "Imagine the hullaballoo if I pull up at the wrong site."

The secretary *could* imagine it because that very thing had occurred before. Not for a policeman, but for a state senator, and there had been a lot of bad press. She gave him precise directions to the site, and was happy to provide the Bonebreaker additional information as well, including the Vasquez family's phone number. He thanked her and promised to drop by the office some time.

With that accomplished the Bonebreaker went to work on the next task, something he'd done before, and that was to create a fake identity for himself. The materials required for that purpose were kept in what he called the costume room.

It was a fully enclosed space that had been painstakingly sealed off from the rats and was located just off one of the halls that connected his many rooms together. By necessity the costume room was better lit than most of the Bonebreaker's underground kingdom. And it was equipped with a dehumidifier, a beat-up makeup table, and a full-length mirror.

A variety of carefully maintained clothes hung along one wall, with floor-to-ceiling shelves on the other. That's where more than two dozen latex masks sat waiting, each on its own styrofoam head. Below them were the belts, shoes, and other accessories required to successfully build a character. In this case the Bonebreaker had chosen to become a police detective, both because that would help him achieve his goal, and to make the LAPD look stupid.

So the rest of the day was spent assembling all of the elements required for his disguise and prepping himself for a return to society. And that was more difficult than it sounded because after staying in the ossuary for long periods of time he found it increasingly difficult to carry out what most people considered normal interactions. That's why he spent a couple of hours chatting with the AI on an interactive computer program intended for ESL students.

By the time darkness fell on the outside world, the Bonebreaker was ready to leave his spiritual retreat, and enter the world of God's apocalypse. He was wearing the full head mask that the manufacturer called "The Doctor." The Bonebreaker had chosen that particular countenance because of its bland, middle-aged quality.

His clothes consisted of a white shirt, a nondescript tie, and a gray suit. All of which were a good fit and were consistent with what Detective Lou Harmon would have worn had he been alive. Fortunately, for the betterment of humanity, Harmon had suffered through the last few seconds of his life in the ossuary twelve years earlier.

Finally, with briefcase in hand, the Bonebreaker was ready to go. That involved a careful exit via one of many escape routes lest he inadvertently leave some sign of what existed belowground. Once outside the Bonebreaker paused to adjust. The area that belonged to him was like an island of darkness in an ocean of lights. The air was cool and tasted different.

Having oriented himself, the Bonebreaker set forth on his mission. A three-minute walk took him to a cyclone fence. One section of mesh was connected to a metal post with hooks that the Bonebreaker had fabricated and installed years earlier. By pulling the fence off the hooks, he could pass through the resulting gap, and close the opening behind him.

Once the Bonebreaker was safely through, he began the six-block walk to a major arterial and the nearest bus stop. It would have been more convenient to steal a car locally. But to do so would attract more police attention to the area, which the Bonebreaker wanted to avoid.

And there were other threats as well . . . Including the gangs that ruled the night. Were some of them to come across a well-dressed businessman walking along a deserted street they would pounce. Then they would die. Because the Bonebreaker was armed with a .22 caliber Ruger Mark III semiauto pistol. A suppressor was attached to the black five-and-a-half-inch barrel, and that made the weapon too long for a holster. So he was carrying the handgun down along his right leg.

Fortunately, the Bonebreaker was able to reach the well-lit bus stop without having to defend himself. The .22 was safely hidden within the outer pocket of his briefcase where he could access it if the need arose. Half a dozen other people were present and none of them were staring at him. A sure sign that the disguise was working.

The bus arrived ten minutes later and the Bonebreaker followed a young man aboard. It was his experience that most people see what they expect to see. And so long as a person doesn't appear threatening, and isn't unusually attractive, they pay very little attention. That was why the Bonebreaker loosened his tie and closed his eyes. Anyone who looked at him would conclude that he was a tired businessman returning home.

The Bonebreaker was forced to transfer twice before arriving in Northeast Los Angeles. A neighborhood that was a long way from the ossuary and therefore a safe place in which to steal a car. There was no particular reason why the Bonebreaker chose the street he did. Or selected that particular house other than the fact that he liked the car in the driveway. Not because it was fancy—but because it wasn't.

He made his way up a short flight of stairs and stood in a pool of light on the porch. Then he put the briefcase down on the "Welcome" mat so he could hold the ID folder with his left hand. Having made his preparations it was a simple matter to press the doorbell button and wait. There was the sound of footsteps followed by a moment of silence. The Bonebreaker held the ID up so the homeowner could see it through the peephole. Detective Harmon was dead—but his badge was still on duty.

The Bonebreaker heard a discreet click as the person on the other side of the barrier turned the bolt. Then the door opened to reveal a middle-aged black woman. She had nice hair, brown eyes, and a pleasant smile. "Yes?" she said. "What can I do for you, Officer?"

The Bonebreaker could smile, but the mask couldn't, so there wasn't any point in trying to do so. "I was wondering about the car parked in your driveway," he said. "Does it belong to you?"

"Why yes it does," she answered. "Why do you . . ."

That was when the Bonebreaker shot her in the face. There was very little sound other than a soft thump as the woman's body collapsed on the floor. "Cora?" a male voice called. "Who's at the door?"

"That would be *me*," the Bonebreaker said, as he entered the living room. The man who was seated in the Barcalounger attempted to rise but was at a significant disadvantage. The .22 produced a gentle pop, and a hole appeared between the man's eyes. "Sorry about that," the Bonebreaker said, as the body slumped back into the chair. "But have no fear—God has a place for you in heaven."

Never assume anything. That was an important rule—and one that the Bonebreaker was careful to observe. The fact that he'd been able to successfully eliminate what appeared to be the two homeowners didn't mean that more people weren't living in the house. Children for example—or a visitor. So the Bonebreaker went from room to room, pistol at the ready. But with the exception of the cat sleeping in a laundry basket the rest of the place was empty.

After searching for and recovering both of the empty shell casings the Bonebreaker went looking for money. Not because he loved it but because he *needed* it, and was pleased to collect a total of $519.24 after going through the man's wallet and Cora's purse.

It was dinnertime by then and the Bonebreaker was hungry. So he went into the kitchen and opened the cupboards. Chicken noodle soup! He was in luck. There wasn't any Melba toast . . . But some rye crispbread would do in a pinch, and Cora had some on hand.

The Bonebreaker made dinner, took it into the living room, and sat in what he assumed to be Cora's chair. The TV was on but it was too late to watch the 5:30 news. So, with soup bowl in hand, the Bonebreaker clicked through the channels until he came to a program about computers. He liked computers and watched the entire program.

Then the Bonebreaker went down the hall to the master bedroom where he removed the mask and hung his clothing in the closet. It was important to keep the suit looking good. After that it was a simple matter to perform some personal maintenance using items from the kit in the briefcase, wrap himself in the bedspread, and lay down on the king-sized bed. He was nearly asleep when the cat landed on the bed. The tabby was purring as the Bonebreaker drifted off.

The Santa Monica Pier was especially pretty at night. The Ferris wheel was set with jewel-like colored lights and could be seen from a long way off. Below it, and all along the pier's length, thousands of other lights glowed, blinked, and strobed as the ghostly sound of an old-fashioned calliope floated across the water. And that was where Lee and Kane had agreed to meet.

The psychologist was there when Lee arrived, standing below the neon sign that had welcomed thousands over the years, and Lee was glad to see him even though the dinner date wasn't entirely voluntary. True to his word, Jenkins had spoken with Kane, but the psychologist wasn't willing to sign a release without interviewing Lee first. And, consistent with the location of prior meetings, Kane had suggested that they have dinner at the beach. Specifically, on the pier.

So Lee went home after work and changed into a seldom-used cocktail dress and a pair of high heels. Was that appropriate attire? she wondered. Or was she trying to turn an exit interview into a date? But if it wasn't a date then why were they meeting over dinner? On the Santa Monica Pier of all places. *What do you want it to be?* Lee asked the woman in the mirror. "You need some lipstick," the other Lee replied evasively. "And some gold hoops."

So as Lee went forward to give Kane an air kiss, she wasn't sure what to expect. "You look wonderful," Kane said. And, judging from the look in his eyes, he meant it.

"Thanks," Lee said lightly. "You look pretty good yourself."

"I made a reservation at Captain Mike's," Kane told her, as they passed under the neon sign. "Have you eaten there before?"

"No," Lee replied, as the crowd closed in around them. "But I like seafood."

"Me too," Kane said. "As long as it's cooked. I promise you won't be disappointed."

Lee felt her cares drop away as they passed the line for the Ferris wheel, a carnie-style booth where people could "fish" for prizes, and a sign pointing people to the aquarium.

Captain Mike's was just beyond that, on the left side of the pier. The façade featured the name and a wood-relief carving of what might have been a Maine fisherman back before the plague. But Maine was part of a red zone now—so there was no telling what a fisherman might look like.

The restaurant's interior was fitted out with all of the predictable maritime kitsch that might be expected of such a place including a huge ship's wheel behind the receptionist, fishing nets that were slung between the fake rafters, and a beachy paint job. "I know, I know," Kane said apologetically. "The décor is a joke . . . But the food makes up for it."

Once they were seated, and had drinks in front of them, the conversation turned serious. "So," Kane said, "how were the San Juans?"

There was enough snark in the way he said it that Lee could tell that Kane was teasing her. "What did Jenkins tell you?"

Kane shrugged. His expression was serious. "You went into the red zone by yourself, you got into a gunfight, and you made it out."

"Yeah, well, that's true," Lee admitted. "I'm sorry I lied to you . . . But I wanted to see my mother—and I knew you'd try to stop me if I was honest."

"You got that right," Kane said, as he sipped his drink. "So how did the visit go?"

"Are you upset with me?"

"Yes."

"How can I tell?"

"My right eyelid is twitching."

Lee laughed. "Oh my God, it is!"

"Like I said," Kane insisted. "How did the visit with your mother go?"

Lee looked out the window. The night was divided between the dark ocean, and the bright, glittering lights of Santa Monica. Her eyes came back to meet his. "I learned that she's selfish, irresponsible, and adrift."

"And?"

"And I let go. She is what she is—and it isn't about me."

"What about your father?"

"Pretty much the same thing."

Kane raised his coffee cup by way of a toast. "Good. I pronounce you to be as emotionally intact as a human with your experiences can be."

Lee smiled. "And you'll notify the police department of that?"

"Yes, of course. And there's one more thing . . ."

"Which is?"

"I hereby resign my position as your therapist."

Lee frowned. "Why?"

"Because it would be unethical to try to seduce a patient."

Lee laughed. "And that's your plan?"

Kane nodded soberly. "Yes, it is."

"I'm armed, you know."

"I suspected as much. That's why I'll have to be sneaky. Are you ready to go? If so, how 'bout a stroll on the pier?"

They left the restaurant and returned to the boardwalk. It was even more crowded than it had been earlier. They passed a ring-toss booth before arriving in front of a store called Ye Old Curiosity Shop. Kane led the way inside, where they prowled aisles stocked with fake shrunken heads, plastic skulls, and the inevitable tee shirts. Kane offered to buy Lee an African mask with a MADE IN OREGON tag on the back, and she laughed.

Farther down the boardwalk, they encountered a so-called living statue. The street performer was wearing a Stetson, Western clothing, and pointing a Colt .45 at a tourist. Both his skin and his costume were a dark bronze color. A second hat lay on the deck in front of him. It contained some bills and a sprinkling of coins.

A clown stood only a few feet away. He was juggling some brightly colored clubs as a street mime pretended to do likewise. A small crowd had gathered as the couple paused to watch. "I wonder how much money they . . ."

Kane never got to finish his question as a man stepped in front of them and the cowboy's .45 went off. The tourist produced a grunt of pain as the slug hit his shoulder and spun him around. He was falling as Lee removed the Glock from her purse.

Lee heard screams, and sensed movement around her, as the cowboy prepared to fire the single-action revolver again. Lee shot him in the chest and turned. If there was one shooter, there might be more. That was when she saw the clown take a swing at Kane. The psychologist ducked and the club passed over his head.

Lee yelled, "LAPD! Freeze!" But the clown *didn't* freeze. He fired a small-caliber semiautomatic pistol as he turned in her direction. Or tried to, except that Kane's body blocked him, and the bullet flew wide.

Lee was about to help out when the mime attacked from behind. The police officer saw a piece of wire pass in front of her eyes—and felt it start to tighten around her neck. She wanted to release the Glock in order to protect her throat but knew that was the wrong thing to do. So she stomped on the attacker's right foot instead and heard the woman swear as the spike-style heel punctured a canvas shoe. Lee took advantage of the opportunity to bring the Glock across the front of her body and point it back under her left arm. The bullet creased the mime's side. She stumbled away, recovered, and was trying to flee when a tourist took her down. Thus freed, Lee turned back to find that Kane was sitting astride the clown's chest, pounding the man's face. "That's enough," she told him. "Good job."

Sirens wailed in the distance as Lee went to get her purse. The boys and girls in blue were going to arrive soon, and she would need to show some ID. Their date was over.

After hours spent filling out reports, and being interviewed by various members of the LAPD, Lee had to sit through a health screening. None of the attackers had been wearing masks, so there was a chance of infection although the doctor didn't think it was likely. Still, if Lee experienced any of half a dozen symptoms, she was to call him right away. And when she asked, the doctor assured her that Kane would receive the same counseling, and both would be notified if any of the blood tests were BN positive. Then Lee was allowed to go home. It was about 2:00 a.m. by that time—so she felt entitled to sleep till 8:00, when the alarm jarred her awake.

She rolled out of bed and padded into the living room. The first thing Lee saw when she turned the TV on was a reporter standing on a mostly empty Santa Monica Pier. The background consisted of a cloudy sky and the gray ocean. "This is the spot where the street performers attacked and tried to kill controversial LAPD Detective Cassandra Lee," the reporter said. "She killed one of her assailants and wounded another. Both were later discovered to be mutants. Lee's companion, Dr. Lawrence Kane, is credited with subduing a third suspect. The LAPD will hold a press conference at 10:00 a.m., and our cameras will . . ."

Lee thumbed the remote, and the TV went to black. "I won't forget." That was what the note from Crystal Bye said. And, judging from the attack, she hadn't.

Lee knew that a camera was on her and kept her face intentionally blank as she left for the bathroom. That's where she made use of her phone to check voice mail. The first message was from Kane. "Hi, Cassandra . . . Just checking in. I hope you're okay. I enjoyed the date . . . Call me when you can."

Lee sent him an e-mail: "Thanks for a wonderful dinner—and for kicking the clown's ass. It was a date I won't forget."

Once she was ready, Lee left the apartment and drove downtown. After parking in the LAPD's underground garage, Lee took the elevator up to the third floor, where she took the usual route through the bullpen. "Hey, Lee," someone shouted. "I hear you capped a cowboy! Yippee ki yay!"

"And a mime!" another voice added.

"What's next?" a third cop inquired. "Little old ladies?"

But Lee refused to take the bait and went straight to Jenkins's office, where he waved her in. "Good morning," he said. "How do you feel?"

"How *should* I feel?" Lee inquired as she sat down.

"Well," Jenkins said, "you were placed on administrative leave pending the findings of a shooting review board. But you've been there and done that."

"Yeah," Lee said. "I have."

"And I see no reason for concern," Jenkins said. "It was a good shoot. Everyone says so. There were lots of witnesses, all of whom agree that the cowboy tried to kill you. So it was a clear case of self-defense and we should get a speedy turnaround."

Lee took a sip of lukewarm coffee. "Good."

Jenkins nodded. "What *isn't* so good is the suspension."

Lee frowned. "Suspension? *What* suspension?"

"The surviving perps are mutants," Jenkins said. "And they claim that you were raising hell in the red zone during the time when you were supposed to be on vacation in the San Juans. And that wouldn't be kosher, since you were not only on administrative leave but theoretically on call. So Internal Affairs plans to take a look at that . . . In the meantime you are suspended."

"So I was placed on administrative leave *and* suspended?"

"I'm afraid so. And that's a first insofar as I know."

Lee understood the spot Jenkins was in. Even though he knew about her visit to the red zone, he had chosen to ignore it. So his job was in jeopardy as well. That made her feel even worse. But maybe she could fix it. Lee chose her words with great care. "I'm sorry, boss . . . I should have told you. The stuff on the Bonebreaker video hit me hard. Then, when my dying mother asked me to come and see her, I felt I couldn't say no. That's how I got mixed up in some Heevy family politics. And, when Heevy sent assassins to kill my half brother, I tried to protect him. Now it looks like they're after me."

Jenkins's expression changed subtly. He was already familiar with most of what she'd said. But now he knew how Lee planned to pitch her story to Internal Affairs. She was going to claim that she'd gone AWOL after suffering a job-related episode of PTSD.

It wasn't an ironclad defense, but in the hands of a lawyer like Marvin Codicil, it could provide Lee with a chance of survival. And protect him as well. He cleared his throat. "Yes, well, I wish you had been more forthcoming. But I understand the strain you were under—and appreciate the fact that you're coming clean."

"So I have to go home?"

"I'm afraid so. And leave your badge here. That goes for the arsenal, too."

"Even though people are gunning for me?"

"Yeah, although the shadow team is still monitoring your home. So that helps. There were more assassins, you know . . . We think three of them were waiting by the gate in case you turned the other way. They took off when the blue suits arrived."

"That's really special . . . Thanks for letting me know."

"You're welcome. The doctor did a nice job by the way . . . Who knew the guy could throw a punch?"

"Yeah," Lee said, as she placed her ID case on his desk. "Who knew?"

"So you two were on a date?"

"No comment," Lee said as she placed her weapons on the desk. "You can have these, but I have a .45 at home."

"You can't carry it."

"Oh, yes I can . . . I've had a concealed weapons permit since I was in college. Dad said every girl should have one."

Jenkins looked at her. "Stay out of trouble, Cassandra."

Lee stood. "Yes, sir." Then she did an about-face and left.

It was a short walk to Yanty's cube, and he was there. "Well," the detective said, "a *double* suspension. You're lucky it wasn't a triple."

"They would if they could," Lee said sourly as she sat down.

"So you're out of here?"

"Yeah . . . I'm afraid so."

"Take this," Yanty said, and handed her a cell phone. It was one of the disposables that he kept for undercover use. Their eyes met. Nothing was said, but Lee understood. The shadow team was monitoring her phone—and it was possible that the assassins were, too.

"Thanks," Lee said as she slipped it into a pocket. "Say hi to Prospo for me." And with that, she left.

TWELVE

The Bonebreaker had to step over Cora's corpse in order to exit the house. Her eyes were open, and she was staring up at him. Both bodies had begun to stink—so it was a good time to leave. The Bonebreaker pulled the door closed and checked to ensure that it was locked.

The unassuming four-door sedan was parked in the driveway, and the Bonebreaker had a set of car keys taken from Cora's purse. Once outside he thumbed the remote and saw the parking lights flash on and off. How long would it be before a relative or an employer tried to reach the couple and, having failed to do so, would come to investigate? At least eight hours. And during that time the Bonebreaker figured he could drive the vehicle without worrying about the police pulling him over.

He opened the driver's side door, got in, and discovered that there was no need to push the seat back. A sure sign that Cora's husband had been the last person to drive the car. Not that it mattered. From the house in Northeast Los Angeles, it was a short drive to Glendale, where the Vasquez family lived. The Bonebreaker had called ten minutes earlier to request what he told Mrs. Vasquez was "a follow-up interview." To which she had responded by telling him that the family was grateful for Detective Lee's efforts to find the killer.

That served to confirm the Bonebreaker's impression that Lee was personally involved in the case—and gave him the opportunity to claim that he worked for her. A ploy calculated to piss Lee off once she learned of it.

It was a short drive to Glendale and the Vasquez residence. The Bonebreaker parked out front and made his way up the driveway with briefcase in hand. He was wearing the latex mask and skintight transparent finger cots that covered his fingertips. Though difficult to see, they weren't invisible. Still, odds were that if Mrs. Vasquez noticed them she would answer his questions nevertheless, and that was all he cared about.

The Bonebreaker rang the bell, and Mrs. Vasquez opened the door half a minute later. She led him into the living room where a young man was seated. That was a surprise and one the Bonebreaker would be forced to cope with. "My husband is at work," Mrs. Vasquez explained. "But Marty dropped by. He is . . . he *was* Rudy's best friend."

There was something about the way she said it, and the look on Marty's face, that claimed the Bonebreaker's attention. A good buddy would be interesting—and a lover even more so. He went over to shake hands. "I'm Detective Harmon . . . It's a pleasure to meet you. Did Detective Lee speak with you?"

Marty wore his hair short, was nicely dressed, and seemed to be more than a little uncomfortable. "No, sir," he replied.

"Well," the Bonebreaker said smoothly, "after Mrs. Vasquez and I finish our conversation, I'd like to ask you a couple of questions. Would that be okay?"

Marty shrugged. "Sure . . . I have to be at work by ten thirty, though. The restaurant opens at eleven."

"No problem," the Bonebreaker assured him. "Thank you."

Then, having turned his attention back to Mrs. Vasquez, the Bonebreaker produced a piece of paper with some scribbling on it. "Please allow me to apologize in advance," he said. "Some of my questions may be similar to those that Detective Lee already asked you. But that's how the process works. You'd be surprised at how many people remember additional details during their second interview."

Mrs. Vasquez nodded dutifully and answered each question. No, she didn't know who would want to kill her son. No, he didn't take drugs or gamble. "Rudy was a policeman," she said proudly. "He would never do bad things."

The conversation lasted about ten minutes and was completely unsatisfactory as far as the Bonebreaker was concerned. Up to that point he had been unable to gather any new information. Still, that meant Lee was SOL too, and that was interesting.

"Thank you," the Bonebreaker said as he folded the meaningless piece of paper and slipped it into the briefcase. "Here's an idea . . . I noticed a cafe out on the main arterial. Marty and I could go there and have a cup of coffee. That would leave you free to get on with your morning."

Both of the other parties seemed to like the idea—which suggested that neither one was entirely comfortable with the other. So the Bonebreaker and Marty said their good-byes and got into their respective cars. The Bonebreaker led the way, and Marty followed.

Five minutes later, the two of them were seated across from each other in the Green Onion cafe. It was a busy place that catered to a lot of what appeared to be regulars. Once their orders were placed the Bonebreaker got to the point. "Is Mrs. Vasquez correct? Rudy didn't use drugs? And he didn't gamble?"

"Heck no," Marty said. "Rudy was a full-on Eagle Scout."

"Okay," the Bonebreaker said. "So, how about Rudy's sex life . . . Was he straight? Or gay?"

"We were a couple until three months ago," Marty answered.

"What happened?"

Marty looked away. "I cheated on him. He caught me, and that was that. Rudy wasn't a second-chance kind of guy."

"I appreciate your honesty," the Bonebreaker said. "So, how about other lovers? Did he have other relationships after you two split?"

The coffee arrived at that point—so there was a short wait before the Bonebreaker got to hear Marty's reply. "I don't know for sure," he said. "But judging from what I've heard, the answer would be no. We met at a club called the Hi-Jinx—and friends tell me that Rudy was spending lots of time there."

The Bonebreaker felt a rising sense of interest. "Hoping to meet someone perhaps?"

Marty shrugged. "Yeah, probably."

The Bonebreaker had what he needed, which was a trail to follow. But it was necessary to go through the motions of asking more questions so he did. And when he cut Marty loose, the young man was clearly eager to leave. The Bonebreaker waited for Marty to exit the restaurant. Then, conscious of his skimpy budget, he left without paying the bill.

Two days had passed since Lee had been suspended. Two miserable days during which Lee wanted to work but couldn't. She awoke to the sound of a repetitive noise. She thought it was the alarm clock at first but then realized that her phone was ringing. She fumbled it on. "Lee here."

"This is Marvin," Codicil said. "I have some good news and some bad news."

Lee groaned. "Okay, give me the good news first."

"The findings of the shooting review board will be announced at 2:00 p.m., and I think both of us will be pleased with the results. You don't *have* to attend—but it would be good form to do so."

Lee yawned. "Good, thank you. I'll be there. And the bad news?"

"I had hoped that the Internal Affairs people would drop the other investigation," Codicil replied. "But they didn't. So you are scheduled to sit down with them at 3:00 p.m. today. I will be present as well. Let's discuss that immediately after the announcement by the shooting review board."

Lee wanted to ask questions but knew why she couldn't. The shadow team was tapping her phone, and for all she knew, Heevy's assassins were as well. And that's why the line had been left active . . . So that the techies could look for an additional tap and try to trace it. "Got it," Lee said. "I'll see you at HQ. Thanks."

Lee got up after that, took a shower, and got dressed. A two-piece suit seemed like the most appropriate choice even though she couldn't wear that and ride the bike, too.

And, since Lee would have to enter the building through the lobby, and pass through a metal detector, the gun would have to remain at home. That left her feeling naked.

Lee took a taxi downtown, made her way through security, and was cleared to go upstairs. Once on the third floor she was able to corral both Yanty and Prospo for a meeting that they weren't supposed to have. It took place in a small conference room behind closed doors. "So, how's it going?" Lee wanted to know. "Have we made any progress?"

"I don't know that you could call it progress," Prospo said soberly. "But it looks like the Bonebreaker paid a visit to Mrs. Vasquez."

"What?" Lee demanded. "How so?"

"A man claiming to be Detective Lou Harmon called, made an appointment, and stopped by the house," Prospo replied. "We found out about the visit when Mrs. Vasquez tried to call you and was referred to me. She wanted to thank you for putting another person on the case."

"The bastard," Lee said tightly. "He chose Harmon in order to piss us off."

"True," Yanty agreed mildly. "And we know it was him because only he could have Harmon's ID. And that supports our theory. The Bonebreaker *didn't* kill Vasquez, and he's trying to tell us that."

"So what did Wolfe and Jenkins say?"

Prospo made a face. "They took it upstairs. But Chief Corso wasn't buying. He says the fact that the Bonebreaker stopped by could mean that he's trying to see how much we know, he's rolling in his own shit, or he's jerking us around."

"So you aren't allowed to work the imposter theory?"

"It's the old chicken-and-egg problem," Yanty said. "We aren't supposed to look at the imposter theory unless we have hard evidence to support it and, since we aren't looking for that sort of evidence, we aren't likely to find any. The whole thing is bullshit."

After the get-together with Prospo and Yanty, Lee made her way to the conference room where the shooting review board was scheduled to deliver their findings. And, in keeping with Codicil's prediction, it was a good shoot. The killing had been justified—and Lee could return to duty.

Unfortunately, the suspension was still in effect pending the findings of the IA investigators into "... what may have been unauthorized travel and activities during the time that Detective Lee was on administrative leave." So any good feelings that Lee might have felt at that moment were erased by the knowledge that her job was still on the line. And that was very much on her mind as she went to meet with Codicil in the cafeteria.

"One down, and one to go," the lawyer said matter-of-factly, as they sat down. "Okay ... The best way to prepare for the interview is to review general concepts rather than rehearse lines. The thrust of your defense is that you suffered a job-related trauma so severe that the department not only put you on administrative leave, but placed you in the care of a psychologist. And that's where you need to open up and show some vulnerability.

"Mark my words, Cassandra ... Your hard-assed-cop persona is fine for the street, but it could hurt you here ... The 'nothing bothers me' manner that you project most of the time will give them the impression that the video of your father's death didn't bother you—and that would imply that you knew what you were doing when you entered the red zone. So keep that in mind. And cry if you can."

Lee wasn't about to cry—no damned way. But she understood what Codicil was telling her and promised to do her best. The interview lasted twenty minutes and Lee kept it simple. She was distraught, and when she received a letter from her dying mother, she took off for the red zone without checking on the rules. Then she found herself at the center of a family feud and left as quickly as she could. The end.

There were two investigators. One male and one female. Lee had met both on previous occasions but wasn't acquainted with either one of them. She marveled at how expressionless their faces were. Had they gone to a special class or something?

The male was a guy named Farrow. Detective Dave Farrow. He had a round face and the manner of a Jesuit priest.

The other investigator was a beady-eyed woman named Marlo Orkov. Her black bangs were so straight, they might have been cut with a laser—and Orkov's long nose was reminiscent of a bird's beak. And, judging from the expression on her face, she was sucking on a sour ball. "So," Orkov said, once Lee had finished her narrative. "You indicate that Dr. Kane can verify the severity of the trauma you suffered. But isn't it true that you are currently having an affair with the doctor? A fact that could influence what he says?"

Lee felt the blood rush to her face and saw Codicil frown from the corner of her eye. She had neglected to mention the relationship with Kane, and he was pissed. "Yes," Lee admitted reluctantly. "I guess it could."

Farrow nodded. "There's something else as well . . . According to the suspects arrested on the pier—you killed a number of people during your visit to the red zone. And you were working for the LAPD at the time."

"Detective Lee was attacked and forced to defend herself," Codicil interjected. "And, as you stipulated, she was in the red zone at the time. Based on the way the department's regulations are written, they apply to members of the LAPD who are operating in the city of Los Angeles. No mention is made of the red zone. That means that Detective Lee was under no obligation to follow departmental regulations while visiting the Republic of Texas."

The look that Orkov directed at the attorney was so pointed that Lee feared it would strike him dead. But Codicil smiled as if immune to anything other than an actual spear. "Is there anything else?" he inquired sweetly.

Farrow shook his head. "We will submit our report in a week or so . . . Until that time Detective Lee's suspension remains in effect. You can and should report to work . . . But your activities will be limited to administrative matters. Is that clear?"

Lee nodded. "Yes, it is."

"Good. This hearing is adjourned."

Lee left the room with Codicil right behind her. Once they were out in the hall, she turned, and he took her to task. "That was stupid, Cassandra. *Very* stupid. If you want to keep your job you must tell me *everything*. Is there anything more that I should know?"

Lee shook her head. "No, that's it."

* * *

Cora and her husband had been found by a relative who, having been unable to reach them via phone, entered the house with predictable results. All of the media outlets carried similar stories. Why had such a nice couple been murdered for what couldn't have been more than a few hundred dollars? It was tragic, it was scary, and the police were determined to find the killer or killers.

Meanwhile, the Bonebreaker had been holed up in a motel waiting to see what would happen. By now the police should know that he wasn't responsible for the Vasquez murder and that a copycat killer was on the loose. All they had to do was announce that, clear his name, and he'd be able to return home.

But no . . . Either the idiots didn't know that somebody was pretending to be him, or they did and had chosen to let the imposter get away with it. That's why the Bonebreaker was going to visit the Hi-Jinx Club. He had abandoned the first stolen car shortly after meeting with Marty and was riding in a taxi. The Bonebreaker waited for the car to pass the club on the right, told the driver to pull over, and paid the exact fare. Tips were a luxury he couldn't afford.

The club wasn't open yet and wouldn't be until midafternoon. So the Bonebreaker had time to kill. Sunshine was a rarity for the Bonebreaker, and as he ambled down the street, he gloried in the warmth of it on his neck and hands. Were it not for the sound of God's voice in his ear and the mission he had accepted, the Bonebreaker would have been in San Diego. He wouldn't need much . . . Just a room within walking distance of a beach. Then he would go fishing every day. Never mind the fact that he didn't know anything about the sport. It was the idea of doing something while doing nothing that appealed to him.

Such were the Bonebreaker's thoughts as he bought a paper and carried it into a small bakery. There, with a sweet roll and coffee at his elbow, he read the *LA Times*. It felt strange to eat while wearing the mask—but it didn't take long to get used to it.

After breakfast the Bonebreaker walked another three blocks to the Rialto Cinemaplex. It was open twenty-four hours a day and was the perfect place to get off the street. And for twenty nu he could watch all four of the movies that were currently playing.

So with the briefcase at his side, the Bonebreaker bought a ticket and made his way through the lobby to Theatre 3, where an escapist fantasy called *One World* was about to start. According to the ads he'd seen on TV, the story was based on the premise that the effort to spread the plague had been foiled by a team of brave CIA agents. A stupid plot to say the least. But a scenario in which the Bonebreaker's family would still be alive. And that appealed to him. The darkness took him in.

The Bonebreaker watched three movies, and consumed a large bag of popcorn, before falling asleep in the middle of the fourth. And by the time he woke up the film was starting over. So he got up, took the briefcase off the seat next to him, and made his way out into the quickly fading sunlight. A glance at his watch confirmed that the Hi-Jinx Club was open, but just barely. And the Bonebreaker knew that a man of his age and appearance would stick out in a nightspot that was mostly empty. Besides, it was dinnertime.

After a short walk he happened across the Athena Restaurant. A menu was posted in the window. There was no chicken noodle soup; nor did the Bonebreaker expect to find any. There was mention of Greek Lemon Chicken soup however . . . And he figured that it might be an acceptable substitute. So he went inside and was shown to a small, linen-covered table. It was positioned so he could place his back against a wall and keep an eye on the front door. Had it been otherwise, it would have been necessary to request a different table.

The Bonebreaker ordered the Lemon Chicken soup and was more than satisfied when it arrived. Not only was it thick, hearty, and flavorful—the triangles of pita bread were the perfect accompaniment. In fact, he was *so* satisfied with the meal that he actually paid the tab.

The Bonebreaker felt an increasing sense of fear as he walked the short distance to the Hi-Jinx Club. Not regarding the possibility of being arrested—because there was very little chance of that. No, the anxiety stemmed from the fact that he would have to mix with a large group of people. Something he perceived as being threatening in and of itself. It had to be done however . . . So he kept going despite the empty feeling in his gut and a case of sweaty palms.

The Bonebreaker heard the primal thump, thump, thump of bass well before he arrived at the front of the club. And the sound was nearly deafening once he went inside. The place was packed with customers, most of whom were male. A DJ was hard at work next to the dance floor, clutching his headphones to his ears, and bobbing his head to the music.

About a dozen people were dancing and the rest were seated at small tables with drinks in front of them. Just as he had expected, the crowd trended younger rather than older, and he felt out of place. He wanted to talk to people but where to start? Maybe the bartender could help.

The Bonebreaker approached the bar, waited his turn, and made his pitch. It was necessary to raise his voice in order to be heard over the music. "Hi! My name is Nathan Como . . . I'm a reporter from the *LA Times*. My editor asked me to write a story about Officer Vasquez—and one of his friends told me that he was a regular here. Could you point me at someone who knew him? I'd like to get some background stuff. You know, so our readers can get a feel for the real person."

The bartender was extremely busy and eager to rid himself of the reporter. "Sure thing . . . See the guys at that table? The one next to the tall plant? Both of them knew Rudy. You're going to say nice things about him, right?"

"Absolutely. Everyone I've talked to agrees that he was a good person."

"All right then. I'll send a drink over. What will it be?"

The Bonebreaker didn't drink. So he named the first thing that came to mind. "A bourbon on the rocks."

"Got it," the bartender said. "It's on the house."

The Bonebreaker felt awkward, and his stomach was churning as he made his way over to the table next to the tall plant. "Excuse me . . . The bartender said you might be able to help me. I'm a reporter for the *LA Times*—and I'm writing a piece about Officer Vasquez. I'd love to get your impressions of him."

"Have a seat," the man with blond hair and wire-rimmed glasses said. "I'm Peter."

"And I'm Jim," the other man said. He had a buzz cut, a nose stud, and lots of tattoos. "We were friends of Rudy's. What a terrible tragedy."

"Yes," the Bonebreaker said lamely as he pulled a chair up to the table. "As you probably know, this is where he was seen last. Were either one of you here that night?"

"I was," Peter replied soberly. "Rudy was in a good mood or seemed to be."

"I see," the Bonebreaker said, as his drink arrived. "So what kind of person was he? How would you describe him?"

Everything that Peter and Jim had to say during the next five minutes was positive—and that was what the Bonebreaker expected to hear. He let the men run on and took meaningless notes as they did so. Then he bought them a round of drinks. "So," he said, as the waitress departed, "what was Rudy doing that evening? Just hanging out?"

"He was basket shopping," Peter replied. "And that's how he wound up with Prince Charming."

"Who?"

"A guy I had never seen before. They were sitting over there." He pointed to a table that was about fifteen feet away. "Rudy was pretty picky—so I figured nothing would come of it. But no . . . They left together."

The Bonebreaker knew that much from watching the news. "Officer Vasquez left the bar in the company of a man with dark hair." And so on and so on. Which meant the Bonebreaker knew no more than he had thirty minutes earlier. And that was what he was thinking about when another man approached the table. "Hey, Peter . . . Hey, Jim . . . I hear we have a reporter in the house."

Peter made the introductions. "Nathan, this is Julio, and Julio, this is Nathan Como. He's with the *LA Times*."

"And you're writing a story about Rudy," Julio said as he sat down. "That's why I came over . . . I ran into Rudy out in the parking lot the night he disappeared. If only I'd had a premonition or something . . . Maybe I could have prevented his death."

The Bonebreaker was interested. "So you saw the man Rudy left with."

"Saw him? Yes. Rudy asked me to take a picture with my phone and e-mail it to him."

The Bonebreaker felt his heart beat a little bit faster. "And did you?"

"Yes . . . Just a sec . . . I'll find it."

The Bonebreaker took a sip of bourbon and wished he hadn't. It was horrible. "Here you go," Julio said. "Look at this."

The Bonebreaker accepted the phone. And sure enough, there was Rudy, smiling into the camera. Unfortunately the man standing to his right was looking away. By accident? Or on purpose? There was no way to know. But the Bonebreaker figured that some sort of picture was better than none.

That was when he noticed that there was a *second* picture . . . One that seemed to have been taken immediately after the first. The two men were turning away. And that picture showed the back end of a pickup truck. "What's going on here?" the Bonebreaker inquired.

"I was going to take a second shot, but Rudy's friend said, 'Let's go . . .' And they turned to go. I meant to delete it."

"I'd like to have the picture of Rudy," the Bonebreaker said. "Would it be okay if I e-mailed it to myself?"

"Sure," Julio said. "Have at it."

So the Bonebreaker selected *both* pictures and sent them to an anonymous e-mail address. "Did you share the photo of Rudy with the police?"

"Yup," Julio answered as he took the phone back. "They said it wasn't good enough to be of any help."

"No," the Bonebreaker said, "I suppose it wouldn't be. Well, thank you very much. I have some great quotes from you guys—and that will give my article some additional depth."

Then, after a round of good-byes, the Bonebreaker left. It was dark outside, and a bit chilly, as he called a cab. The car took ten minutes to arrive. Lights were mounted underneath the chassis so that the *especiale* seemed to float over a pool of lavender light.

The Bonebreaker got into the backseat and gave the driver a destination that was about half a mile away from the ossuary. Then, as the cab pulled away from the curb, he checked his e-mail. Both photos were waiting. But it was the second that he cared about. Because there, attached to the truck's back bumper, was a California license plate.

THIRTEEN

When Lee went to work on Monday morning, she found herself in a strange state of suspended animation. Although she'd been cleared by the shooting review board, Lee was still under a partial suspension, and deskbound. So there she was, feeling frustrated, when two dozen red roses arrived. And since the receptionist who brought them had been forced to cross the bullpen in order to reach her desk, the flowers caused quite a stir. "Oh my God," someone said, as the bouquet landed on Lee's desk. "Look at that! Doesn't he know that she prefers ammo?"

"Who *is* this guy?" another detective demanded. "Maybe we should run him for wants and warrants."

"Clear the area," a third said, "and call the bomb squad!"

Lee offered all of them a one-fingered salute before thanking the receptionist and plucking the card off the packaging. It read:

Dear Cassandra,

Please join me at 11:30 for lunch at Alessandro's. My phone is off, so you can't say no.

Love, Lawrence

Lee knew that Alessandro's was only two blocks away and

had clearly been chosen for her convenience. And had she not been on suspension, she would have said no. But she was on suspension, she needed a morale boost, and Kane was the answer. *Are you getting serious about him?* the voice inquired, as she checked her watch. "No, maybe, yes," she replied. "No, make that *hell* yes." There were catcalls as she departed for lunch.

The Bonebreaker wanted to gather all the information he could prior to the meeting with Lee. It took only a few minutes for him to sign into a tracing service with a false name, transfer five cred coins, and enter the imposter's license-plate number in the search box. The results came back quickly. It seemed that the vehicle in question was registered to Mr. Alvin Hoffler. And his address was in Nuevo, California, a community the Bonebreaker had never heard of.

A quick check revealed that it was about an hour east of LA. So far so good. All he had to do was create a new disguise, steal a car, and drop in for a visit. After he killed Hoffler, the Bonebreaker would have a late dinner and return home. Mission accomplished.

So the Bonebreaker spent the balance of the day getting ready and left the ossuary just after dark. His persona was different this time. The mask was called "The Farmer" and made the Bonebreaker look as though he'd spent years out in the sun.

He exited the area via an old storm drain. It was dry but still hard on the knees. The trash-strewn concrete pipe led under a street and into an open channel. That allowed the Bonebreaker to stand and make his way up onto the sidewalk. From there it was a ten-minute walk to a bus stop. A short ride took him into what most people thought of as a bad neighborhood. That was where he got off the bus and wandered down a half-lit side street. There were houses, but only half of them appeared to be occupied, and they had bars over their windows.

The straw cowboy hat, the denims, and the canvas shopping bag were bait. And it didn't take long to get a nibble. A car passed, then braked. Two men got out and came his way. The Bonebreaker paused and began to back away. "Hey, farm boy," the one on the right said. "We're a little light on cash . . . How 'bout you lend us a twenty?"

"Yeah," the guy on the left said. "And we'll pay you back in a couple of years." Both of them laughed.

The gangbanger on the right was a tiny bit closer, so the Bonebreaker shot him first. One in the head and one in the chest. What professionals referred to as a double tap. The little bullets didn't pack much punch, but dead is dead.

Leftie, as the Bonebreaker thought of him, had good reactions. By that time the street thug had jerked the nine-mil from the waistband of his pants and was bringing it to bear. But the .22 was already on target and spitting bullets. The thug jerked spastically as six rounds hit various parts of his anatomy. Then he said, "Shit," and fell over backwards.

The Bonebreaker had two bullets left in the magazine and waited to see if a third person would emerge from the car. None did. So he wandered about picking up empty casings until he had all eight. There hadn't been much noise, so it was possible that the locals were entirely unaware of the murders, but the Bonebreaker figured that some of them knew . . . And didn't want to get involved.

The car was in park, with the engine running. All the Bonebreaker had to do was slide in behind a ridiculously small steering wheel, grab the glowing skull, and pull the shifter into drive. The main risk at that point was that the owner of the vehicle was wanted for something—and the police were looking for the car. But that was a chance the Bonebreaker was willing to take.

Thanks to light traffic it took an hour and seven minutes to reach the town of Nuevo on Interstate 215. And that was ten minutes less than what the Bonebreaker had expected. Nuevo wasn't much of a town and it didn't take him long to reach the Hoffler residence. The ancient double-wide was parked on a dry lot between a couple of small homes made of cinder blocks. A pickup truck was parked in the driveway though . . . And that was promising.

The Bonebreaker pulled in, killed the lights, and took a moment to refill magazine number one. Then, with a fully loaded pistol in hand, he got out of the car and crossed the street. A dog began to bark from the lot on the right—and the Bonebreaker made a mental note to keep an eye out for the animal.

Gravel crunched under the Bonebreaker's boots as he walked up the drive and paused to inspect the license plate on the back end of the truck. It appeared to be brand-new, and the numbers were different from the plate in Julio's photo. *Why?*

He made his way past the truck and up to the front porch. As he stood in the spill of light from the naked bulb over his head, and rang the doorbell, the Bonebreaker could hear the sound of a TV inside. When there was no reaction he pressed the button again. "I'm coming, goddamn it," a male voice said. "Hold your fucking horses."

Then there was a squeal of unoiled hinges as the door opened and an old man appeared. He was about six feet tall, had at least two days' worth of stubble on his sallow cheeks, and was holding a sawed-off shotgun. It was pointed at the Bonebreaker's midriff. "Yeah?" the geezer inquired. "Who the fuck are *you*? And why do I care?"

Suddenly the Bonebreaker found himself in the unaccustomed position of being both surprised and seriously outgunned. And judging from his attitude, and the smell of alcohol associated with him, the old man wouldn't hesitate to jerk both triggers. The Bonebreaker swallowed. "Sorry to bother you," he said hesitantly. "I'm looking for the owner of a truck with license plate 3HUA17."

"What the fuck for?" the old man demanded.

The conversation wasn't going the way the Bonebreaker had planned—so he was forced to improvise. "I scraped a fender on a truck with that number," he said lamely. "And I want to pay for the damage. Are you Mr. Hoffler?"

"Yes," the man said. "I am. You must have written the number down *before* some bastard stole my plates. I didn't notice no scrape though."

The Bonebreaker was already backing away while holding the .22 tight against his leg. "I guess there was some sort of mix-up then. Sorry . . . Have a good evening." And with that he turned and left.

"Shit, shit, shit," the Bonebreaker said under his breath as he returned to the car. The imposter was still on the loose—and his best lead was in the toilet. Life sucked.

The lights were low, the dance music was loud, and Jennifer Baxter was sitting alone. That wasn't unusual because while Baxter had a good figure she wasn't especially pretty. "Handsome" was the adjective her mother liked to use. And Baxter felt a twinge of pain every time she heard it. Men were handsome. Horses were handsome. But girls? Never.

There had been men in her life though . . . Not a lot, but some, most of whom had been met online. But Baxter was tired of sitting in front of her computer reading carefully worded profiles. So she was at a club called Jambo's. Located on the Sunset Strip, it had a Caribbean theme and was momentarily hip. Two drinks. That was her limit. Then she'd go home. Roll call for the West Bureau's Pacific Area was at 0700, and she was always on time.

That's what Baxter was thinking about when a good-looking guy with dark brown hair made eye contact with her from a stool at the bar. He smiled, and she smiled in return. Thus encouraged, he got up and made his way over to the tiny two-person table. "Hi, can I join you?"

"Sure," Baxter said as she wondered what was taking place. This guy was an eight and she was a six. Okay, a five-point-five . . . So she was wary.

"My name is Mike," he said. "And you are?"

"Jennifer. But my friends call me Jenny."

"It's a pleasure to meet you, Jenny," Mike said formally. Then he smiled self-consciously. "Sorry, I'm not very good at this sort of thing."

"Good," Baxter said. "Neither am I. So what *are* you good at?"

"I'm a vet," Mike said. "Not a dog-and-cat vet, although I treat some of those, but I have what's called a large-animal practice."

"Like horses?"

"Exactly. And cows, donkeys, and a llama named Alfred. I

had to hit the books in order to take care of him. Did you know that llamas evolved on the plains of North America?"

Baxter *didn't* know ... But soon found herself laughing at Mike's vet stories and, after some prompting, told him that she was a cop. Baxter knew from previous experience that her profession was a turnoff to some—especially those who had a few grams of cocaine on them. On the other hand it was a turn-on for guys who were into S&M. They wanted her to cuff and whip them.

But Mike wasn't interested in her handcuffs or role-playing. He asked questions about her work, laughed at her cop stories, and was clearly having a good time. So they had a round of drinks. And eventually Baxter went to the ladies' room. When she returned Mike was gone. That hurt, and she was reaching for her jacket, when he returned carrying a bowl of the crispy palm fritters that Jambo's specialized in. "I don't know about you," he said, "but I could use something to nibble on."

Baxter felt a sense of relief as she let go of the jacket. They talked some more, and by the time Mike suggested that they visit a bar farther up the strip, Baxter was feeling a bit woozy. *I won't have any more drinks,* she thought to herself. *But it's too early to bail out. Half an hour. Then I'll go home.*

So Mike paid the tab—and they left together. "Let's take my rig," Mike suggested. "I'll bring you back later."

By that time, Baxter felt too dizzy to drive and was happy to accept his offer. Mike's "rig," as he called it, was a big 4x4 pickup with a canopy on the back. "I have to carry a lot of vet gear," he explained. "So she takes a beating."

It required an act of will to climb up into the crew cab. And once there Baxter felt as if she was going to faint. "I'm sorry," she said. "I don't feel ..." Then came the long, dizzy fall into nothingness.

Mike saw Baxter's head slump forward onto her chest and grinned. The Zolpidem was working. But was she well and truly out? He reached over to pinch her arm. Yes, indeedy ... Out like a light. So Mike leaned over to kiss her unresponsive lips—and to squeeze a firm breast. That was when he found the snub nosed .38 in the shoulder holster. Just like Vasquez . . . Except he wore his on his belt. The cops were still chasing their tails on that one . . . Still looking for the Bonebreaker! Mike laughed out loud. *They're so stupid*, he thought, *and as long as they keep looking for the Bonebreaker, I'll be in the clear.*

Mike put the revolver in his pocket. *Who knows?* he thought. *Maybe I'll shoot her with it! Not in the head, but in an arm, or a leg.* But the fun stuff would come later. At the moment it was time to secure her wrists, her ankles, and strap her into the seat. And thanks to the truck's tinted windows, nobody would be able to see what he was doing.

Once Baxter's restraints were in place he started the engine, turned the lights on, and pulled out of the lot. Six blocks later he pulled around a corner and into a patch of shadow. It took less than five seconds to put the surgical gloves on and jump out. A couple of magnets held the stolen plates in place—and once removed they could be thrown away. Then it was a simple matter to mount the correct ones on and reenter the cab. Life was good . . . And death was even better.

Everyone, mutants included, had come to call the area "Freaktown." That didn't make it right of course. But all of the efforts to rename the neighborhood had failed. And for the moment the area that catered to visiting mutants was stuck with the name. Even if it was offensive to those who had to stay there.

And in spite of the danger of being infected with *B. nosilla*, some of LA's norms chose to visit Freaktown for a variety of reasons. Some liked to visit the clubs where they could mix with mutants, some wanted to listen to a form of jazz called "Red Rag," and some went there to eat the famously spicy freak food. And, in spite of the LAPD's continual efforts to close the brothels down, mutant prostitutes were quite popular.

So as Lee drove down the main drag she saw lots of neon. She could hear the thump, thump, thump of bass through the open window and could see the groups of people congregated around the neighborhood's most popular bars. Most of them were wearing spit masks. But spit masks with a difference. They came in all shapes and sizes and were highly personalized. So much so that no two were alike. That allowed for a high degree of anonymity as well as protecting them against *B. nosilla*. And as any cop knows, when people believe they can't be identified, they are much more likely to act out. The result being public nudity, fistfights, and the occasional riot. And who had to try and keep the lid on? The police department, that's who—and it was a largely thankless task.

The car's nav system told Lee to turn right and she did. The address had been supplied by the Bonebreaker twenty-one minutes earlier. She'd been brushing her teeth at the time, getting ready for bed, when the cell phone rang, and her heart jumped. "Half an hour," he said in her ear. "You, and you alone. Here's the address."

So there she was, turning onto a street that led away from the action, and into the surrounding darkness. There were some lights to be seen in the surrounding buildings but not many. No one lived in the so-called back blocks unless they had no other choice. "Take a left at the next corner," the navigator told her, and Lee obeyed.

"Turn right in one hundred feet," the voice advised. "You have arrived at your destination."

Most of the streetlights had been shot out, but there, in the spill of a solitary lamp an empty lot could be seen. Judging from the look of it the open space had been home to a building at one time. But it had burned, been demolished to make way for a defunct redevelopment project, or cleared to discourage squatters.

Whatever the reason, the lot was empty except for a lone vehicle—and when Lee saw it, she assumed that there had been some sort of mistake. Surely the Bonebreaker wouldn't be the sort of person to drive a low-slung, gangster-style *especiale*, complete with bright yellow paint and red flames! Yet there it was.

Lee was about to pass the lot and regroup when the *especiale*'s lights flashed on and off. Maybe it was him. Or maybe it was a drug dealer who thought she was someone else. Lee braked, took hold of the Glock with her right hand, and steered with her left. Then she entered the lot and pulled in nose to tail so that her window was only a foot from his. It was a cop thing. A way to chat with another officer without getting out and without losing contact with the dispatcher. And there, looking out through the other window, was a farmer. Or what *looked* like a farmer. Although Lee felt sure that it was a disguise. "There you are," the man said cheerfully. "Right on time. I think punctuality is important. Don't you?"

"Yes, I do," Lee replied. "Although I suspect it's one of the few things we can agree on."

"Don't be too sure of that," the Bonebreaker replied over the soft mutter of his engine. "Are you holding a gun?"

"Yes, I am. A .45."

The Bonebreaker laughed. It had a dry, raspy quality. "Me too. See? We're more alike than you'd care to believe."

"Maybe," Lee allowed. "Although you're a serial killer, and I'm not."

"Ah, but you are," the Bonebreaker responded. "The word 'serial' means 'of, forming, or arranged in a series.' And I think it's safe to say that you have killed far more people than I have! The latest being only a few days ago. And you enjoy it, don't you? Of course you do . . . You enjoy it because it's what you do well."

Lee knew that the first part of his statement was true. How many people had she killed anyway? It was something she didn't want to think about. But was the Bonebreaker right? Did she *enjoy* it? No, not in the way he meant. *He's trying to mindfuck you*, Lee told herself. *Be careful.*

"Perhaps you're right," she replied out loud. "And who knows? Maybe I'll run up the score tonight. You were masquerading as Detective Lou Harmon when you met with Mrs Vasquez. Tell me why I shouldn't send you to the place where all of your victims are waiting for you?"

"Because you need my help solving the Vasquez murder," the Bonebreaker replied. "You'll have to choose. Which do you want more? Revenge for what I did to Harmon? Not to mention your father . . . Or to catch the man responsible for offing Vasquez? The man who might kill *more* cops. It's up to you."

"You make me sick."

"The feeling is mutual. So what's it going to be?"

"If you have a photo of the vehicle Officer Vasquez left the Hi-Jinx Club in I'd like to see it." It was a peace offering of sorts. Because the truth was that Lee *did* need him, and more than that, was waiting for him to make a mistake.

The Bonebreaker gave her the printout with his left hand since his right was full of gun. Lee turned the overhead light on in order to risk a look. The picture showed the back end of a pickup truck. It was equipped with a heavy-duty bumper and a California license plate. "I traced the number to a Mr. Hoffler in Nuevo," the Bonebreaker said. "But the plate was stolen."

Lee turned the light off. "That means the imposter had the foresight to steal plates and put them on his truck *before* he took Vasquez," Lee mused.

"And that supports my thesis that he isn't acting on impulse," the Bonebreaker said. "That makes him even more dangerous."

"Like you."

"Yes, like me."

"Okay, what do you want?"

"I want you to run a computer check on all of the pickups registered in the town of Nuevo. If one of them matches the vehicle in the picture then bingo! We have him."

Lee had already made up her mind to do that. Because there were few, if any, standard-production cars left, every vehicle was photographed as part of the registration process. Sure, there were likely to be hundreds of pickups in a town like Nuevo. But it wouldn't be all that difficult to sort them manually.

Plus there was something else. Something the Bonebreaker hadn't mentioned. There was a black-on-white DMV sticker on the bumper . . . And a vise. What did that suggest? A plumber, perhaps? She'd seen utility trucks that had a vise mounted on the back bumper. "Okay," she said. "I'll take care of it."

"And you'll let me know what you find out?"

"I'll give you a general idea, yes. But I won't give you a name and address."

"Why not?" the Bonebreaker inquired innocently.

"Because you'd go over there and kill him."

The Bonebreaker shook his head. "No way . . . If I kill him, no one will know why he died. But if *you* take him in, or kill him, everyone will know that he was an imposter."

"Okay, I get that . . . But my answer is the same. I guess we're done here."

"I guess we are."

Lee took her foot off the brake and pulled away. The Bonebreaker waited until her lights disappeared. He assumed Lee had memorized his plates and might or might not be in the process of putting out an APB on the *especiale*. He got out, opened the trunk, and removed a can of gas. After splashing it all over the car, he lit a match and gave it a toss. There was a loud whump, and a ball of fire lit up the lot. The Bonebreaker admired it for a second, turned, and walked away. The meeting had been a success.

Yanty was getting ready for bed when a cell phone began to chime. There were three phones on top of his dresser--and it took a moment to figure out which one to answer. He thumbed it on. "Yeah?"

"This is Lee," the voice on the other end of the line said. "I'm going to send you a photo of a back bumper and a plate. According to my source, this is the vehicle that Vasquez was in the night he disappeared. But the plate was stolen from a vehicle in Nuevo. That suggests that the perp might live there. So I suggest that you run a check on all of the pickups in the area. Who knows? Maybe you'll get a match."

"You're kidding," Yanty replied. "I'm supposed to match trucks from a single photo? A bumper photo at that?"

"Yes," Lee said. "And it may not be as difficult as you think. The truck we're looking for has a black-on-white sticker with the letters 'DMV' on it. And DMV typically stands for Doctor of Veterinary Medicine. Plus a vise is mounted on the right side of the bumper. So those items could be visible in the DMV photos."

"They could be," Yanty agreed, "but I doubt it. Assuming the truck belongs to a vet, he or she probably added them *after* completing the registration process."

"True," Lee admitted. "But it's worth a try."

Yanty was silent for a moment. "Are you still on suspension?"

"Yes."

Yanty groaned. "Who is the source you mentioned?"

"I'm sorry, Dick, I can't tell you."

"But they're for real?"

"Yeah, definitely."

"Okay," he said reluctantly. "I'll see what I can do."

"Thanks," Lee said. "I won't forget." There was a click as the call ended.

Yanty was pulling his pants on as his wife entered the bedroom. "What are you doing?"

"Going to work."

"*Why?*"

"Because I'm an idiot, that's why."

She smiled and kissed him on the cheek. "Be careful, honey." And with that she went to bed.

Baxter had a headache when she woke up. And she was cold. So very, very cold. The reason for that became evident as she opened her eyes. She was lying on a concrete floor and she was naked. *Why?*

The bar, the man, and the drinks. Baxter felt a sinking sensation as all of it came rushing back. She'd been stupid . . . And her first reaction was a feeling of embarrassment. How would she explain this to her cop friends? The teasing would last forever.

Then, as she struggled to stand, the reality of the situation set in. There was a strong possibility that she'd never see her friends again. And a good chance that the man who called himself Mike was going to kill her. Baxter felt an emptiness in the pit of her stomach. She was afraid. *Don't be afraid,* she told herself. *Escape.*

Baxter forced herself to concentrate as she examined the six-foot-by-six-foot cell. What light there was came from a small window high above her head. The ceiling, the walls, and the floor were made of concrete. There was a drain in the middle of the floor. So Mike could hose the room down if he needed to.

Baxter shuddered. And there, next to the metal fire door, sat two bowls. Both were made of stainless steel. One was filled with what looked like Cheerios—and the other was filled with water. Her spirits fell.

Then Baxter noticed an unexpected odor. A smell that reminded her of Uncle Harry's horse farm. She remembered the conversation in the bar. "I'm a vet." That's what Mike had said. Not a dog-and-cat vet but a large-animal doctor. And that's where she was—locked inside some sort of barn.

Baxter shivered. Is that what she was to him? An animal? She wrapped her arms around herself in a futile attempt to stay warm. The tears wanted to flow, but she refused them. "I'm a cop," Baxter whispered to herself. "And cops don't cry."

Lee couldn't sleep and got up early. A run . . . that would feel good. Then she'd go to work and see what, if anything, was new. She made coffee and turned on the TV. The weather came up first, followed by the news that an Aztec spy ring had been uncovered in San Francisco, and an update on the *B. nosilla* breakout up in Oregon.

Then came the lead-in that caused Lee to turn the volume up. "An LAPD officer is missing this morning. Officials tell LA-7 that Patrol Officer Jennifer Baxter failed to show up at work today—and was last seen at a club called Jambo's. A police spokesperson says that it is far too early to speculate regarding what happened to Baxter. But coworkers tell Channel 7 that she's very reliable—and they suspect foul play. Some even went so far as to suggest the possibility that Baxter was abducted by the serial killer called the Bonebreaker. This follows the recent murder and dismemberment of Officer Vasquez . . . A killing that's consistent with the Bonebreaker's MO."

Lee swore and went to get the disposable cell phone that Yanty had given her. She took it into the bathroom. There weren't any e-mails from Yanty . . . But there was a message from ENOB9. "It wasn't me. I was with you!" Lee didn't know whether to laugh or cry. She was the Bonebreaker's alibi!

But that didn't matter . . . What mattered was Jennifer Baxter.

Lee hurried to get ready for work, called a taxi, and was lying in wait when Prospo arrived in the office. "Lee? What's up? Besides you, that is?"

"I heard about Baxter. I came in."

"Don't worry, we're on it."

"Do you think the Bonebreaker took her?"

There was a pause. Prospo looked left and right as if to make sure that none of the other detectives could hear him. "I'm not sure that we should discuss stuff like that. Not until they lift the suspension."

"The simple answer is no, we shouldn't," Lee replied. "So, like I said, do you think the Bonebreaker took her?"

Prospo laughed. "You have ovaries . . . That's for sure. No, *I* don't. But a yo-yo who *claims* to be the Bonebreaker called in, and the brass bought it."

"The *real* Bonebreaker would never do that," Lee said. "He takes, he kills, and he dumps the body. *Then* he brags about it."

"Tell it to the chief . . . The last thing he and the mayor want is a *second* serial killer for the media to criticize them about."

"So we'll have to do it the hard way," Lee replied. "You're working the Baxter case?"

"Yanty and I are working both the Vasquez and the Baxter cases."

"Good. I want to visit Baxter's home."

"I can't do that," Prospo responded. "Talking to you about the case is one thing . . . Letting you into Baxter's apartment is something else."

"She could be alive," Lee said.

"That's pure speculation."

"Yup, but it could be true, and you know it. She's one of us, Milo. Fuck the rules."

"Can my family move in with you if the department fires me?"

"My tent is your tent."

"Okay . . . It'll take a while to set it up. I'll let you know."

Once roll call was over Lee went to her desk and tried to do some paperwork. But it was difficult to concentrate and she was thankful when Prospo showed up. It was noon by then. "Come on," he said with a wink. "Let's get some lunch."

"I checked the schedule," Prospo said, on the way down to the parking garage. "None of our people will be there for the next hour or so."

"We'll keep it quick," Lee promised. "Thanks, Milo. You're okay in spite of what Yanty says."

Prospo laughed as they got in his creeper and headed up the ramp. It was midday, and that meant traffic was as light as it would ever be. And, since patrol officers weren't about to stop one of their own for going ten miles an hour over the limit, they made good time. Baxter's apartment was in West LA—a location that put her fairly close to work.

The building was a boxy nondescript affair that styled itself as Las Palmas even though the nearest palm tree was half a block away. There were a couple of stumps out front though—so maybe there had been palms at one time.

There was a row of parking spots and Prospo pulled into the one labeled "106." "They found her car at the club," he said.

"Just like Vasquez," Lee observed. "And, assuming that we're dealing with the same person, he's attractive to both men *and* women. So maybe he swings both ways . . . Or maybe he's a good actor. Do the descriptions match?"

"Mostly," Prospo said. "But it's hard to be certain. There were a lot of people in the Jambo club that night and the eyewitness accounts are vague."

"No photos then?" Lee inquired, as they followed a short flight of stairs up to the apartment house.

"Some grainy stuff," Prospo replied. "But nothing definitive. Follow me . . . I have a key."

Once inside the apartment Lee put her hands in her pockets rather than run the risk of touching anything. And she was careful to watch where she stepped as well—even though there was no reason to believe that a crime had been committed on the premises. Not yet anyway—but they wouldn't know for sure until the techs finished their work.

Lee's purpose was to learn more about Baxter. What kind of person was she? And, more importantly, what kind of *cop* was she?

The answers to both questions were quite apparent. Unlike

Lee's apartment, which was decorated man-style, Baxter's was girly. There were colorful prints on the walls, some droopy flowers on the kitchen table, and all of the furniture matched.

But it was easy to see that a cop lived there as well. A framed target was hanging in the hallway that led to the bedroom. All of the hits were in, or close to, the bull's-eye. A commendation hung next to it. That reminded Lee of the award she'd seen at Rudy Vasquez's apartment. And, judging from a black-and-white photo of Baxter posing in front of her cruiser, she was in good shape. A factor that might help her survive. "Okay," she said finally. "I've seen enough. Let's get while the getting is good."

Lee still couldn't drive a police car so Prospo took her home, promised to let her know about any major developments, and returned to HQ. Lee felt somewhat lost as she made her way up to the apartment. She left a message for Jenkins, letting him know where she was, and checked her e-mail. There was nothing of interest other than an update from Codicil. The IA investigators had yet to file their report but were supposed to do so soon.

The suspension was driving Lee crazy! She wanted to *do* something. So she called Yanty, knowing full well that he would let her know if he had anything to share. Her call went through this time. "Dick Yanty."

"Hi, Dick. Lee here. Any news?"

"Nothing so far," Yanty replied. "It turns out that there are a total of 356 pickups in Nuevo and the surrounding area—and I'm going through them as fast as I can. But now that we have the Baxter case to work on as well it's hard to find the time. Lieutenant Wolfe is all in—she's throwing everything we have at the case."

This is about the Baxter case, Lee thought to herself. But she knew Yanty was doing all he could. "Good," she replied. "Sorry to bother you. I promise not to call during the next half hour."

Yanty laughed. "No problem . . . I understand."

They said their good-byes and hung up. That left Lee with nothing to do. So rather than mope she forced herself to clean the bathroom. A chore she hated but one that left her with a feeling of satisfaction once she was done.

Then it was time to have lunch, watch the news, and take a

nap, the last being a treat she rarely got to enjoy. There was a lot of noise during the day, and there was a lot on her mind, so it took a while to fall asleep. But eventually she did. And she was hunting the Bonebreaker when one of her phones began to ring.

Lee sat up, realized that the call was coming in on her personal phone, and immediately thought of Kane. He'd been at a conference in San Diego. But when she eyed the screen, Lee saw a number she didn't recognize. "Hello, this is Cassandra Lee."

"And this," the voice on the end of the line said, is "Crystal Bye."

Lee was still sleepy and didn't recognize the name at first. Then it came to her . . . The assassin! Was the shadow team listening in? They were supposed to be. "Why weren't you on the pier?" Lee inquired sweetly. "It would be nice to meet you. We could compare guns or something."

"I was busy elsewhere," Bye replied. "But I'm here today . . . Look out your front window."

Lee grabbed the .45 on her way to the living room. The curtains were closed. As were the blinds beyond them. What would happen if she opened them? Would a sniper put a bullet in her head?

Lee stood to one side of the window and lifted a slat. That was when she saw the white van. The sign on the side read, AL'S PEST CONTROL. Was that Bye's idea of a joke? Or just a coincidence?

The vehicle was parked on the far side of the street in front of a deserted home. And there, standing in front of it, was a slender woman dressed in black with shoulder-length white hair. "Stay there," Lee said. "I'll be right down."

Bye laughed. "Stalling won't work, bitch . . . Your story is over. Bye-bye."

Suddenly a man carrying a pipe stepped out from behind the van. No, *not* a pipe . . . A rocket launcher! He brought the weapon up to his right shoulder and peered into a sight.

Lee turned and ran. She was halfway to the front door when the rocket struck. There was a loud explosion. A hole large enough to drive a car through appeared in the wall, flying shrapnel ripped into the walls, and the apartment erupted in flames.

* * *

Crystal Bye smiled enigmatically and nodded to the man with the rocket launcher. Mission accomplished. Then they got into the van and drove away. A police car with its siren bleating passed them going in the other direction. A fire truck followed. It was just another day in LA.

FOURTEEN

The force of the explosion threw Lee forward. She hit the floor hard. The phone flew out of her hand, but she was able to retain the .45, and that was good since Bye could be waiting outside. Lee did a push-up and stood. She could hear the fierce crackle of flames and feel the heat pressing against her back as her fingers fumbled with the door locks. All three of them were there to protect her. But now, as she was forced to take some of the thick black smoke deep into her lungs, there was a very real possibility that the locks were going to kill her.

Finally, as the last bolt was retracted into the door, Lee pushed it open. The .45 was up and ready to fire, but there weren't any targets. Lee gave thanks as she jammed the weapon into the small of her back and took a sharp turn to the right. Five other people lived in the four plex. That included the Dewey sisters, both of whom should be at work, and Mr. Henry. He had the apartment next to Lee's and was carrying a metal file box as he stumbled through the drifting smoke. She grabbed his arm and guided the old man down the stairs to the ground.

A fireman appeared out of the smoke. "Apartment 101!" Lee shouted. "Mrs. Reed is eighty-six years old and very slow."

"Got it," the man said. "Get away from the building." Then he vanished into the smoke.

Confident that Mr. Henry would be okay, Lee hurried off to make sure that the Dewey sisters really were at work and not home on vacation. The flames were confined to the second floor at that point—and the fire department was putting water on the blaze as Lee banged on the door marked 102. There was no response.

That was when Lee remembered the Road King and went to roll the bike down onto the street. The ignition key, her wallet, and everything else she owned was in the apartment. *Used to own,* Lee corrected herself, as she looked back.

A column of thick black smoke was rising from the scene, and in spite of the fire department's fast response, the dingbat's top floor had been destroyed. That was when Carla Zumin arrived, recognized Lee immediately, and ordered her camera operator to roll. "What happened?" the reporter inquired, as she shoved a mike into Lee's face.

"Somebody fired a rocket into my apartment," Lee answered. *"Why?"* Zumin demanded.

Lee turned to look into the camera and smiled. Half her face was covered with soot. "It's just a guess, mind you," she said. "But maybe they don't like me."

At that moment Lieutenant Wolfe and two members of the shadow team arrived and shooed Zumin away. But the reporter didn't care. She had what she needed . . . And it would hit the airwaves soon.

Dr. Michael Valentine was a busy man. That was because he was very good with horses, there were a lot of the animals in and around Nuevo, and all of them needed regular care. Care that included biannual vaccinations, worming, and occasional surgery.

There were other vets of course—but "Dr. Mike," as his clients called him, was the most personable of the bunch. He was also the easiest to look at. And that was helpful with most of his female clientele and some of the men too.

He was no fool though. Dr. Mike knew better than to attract attention to Nuevo by committing crimes there—and had always been careful to victimize people who lived elsewhere. To achieve sexual gratification Dr. Mike had to inflict pain. A predilection that had begun back in his college days with BDSM role-playing that evolved into a series of date rapes. During the years that followed, there had been some of what he categorized as "real" rapes and two related murders.

But as time passed Dr. Mike discovered that it took increasing amounts of violence to provide him with the level of gratification he sought. And that was how he came to play the part of the Bonebreaker. Because by using the predator's name he could have his fun and point the police in a direction they were inclined to go anyway.

Such was the logic behind both the Vasquez abduction and his most recent acquisition, a policewoman who was like a present waiting to be opened. But, he'd been too busy to enjoy her. This would change soon however. Those were Dr. Mike's thoughts as he pulled into the parking lot that fronted a one-story building. If one looked closely it was still possible to see the faded name that had been painted on the front of the building prior to the plague—OLSON & SONS MEAT PACKING, INC.

Below that a *new* sign had been hung: VALENTINE ANIMAL BOARDING. His primary business office was five miles away. But the old building was the perfect location for a secondary office and a place to house large animals on a temporary basis. Meaning a horse hotel where clients could leave their animals while they went on vacation. It was a profitable sideline as well as a place to live out his darkest fantasies.

Dr. Mike parked his truck in a slot marked RESERVED and made his way up to the front door. A keypad was mounted next to the entrance and, when he entered the four-digit pin code, a click was heard. Valentine turned the knob and went inside.

His assistant was a vet tech who went by Fred rather than Fredericka. She looked up from her computer as Dr. Mike entered the office. Her face was somewhat plain, but her eyes were an icy blue, and had a hypnotic quality to them. They had worked together for years, had rough sex on and off, but weren't entirely compatible since both were sadists. "Good morning, Mike . . . I was just going over the reservation list. We have a horse and a donkey coming in today."

"A donkey? Oh yes, that would be Eeyore . . . Be sure to carry out a complete check on both animals. We wouldn't want our customers to claim that they were harmed while in our care."

Fred had heard the instructions hundreds of times before. She nodded dutifully. "Will do."

"So," Dr. Mike said, "how is our *human* guest?"

"She's pretty tough," Fred replied. "The bitch tried to deck me when I went in to put water in her bowl. I had to tase her."

Dr. Mike chuckled. "Well, that's how we like 'em, right Fred? The stronger they are, the longer they last. I'm going to head back and have a chat with her."

"Take the taser," Fred suggested, as she took it out of a drawer.

"Thanks," Dr. Mike said, as he accepted the weapon and left. The interior of the building had been gutted and divided into twenty-four stalls, about half of which were empty at the moment. The thick smell of animal feces hung in the air as Dr. Mike made his way back to the storage room, but the vet didn't notice. The odor had been a natural part of his working environment for years. All of the stalls were clean thanks to Fred's unending efforts and it was clear that the "guests" had been fed. Dr. Mike saw a horse blanket hanging on a rail and took it as he walked past.

The storage room was labeled as such and secured with a sturdy padlock. There were two keys—one for Fred and one for Dr. Mike. He used his to open the lock and remove it from the hasp. Then, taser at the ready, he pushed the door open.

Hearing his arrival Baxter was on her feet, back to the wall, ready for anything. Most women would have attempted to cover their private parts, but not Baxter. Her fists were up and ready to throw punches. "You aren't very pretty," Dr. Mike observed, "but you have a great body. I plan to enjoy it thoroughly. Here, I brought you a present."

Baxter's eyes remained on Dr. Mike, and she made no attempt to catch the blanket as it fell to the floor. "The least you could do is say 'thank you,'" Dr. Mike said irritably.

"Why?" Baxter said. "Why are you doing this to me?"

"Why does a pet dog kill the neighbor's chicken?" the vet responded rhetorically. "Not for food . . . He has that. No, he kills the chicken for the fun of it. Because deep down, underneath the collar, he's a predator. In this case I'm the predator, and you're the prey. Learn to accept that. You'll feel better if you do." And with that, he withdrew and slammed the door.

Baxter listened to the rattle of the padlock as it mated with the hasp, followed by the sound of departing footsteps. Then she bent over to retrieve the blanket, which she wrapped around her shoulders. It was scratchy, and smelled like the animal it belonged to, but it was better than nothing. Perhaps the additional warmth would enable her to sleep for a while.

With that in mind Baxter lay on the floor with her back to the outside wall. And it was then, with the help of the light from the window above, that she saw the name. It had been scratched into the concrete floor with something like a nail. "VASQUEZ." She began to cry.

A couple of hours had passed since the rocket attack—and Lee was on the third floor of police headquarters in Jenkins's office. According to a patrol officer on the scene, everything she owned with the exception of the motorcycle was gone, and that was true for Mr. Henry as well. Lee planned to follow up and see how the retired bus driver was doing. He had his file box, and she hoped there was a paid-up insurance policy inside.

Jenkins and Lee turned to look as Wolfe entered the room. "The folks in HR are going to arrange for a temporary driver's license—and an emergency clothing allowance. It won't be much, but tee shirts and jeans aren't that expensive."

Lee gave Wolfe the finger, and they laughed.

"We'll arrange for a hotel as well," Wolfe added. "And a security detail."

"Thank you," Lee said gratefully. "But forget the security. This Bye bitch is capable of *anything*. So it would take an army to protect me, and I don't want to suck resources away from the Baxter case. Our first priority is to find her."

Lee looked from Jenkins to Wolfe and back again. Neither one of them said anything. "Good," Lee said. "That's settled.

Now . . . How about my badge? When can I have it back?"

Jenkins opened a desk drawer, removed an ID case, and pushed it across the surface of his desk. The pistols followed. "There you go."

Lee was surprised. "So the dynamic duo cleared me?"

"Hell no," Jenkins replied. "They wanted the department to fire your ass."

"Then why am I back on the job?"

"Because Chief Corso overruled them," Wolfe replied gravely.

"Corso? You've got to be kidding."

"Nope," Jenkins said. "When the IA people asked why, the chief said that you were badly traumatized prior to entering the red zone, and there's no way to know if you were fully aware of the rules. Then he went on to say, and this is a quote, that 'keeping Detective Lee on the force is in the best interests of the department.'

"Here's my guess as to why," Jenkins continued. "You're something of a folk hero at this point. And the chief is afraid there will be all sorts of blowback if the department dumps you."

Wolfe nodded. "I agree. But I think there's something more to it as well. Corso is a cop deep down. And even though you're a huge pain in the ass, he knows that you deliver the goods. And, in the wake of the rocket attack, no one is likely to question his judgment."

"Thanks," Lee said. "I think. So, given that I'm a pain in the ass, what I'm about to ask for won't surprise you."

Jenkins sighed. "What now?"

"I want Yanty and Prospo back . . . And I want permission to look for a Bonebreaker imposter."

Wolfe opened her mouth to speak—but Lee raised a hand. "The rest of the team can continue to search for the real deal— and I hope they find him . . . But let's put money on *both* possibilities."

Wolfe looked at Jenkins and he frowned. "The chief wouldn't like it . . . Two serial cop killers would scare the shit out of everyone, our people included."

"So don't tell them," Lee said.

"Don't overplay your hand," Jenkins cautioned. "There's a

limit to how much of your bullshit I'm willing to put up with."

Lee tried to look penitent. "Yes, sir. I hear you."

Wolfe rolled her eyes but Jenkins didn't notice. "Okay," he said reluctantly. "Take your best shot but don't talk about the imposter theory. Just do what you need to do. And keep us in the loop."

"I will," Lee lied, as she checked to make sure that the Glock was loaded. "So I can go to work?"

"Yes," Jenkins replied. "You can go to work."

Lee smiled sweetly, and said, "Thanks." Then she was gone.

Jenkins looked at Wolfe. "So, what do you think? Did the chief make the right call?"

She nodded. "Lee is like a hand grenade. You throw it at the bad guys, and who knows what will happen? So Corso figured, 'What the hell? I *have* a grenade . . . I'll use it.'"

Jenkins laughed. "Let's hope none of us gets caught in the blast."

The Bonebreaker was doing fifty miles an hour when the sedan pulled out in front of him. That forced him to stand on the brakes and caused the dead mailman to slide forward. There was a thump as his shoes struck the engine compartment positioned between the front seats.

The Bonebreaker swore and slammed a fist down on the horn. The man in the car flipped him off and sped away. The Bonebreaker was sorely tempted to follow the driver and shoot him. But he was on a mission and couldn't allow himself to be distracted.

The whole thing seemed so simple at first. While he didn't have the technical resources that Lee could muster—the Bonebreaker figured there was a decent chance that he could find the truck on his own. He hadn't mentioned it to Lee, but the "DMV" bumper sticker could indicate that the truck's owner was a Doctor of Veterinary Medicine, and there were only five of them in the Nuevo area.

Plus there was the matter of the vise to consider. While reading about vets the Bonebreaker discovered that routine hoof care was typically provided by specialists called farriers. And, judging from pictures he'd seen online, most of them had specially equipped vehicles. Trucks that often had a vise mounted somewhere. For working with horseshoes? Probably.

So what did that mean? Was the person who owned the truck a vet, a farrier, or both? The Bonebreaker figured he'd start with the vets. All he had to do was look them up online, drive to their various offices, and check the trucks that were parked nearby.

With that in mind he had left the ossuary just before dawn, taken a bus to an adjacent neighborhood, and was looking for a vehicle to steal when he saw the mail van. It was sitting in the parking lot in front of a strip mall. And that was when it struck him. No one paid any attention to mail carriers. They were part of the urban wallpaper—always there but nearly transparent.

The driver was sitting behind the wheel sorting mail. So when the Bonebreaker strolled over to the passenger side of the van and jerked the door open the mailman turned. "What are you . . ." as the .22 caliber bullet hit him in the face. The mailman's head jerked, and as his body went limp, it fell toward the Bonebreaker. The serial killer took advantage of that by climbing inside and muscling the body into the back of the vehicle. There was a central aisle with shelving on both sides, and that was the perfect place to put the corpse.

The Bonebreaker wasn't dressed like the carrier, but the man's postal jacket was a good fit and enough to give the right impression. What money the dead man had went into the Bonebreaker's wallet along with a pearl-handled pocketknife.

From there it had been a ninety-minute drive to Nuevo, where the sedan pulled out in front of him. Then the *real* work began. That involved visiting each vet's place of business to look for the truck. But it soon became apparent that what seemed like a straightforward operation wasn't. Because even though there was no sign of the vehicle at Dr. Tolly's office, that didn't mean much. Maybe she had *two* trucks, was out visiting a patient, or was on vacation. Or maybe all sorts of things. And if the Bonebreaker entered Tolly's office asking questions, he would not only attract attention to himself, he might tip the killer off as well.

So all the Bonebreaker and the dead mailman could do was make their rounds and hope for some good luck. Or, perhaps God would intervene on his behalf, although the deity had been very stingy with assistance of late. Police work was hard.

In keeping with the LAPD's thrifty ways Lee had been booked into an unassuming hotel located near work. After checking in, Lee went up to a small room, where she took a shower and made full use of the complimentary shampoo, soap, and skin lotion.

Then, having freshened up to the extent she could—Lee took the elevator down to the lobby, where Kane was waiting for her. He came forward to give her a kiss. "Cassandra! I'm so glad that you're okay."

"Thanks for coming," Lee said. "It's like I told you on the phone, I need *everything*, and I can't drive a police car until my temporary license comes through."

"No problem," Kane said. "I'll take you to dinner. Then we'll go shopping."

"That sounds good," Lee said. "Except that we need to stop by Grady's Gun Store first. I need some ammo and a couple of holsters. Unless you'd like to date a lady who walks around with a Glock stuck down the back of her pants."

Kane laughed. "That would never do. How about money? I'd be glad to loan you some."

"I have that covered," Lee told him. "I made it to the bank just before closing time."

"Good," Kane said. "We're off."

An hour and twenty minutes later they were sitting opposite each other in Caputo's Italian Restaurant. A very nice place that was adjacent to the Grove Shopping Mall. Lee had no choice but to carry her weapons and the holsters in a shopping bag until she could buy at least one jacket. "So, you're back on the job," Kane said. "What's next?"

"Some clothes and girl things," Lee replied. "Plus a place to live. Remember what you said about the room dedicated to my father? That's gone now. Along with everything related to him."

"Yes," Kane said. "I *do* remember. So you have an opportunity to start anew."

"Exactly," Lee said, as she took a sip of wine.

"Here's an idea," Kane said. "Why not stay with me while you look for an apartment? You're already familiar with the guest room—not to mention the resident chef."

Lee eyed him over the rim of her glass. "Is this yet another part of your plan to seduce me?"

Kane nodded. "Yes, but the process is taking forever."

Lee laughed. "Sorry, I promise to become seducible in the near future."

"So you'll come?"

"Maybe, but there's something I want you to consider."

"Which is?"

"I'm a target. Something you experienced during our *first* date. The same thing could happen again."

Kane smiled. "I'm aware of that. You warned me earlier."

"Yet you're willing to hang out with me anyway?"

"I'm here, aren't I?"

"Yes, and I'm glad you are."

The food arrived at that point, and it was very good. Once the meal was over they went to the mall where, in keeping with Wolfe's prediction, Lee bought a week's worth of jeans, tee shirts, and a couple of waist-length jackets. Some underwear and a pair of combat boots completed the interim wardrobe. Then Kane drove her to his condo, helped carry her shopping bags upstairs, and promised to wake her at 5:00 a.m. A cop was missing—and Lee was determined to find her.

Baxter produced a grunt of pain as the riding crop cut into her left breast. Dr. Mike nodded knowingly. "That hurt, didn't it, bitch? More than you're letting on. And it will get worse tomorrow."

The so-called Equipment Room was located at the back of the concrete building and was furnished with thousands of dollars worth of S&M gear. That included an X-shaped rack, an adjustable torture table, and all manner of "gear."

Ropes had been fastened to the leather cuffs on Baxter's wrists. And by passing them through ceiling-mounted pulleys, Dr. Mike had been able to hoist the policewoman up so that her feet were six inches off the floor. Then, by pulling her ankles apart and securing them to ring bolts set into the concrete, the vet had been able to expose every part of her. And not just for *his* enjoyment. No, thanks to the video Fred was making, hundreds if not thousands of other people would get to see *Torment 3*.

Like Dr. Mike, Fred was wearing a black hood to protect her identity. But, except for a garter belt, fishnet stockings, and a pair of red high heels, she was naked. Something that would be apparent to viewers after the footage from a stationary camera was cut into the final production.

Meanwhile Fred was getting medium and tight shots using a handheld camera. She zoomed in to capture the red welt left by the riding crop as well as the hypodermic needle that was sticking through Baxter's nipple. All of which was preliminary to the final scene, which would be recorded soon. Once the final denouement was over, Fred would edit the snuff film and sell it to a distributor in the red zone. He would charge collectors up to five hundred eagles per copy. It was, to Fred's way of thinking, an enjoyable way to make some extra money.

Baxter didn't know which was worse. To see the next blow coming—or to be caught by surprise. But that was a tactical issue. Of more importance was to save as much of her personhood as she could. The LAPD was searching for her, of that she was sure, but what would they find? A basket case? Or a person who could recover from what she'd been through and live a normal life? *You aren't going to die tonight*, Baxter told herself. *Dr. Mike said that the pain will get worse tomorrow. And that's a good thing.*

The cop struck her right breast, causing Baxter to utter a yelp of pain. "She felt that one," Dr. Mike said to the camera. "Now watch *this*."

* * *

Kane dropped Lee off at 6:30 a.m., and by 7:00, she was in a meeting with Yanty and Prospo. Both looked tired. "Good to have you back," Yanty said. "Even if you are a crap magnet."

"I like the new look," Prospo added. "Oh, wait a minute, it's the *same* look."

Lee grinned. "Thanks . . . I feel better now. All right . . . What, if anything, have we got?"

Prospo looked at Yanty, who shrugged. "The truth is that we don't have anything worth talking about. We finished the photo comparison process an hour ago. There were three bumpers that had some sort of vise bolted to them—but only one that was located on the right side. That belonged to a plumber in Nuevo, but the truck was totaled two months ago."

"And the DMV sticker."

"*Nada.*"

"Shit."

"Yeah."

All of them were silent for a while. Lee felt as if she should provide some sort of guidance. Some glimmer of hope. But she had nothing to offer. Finally she gave the only instructions she could. "Okay . . . Let's pull up pictures of the trucks that belong to the vets in LA County and check them out."

Yanty groaned. "You must be kidding."

"Got a better idea?"

"No."

"Then let's get to work. There are three of us this time, so the work will go more quickly."

It took more than an hour to pull up all the vet licenses for LA County, compare the names to DMV database, select the vehicles identified as trucks, download the related photo files, and divide by three. Then came the mind-numbing work of plowing through Lee's share of the list. She was two and a half hours into the process when her new disposable phone rang. She eyed the incoming call, saw that it was from ENOB9, and placed her thumb on the green bar. "Yeah?"

"I have the bastard," the Bonebreaker said.

Lee felt a sudden surge of hope. "What does that mean?"

"I'm in Nuevo, and when I pulled into the drive-through for

the local burger joint, I found myself behind a pickup. It has a utility bumper complete with the DMV sticker on the left and a vise on the right."

Lee's heart began to beat like a trip-hammer. "Where are you now?"

"Where the hell do you *think* I am? I'm following the truck."

"Have you got a license number for me?"

The Bonebreaker read it off, and Lee wrote it down. "What kind of vehicle are you driving?"

The Bonebreaker laughed. "Get serious."

"Okay, I'm on the way."

"Come alone," the Bonebreaker said. "If cops swarm the area the deal is off."

Lee swallowed. "Give him plenty of room, and if he stops, let me know immediately."

"Stop talking and get your butt in gear," the Bonebreaker replied. Then the line went dead.

Lee ran the license number, and bingo, there it was: Dr. Michael Valentine. She entered the name into her browser and got a second hit. Valentine was a vet all right—with offices in Nuevo. Now she was in a bind. The Bonebreaker wanted her to go to Nuevo alone, but that was a bad idea. It could be a trap for one thing. A way to get her alone so he could kill her.

But that was just the tip of the iceberg. She had her badge back but was sure to lose it again if she ignored the LAPD protocols that applied to such situations. And there was zero chance that Corso would save her ass the second time around.

Plus there was the fact that the town of Nuevo was outside of the LAPD's jurisdiction. And that meant all sorts of shit would fly if she rolled into town and made an arrest. So Lee made the decision to do something radical, for her anyway, and that was to consult with her boss. Wolfe was in her office. She looked up from her terminal. "Yes?"

"I need help," Lee said. "And I need it fast."

Wolfe's eyes widened. "What's up?"

"One of my informants is tailing the vehicle that Vasquez was abducted in and was probably used to dump his body. It belongs to a vet named Dr. Michael Valentine. He has offices in

Nuevo, and if he's holding Baxter, then every second counts."

Wolfe frowned. "Nuevo is outside our jurisdiction."

"Correct. And, if my informant sees any cops, he's going to break it off."

"Is your informant wanted?"

"Big-time."

This was a critical moment from Lee's perspective. Would Wolfe step up? Or create a committee and convene a meeting? The answer came quickly as Wolfe stood and made a grab for her purse. "We'll take my car. You drive while I take care of the logistics."

Lee didn't have the temporary driver's permit yet—but decided to ignore that as they ran for the elevator. It took them down to the parking area where they hurried over to Wolfe's sedan. Lee had the siren and grill lights going by the time they hit the street. She was on I-5 within a matter of minutes and swore steadily as some of the motorists took their own sweet time about pulling over. The car sped south to the junction with 60 and turned east. From there it was a straight shot. As Lee drove Wolfe made use of her cell phone and the car's radio to get the necessary arrangements in place. And because it was her, rather than Lee, there was very little pushback.

Lee was going eighty, and waiting for a semi to pull over, when her phone rang. She brought it up to her right ear. "Yeah?"

"The truck pulled into the parking lot in front of an outfit called Valentine Animal Boarding, and a man got out. He entered the building."

Lee already had two addresses for Valentine, but it made sense to check. "What's the street address?"

The Bonebreaker told her, and Lee was careful to repeat it so Wolfe could hear it. "Thanks," Lee said. "Let me know if he leaves."

"Bullshit," the Bonebreaker said. "I'm out of here." The line went dead.

"Asshole," Lee said, as she placed the phone on the center console.

Wolfe looked at her. "Meaning the informant?"

"Yeah . . . He took off. But we've got the perp, assuming

he stays where he is," Lee said. "What were you able to put together?"

"We have a green light from Jenkins, and once I give them the address, the county mounties will throw a perimeter around the place. Hopefully your guy won't notice—but it sounds like he's out of there anyway."

"Outstanding," Lee said, as she passed a huge RV. "Did you bring a weapon?"

"Of course."

"Good. You might need it."

Lee managed to cut a trip that was supposed to take an hour and twenty minutes down to forty. She killed the lights and the siren as they passed through the screen that had been thrown up by the sheriff. By that time Wolfe had authorized them to tighten the cordon—and send a unit to Valentine's clinic.

"Okay," Lee said, as they neared the location. "There were at least two people involved in the Vasquez murder—so we'll need to be on the lookout for a second perp."

"Roger that," Wolfe said, as she checked her Glock.

"Bingo!" Lee said, as she pulled into the lot. "There it is. See the DMV sticker on the bumper? And the vise? My informant was correct."

"It looks like all of the tires are flat," Wolfe observed. "Your guy perhaps?"

"That's how it looks," Lee agreed, as she turned the engine off.

"We don't have a warrant so we'll have to bullshit our way in," Wolfe said as she put the pistol away. "I'll take the lead." All Lee could do was nod.

Gravel crunched underfoot as they got out of the car and made their way up to the front door. A sign read, "Push the button for service," and Lee saw that a keypad was mounted next to the entrance, and a camera was peering down at them. That was a whole lot security for a boarding facility. A disembodied voice said, "Yes? How can I help you?"

"I have a horse," Wolfe replied. "And I'm looking for a place where I can leave him for a month or so."

"I'm sure we can help you," the woman said. "Please come in." There was a click as the lock was released. Wolfe opened the door and entered first. They found themselves in a sparsely furnished office. A woman was seated behind the reception desk—and Lee could see a glassed-in office beyond that. A man was seated with his back to the visitors. The perp? Lee felt her pulse begin to race.

As the receptionist turned to look at the policewomen, Lee saw the look of instant recognition on her face. Because she hadn't bothered to study the images on the security monitor? But was *very* familiar with the news coverage related to the Vasquez murder? Yes!

Lee was about to intervene when the woman brought a taser up from a drawer and shot Wolfe in the chest. She jerked spasmodically and fell.

Lee knew the weapon could be fired up to three times in quick succession and went for the Glock. The pistol came out of the new holster smoothly and jumped in her hand. The slug passed through one of the receptionist's sky blue eyes and killed her instantly.

Then Lee heard a loud bang and turned to see that the man had disappeared. The noise had been caused by a door's hitting the wall as he escaped into the back of the building.

Lee glanced at Wolfe, saw the agonized expression on the other woman's face, and knew she'd be out of action for at least ten minutes. That left Lee with no choice but to proceed alone.

As Lee approached the open door, the fire alarm came on, causing her to wonder if the perp was trying to burn the place down. But as she stepped into the area where the animals were stabled it quickly became apparent that the suspect had something else in mind. Since escaping the office the perp had been able to open at least a dozen stalls. So when the alarm went off many of the animals bolted out of their enclosures and went looking for a way to escape the shrieking noise.

Lee had to jump aside as a badly panicked horse charged straight at her. Then she had to run from stall to stall as a menagerie of mules, donkeys, and goats thundered back and forth, all adding their own unique noises to the hellish cacophony inside the barn.

The perp was trying to slow her down. That much was

obvious. But *why*? To escape out the back? If so, that was fine with Lee. He wouldn't get far. Not with four flat tires and a bunch of deputies waiting for him.

But what if the bastard had something else in mind? What if Baxter was being held in a room somewhere? Maybe he planned to use her as a hostage. Or, worse yet, the sick son of a bitch might kill her!

Lee managed to sidestep a braying donkey as she pushed forward. Then a bullet blew a splinter out of the support post to her right, and Lee caught a brief glimpse of a man standing on top of a divider, pointing a pistol at her. Then he was gone as a cloud of dust rose to envelop the scene.

Lee swore, dropped into a crouch, and continued to advance. There was a second gunshot as she dashed across an aisle and a horse screamed in pain. And that produced even *more* panic. But Lee was almost at the back of the barn by then. And, as someone turned the alarm off, she advanced with the Glock at the ready. That was when the man appeared with an arm wrapped around Baxter's throat. She was nude, Lee could see ugly-looking welts on her body, and it looked as though the vet was supporting most of the police officer's weight. He was also holding a gun to Baxter's head. "Back off!" he grated. "Back off, or the bitch dies."

"If she dies, *you* die," Lee countered. "So let's cut the crap. If you were going to blow her brains out you'd have done it by now. So release Officer Baxter and put the weapon down."

"No!" he said emphatically. "I want . . ."

Lee never got to hear what the perp wanted because that was the moment when Baxter came back to life. Her head came up, she snarled, and turned in on Valentine. That threw him off-balance. He fired and the bullet creased Baxter's skull. The vet tried to react, but was too slow, as Baxter grabbed his shirt and brought a knee up into his crotch. As he bent over in pain, she made use of both hands to club the back of his neck.

The revolver came loose as he fell and Baxter hurried to scoop it up. And then, with the gun pointed at his back and blood running down her cheek, she began the legal litany. "You are under arrest. You have the right to . . . to . . ." Then she collapsed.

FIFTEEN

About a hundred people were gathered on the plaza in front of the angular LAPD headquarters building. The press conference began at precisely 5:30 p.m., so that the local TV stations could carry it live.

The chief of police was present . . . As were Jenkins, Wolfe, and Lee. But rather than talk about the team, Corso chose to tell the story of a brave police officer named Jennifer Baxter who, even after being tortured for days, still found the strength required to turn on her captor at the last moment. And would have arrested him herself had it not been for the extent of her injuries.

Very little attention was paid to the events that led up to that moment, or to Lee's role in the arrest, and that was fine with her. Baxter deserved the praise that was being heaped on her—and the last thing Lee wanted was more publicity.

As for Dr. Michael Valentine, AKA the Bonebreaker, he was being held on multiple counts of murder. And thanks to the fact that he and his assistant had chosen to videotape their crimes, a guilty verdict was a foregone conclusion.

So after updating the press on Baxter's condition, Corso opened the press conference to questions, most of which were directed to him. But Carla Zumin saw Lee and was quick to pounce. "So, Detective Lee," she said. "Congratulations regarding your part in the rescue. According to the department's press release, the critical tip came in to *you*. Who provided that tip? And why did they contact you?"

"I can't share that information with you at this time," Lee said stiffly.

Zumin smiled sweetly. "Please let me know when you can. It seems there might be a hidden hero in all of this."

The presser came to a conclusion a few minutes later and Lee was free to go home. More than that she *had* to go home pending the finding of another shooting review board. Everyone agreed that it was a no-brainer. Even so the process would have to be coordinated with the Riverside Sheriff's Department—and that was likely to drag it out. Kane saw that as a plus—and said so as he drove her home. "You could use time off," he said. "The break will be good for you."

And it *was* good for her. Lee made use of the time to rent a storage unit for her bike, to file an insurance claim, and to check on her former neighbors. Mr. Henry blamed her for the loss of his home, but he had renter's insurance and would be okay. The others were more generous and wished her well.

But even with all of that, there was plenty of time to spend with Kane, and Lee could tell that this man was different. Maybe it was because of his profession, but whatever the reason, Lee felt that Kane understood her in a way that no one else had.

So one thing led to another, and Kane's plan to seduce her finally paid off. And when that took place, it seemed like the most natural thing in the world. Almost as if they had made love before. And Lee liked that because in the past she had climbed to the top of some romantic mountaintops only to fall into the valley below.

That's why Lee was a little disappointed when the e-mail arrived. "You have been cleared for a return to duty," the message said. "So quit goofing off and get your butt in here." It was from Jenkins.

Kane made dinner and they ate on the deck. This was when Lee realized that she had yet to look at a single apartment. Was this because she'd been so busy putting her life back together? Or was it because some part of her didn't *want* to find a place of her own? And what would that mean? Lee chose to ignore the questions and watch the sun go down.

The next couple of days were busy, but routinely so, until Lee got a call from Kane. "Hey, hon," he said. "What time will you be home?"

That wasn't unusual since she often ran late—and Kane did most of the cooking. Lee looked at her watch. "I'll be there by five thirty."

"That's good," Kane replied. "I thought we'd go out for sushi. I'll make the reservations. See you then."

The line went dead, and bells began to ring in Lee's head. Kane loved seafood but *hated* sushi. And he never hung up without saying something lovably sappy. What should she do? Ignore her suspicions? Or take them seriously?

You should take them seriously, the voice inside her answered. *Maybe the Bonebreaker is waiting for you . . . Or maybe Crystal Bye is holding a gun on Kane. Something is wrong.*

Shit, shit, shit, Lee thought to herself as she went to see Wolfe. Would the other policewoman pooh-pooh her concerns? Or take them seriously? Of course Wolfe had been straight up on the Baxter thing—so maybe she'd be equally reliable this time.

The answer came quickly once Wolfe understood the situation. "I'll talk to the SWAT team," Wolfe said, as she dialed her phone. "They have the resources we need."

Lee had to agree even though she was still worried about the possibility of a misunderstanding. As Wolfe spoke to Lieutenant Mick Ferris, Lee glanced at her watch. An hour and a half. That's how much time they had before she was supposed to arrive at the condo. What would happen to Kane if she was late? What if somebody killed him because of *her*? Lee felt sick to her stomach.

"Ferris is on his way," Wolfe said, as she put the phone down. "Everything needs to look normal. Someone has you under surveillance. So if you leave early, or if you leave late, they'll know."

That made sense . . . And Lee was reminded of Bye and the helicopter in Las Vegas. "Maybe it's Bye," Lee put in. "If so, she had a helicopter in the red zone. And there's a pad on the roof of the building that Kane lives in."

Wolfe swore and placed another call. Then she was back. "Our birds crisscross the city all day. One of them will let me know if a helicopter is sitting on the roof."

No introductions were required as Ferris entered the office since both women had worked with him in the past. He had a young-old face, a salt-and-pepper buzz cut, and a lean frame. With the seconds ticking away there was no time to waste on small talk. "Tell me everything you know about the building," Ferris said, "starting with the location. My team is checking to see what's available online."

Lee gave him the address, a brief description of the building, and mentioned the presence of the structures that flanked it. "Good," Ferris said. "I'll be back in a sec . . . But first I need to put some people into the neighborhood."

"We think the perps have the area under surveillance," Wolfe said tactfully.

"I won't send the war wagon," Ferris replied, "if that's what you're worried about. My team will infiltrate the area two at a time in civilian clothes. Excuse me . . . I need to get them under way." And with that Ferris stepped out of the office to use a handheld radio.

"Okay," Wolfe said. "So let's talk about *your* role—and how this is likely to go down. There are a couple of possibilities. You go home, enter the condo, and someone shoots you. Or you go home, enter the condo, and he or she talks to you. *Then* the perp shoots you—followed by Kane."

"Thanks for the pep talk, I feel better now," Lee said.

Wolfe shrugged. "I'm about keeping it real," she said. "Since there's no reason to waste time on scenario one—let's talk about scenario two. If they want to talk chances are they will take your weapons—or force you to surrender them."

"Makes sense," Lee said, as her spirits continued to fall.

"But," Wolfe said, as she went over to a steel cabinet, "I'm going to loan you a backup to your backup. I wore it every day when I was undercover." Keys rattled as Wolfe opened the cabinet and gave Lee a look inside. There were all sorts of weapons in the lieutenant's miniarmory. A collection that probably dated back to the days when Wolfe had been a kick-ass detective.

"*This* is what I had in mind," Wolfe said, as she withdrew a two-inch-wide hand-tooled belt. Lee noticed that the buckle was a large Western-style oval with a large chunk of turquoise fastened to it. How that might help wasn't apparent until Wolfe pressed the spring-loaded front piece—and it popped open to reveal a tiny derringer. "It's single action, I'm afraid," Wolfe confessed. "And it fires .22 long rifle cartridges. But something is better than nothing. Try it on."

Lee removed the one she was wearing, wrapped the new belt around her waist, and discovered that two simple hooks were used to fasten it. And judging from the wear marks Wolfe had the same size waist that she did. Once the rig was secured, Lee tried touching the blue stone with her left hand and grabbing the little revolver with her right. It worked quite well. "Thanks," Lee said. "I appreciate it."

"It looks good with jeans," Wolfe said lightly. "And tee shirts."

Lee laughed as Ferris entered the room. "So here's how we're going to handle it," he said. "Lee will leave the building with a cop in the trunk of her sedan. She'll drive home, enter the parking garage, and let him out. That has to happen smoothly in order to avoid detection—and let's hope there isn't a car right behind hers.

"Lee will park her vehicle and go over to the lift. My officer will arrive separately in case the perp or perps placed a wireless camera down there. The elevator will take them up to three where my guy will get off. Lee will proceed to four. I can't predict what will happen next . . . That will depend on what we hear via the wire Lee will be wearing."

Lee cleared her throat. "And if they shoot me off the top?"

"We'll make sure they die," Ferris said grimly. "By the way . . . It turns out that a chopper *is* sitting on the roof of the building. So we put *two* air force gunships on standby. And there's a good chance that Kane is being held by Crystal Bye rather than the Bonebreaker."

"Okay then," Lee said grimly. "It'll be nice to see her again."

Ferris smiled. "We'll have snipers in the surrounding buildings. You described Kane's unit as having large windows. So it may be possible to solve a few problems from afar . . . Hit the deck if we do."

A tech arrived at that point. She was carrying a mike and

transmitter, both of which could be concealed beneath the body armor that Lee was told to put on. "Most cops wear it," she said. "So no one will be surprised. And you'll need to insert these nostril filters just in case."

Lee knew the filters were a good idea, but knew it would be damned hard to avoid breathing through her mouth in such a stressful situation, and was worried about Kane's health, too . . . If the mutants were holding him captive Kane was in double jeopardy.

After a few minutes in the nearest restroom Lee emerged ready to go. Or if not ready, then somewhat prepared. At that point all she could do was head down to her car, get in, and drive home. What was it like to make the trip in the trunk? she wondered. It would be dark—like the interior of a coffin. And what about Kane? Was he scared? Was he going to die because of her? If so, they would go out together.

Lee pushed the thought aside as she threaded her way through traffic. It had been a sunny day, but the air was starting to cool, and it would be dark before long. Was that part of Bye's plan? To escape during the hours of darkness? *No, the whole thing will be over before sunset,* she thought to herself as the cluster of condo buildings appeared up ahead. "We're almost there," she said for the benefit of the man in the trunk. "Get ready."

Lee eyed the rearview mirror as she turned off the street and steered the car in under the building Kane lived in. There were no vehicles behind her, so she braked and pulled the trunk release. The cop vaulted out of the car with briefcase in hand. There was a thump as he closed the lid—and that was Lee's signal to pull forward. "He's out of the car," she said for the SWAT team's benefit. "And I'm about to park."

Lee was as frightened as she'd ever been as she got out of the car. It was one thing to walk into a dicey situation with at least a few advantages and something else to go in with none. Everything was hyperreal. The faint smell of exhaust. The pores in the concrete walls. And the rasp of her own breathing. In fact, the whole experience was so intense, it was like being on some sort of upper.

A glass door swished out of the way as Lee entered the elevator lobby—and the cop with the briefcase appeared seconds later. He smiled and nodded. It was Tanaka! A guy she had worked with before and was a cool customer. A morale booster for sure.

The elevator arrived and the officers got in. They knew it might be bugged and were silent as it rose. A tone sounded as they arrived on three, and Tanaka got off. Lee knew he would report in and struggled to control the way her hands were shaking as the lift stopped on four.

There were four large condos on the "Vista" floor but only two that looked out onto the ocean. Lee turned right and approached Kane's front door. They could see her through the peephole if nothing else. Would someone open the door and jerk her inside? No one did.

What if she was wrong? What if Kane was standing in the kitchen making predinner drinks? Lee inserted the key and gave it a turn to the right. Then she opened the door. That was when hands grabbed Lee, pulled her into the condo, and threw her down. Hands explored her body, found the pistols, and took them. A couple of men hoisted her up onto her feet. Hoods concealed their faces. "She's wearing body armor," one of them said. "But that's all."

Crystal Bye stood with her hands at her sides. Both her snow-white hair and her makeup were perfect. And when she smiled Lee saw that her teeth were flawless as well. "Body armor, huh?" the assassin said. "Well, that won't keep me from shooting you in the face, now will it?"

It's option two! Lee's inner voice chortled. *Stretch it.* "No, it won't," Lee replied as she took a look around. The place was a mess. It looked as though Kane had put up a fight. Was he still alive? It was as if Bye could read her mind.

"Your boyfriend took a beating but he's still with us. We'll pop him on our way out."

"*Five* of you?" Lee said contemptuously. "It takes five assassins to smoke a psychologist and one cop?" The SWAT team would hear that of course—and know what they were up against.

"There are five of us," Bye agreed. "But all it will take is one bullet to shut your mouth." The long-barreled pistol came up, and was aimed at Lee's face, when a window shattered. The report was like an afterthought. And the *second* bullet, the one that could fly straight and true because there wasn't any glass in the way, hit a mutant in the head. Blood sprayed the floor as he went down.

That was Lee's signal to throw herself sideways. She landed hard, and her fingers were clawing at the fancy belt buckle as the surviving assassins hit the floor, and more slugs tore into the walls. "It's a trap!" Bye shouted, as some of her people went to the shattered window and fired their handguns. That was a mistake and one of them was thrown back onto the floor.

By that time Lee had the tiny pistol in her hand. Each action seemed to take forever as she pulled the hammer back, took aim, and fired. There was a pop, and the bullet hit a spot two feet above Bye's head! The derringer was worthless.

Lee rolled to the left as Bye fired. The bullet came within an inch of Lee's face and ripped a splinter out of Kane's hardwood floor. Lee pushed herself up and over as she came into contact with the dead man's body. Then she scrabbled for his gun, got a grip on it, and began what promised to be a time-consuming turn.

Bye fired again. But, like Lee, the assassin was on the floor—and the body separated them. The corpse jerked and geysers of blood shot up into the air as each bullet hit. Lee, who was still in the process of turning, fired five times in rapid succession. Not with any hope of hitting her opponent—but in an effort to force Bye's head down. And the strategy worked. Suddenly, Lee was there, sighting over the body, her finger pressed against the trigger. Time slowed, and a .9mm slug flew straight and true.

Given the angle, the bullet hit the top of Bye's right shoulder, broke her clavicle, and went deep into her chest. Her eyes widened, a look of surprise appeared on her face, and Lee nodded. "Bye-bye, bitch."

Suddenly, the front door burst open, and Tanaka entered. He was holding an Uzi Pro. It burped three-round bursts as the last two assassins turned to fire at him. They staggered and fell. The acrid odor of gunpowder was thick in the air as Lee spoke into the mike. "Tanaka is here . . . The condo is secure. I'm about to stand up."

Lee stood, thanked Tanaka, and went looking for Kane. He was lying faceup in a blood-smeared bathtub. His face was puffy, one eye was swollen closed, and plastic ties had been used to secure his extremities. He turned to Lee and attempted to smile. "Sorry, hon . . . Dinner's going to be late."

The sun-splashed lounge chairs were positioned in front of a glittering pool beyond which the vast expanse of the Pacific Ocean could be seen. A freighter was working its way north, but, other than that, there were only the wheeling gulls to capture her eye.

A month had passed since the shoot-out in the condo, and a great deal had occurred. Lee had been cleared by yet another shooting review board, neither one of them was BN positive, and Kane's newly refurbished home was up for sale. "I'm ready for a new view," is the way he put it. But Lee knew it was more than that. Neither one of them could sit down in the living room without remembering what had taken place there.

As for the future . . . Well, that was something the couple planned to discuss while they vacationed in Santa Barbara. Maybe this and maybe that . . . Time would tell. Lee glanced at Kane and saw that he was reading. She closed her eyes. The sun was warm, and the ocean breeze was cool. Dreams beckoned.

It was cold in the ossuary . . . And the only sound was the steady drip, drip, drip of water finding its way down from above. But the Bonebreaker didn't care about that. He was focused on the beautiful white femur that lay on the table before him. The inscription was finished and that meant he would send the final product to Cheyenne Darling soon. It was a present . . . Something she could place on a bookshelf in her living room. After that? God wanted to confront Cassandra Lee next . . . And it was the Bonebreaker's duty to send her along.

Don't miss the third Mutant Files novel
GRAVEYARD
Coming February 2016 from Titan Books!

Sunday school teacher Misty Roker was having a nice day until her students found a body behind St. Patrick's Church in south LA. Roker was in her classroom, putting instructional materials away, when sixteen-year-old Emily Stills burst into the room. "Miss Roker! A man is lying in the parking lot—and there's something wrong with his face!"

Sunday school was over, but the children's parents were still attending Mass, so Misty instructed Emily to remain in the classroom while she went outside to investigate. A tiny playground had been built behind the church a few years earlier. It was fenced in and the children were gathered at the gate that provided access to the parking lot. Their backs were turned, and Misty could tell that they were staring at something. She clapped her hands. "Go inside, children . . . Emily is waiting for you."

As the children turned in her direction Misty could see the worried looks on their faces and felt the first stirrings of concern. She had assumed that a drunk was passed out behind the church. That would require some explanation but she could handle it. Now, based on the complete lack of chatter, Misty sensed that something much worse was in the offing.

As her charges filed inside Misty approached the gate. The man was lying a few feet away, eyes wide open, staring up into the bright sun. That was when Misty noticed the facial discoloration, the swelling, and the hundreds of tiny stitches that ran around the circumference of his face and formed clusters here and there. What the heck?

Misty opened the gate and knelt by the man's side. Because the Sunday school teacher was a nurse she knew how to check the man's vital signs and proceeded to do so. The results were unequivocal. He was dead—and had been for some time.

Misty fumbled for her phone, dialed 911, and reported the find. "My name is Misty Roker. We have a man down behind St. Patrick's Church. He's unresponsive, cyanotic, and I can't detect a pulse."

The dispatcher promised to send an aid unit, and as Misty waited for the medics to arrive, she noticed the white envelope. It was protruding from the man's shirt, and when Misty pulled it free, she saw that Father Benedict's name had been written on it. Deep down Misty knew that she shouldn't open it, but curiosity got the better of her.

The envelope wasn't sealed. So all Misty had to do was pry it open. That was when she saw five one-hundred-nu notes and a single piece of paper. She opened it up and read what was typed on it:

Dear Father Benedict,

This man has gone to a better place. His name is Joel. Please use the money to cover his burial expenses.

Thank you,
Alcmaeon

Misty frowned. *Alcmaeon?* What kind of name was that?

By that time a siren could be heard in the distance. So Misty stuffed the note back into the envelope—and slid it back into Joel's shirt. The EMTs arrived a minute later along with a police car. The medics went through the motions of checking Joel out, but he was dead, and all three of them knew it. The envelope went to one of the patrol officers, who was careful to hold only the edges of the object before sliding it into a larger envelope.

Then, after taking Misty's name and contact information, he turned her loose. Sunday school was over.

Cassandra Lee and Lawrence Kane were looking for a place to live. The decision to live together had been made during a recent vacation, and now they were looking at condos in Santa Monica, an area that both of them liked.

But they were very busy people, which made finding the time to tour properties difficult. And, now that Kane's existing condo was up for sale, the task was urgent. So they'd gone to see two different homes in the morning and were about to discuss them over lunch.

The restaurant was called Mac's and it was located about a mile away from the famous Santa Monica Pier. It had large windows that looked out over the highway to a sandy beach and the pale blue ocean beyond. "So," Kane began, once they'd been through the buffet line and taken their seats. "What did you think?"

Lee nibbled on a huge strawberry. It was delicious, and the process gave her an opportunity to stall. In spite of the fact that they'd been through a great deal they hadn't known each other all that long—and she wanted to provide a considered response. "Well, the first place is the larger of the two, and I liked that. But it needs a new kitchen."

Kane had a straight nose, even features, and was wearing a white polo shirt over jeans. He nodded. "True . . . And the head chef needs a good place to perform his culinary miracles. It might be fun to do a reno. Then we could have the kitchen exactly the way we want it.

"How 'bout number two?" he inquired. "It's smaller, but it comes with *two* parking slots plus a place to keep your bike."

Lee's Harley Road King Police Edition motorcycle was a problem since most condo buildings provided two parking places max, and she hoped to keep the bike nearby. Lee was about to respond when her phone started to dance across the table. Kane made a face. But he knew that Lee was on call. "Hello, Detective Lee."

"Sorry," Deputy Chief Jenkins said. "Life sucks."

"No kidding. What have you got?"

"Something weird," Jenkins said. "That's why I called you."

"Screw you," Lee replied. "And the horse you rode in on."

Jenkins laughed. "Somebody dumped a body in the parking lot behind St. Patrick's Church."

"Okay," Lee said. "But that doesn't qualify as strange. Not in LA."

"True," Jenkins admitted. "But, based on a preliminary evaluation by the coroner, this guy probably died as the result of a botched face transplant."

"That *is* weird," Lee agreed.

"Oh, but there's more," Jenkins responded. "The dead man is *B. nosilla* positive."

Lee was surprised. The John Doe was a mutant! Thirty-one years earlier, back in 2038, a terrorist called Al Mumit (the taker of life) had turned a spore-forming bacteria called *Bacillus nosilla* loose on the world.

The bioengineered bacteria was delivered to *Kaffar* (unbelievers) all around the world by 786 *Shaheed*, or martyrs, each of whom had been selected because they had light-colored skin, were elderly, or only a few months old.

The results were even better than what Al Mumit had hoped for. Billions fell ill as *Bacillus nosilla* spread, and of those who contracted the disease, about 9 percent survived, with slightly better odds in developed countries. And of those who survived many but not all went on to develop mutations. Some of the physiological changes were good, but many were disfiguring, or in some cases lethal.

In Los Angeles, hundreds of thousands of people were declared communicable, some mistakenly, and herded into hastily organized "recovery" camps. Over time the recovery camps morphed into "relocation" camps and untold thousands of people were loaded onto trucks and sent east into the states of Idaho, Nevada, and Arizona. The sudden influx of mutants caused the "norms" in those states to flee west—and those who were *B. nosilla* negative were allowed to stay.

Meanwhile other parts of what had been the United

States were going through a similar process. The result was a patchwork quilt of so-called red zones, where mutants lived, and the green zones, occupied by norms. It wasn't long before zones and collections of zones gave birth to nation-states like Pacifica, which consisted of Washington, Oregon, and California.

Meanwhile the Republic of Texas annexed Idaho, Utah, and Arizona. And *that*, Lee knew, was likely to be the area where the dead man had come from. "This is going to be tough," she predicted. "Assuming this guy came in from the RZ, he'll be hard to identify."

"Patrol officers responded," Jenkins put in, "and they found a note on the body. According to the person who wrote it, the deceased is named Joel. But I agree. That isn't a whole lot to go on. Head out to St. Patrick's and collect what information you can."

"I'm on my way," Lee replied.

"Yanty will meet you there," Jenkins said. "I'll see you in the morning." Lee heard a click.

Lee looked at Kane as she put the phone away. "Sorry, hon . . . Gotta go."

Kane had been through it before. He smiled. "No problem . . . Let me know if you'll be home for dinner. So, if you had to choose between the condos we looked at today, which one would it be?"

"The larger one," Lee replied, as she took a final sip of coffee. "It had an incredible view of the ocean. There's a room for your office, and a kitchen reno would be fun."

"And your bike?"

"There's bound to be a storage unit somewhere nearby."

"That's very nice of you."

"I can be nice," Lee said, as she got up from the table. "Sometimes."

Kane laughed. "Shall I get a box for your food?"

"Please," Lee said. "I'll call you." And with that, she left.

Since Lee was on call, both of them had driven cars to Mac's. Lee's vehicle was a so-called creeper, which was street slang for an unmarked car. Except that most of them not only had been tagged a dozen times—but were often decorated with the letters TIACC. "This is a cop car." Her sedan was no different.

Lee's vehicle was equipped with a nav system, which she rarely used. After college she'd gone straight into the police academy, graduated near the top of her class, and spent four years as a patrol officer before making detective. And, like most street cops, she knew the city like the back of her hand. So she chose to take 10 east and exit onto National Boulevard, which morphed into Jefferson Boulevard. The latter was a four-lane road that delivered her to the church with a minimum of fuss.

St. Patrick's was a large building with a green roof, towers that were somewhat reminiscent of the Spanish missions, but with a more modern aesthetic. *That's Kane talking,* the voice in her head said. *Since when did you care about architecture?*

So? Lee answered. That's how it is when you have a relationship with someone. They rub off on you.

Or they come to own you, the voice suggested.

That's bullshit, Lee thought, as she pulled in behind the church. Maybe *you* would like to spend the rest of your life with a bunch of cats. Personally, I'd prefer a man.

"This is 1-William-3. I am Code 6. Over." There was no need to say where she was, since the dispatcher could see the creeper's location on the computer screen in front of her.

Church was over—so there were only a few cars in the parking lot. The body had been removed by then, but a police cruiser was still on the scene, as was the middle-aged crime-scene investigator who everyone called "Moms." She was busy taking pictures of the area while the bored patrol officers looked on.

Detective Dick Yanty had seen Lee pull in and made his way over to meet her. He was balding, wore wire-rimmed glasses that had a tendency to slide down his nose, and was wearing the usual plaid sports coat. Technically both of them worked for Lieutenant Brianna Wolfe, but both Yanty and a detective named Prospo had been assigned to work with Lee on the Bonebreaker case. "The Bonebreaker" being the name the media had bestowed on the serial killer who was responsible for killing Lee's father and eight other cops over the last sixteen years. "Hey, Lee," Yanty said. "Does this suck or what?"

"It sucks," Lee agreed solemnly. "So what, if anything, do we have?"

"First there's *this*," Yanty said, as he handed her a sheet of paper. "It's a copy—so don't worry about prints."

Lee read it:

Dear Father Benedict,

This man has gone to a better place. His name is Joel. Please use the money to cover his burial expenses.

Thank you,
Alcmaeon

"*Alcmaeon?* Who the hell is that?"

Yanty pushed the glasses up onto the bridge of his nose. "What did you do while you were in college? Everybody knows who Alcmaeon of Croton is."

"That's bullshit," Lee replied. "You ran a search on it."

Yanty grinned. "Yes, I did. It seems that Alcmaeon of Croton lived in the fifth century bc—and was one of the most eminent medical theorists of his time. Although he wrote about medical stuff, most of the time he studied astrology and meteorology, too."

"So he was a nerd."

"Yup."

"That's interesting," Lee said. "And it seems to support what Jenkins told me."

"Which was?"

"The coroner thinks Joel might have died of complications following a botched face transplant. We'll know after the autopsy. But try this on for size . . . The hack who botched the operation felt guilty about Joel's death. So he dumped the body here, along with some money to pay for a burial."

"And signs the note Alcmaeon because he or she identifies with the old goat for some reason," Yanty put in.

"Exactly," Lee said. "And how much you wanta bet that the perp is Catholic?"

"Perhaps," Yanty replied cautiously. "But maybe Joel was Catholic—and the doctor knew that."

"Good point," Lee said. "How 'bout video? Do we have any?"

"Yes," Yanty replied. "The church is equipped with a full-on security system, so we could get lucky. A guy named Mike agreed to work on that. Come on . . . Let's see if he found anything."

Lee followed Yanty through a small playground and into the church. They found Mike in a nicely furnished office sitting in front of a monitor. He turned to look over his shoulder as they entered the room. Lee assumed that Mike was one of the parishioners. He had mocha-colored skin, short hair, and a serious expression. "I have it," he announced. "At least I think I do."

"This is Detective Lee," Yanty said. "You sound doubtful . . . What's the problem?"

Mike nodded to Lee. "They say a picture is worth a thousand words," he said. "Watch this."

So the police officers stood behind Mike as he started a black-and-white video clip. Lee could see a time and date stamp in the lower left-hand corner of the screen. It read: 05/12/69 04:12.

As the three of them watched, a white box truck drove into the lot behind the church, did a U-turn, and came to a stop. Lee expected to see someone get out, open the back, and remove Joel's body. They didn't. The truck drove away. And there, lying on the pavement, was the corpse. "Damn," Yanty said admiringly. "That was slick!"

"The perp cut a six-foot-long hole in the bed of the truck," Lee said. "It had to be on one side or the other to avoid the drive shaft."

"And that means he or she has done this before," Yanty said. "Or plans to do it again."

"Precisely," Lee said. "Mike, can you zoom in? If so, I'd like to take a look at the license plates coming and going."

It turned out that Mike *could* zoom in, and he proceeded to do so. The results were disappointing. There weren't any plates. That meant the driver had been careful to remove them prior to the drop with plans to replace them later. "So we have *nada*," Yanty said. "Shit." Lee was in full agreement.

Lee managed to clear the crime scene by three and made it home by four. Except that the condo didn't feel like home after what had taken place there a month earlier. But Lee was determined to ignore that . . . And Chef Kane helped her do so by serving cocktails, tossed green salads, and some perfectly browned sole.

Then it was time to sit on the deck and watch the sun go down. "We need a view like this one," Lee said as she sipped her coffee. "What a great way to end the day."

That led to a discussion of all the properties they'd seen over the last two weeks and how to rank them. Later, as Lee lay next to Kane, she thought about the way her life had changed. There were things to look forward to now—and a person to share them with. That was new, and for the first time in a long time, Lee was happy.

Lee had never been good at getting up in the morning and was often late for work—until she moved in with Kane. Every morning, he woke her with a kiss on the forehead or a pat on the bottom, depending on what part of her was available.

Then, as Kane went out for his morning run, Lee would shower and get ready for work. Then they usually had a cup of coffee together prior to going their separate ways. So Lee was standing in the kitchen and Kane's coffee was ready as he reentered the condo at precisely 6:32 a.m. He was dressed in a tee shirt, blue shorts, and running shoes. "You're right on time," Lee observed. "A shrink with OCD . . . Someone should write a paper about that."

"A cop who breaks all the rules," Kane countered. "Someone should write a paper about *that*. And maybe I will." They laughed.

Kane took a sip of coffee and gestured to the small flat-screen TV that sat on the countertop. "So what's in the news this morning?"

"It sounds like peace could break out at any time," Lee replied. "The Aztec ambassador is scheduled to meet with a representative from the Republic of Texas in El Paso. And our secretary of state will be there too."

Both of them knew about the conflict between the Republic of Texas to the east and the Aztec Empire to the south. The tecs insisted that all of the lands that had once been part of Mexico should be returned to them regardless of the treaties signed in the past.

So their army had crossed the border at a point halfway between San Luis and Nogales and had been slugging it out with the Republicans for months. The fighting had been confined to Texas and Arizona thus far. But there was a very real possibility that Pacifica would be dragged into the conflict because the Aztecs believed that California belonged to them. "I'm glad to hear that everybody's at the table," Kane said. "Maybe they can work something out. How about you? Will this be a normal day?"

"I hope so," Lee replied. "I'll call or text you if things go off the rails." Lee gave him a coffee-flavored kiss followed by a wave as she headed for the door.

Lee knew that there were a number of people who would like to kill her, including the Bonebreaker. So she was careful to scan her surroundings as she left the condo, entered the elevator, and rode it down to the parking garage. The car appeared to be undisturbed but appearances could be deceptive. So Lee removed a handheld GPS and cell-phone detector from her purse, turned it on, and circled the vehicle. If a tracker had been placed on the sedan during the night the device would warn her. None had.

So Lee got in, started the engine, and drove to a restaurant called Maria's, where she ate a breakfast burrito before completing the trip to work. The LAPD headquarters building was known for its angular appearance—and cost $437 million old bucks to construct back in 2009. Unfortunately, the façade had been damaged by a rocket attack in 2065 and was still awaiting repairs.

Lee entered the ramp that led to the parking garage, paused to show her ID, and continued down until she located an empty slot. Then she rode an elevator up to the sixth floor, which was home to the Chief of Detectives, her staff, and about sixty detectives. All of whom occupied the maze of cubicles generally referred to as the bullpen.

Of the larger force, only twelve men and women were

members of the elite Special Investigative Section (S.I.S.), charged with getting the city's most dangerous criminals off the street. That was the unit Lee belonged to—and she made it to roll call with a minute to spare. The conference room was about half-full, and that was typical, since five or six detectives were out of the office at any given time. But Yanty was there, as was Prospo, and both of them looked glum. The likelihood was that they knew something she didn't.

Lee plopped down next to Prospo and was going to interrogate him when Jenkins entered the room. He had black hair, startling green eyes, and brown skin. He was dressed in a nicely cut gray suit. "I wish I could say 'good morning,'" Jenkins said soberly, "but I can't. All of you have met Cheyenne Darling—and are cognizant of the relationship she had with Deputy Chief McGinty."

Like Lee's father two years earlier, Deputy Chief of Detectives Ross McGinty had been murdered by the Bonebreaker, and his body had been dumped next to a freeway. Most of him anyway . . . the Bonebreaker liked to keep his victims' extremities.

Furthermore Lee knew that although McGinty and Darling had been lovers they didn't live together because he feared for her safety. And McGinty, like her father, had been subject to bad dreams and bouts of depression.

"Darling was visiting friends yesterday," Jenkins continued. "And when she came home, a package was waiting for her. It appeared to be from her sister, so she opened it. And there, nestled in shredded packing paper, was Chief McGinty's left femur."

ABOUT THE AUTHOR

William C. Dietz is an American writer best known for military science fiction. He spent time in the US Navy and the US Marine Corps, and has worked as a surgical technician, news writer, television producer, and director of public relations. He has written more than 40 novels, as well as tie-in novels for *Halo*, *Mass Effect*, *Resistance*, *Starcraft*, *Star Wars*, and *Hitman*.

williamcdietz.com